Pants on Fire

An Iris Raines Mystery

Denise Diana Huddle

Crimes & Passion, LLC

Editing by Laura Barth
Proofreading by Beth Attwood
Cover design by Damonza.com
Contact email: denise@denisedianahuddle.com
ISBN: 979-8-9994822-2-8—Ebook
ISBN: 979-8-9994822-1-1—Paperback

In memory of Harold Flemming Duncan, Jr., Esq.

Prologue

D*on't lie to your PI. It's a maxim for successful living...right up there with* never stiff the hitman *and* don't blow-dry your hair in the bathtub. *Yet every day clients walk into the offices of PIs and lie just like rugs on the floor. How can they believe we're going to resolve their current imbroglio without uncovering their own role in it?*

If you've been a PI since lunch, you know that people do not end up slogging upstream, ass-deep in a river of alligators, without having somehow gotten into the water in the first place. However much of an asshole they may be, when we join their team, they become our *assholes, and we keep their secrets and do every legal thing in our power to save them. It's the job. We explain this to them* ad nauseam. *But they lie to us anyway.*

Knowing this, my bullshit antenna is constantly scanning the environment for deception, like the spinning radars perched on the masts of warships. But this time I had no inkling—not until the first bullet hit my windshield.

Chapter 1

Tuesday, September 7, 3:15 p.m.

When they mail your PI license, they should attach a note: "Congratulations. You are now licensed to spend the better part of your professional life prying public records out of the vaults of clock-watching clerks and paper-pushing bureaucrats."

I parked my beautiful new jet-black Genesis GV80 in the carport, got out, and stretched. I'd driven the hundred and fifty miles south to Laredo that morning and spent the day extracting probate copies from a clerk who was only slightly less helpful than a broken toaster before I turned around and hauled my happy ass back to San Antonio. The muscles between my shoulders felt like someone had crocheted them into a granny square.

My Saint Bernard, Festus, came bounding through his doggie door and down the stairs in his awkward gait. His leg had been shattered when he was hit by a fire truck a year before. Our receptionist, Francine, had found him outside the burned-out remains of our office building and brought him to me, and we'd been best friends ever since. The finest surgery available had gotten him back on all fours, but he would always limp.

My apartment was the second story of a 1920s Victorian in Alamo Heights, one of the toniest bedroom communities in San Antonio. The arsonist who'd torched the Hampe Ewald the year before had also blown up the Victorian—and almost got me along with it—when he'd realized I had learned his identity. My father (and superlitigator) Addison Raines had leaned on the insurance company pretty hard, and my downstairs neighbor, Ron Forsythe, and I had made out fine. We'd pooled our money and bought what was left of the building from our landlord and rebuilt. As awful as it was, it had given me the opportunity to construct an enclosed play area for Festus.

The second I opened the gate, he stood up on his hind legs, towering over me, and licked my face. I threw his ball, and we played tug-of-war. Back upstairs, I poured kibble into his bowl, fluffed his ears, and said, "Sorry, pal, but I have to go to the office. I'll be back in no time."

I slipped out the back door and drove the mile north on Broadway to the Hampe Ewald. Hefting my briefcase, I walked through the baking heat into the building. Originally built back in 1961, the lobby exuded a midcentury vibe. But the terrazzo floors and marble wall panels had actually been installed during the restoration after the fire.

The new stuff was nice, but it didn't have the lingering smell of sweat and cigar smoke and Old Spice that permeated buildings of the *Mad Men* generation. I boarded the mahogany-paneled elevator car and headed up to the offices of Raines & Raines, the law firm owned by the brothers who'd adopted me after one of their clients had dumped me on their doorstep thirty-plus years ago. I operate my PI agency, Raines Investigations, in a smaller suite of offices next to my fathers.

As I exited the elevator, the law firm's receptionist, Francine, called out, "Hey, Iris?"

I headed to her desk.

"Mr. Raines needs to see you in his office."

"Justis or Addison?"

"Addison."

I dug the sheaf of probate documents I'd fetched from Laredo out of my briefcase and handed them to her, and she made a beeline for the oil and gas section.

I found my father leaning back in his chair with his ostrich-skin cowboy boots kicked up on his rosewood desk, flipping through a pleading. I stuck my head into his office. "Knock, knock."

He swung his long legs to the ground, sat up in his chair, and motioned me in. "Hey, champ."

I plopped down in one of his brown leather client chairs. "What's up?"

He passed me a file. "We had an emergency meeting this morning with a new client. He's in a world of shit, and I need you to get on it—full court press." I thumbed through the contents of the folder.

Addison continued. "A disgruntled executive left with all the recipes from Circus Burgers. Opened up a bunch of competing stores called Big Top that are undercutting the hell out of Farragut."

Everyone in town knew who Quinten Farragut was. While the circus décor in his chain of hamburger restaurants was ridiculously hokey, the burgers were prime meat garnished with hickory-smoked bacon and guacamole served on homemade buns, and the signature fries were smothered in melted cheese. The chocolate shakes were thicker than cement slurry. And if you didn't care if you ever zipped up your skinny jeans again, you could top your meal off with a gooey Rice Krispies treat. I grabbed dinner there at least once a week. Just thinking about one of those Circus Burgers made my mouth water. Besides a pimento cheese sandwich from the refrigerator section of a truck stop on I-35, I hadn't eaten anything since breakfast. "They should serve that Three-Ring Meal with a little shoehorn to wedge the last drop of fat into any available space left in your coronary arteries."

"I'll mention that next time I see him."

I looked up from the intake form. "So what's the emergency? And what does he need with us? He's bound to have counsel already since the suit's ongoing." I flipped more pages. Then I saw it. My head snapped up. "Strite, Streckfuss?"

Addison nodded. "Yep. He settled the suit for next to nothing August 17 and canned Strite, Streckfuss the next day, leaving him without outside counsel. He knows Justis from the Plaza Club and called him this morning in a twist."

Strite, Streckfuss & Storey was our archenemy. During the litigation surrounding the fire at the Hampe Ewald, I had been instrumental in getting their chief investigator locked up in Huntsville for ten to twenty for witness tampering and aggravated assault. Rudolph Streckfuss was a red-faced hardball player with rubbery lips and the legal ethics of a pit viper, but he was a damn smart lawyer. I tossed the file on the desk. "How the hell did Triple S get hammered in that case? It looks like a slam dunk."

Addison shook his head. "According to Farragut, it wasn't a matter of legal skill. Seems they spent him out of house and home. He couldn't finance the litigation any longer and had to salvage what he could before he ran out of cash. Now he's in deep kimchee. The stores are floundering, the competition is nipping at his heels—and to top it off, someone's sabotaging his ranch." He passed me a series of police reports detailing various acts of vandalism on the ranch over the past two and a half weeks. I flipped through them. Fences cut, equipment damaged, fires set in pastures...

"The Wind Rose Ranch? Jesus." An iconic ranch about forty miles south of San Antonio, it was widely considered the most over-the-top display of wealth in the world of Texas megaranches.

He peered at me over his reading glasses. "It's the crown jewel of his real estate portfolio."

I rolled my eyes. "There's a fake Venus de Milo in the master bathroom. Didn't you see that spread in *Texas Style*?"

"There's no accounting for taste." He tossed his gold pen on the desk.

I scanned the photos. "Does Farragut have any idea where this is coming from?"

"Not a clue."

I studied an image of a scorched pasture. "Or so he says..."

Addison nodded. "Or so he says." He leaned forward and rested his forearms on the desk. "The locals aren't doing jack. We need you to get to the bottom of it in case we have to sell the ranch to keep the business alive. Any ideas?"

I drummed my fingers on the arm of the chair while I mulled it over. "The fastest way will be to install a bunch of hidden infrared cellular cameras and see if we can catch the bastards in the act."

He picked up his pen and made a note on his legal pad. "Do you have the equipment?"

I shook my head. "If we're in a time crunch, I can go buy a bunch of trail and game cameras and use them. It won't be cheap."

"Do it. And start now."

I cocked my head. "If he couldn't afford Strite, Streckfuss, why do we think he can afford us?"

Addison cleared his throat. "He's paying us with stock in the company."

I fought the urge to bug out my eyes. My fathers had taken an ownership position in the Hampe Ewald instead of cash legal fees when the new owner had bought it in a complicated and expensive transaction just months before it burned. When it came out that the developer had let the insurance coverage on the project lapse months before the fire, my fathers would have been ruined if we hadn't found a way to hang the whole mess on the electrical contractor's shoddy work.

"Look...we learned our lesson with the fire. It was a bitch getting through it, but now the money we're making from our minority share of the Hampe Ewald is covering most of the overhead around here. Justis and I think this idea of working for passive interests in businesses outside of the firm is going to play a major role in our future growth."

I gathered up the documents and slid them back into his file. "Speaking of, where is Papa J? I didn't see his car in the parking lot."

"He's down at the federal building. Darnell Carter got picked up on racketeering and interstate commerce charges this morning. Jerks at the US attorney's office didn't even give us a heads-up and let him surrender. Justis has been down in the magistrate's office since lunch trying to get bail set."

Darnell Washington Carter was a frequent target of local, state, and federal law enforcement types. He was also by far the most colorful character on my fathers' robust client roster. "That's just bad form."

"They'll get theirs. In the meantime, we need you full steam ahead on this Farragut mess. If CB goes under, we don't get paid."

It'll be a cold August day in South Texas when I question my fathers about how they run their law firm, so I just nodded and stood up. That granny square between my shoulders felt like it had shrunk in the dryer. I rolled my head and massaged my neck then checked my watch. "I'll run to pick up the equipment now. Then I'll head down to the ranch tonight and install the stuff when no one is around." Picking up my briefcase, I said, "Tell Farragut you need the gate combos, but don't tell him when I'll be there or what I'll be doing. God knows where he's got security leaks, and this camera strategy will only work if nobody knows they're there. Speaking of, do you know what kind of security he's got?"

Addison nodded. "A couple of ranch hands live in a trailer on the eastern periphery of the property. Otherwise, it's just gate locks."

I went to my office, packed up my gear, and headed out to buy the cameras. On my way, I called my best pal, Sean Galen. Sean has a PhD in computer science and calls himself an "IT specialist." In reality, he performs all kinds of black-box cybermagic for alphabet soup agencies he doesn't talk about. And he just happens to have an armored Escalade with four-wheel drive and bullet-resistant glass he acquired a few years back when he had a spat with some guys with access to rocket-propelled grenades. He picked up on the first ring. "Hey, sugar."

I merged onto Loop 410 West. Rush hour was dying down, and the Loop was more like a highway than a parking lot. "I've got to go hang some sneak-and-peek gear down on a ranch south of town—I'm trying to bust some assholes vandalizing the place. It's the Wind Rose Ranch, no less. I may need four-wheel drive. Can I use the Escalade?"

"Hmm...I guess that depends on whether you're going to let me feed you and my goddog before you go."

Sean could cook like Pavarotti could sing. My stomach let out a loud growl. I sighed. "Oh, that I could, but I have to take a rain check. I'm going to clean out all the cellular game cameras at the Bass Pro Shop, then head your way to pick up the Escalade. After that, I still have another hour from your place to the ranch." I checked my watch. "I'll just grab something and eat it in the car."

"No grabbing. For you, my darling, I will prepare a to-go meal. See you soon."

After I bought the cameras and arranged through the store to have the cellular service for them activated, I stopped by my apartment, changed into my field clothes, and strapped on my shoulder holster, stuffing extra ammunition for my Glock into the pockets of my field pants. I loaded Festus into the Genesis and zipped south on 281. We pulled into the underground parking garage of Sean's luxury downtown loft at 7:30.

Sean's private elevator opened, and he emerged barefoot in khaki shorts and a T-shirt that read "*User* is the IT term for *Idiot.*" He was carrying a lunch bag and a car fob. Festus drooled and spun around in the seat, bucking like a rodeo horse, whining and pawing at the car window. Sean opened the door, produced the obligatory cookie, herded the dog into the Escalade, and then handed me the fob. When I caught a whiff of one of Sean's amazing gourmet burgers mixed with the aroma of his cottage fries, I was afraid I was going to start drooling like Festus. I smiled at him. "You made me a Galen cheeseburger combo!"

He nodded. "Not quite. They're bite-size sliders, mini versions of the real thing. Ideal for car trips."

I thought of Sean and how much he had loved me since we were children. "How'd you know I was craving a burger?"

He smiled. "It seemed thematically appropriate." Opening the Escalade's door for me, he said, "You need help with the installation?"

I shook my head. I would have loved to have him ride shotgun, but lately Sean had been pushing hard on a project of some sort. Though he never talked outright about such things, I knew the signs. He was tired and distracted and unavailable for many of our usual visits. I kissed his cheek and waggled my cell. "Don't worry about it. Festus will help me out. You can see me on Find My. Thanks for the goodies."

He ruffled Festus's ears through the window and winked at me. "Be careful, sugar. You damn sure don't want to run into those assholes in the dark."

I pulled the shoulder belt across my chest and clicked it into the latch. "No doubt."

He slapped the hood of the car, and we headed to the Wind Rose Ranch, three counties to the south.

Full dark was coming on when Festus and I pulled up to the gate on the southeastern corner of the ranch. Through binoculars, I studied the gaudy mansion ringed by its twenty-eight massive Corinthian columns. Two hundred yards to the west, a mile-long paved driveway dotted with palm trees reminiscent of Sunset Boulevard led to a roundabout in front of the house. The whole residential compound was lit up like Times Square. I used the combination Addison had texted me to open the gate and pulled onto the dark ranch road at the southeastern entrance.

Designed to monitor game and livestock, the cameras were easy to attach to trees and fence posts. I set one along with its solar-charging panel to record activity at the gate I had just come through. Once I verified via my phone app that the camera was working and focused on what I wanted to see, I pulled on night vision goggles and drove without headlights, following the ranch road north to the eastern entrance where I set another camera. The night was still and muggy, and I was sweating through my T-shirt. The sound of cicadas buzzed through the brush, and a rustling in the grass made me wish I'd remembered my snake leggings.

At the northeast end of the property, the gate was held shut by only a latch. Why wasn't it locked? A little warning trill trickled through me. I scanned the area with the night vision goggles, but the glowing green shapes of some deer bedded down for the night were the only signs of life. My hands were slick with sweat as I checked the load in my Glock and slid it back into the leather shoulder holster. I took a deep breath and went to work setting the last gate camera. Finished, I drove west then followed the ranch road south as it skirted the residential campus, stopping even with a four-car garage that sat just southeast of the twenty-nine-thousand-square-foot antebellum-style home that resembled a *Gone with the Wind*–themed hotel more than a personal residence. More palm trees surrounded a Grecian-style pool and hot tub west of the main house. Tennis courts and three storage buildings lined the northern edge of the compound. Between the storage buildings and the garage, a stable rounded out the residential campus. I surveyed the area with my binoculars but didn't see a soul.

Shouldering my gear bag, I crawled quietly out of the truck with Festus on my heels. I felt exposed as we scurried across the brightly lit compound. In addition to the ridiculous architectural hodgepodge, ten-foot elephants in a trunk-to-tail conga line were carefully sculpted out of evergreen hedges along the driveway that ran between the main house and the garage then past the stables toward the storage buildings on the north edge of the property. Interspersed between these monstrosities were countless other topiaries of circus animals positioned near the entrance to every structure. I had to figure out how to hide the cameras in the shrubs where their view wasn't blocked by the foliage, but they would not be seen by the gardeners. After a few tries, I discovered a way to attach them near the base of the shrubs. With that sorted out, I got the cameras up and running in no time.

We slid behind the stables, hiding in the shadow cast by the eaves. Pressing my back up against the wooden slats of the building, I took five deep, calming breaths before I summoned my nerve, stepped back into the light, and slipped through the door into the barn. The earthy smell of horses mixed with manure and hay filled my nostrils. Festus sniffed the air. The animals were quiet, save for a few random snuffles and snorts. Festus sat at attention while, using the night vision, I crept up a wooden ladder and set a camera in the loft overhanging the horse stalls, then made my way carefully back down the rungs. I had just taken my first step outside the stable entrance when Festus, a couple of feet ahead of me, let out a low growl.

He was staring into the darkness southeast of where the Escalade was parked. I whispered to him, and he followed me as I quietly eased back through the open door into the stable. My heart pounded in my chest like a herd of stampeding elephants—and not the topiary kind. I fought to steady my hand, dug the binoculars out of my gear bag, and focused them in the direction Festus had been staring.

I yanked my phone out of my pants pocket and dialed 911. Grasping the phone in my sweating hand, I listened to my pulse pounding in my ears as the operator answered. Whispering, I said, "Private Investigator

Iris Raines, Texas License A07941 reporting illegal activity on the Wind Rose Ranch off Highway 181 at mile marker 36. Ten men and two pickup trucks approximately three hundred yards east of the residential compound. Intruders armed with AR-15s." After I rattled off the gate combo and hung up, I pulled my video camera out of my gear bag, dialed in the low-light setting, and started recording.

The men seemed oblivious to my presence. Setting the camera to continue recording, I inched farther back into the stables to establish a defensive position until the cops arrived. As I settled against a stall, one of the horses let out a loud whinny. In seconds, the stable was a cacophony of neighs and whinnies from the frightened Arabians. With Festus right next to me, I pressed myself closer to the stall wall, willing myself to be invisible. I squelched the tsunami of panic rising in me by reminding myself all I had to do was hold out until the sheriff's people got there.

Then the spotlight hit us.

One PI with a Glock was hardly a match for ten men with automatic weapons. But my distance to the Escalade was less than half of theirs. I grabbed my gear and snapped my fingers for Festus. We raced out the back door of the barn and hauled ass to the truck. The white-hot electric buzz of panic propelled me forward as bullets whizzed by. I glanced over my shoulder at Festus. A few feet behind me, he was running full out. A shot of terror stabbed my chest like a bolt of lightning at the thought that he might get hit. I flung open the driver's door, and a hundred and forty pounds of brown and white fur barreled past me and bounded over the center console. I slung my gear into the truck, pulled myself into the driver's seat, and slammed the door. Bullets hammered the reinforced exterior. I hit the Start button, and the giant V8 roared to life. As I yanked the truck into gear and floored it, I watched in the rearview as the men jumped into their trucks and hit the off-road spotlights mounted on their roofs, kicking up dust as they raced after us.

Shit. Shit. SHIT. With a death grip on the steering wheel, I fled north, then followed the ranch road east, away from the compound. The air conditioner was sucking the caliche powder into the truck, and I coughed as my mouth filled with the fine limestone grit. I killed the AC with one hand as I steered the SUV around a tight curve in the gravel road with the other. Heading south, I sped toward the nearest stretch of barbed wire. The Escalade bounced on the rocky road as I pushed the accelerator to the floor. My stomach lurched as the back of the truck fishtailed around. I hit the shift-on-the-fly four-wheel drive, and the truck bucked as the drive train locked in with a metallic clank.

The men were gaining on me, and a shot hit my rear windshield. The thick bullet-resistant glass held, but a spider web of cracks shot out from the point of impact. Then shots hit the front windshield, and a third truck appeared in front of me and hit its lights, speeding straight toward me.

Bullets slammed into the truck in a terrible rat-a-tat-tat until one finally penetrated the glass and whizzed by my right shoulder. The world around me dropped into hyperclear slow motion as instinct took over. Festus hunkered on the rear floorboard, and I yanked the wheel to the right and swerved the Escalade out of the path of the oncoming truck. I punched the emergency call button and dived down in the seat, struggling to stay below the windshield as I strained to see where I was driving. The emergency operator's voice was barely audible over the hailstorm of bullets hitting the truck. I shouted over the din, "Private Investigator Iris Raines at Wind Rose Ranch. I'm under fire. Repeat. Under fire from three pickup trucks carrying at least ten men with automatic weapons.

Require immediate law enforcement assistance. Repeat—require immediate law enforcement assistance. Approach and use southeast ranch gate off 181. Gate lock combo 5826. Repeat—combo 5826."

There were multiple holes in the thick glass of the Escalade now. Using what limited visibility I had, I picked the spot in the fence where I was going to make my break. If I made it to the road, I had a fighting chance these assholes wouldn't want to commit cold-blooded murder on a busy state highway. I floored the truck. As I sped toward the fence and braced for impact, I was suddenly awash in a flood of white light. Over the racket of the shots, the distinctive *whump, whump, whump* of a helicopter thundered down from above.

The shooting stopped, and I slammed the truck to a fishtailing halt in a swirling cloud of caliche and stared out the shattered windshield at the two helicopters hovering overhead. The pickup trucks scattered, and the choppers split and followed them as they off-roaded in different directions, keeping them illuminated in their blinding spotlights. Festus clambered over the console into the front seat. I cheered as one truck careened into a ditch by a stock pond. Packages of some kind flew from its bed as the pickup flipped over and landed on its roof. The other two trucks descended on their disabled compatriot and disgorged their occupants. Some of the men began gathering the fallen packages while others fired on the helicopters.

I bailed out of the truck, positioned the armored passenger door between me and the bad guys, and shot at the men who were firing at the helicopters. I hit at least three of them before they all abandoned the remaining packages, piled into the two operable trucks, and sped into the darkness. One helicopter gave chase while the other hovered over my position. Black SUVs bearing the markings of the DEA came racing up the ranch road as a booming voice blasted from the chopper's speakers. "Federal agents. Drop your weapon and get on your knees. Do it now, or we will shoot."

I dropped my Glock and kicked it away before I knelt down on the hardscrabble South Texas dirt and held my hands high over my head. The helicopter's propeller wash blew caliche dust into my face. My eyes poured water, and I couldn't stop coughing. But I kept my hands up so the assholes wouldn't shoot me.

Chapter 2

Tuesday, September 7, 11:45 p.m.

DEA agents in raid jackets with weapons drawn jumped out of the black SUVs and ran toward me. Two of them grabbed me, threw me facedown on the ground, and handcuffed me. The sharp limestone rocks of the road cut into my face, and I tasted dirt in my mouth. The cold metal handcuffs cut into my wrists.

Out of the corner of my eye, I saw another agent draw a Taser and aim it at Festus, who was running to my aid. I screamed his emergency halt command: "Festus! Danger!" The agent's knee dug into my back as I wedged my head to the side and saw my dog's enormous form plop onto the cracked dirt. Terror flooded through me. Festus's only concern was saving me from these strangers. He would trade his life for mine in a second.

I gasped for breath. "Don't hurt my dog. He won't move." Festus lay wide-eyed, frozen in his danger position. I forced myself to relax and didn't offer the slightest resistance as two of the agents grabbed my elbows and yanked me to my feet. I could manage my body posture, but I couldn't stop the stress pheromones that were oozing from my every pore. Festus could detect those a mile away—and I could see in his eyes he didn't like what he was smelling.

Just as a low growl escaped his giant chest, a man stepped forward from the knot of agents surrounding us. Tall and muscular with light brown hair and a neatly trimmed beard, he was wearing a Kevlar vest that read Special Ranger across the chest. A patch on his jacket sleeve had the profile of a dog and K-9 embroidered above it. His voice was calm but commanding. "Hold on, fellas. Let me see if I can help out." He looked at me and said, "Can you instruct the dog to let me frisk you?"

I nodded again. "Festus, hold." He dropped his bowling-ball-sized head to his paws.

The special ranger frisked me and nodded to the agents. "I think I can handle this if you'll back away from her." The DEA men grumbled, then grudgingly stepped back. "If you'll call the dog and follow me to my truck, we can put him in my kennel, and he'll be safe."

Relief washed over me at the prospect of getting Festus out of harm's way. I whistled, and he fell in beside me. Flanked by the two DEA men, we followed the special ranger to his truck. He opened one of the climate-controlled kennels built into the truck bed, and I coaxed Festus inside. When the ranger closed the door, I let out a deep sigh. Festus was safe. "Thank you."

He checked the climate control on the panel by the kennel doors and said, "I'm Special Ranger Finneas Rhodes. I work out of the King City office. I'll take care of the dog until you get this straightened out." He handed one of the DEA men his card. "Give this to her when she's ready." He turned and walked away.

"I am a private investigator," I said to the DEA agent on my right. "My license is in my shirt pocket. Please call Deputy Chief Grover Delacourt at SAPD. The desk sergeant will patch you through to his cell. He'll vouch for me."

"We don't give a damn who you claim will vouch for you." The agent pushed me into the back seat of one of the black SUVs and slammed the door. My shoulders screamed in pain as I struggled to take the pressure off of my cuffed wrists wedged behind me. I stared through the iron grate that separated the back seat from the front. There were no handles on the doors. The car reeked of fear and sweat and cheap disinfectant tinged with vomit. I staved off pangs of claustrophobia.

The agents got in the front seat, and we bounced over the rocky ranch road. In minutes we were on 181, headed north to San Antonio. The driver didn't utter a word during the entire trip, while the agent riding shotgun yammered on about some fishing tournament they'd attended the weekend before. Penn and Teller.

An hour later, I found myself cuffed to a table in an interrogation room at the federal building just south of downtown San Antonio. The tubes of fluorescent lights in the ceiling buzzed and hummed behind the wire cage surrounding the fixture. Three cheap plastic chairs surrounded the metal table screwed into the floor in the middle of the stark white room. My chair faced a rectangular one-way mirror. Teller sat opposite me, as quiet and unmoving as Mount Rushmore.

Around 5:00 a.m., the lock on the heavy metal door rattled, and a man wearing a DEA badge came into the interrogation room. He nodded to Teller, who left without a word, the door clanking shut behind him.

The man tossed a file on the table, unlocked the handcuff, and removed it from my wrist. His badge was dangling from a brass bead chain around his neck. "Agent Butler." He sat down opposite me. "Deputy Chief Delacourt was pretty pissed we woke him up. He says you're a pain in the ass, but he's sure you're not a member of a drug cartel. He also says to tell you he's going to call you at four a.m. tomorrow and wake your ass up just to even the score."

I rubbed my wrists. The ride up from the ranch in handcuffs had left both of them bruised and swollen, and I was pretty pissed myself. I could understand the field guys scrambling to get control of a chaotic situation on the ground, but Penn and Teller were just assholes and had pushed it way too far. This guy was their boss, and he was going to defend his people and rely on Grover to keep me from making a stink.

He leaned back in his chair. "So what were you doing on the Wind Rose last night?"

Stretching my arm across my body and pulling the elbow to my chest, I tried to work the kinks out of my shoulder. "I was at the ranch on a routine matter. I'm in the employ of the law firm of Raines & Raines. I can't discuss my investigation without a release from them."

Completely ignoring my response, Butler opened the file and examined one of the reports inside. "Do you normally drive an armored car when you're out on 'routine matters,' Ms. Raines?"

I rubbed my wrists some more. "Agent Butler, without a lawyer and my client present, I cannot answer these questions."

Butler leaned back in his chair. "You know, normally I'd leave you cuffed to this table until your attitude adjusted, but since Deputy Chief Delacourt vouched for you, I'm going to let it slide. I trust he can always reach you?"

I forced my voice into a neutral register and said, "He can."

He flipped the folder closed. "Well, then...there are a couple of things you should know. First, tonight's adventure resulted in our confiscation of ten kilos of heroin worth about half a million bucks. Second, you shot at least three of those cartel boys while they were using our helicopters for target practice. Based on the amount of blood we're finding at the scene, you did more than wing a couple of them. I imagine that is one pissed-off bunch of hombres—out $500K and shot to shit. You best keep your head low because if those assholes get wind of who you are, I wouldn't want to be your life insurance company." He pushed a fob across the desk. "What's left of your armored truck is parked out front."

Chapter 3

Wednesday, September 8, 6:30 a.m.

I dragged myself across the parking lot of the federal building just as a smudge of pink watercolor was creeping up in the inky sky. Once inside the bullet-riddled truck, I was amazed I could see through the fractured windshield well enough to drive. I retrieved the special ranger's business card and dialed. He picked up right away. "So, they haven't sent you to the Supermax yet?"

I laughed. "In fact, they have, and this is my one monthly phone call. How's my dog?"

"He's fine. He's had breakfast and a walk, and he's getting on nicely with my German Shepherd, Isabella. She's lobbying for us to keep him."

"Not a chance. Where are you? We can meet wherever is most convenient for you."

"I'm at the SA ranger's office over by Trinity University."

I checked my watch. How the hell was it just 6:30 in the morning? It seemed like it should be next week. "How about you meet me at the coffee shop over at the Pearl? They allow dogs on the outdoor patio. I'll buy you breakfast and retrieve my pooch."

I cranked up the battered Escalade and headed north on 281. The trendy Pearl complex was just a stone's throw from Trinity University and only four miles up 281 from the federal courthouse. Mercifully, I was driving against the morning rush-hour traffic, or I wouldn't have made it there in time for lunch. I parked and walked up the sidewalk to the restaurant. When I was still a good fifty yards away, Festus spotted me and began to howl. I used what little energy I had left to jog over. I didn't want us to get thrown out before I even arrived. When I reached him, he reared up and put his paws on my shoulders and gave me a tongue bath. I was so glad to see him, I buried my face in his long, thick fur and hugged him tight. Satisfied I was alive and well, he sat down on the redbrick patio and watched me intently. I brushed dust and grass cuttings from his paws off my shirt. "Ranger Rhodes, I can't tell you how much I appreciate you taking him last night. Those assholes were about to tase him."

He ruffled Festus's giant ears. "Finn, please."

I sat down across the hammered copper table from him. "Finn it is, then."

He returned to his chair. "Most cops are scared of dogs, especially big ones. Festus is very well trained. He took that d-a-n-g-e-r command under intense stress where you were clearly in peril. Who trained him?"

"A tech at my vet's office used to train guide dogs. He took Festus on when he was just a puppy. The guy's amazing." I set my purse on one of the empty chairs. "Where's your dog?"

He tipped his head toward the parking lot. "She's in the kennel. Policy prohibits us taking them out during duty hours unless they're working."

"That's pretty hard-core."

Finn shrugged. "She's a working animal, not a pet. Last year, she busted an eighteen-wheeler carrying twenty pounds of coke and two hundred grand in cash hidden in a trailer load of coffee beans."

"And what did Isabella get out of the deal?"

"She got an extra ten-minute play session with her dope-scented towel."

"Sounds to me like she needs a business manager. Negotiate her a better deal."

"When she retires in three years, I'll get to keep her. Then, she'll be a pet. And I'll spoil her rotten."

I pulled two menus out of the rack on the table and passed him one. "I'm starving. Let's order. Breakfast is on Festus."

A waitress arrived and poured coffee. I made my selections and studied Finn while he ordered. He was all of six-three. Rock-hard muscles rippled through his uniform shirt. He could probably bench a Mini Cooper. His green eyes were brilliant emeralds, and his voice was deep and strong. He had a calm, deliberate way about him. Just sitting here with him at breakfast, I felt the night's adrenaline surge waning away. I tucked my menu back in the rack. "All I know about special rangers is they investigate agricultural crime. I have no idea what brought you to the party last night."

Festus sat next to Finn and rested his giant head on Finn's thigh. Finn scratched his ears. "Special rangers are commissioned peace officers employed by the Texas and Southwestern Cattle Raisers Association. We investigate everything from stolen livestock and agricultural equipment to white-collar crime like scams at livestock auctions. When anything happens on a member's ranch in my district, I'm automatically contacted. The owner of the Wind Rose is a member of the association, so that made it my problem, too. I could tell from the radio traffic it was a real shitstorm."

The waitress brought a large round tray loaded with our plates. The spicy scent of the chorizo smelled so good, I could barely keep myself from snatching the plate off the tray. "I feel like I haven't eaten in a week." I dug into eggs scrambled with cheese and sausage then slathered butter and grape jelly on a huge buttermilk biscuit while Finn calmly ate his egg-white omelet and turkey bacon. I eyed his plate. "Lucky you're from out of town. Your buddies from the gym catch you out with someone eating like I am, they'll suspend your membership and make you drink five kale smoothies as penance."

He smiled. It was a kind, pleasant smile that didn't seem to have a scintilla of contrivance in it. "Well, if they didn't like it, they could just blow. I'll eat with any beautiful woman I want to whenever the urge strikes me. Especially if she has a cool dog."

I couldn't help but smile back. "Charmer."

He took a sip of coffee and set the mug back on the table. "Those DEA guys were out of line last night. The dispatcher repeatedly identified you as a PI."

I put my fork down. "You know what baffles me? I didn't see a single sheriff's car last night."

He shrugged noncommittally. "Weird shit happens when the feds are in town." He munched on a strip of turkey bacon. "You were something last night. Those cartel dudes are bad motherfuckers. The DEA was just pissed because their guys unloaded enough ammo to empty a Remington warehouse and didn't hit a thing while you shot up a bunch of narco-terrorists firing ARs, and did it with a Glock. Plus you're a PI—and a woman, to boot. They may never get over it."

I smiled. "You can't beat motivation, and I was pretty fucking motivated while those assholes were trying to kill me." I checked my watch. "I've got to drop the dog off at my apartment and get to the office." I picked up the check.

He nodded. "And I've got to get back to King City. There's a cattle auction this afternoon, and I have a tip there may be some stolen bulls there I'm trying to recover."

I handed the waitress the check and cash and told her to keep the change. I stood and took Festus's leash. "We can't thank you enough."

He smiled again. "It was my pleasure. You have my card. The Wind Rose is in my portfolio, so shout out if you need me."

I loaded Festus into the pockmarked Escalade and headed back south on 281. As I pulled into downtown, I called Sean.

"Hey, sugar! How's tricks in South Texas?"

"Well...I'm working a good news/bad news deal here."

He laughed. "Okay, I'll bite. What's the good news?"

"The armor on your Escalade can hold up to an attack by a bunch of drug dealers with AR-15s."

His tone turned serious. "What happened?"

I ran him through the highlights. "The truck is beat to hell. My liability and property damage policy should cover it, though."

"I don't give a fuck about the damn Escalade. Where are you? I'm coming to get you."

"That's sweet, but I'll be pulling into the garage in five."

No sooner had I parked than Sean emerged from his elevator and jogged over to me. He helped me out of the SUV without so much as a glance at the damage. "Are you sure you're all right? Tell me every bit of it."

I ran him through the details. "What a clusterfuck."

He whistled for Festus and started toward the elevators. I said, "Sorry, but I've got to hustle. I need to catch Justis and Addison before they get tied up for the day. I don't want to tell them about this over the phone."

He nodded. "Don't worry about the truck. It's insured, and I'll deal with it." He helped me transfer my gear to the GV80. "Go see your fathers, then get some sleep. We'll meet up this evening and figure out what to do next."

Oh, that it had been that easy.

Chapter 4

Wednesday, September 8, 8:00 a.m.

I headed home to drop Festus off and change. When I hit the kitchen, I texted my fathers. *I'll be at the office in thirty. Need to see you both. Urgent.* My fathers have always done pretty well at squelching their "daddy's little girl" tendencies when it comes to my work, but this was going to test their limits.

Half an hour later, I found Addison in his customary pose, leaning back in his chair with his cowboy boots propped up on his desk. The wall of windows running behind him afforded a panoramic view of the airport. Four floors down, the cars on the Loop sped by like an army of multicolored ants. Addison was noshing on a blueberry cheese Danish. His older brother, Justis, dressed in his standard navy suit and Harvard tie, sat in one of Addison's client chairs drinking espresso from a tiny bone-china cup. Justis stood. "Iris. Are you all right? Your message sounded rather ominous."

I loaded the espresso machine sitting on Addison's side bar. "I'm okay, but it's been a long night." The machine gurgled to a stop, and I removed the little cup and said, "We've got way more trouble than we ever imagined on this Farragut case." The aroma of the rich coffee was heavenly. I reloaded the machine. No way one espresso shot was going to do it. "I spent half the night under arrest at the federal building with a bunch of DEA assholes."

Addison's boots hit the floor. *"Under arrest?"*

I sat down next to Justis and told them all about the night's events. When I finished, Addison's stare could have stopped a train. "Before we go one step further. Are. You. All right? Nothing matters to us more than that."

I nodded. "I've been up all night, and my wrists are sore from the cuffs because the DEA jerkoffs made me ride all the way back to San Antonio sitting on my hands, but yes, I'm fine." I sipped the espresso.

Justis muttered, "Oh, goodness."

Addison was less discreet, throwing his pen on his desk and hissing, "Fucking Christ."

When he and Justis finished peppering me with questions, I pulled an SD card out of my briefcase and passed it to Addison, who plugged it into his computer. Justis and I huddled around Addison's chair and watched forty-five seconds of zoomed video showing clear face shots of at least five of the attackers. Sometimes I just love myself—I can be one wicked bitch with a surveillance camera. We reran the video several times.

When we finished, Addison slammed his palm down on the desk. "Sonofabitch. That asshole sent us running into a minefield without a map—never mind almost getting our daughter killed."

I cleared my throat. "Well, whatever Farragut knew or didn't know, we're in this now. When those cartel people ID me, they'll be hot on my trail. Either we figure this out ourselves or I trust those feds to get it done, and considering the mess they made of it last night, I'm much more inclined to rely on us to bust this up than them."

Justis carried his coffee cup to the window. He took several sips while he watched an American plane swoop in for a landing. "Iris, where was this SD card while you were in custody?"

I thought back to me and Festus racing to the Escalade. I pictured myself opening the door... "I threw the camera and tripod onto the front seat when I reached the Escalade. It was right there when I got the truck back this morning."

He turned to me. "So the government was in possession of the Escalade—and the SD card—for a period of hours last night. They had access to the video and gave it back."

Addison tore another piece off his Danish and tossed it into his mouth. "So we have no obligation to turn it over to law enforcement." He licked his fingers. "I say we just lock it in the vault for now."

I grabbed a chocolate-filled donut doused with powdered sugar from the sideboard and hit the button on the espresso machine. I took a bite of the donut while the machine hissed and sputtered. "I didn't see any distinguishing marks, no visible license plates, nothing we could use to track them." I carried the rest of the donut and my coffee back to the client chair. The sugar and caffeine were kicking in. My pulse had a wiry trill to it, but the cogs and gears in my brain were grinding and turning like an old car coughing to life.

Justis sat back down next to me and patted my hand. "Iris, you go home and get some rest. Addison and I will contact Farragut about last night's events...though I'm sure he's already heard from staff at the ranch."

An idea tickled my semiaddled brain. I held up a finger. “Wait...” *What the hell was wrong with that statement?* Then the answer popped like an old-fashioned flash bulb. “He’s bound to have.”

Addison knitted his brows. “Bound to have what?”

The caffeine and chocolate were colliding head-on with exhaustion and an adrenaline crash. I shook my head to clear it and forced myself to concentrate. “Bound to have heard. Between the helicopters and those SUVs parading down 181, half the people in Kenton County know something went down at the Wind Rose last night. No way Farragut hasn’t heard about it. So, why hasn’t he called here, pissing and whining to you two?”

Addison smacked his palm on the desk. “That is a damn good question. Time we get that jackass on the phone and find out what the fuck is going on here.”

“Always a good thing to know.” I poured some of the syrupy chicory coffee from Addison’s pot into a foam cup and headed home. As I crossed the parking lot, I scanned the area for threats and fast-walked to the Genesis like a rat sprinting through the light for a piece of cheese. I wondered how long it would take the cartel to figure out who I was and set a trap.

Chapter 5

Wednesday, September 8, 6:00 p.m.

Back at the apartment, I stripped off my suit, took a shower, and crawled under the covers. The crisp cotton sheets felt cool against my skin, and the feather pillow was soft against my bruised face. Curling up in the cozy bed was a strong contrast to being laid out on the hard ground while Penn and Teller lived out their Dirty Harry fantasies on me. Festus climbed up onto the bed and sniffed me all over before he snuggled up against me, grunted, and fell asleep. I nodded off minutes later, my hand draped over his silky head.

Seven hours later, I woke up to him licking my face. The past three years had been tough, building to a crescendo when a serial killer shot and almost killed me the year before. After I recovered, I took advantage of every moment of joy that came my way. There was nothing quite as good as waking up to my wonderful, loving dog. We tussled and played peek-a-boo with the covers. I rubbed his velvety, freckled muzzle. "You need a walk?"

He ran to the hook where I keep his leash and barked. I pulled on some clothes, and we headed out for a constitutional. While we walked, I called

Addison. "So, what does the asshole of the week have to say about last night's events?"

Addison let out a sigh. "Seems he was at some management/staff bonding retreat at the YO Ranch up in Kerrville last night. Some hippie bullshit where they take your cell phone and make you confess your deepest fears and catch each other falling backward."

"Sounds productive. Maybe you should host one of those for the firm."

"Sure. That's just what a bunch of bloodthirsty litigators would really dig. I'll get Bernie right on planning it." Bernie was Addison's head bone-crusher in Litigation. "Anyway, Farragut said he stayed over at the hotel. Didn't head home until after breakfast this morning. Claimed he hadn't heard a word about the trouble at the ranch. Swore up and down he didn't have any idea about what the cartel guys were doing there except to say illegals come through Kenton County all the time on their way up from the border."

"Give me a second. I need to turn off the alarm on my bullshit detector."

I could hear the smirk in his voice. "Did somebody wake up cranky from her nap?"

"No. It was when I realized for sure our client is a lying chain-yanker that the cranky thing set in."

"Okay...tell me what you're seeing."

"I didn't have a chance to check their passports, but these were not some poor bastards slogging across the river to pick lettuce. They had AR-15s and at least a half mil in heroin, and they were parked and milling around like they were waiting for someone. I think the two trucks I saw first were being backed up by the third truck that came out of nowhere. That's organization."

Addison said, "That's the way we see it, too."

Festus stopped to check some nosemail and leave a reply. Addison continued. "But maybe our guy doesn't know anything about it..."

Festus was back on the move, heading home. "And maybe I'm Mother Teresa."

Addison laughed. "Okay, so much for that theory..."

Festus and I walked up the stairs to our condo, and I unlocked the door. "I'm going to see Sean tonight. We'll kick it around. Let's talk in the morning. Do I have your permission to run this by Marvin?"

Addison paused for a few beats then said, "Yeah. I think that's a great idea."

I gave Festus a biscuit and checked Find My for Sean. He was at Club 12 where he attended many of his Gamblers Anonymous meetings. I glanced at my watch. His usual meeting would let out in fifteen minutes. Deciding to surprise him, I loaded Festus into the back seat and headed west. Bob Dylan was singing "The Times They Are a Changin'" on Sirius.

When I pulled to the curb outside the building that was the epicenter of the San Antonio twelve-step community, I spotted Sean in a knot of people outside the main door. At six-foot-four, he towered above the small crowd. Some were smoking furiously, others nervously shifting from foot to foot. With ten years of abstinence from games of chance, Sean was a leader in the Gamblers Anonymous community and made certain he hung around after meetings in case any newcomers who were too shy to talk during the formal gathering needed someone to listen. Not wanting to interrupt, I sat in the SUV until the group dispersed.

Then, I saw her. Just the sight of her sent gerbils running through my guts. What the hell was she doing here?

I killed the engine, and Festus and I made a beeline toward Sean.

He was leaning on a limestone planter, talking to a tiny woman with platinum-white hair cut in a radical bob. A sick feeling roiled in my stomach as I recognized the hair and the pixie form. She was perched up on the planter like a fairy demon, looking up at Sean and talking animatedly. I didn't like Sean's expression when he saw me—a microsecond of caught-in-the-act flashed over his face before he smiled and pulled me into a hug.

"Hey, sugar! What a surprise. We're just finishing up here..."

When she cleared her throat, I turned and glared straight into her lupine-blue eyes. She didn't flinch, but her lips slithered into something between an obsequious smile and an outright sneer. "Hello, Iris. It's been a while."

I barely managed an icy "Dorinda."

Opting for a hasty retreat, Sean bent over and gave the blonde a distant hug. "Catch you at the next meeting." She didn't hug him back and sat silent, hostility oozing from her pores as she shot a dagger-filled look at me, said, "Sure," then hopped off the planter. Sean and I stood side by side and watched her walk away.

He scratched Festus's ears and turned to me. "What a great surprise! Why don't you follow me back to the loft, and I'll fix us a spread? The night is going to be glorious. We'll eat upstairs by the pool."

What the hell? I'd just found him chatting it up with the Antichrist, and he was talking about dinner by the pool? I couldn't think of anything to say.

He picked up the slack. "I know, I know. There's nothing to worry about. We'll talk about it over dinner."

I swallowed bile and bit back the urge to get into it right then. I nodded. "I'll see you there."

Sean and his partner of eighteen years, Robbie Hazelwood, had two floors of what used to be the Robert E. Lee Hotel. The bottom floor was all open, divided by furniture placement and support columns into a kitchen space, a living-dining area, and a gym. Sean's bedroom occupied a loft overhang that was bigger than my whole condo. The rest of the second floor was Robbie's flat. Underneath Sean's bedroom loft, what appeared to be a wall of bookshelves masked the entrance to a steel-reinforced, fireproof safe room that was accessed through the kitchen. That was where Sean conducted a lot of his more sensitive work.

Festus took up his usual position on the floor in the kitchen, immediately below the cookie jar containing gourmet dog treats. Festus yapped, and Sean tossed him a couple of the cookies then slid a casserole dish into the convection oven. "I made the chicken in poblano crème sauce you like so much."

"Sounds great. Where's Robbie?"

Sean pulled lettuce and veggies from the stainless steel refrigerator. "He's on a job over in Houston."

He tossed a salad while I recounted the events of the previous night. Grinding pepper onto the salad, he said, "No doubt it was a meet. I take it your fathers aren't going to the cops with your video for fear it'll end up incriminating the client?"

I nodded.

He drizzled the salad with olive oil. "Then, we need to get a handle on your security until we bust these bastards. And I think we should call Marvin. He's plugged in to everything about the drug trade around here."

"I talked to him earlier. He's tied up on a job tonight, but he'll get into it tomorrow."

The oven dinged, and Sean served our plates. We carried them into the elevator and up to the private rooftop garden Sean had created for him and Robbie when he bought the old hotel and turned it into San Antonio's premier loft condos. The oasis was complete with an outdoor kitchen and bar, a heated pool, and a hot tub. Sitting at the bar, we ate and talked about local events while a crackling electric tension danced under the surface of our chatter. We finished eating, and he took a plate of dessert pastries out of the refrigerator and carried them to a table and chairs by the pool while I made espresso at the bar. An awkward silence blanketed us as we sipped our coffee laced with Baileys. I put my cup down and turned to him. Keeping my voice level, I said, "How long has she been here?"

He fiddled with the handle of his mug. "A couple of weeks."

I locked eyes with him. "Why didn't you tell me?"

"I didn't want you to worry. Dorinda's been in recovery for ages. She's in town working on a defense contract at Lackland. Club 12 is the biggest meeting site in town. It was natural she'd end up there. There's nothing more to it."

The night was clear, and a million stars dotted the black velvet sky. I took his hand. "Sean, I've loved you since the first day I met you when I was six. You, Addison, Justis—you're the most important people in my life. You guys are the only family I have. I never want you lost in the abyss of your addiction again."

He took another sip of his coffee. "Iris, I know you blame Dorinda for my gambling problem. But, sugar, I have a gambling problem because I'm an addict, not because I met Dorinda at Stanford and we gambled ourselves to rock bottom together. That was a symptom of the problem, not the cause."

I stood up and walked to the railing of the rooftop garden that overlooked downtown San Antonio. I counted at least three buildings Sean owned outright besides the one I was standing on. When it came to Dorinda, Sean had a blind spot the size of Alabama. I forced myself to keep my voice calm. "Sean, you've got too much to lose now. Back at Stanford, you had a couple of software patents and some computer gear. Now, you own half the real estate in downtown San Antonio, drive a Ferrari, and fly your own jet. You've got an international reputation in the cyberintelligence world. Think about your security clearances...your clients. You can't risk a relapse. You've come too far."

He avoided making eye contact with me as he picked up our cups and headed to the kitchen for refills. Without turning to me, he said, "And I'm fine. I know how valuable all those things are. If nothing else, the fear of having to fly commercial is enough the keep me straight." His voice was dripping with denial.

I followed him to the kitchen and perched on a bar stool. "Dorinda's a trigger, and you need to avoid her like the plague."

He poured more coffee into our cups and topped them off with Baileys. "Well, you don't have to worry much longer. Her gig at Lackland is up in a few weeks."

"Her showing up at your meeting is not a coincidence. She stalked you to that rehab in Boston. Nobody knew where we were. We did everything to make sure there was no record of your admission so it couldn't affect your clearances. Yet, that bitch came all the way from California and broke into the hospital to get to you. Hell, it took her being arrested to finally get rid of her. And now, she just *happens* to show up at the same meeting you attend. That's ludicrous." The heat of my rage at Dorinda Crandall was rising in me like Old Faithful. Any minute, I was going to spew steam out my ears.

We sat in silence for what seemed like an eternity. "What's Robbie's take on this?"

Sean fiddled with a wet paper napkin, tearing it into little bits. "I haven't discussed it with him. He'll get all bent out of shape just like you are now, and there's no reason for it. I'd appreciate your discretion on this point, if you don't mind."

I walked around the bar and stood right next to him. "Sean, things are finally starting to level out around here. I've hit my stride with therapy, and I'm making real progress on getting past what happened with Kerabos and with Geare. I'm sleeping through the night for the first time in two and a half years. I'm living alone without having to call you every time the house creaks. They've released me from physical therapy, and I actually did a few crunches at the gym last week without puking from the pain. You're crushing it at work, and you and Robbie seem to have gotten to a really good, solid place. You've got more than enough money to last the rest of your life. So please...I'm begging you...don't rock this boat. Change meetings, and tell her to leave you alone. If there really is a contract at Lackland and it really is almost over, soon she'll go back to wherever she came from, you'll be back at Club 12, and we'll all go on down the road."

He kissed the top of my head. "I'll take it under advisement."

I stayed a few more minutes, and we yakked about trivial things until Festus and I headed home.

In the car, I said to my beautiful dog, "There's a bad moon rising, buddy."

He rested his giant head on his paws and let out a whine.

Chapter 6

Friday, September 10, 9:15 a.m.

I was sitting at my desk plowing through a list of missing heirs that Oil and Gas needed me to find. The damn thing was longer than the descendancy of Abraham and Sarah, and I welcomed the interruption when Addison called. His voice came through the phone in his trademark tone of understated urgency that cuts through bullshit like a Ginsu knife. "Iris, could you join us at the Circus Burgers store on San Pedro—now, please?"

"On my way."

I grabbed my purse and briefcase and headed down the stairs.

Ten minutes later, I knocked on the locked front door of the San Pedro store. The sunshades were down, and I couldn't see inside. Someone had taped a handwritten sign in the window—*Closed for Repairs.* Addison opened the door. Workers in white Tyvek suits and face masks were bustling about with red hazmat bags and swab kits and spray bottles of cleaner working under the direction of a large, bald man who was issuing orders like a drill sergeant. Images from Three Mile Island and

Chernobyl raced through my mind. "What the hell? Is it safe to come in?"

Addison motioned me toward the game room behind the main dining area. "It's fine. Just don't eat anything."

Justis and Quinten Farragut were huddled at a table behind the video games and shuffleboard courts. I recognized Farragut from photos I'd seen in the newspaper, but those images hadn't captured his flaming rosacea and disheveled air. Farragut got to his feet, and Addison introduced us. He was at least six-five and couldn't have weighed an ounce under two-fifty. We shook hands…and I bit back the urge to say, "Thanks for almost getting me killed, you lying jerkoff." Instead, I sat down, pulled a legal pad from my briefcase, and asked, "How can I help?"

Justis motioned to Farragut. "Why don't you bring Iris up to speed."

Farragut looked like ten miles of bad road on a low tank of gas—his suit was rumpled, his tie was askew, and his face was etched with worry. "About one yesterday afternoon, we heard from a customer saying her brother had become ill that morning after they both ate here the evening before. That would be Wednesday night, the eighth. We didn't think much of it. The woman who called was fine. There are always bugs going around town, and restaurants get these calls all the time." He mopped his brow with his handkerchief.

I made a note. "What was CB's response when this woman called?"

He burrowed his finger behind his shirt collar and undid the button. "We have a protocol for these situations. The manager immediately relayed all the information from the caller to Risk Management. A sanitation specialist was here by two-fifteen yesterday afternoon. Just look around." He dipped his head toward the bald man and his platoon of white-clad minions. "Our sanitation people are like pit bulls on a porterhouse when it comes to foodborne illness. When our man determined nothing was out of order, I was satisfied we were clear. We left the store open and went on about our business.

"At four yesterday, we got another call. Same deal. Somebody sick who had eaten here Wednesday night. The head of the food safety department—" He tipped his head to the dining room again. "That's Frank, the guy running things—well, Frank immediately came to the store. When he couldn't find anything irregular, he shut the store down for a total evaluation and cleaning." Frank motioned to Farragut, and he loosened his gaping tie some more, heaved himself off the chair, and lumbered to the beverage station to confer with his sanitation chief.

We watched as Farragut pointed to various pieces of equipment, and the bald man shouted orders. Two workers began disassembling the soda machine. Farragut came back and settled onto the chair like a linebacker sitting in a kindergarten desk. "I'm having them take the soda machine back to the warehouse to sanitize it." He wiped his forehead again. "I hate self-serve stations. They really save on the labor matrix, but they are cesspools for bacteria."

Yum... I made a note to remember that the next time I refilled a soda.

Justis prompted, "Go on, Quinten."

"About eight this morning, I get a call from an ER doc at Santa Teresa in the Med Center. Said they had fifteen people in the ER with what looks like some bizarre foodborne illness. Three more at St. Elizabeth's ER with the same thing. They've diagnosed the patients with liver issues, some in acute liver failure. They all have hypoglycemia, some of it dangerously severe. A bunch of the folks are headed to the ICU. One poor guy with a kidney transplant may not make it. The only thing the sick people have in common is having eaten here two nights ago." He pulled a roll of Tums from his jacket pocket, peeled one off, and stuffed it into his mouth. His color was dusky, and I hoped to God he didn't have a heart attack right there.

Justis said, "Quinten, are you all right? Do you need us to call for medical help?"

Farragut chewed the antacid while he pulled an orange prescription bottle out of his suit coat pocket and poured a tablet into his hand. He tossed the pill into his mouth and dry-swallowed it along with the last of the Tums. "I'll be okay." The sweating slowed down, and his color returned to its original red flush.

Justis tipped his chin a micron, telling me to proceed. "Mr. Farragut, has anything even remotely similar happened in any of your other stores in recent memory?"

He chewed his lip. "We had a guy get pretty sick up in Tishomingo, Oklahoma, last month. It's a low-volume store in a rural county. Same kind of deal—somebody called saying a relative was sick after eating in the store. We sent one of the sanitation guys up there on the company plane. Had him there in three hours. The place was clean as a whistle. The sick guy was in the hospital a couple of days, but he recovered fully. The docs never determined what was wrong with him, and no more cases showed up. Smooth sailing up there ever since."

Justis and Addison exchanged glances. Justis spoke. "Quinten, out of an overabundance of caution, we're going to recommend you close that Oklahoma store, if for no other reason than the optics."

Farragut nodded. "Sure. Whatever you think." When nobody said anything else, he looked at Justis. "You mean now?"

"It's probably best," Justis said. "Why don't you just give the manager a call. We'll be happy to wait."

Farragut fished his phone out of his pocket. "What do I say is the reason?"

Justis and Addison both glanced in my direction. I hate leaving the impression I can lie through my teeth at the drop of a hat, so I bit my lip and feigned difficulty concocting the story. I checked my watch. "The store's not open yet, right?"

Farragut shook his head. "The employees won't get there until 10:00."

"Have the manager call the staff and say they've had an electrical problem and lost power to the store. Stick a handwritten sign on the door about a power failure. Everybody's off work until the electricians fix the problem. Keep the juice on to the refrigeration, but make it look like the place is experiencing a total blackout. Tell the manager to keep his mouth shut and not talk about it to anyone but you until you tell him differently."

Farragut popped another Tums and said, "The manager's a good guy. He'll play ball." He called the Oklahoma store and relayed the instructions.

When he hung up, I tossed a glance to my fathers, then said, "We're going to need an outside expert." When Farragut drew in a ragged breath, I held up a hand to stop him before he got started haranguing me about the quality of Frank and his sanitation department. "Mr. Farragut, these poisonings could be a result of sabotage. If that's the case, we don't know who's behind it, so we need someone outside of your ecosystem investigating the case. Also, we may eventually need an unbiased third-party expert witness if you face litigation resulting from these incidents."

Farragut's eyes went wide. "Are you saying my people shouldn't be cleaning the store? I've got to sanitize before I have a rat's chance in hell of those twits at County Health letting me reopen. My people are swabbing every surface before they clean it."

Justis added, "The health department was here earlier and collected their own samples before the cleaning started."

An ear-splitting racket shook the store as a wire shelving unit stacked with pots and pans toppled over, and a pack of the white-clad cleaners scampered into the kitchen. When I could hear myself think again, I said, "I'm fine with what you're doing. I just want some experts outside your organization to advise us and review everything. I do, however, recommend that you not dispose of any unused food left in your refrigerators. I'd like the consultants to have access to that."

Farragut said, "No problem. We can dump it later."

Workers carrying various parts of the disassembled soda machine headed to the front door. Farragut pushed himself out of the chair and hollered, "Hold on there! Frank! Goddamn it." The workers froze as Farragut lurched across the dining area. He spoke to the sanitation chief, who nodded quickly and directed the workers to the back door. Farragut returned and sat back down. "Damn moon suits. Legal insists on them if the employees face any possible risk of exposure to a pathogen. Idiots were going to haul that equipment out into the front parking lot wearing those getups for the whole damn world to see. I swear to God, sometimes I wonder how these people find their way home."

Addison scrubbed his jaw then said, "We definitely need outside experts, but we need somebody fast. Iris? Suggestions on who we should hire?"

I thought about it for a minute. "There was a case a couple of years ago...an old woman killed her husband with some bizarre poison and then sued a chain of steakhouses in Ohio, claiming it was from their salad bar."

Farragut's eyes lit up. "I read about that. Guy who owned the chain was damn near bankrupt before the cops figured out the old lady killed her husband for his life insurance."

I pulled out my phone and tapped keys. "But it wasn't the cops that figured it out. I saw a case study on it. The restaurant chain hired a forensic food safety expert..." I pulled up the criminal case on LexisNexis and scanned the docket. "Cibius Forensics." I Googled some more then scribbled the phone number down and passed it to Justis. "Better if you make the initial contact and clarify they work for you, not me. I'll follow up afterward."

He folded the slip of paper and stood. "If you'll excuse me, I'll go make the call in my car."

Addison rested his forearms on the table and leaned forward. "Anything else you can think of, Iris?"

I struggled to concentrate amid the clanking pandemonium as workers raced around culturing every surface before others swooped in with disinfectants. "Have you determined which menu items the sick patrons ate in common?"

Farragut shook his head. "The doctors and County Health are still working on it. Apparently some people are too sick to answer questions. They think the symptoms may be consistent with a rare and severe form of *Bacillus cereus*, but that comes from rice and pasta, and we don't serve any of that. It'll be a day or so before they get cultures back on the hospitalized patients."

"Do you have a list of the sick diners?"

He pulled out his phone. "Our people have been at the hospitals since the first call came in from the ER." He tapped the screen and scrolled. "I have the list right here."

I stood and looked over his shoulder. "We need to go through credit card receipts."

I gave Addison the we'll-talk-about-this-later nod as Farragut looked up at me with wide eyes. "They're in the office."

He led us to the back of the restaurant and let Addison out the service entrance leading into the employee parking area where Justis sat in his Lincoln talking on his cell. After Addison climbed into his brother's Continental, Farragut bolted the back door and unlocked the manager's office, motioning for me to follow. I took a seat on a rolling stool while Farragut pulled a box of credit card receipts out of a floor safe. He sat at the desk and read off the names on the receipts while I checked the list of sick people. In half an hour, we had receipts for fifteen of the eighteen hospitalized customers.

He put the stack of receipts back in the box. "The rest either paid cash or had their meal charged to a credit card other than their own."

"Can you lay those receipts out on the desk? I need to photograph them."

I snapped pics of each of the receipts and stored them on the firm's cloud account. Farragut stared over my shoulder while I worked. When I finished, he said, "Cheesy fries. That's the only thing they all had in common."

I slipped my phone back into my briefcase. "Mr. Farragut, you mentioned that *Bacillus cereus* comes from rice and pasta. I'm worried that the poisoning is coming from a type of food you don't serve."

He knitted his bushy eyebrows above his jowly face. "Why isn't that good news...like they got it somewhere besides CB?"

Ah, the delusions of desperation. "Mr. Farragut, it seems unlikely to me that a group of fifteen people with almost identical symptoms all ate exactly the same thing at the same place at the same time and got sick as a result of eating somewhere else."

His shoulders slumped and his face drooped. "When you put it that way, I see your point. But I still don't get why the fact we don't serve rice or pasta bothers you."

I felt like my answer should come with a warning label. *Danger: Risk of bursting delusional bubble.* Maybe I hadn't spelled it out clearly enough earlier. I took a deep breath. "Sir, if all the victims were poisoned in this store by an organism that grows in food you don't stock or sell, the pathogen didn't get into the meals through normal channels like a bad batch of premade pasta salad or a tray of rice that sat out too long. That leads me to worry that it didn't end up in the food accidentally."

The sweating started again. He fumbled the pill bottle out and dry-swallowed another small white tablet. *Dear God, please don't let him kick off on my shift...* "Sir, do you need me to call for help?"

He grunted a mirthless chuckle. "I definitely need help, but not the kind that comes in an ambulance. What I need is a pack of Marlboro reds, a fifth of Jack, and a fucking lap dance. Instead, I'm chowing Xanax like Pez and refilling my nitro every day while I hope to Christ you and your family can save my business."

What do you say to that? I opted for, "Well, okey dokey. We're going to do our best." I noticed a bank of monitors mounted to the ceiling above the manager's desk. "Now we need to figure out how the contaminant got into the cheesy fries. Do you have security cameras?"

He nodded and used the manager's computer to log on to a cloud account where the video was stored. "I'll send you a link to the encrypted folder with the video in it. We save it for ninety days." I rattled off one of Sean's secure addresses. He typed and finally hit the Enter key with a flourish as access to the video whooshed through cyberspace. He looked at me. "What else?"

"I'm going to need a list of new hires—employees you've taken on at this store in the past month. And their personnel files."

He tapped more keys on the computer, hemmed and hawed, and typed more. "I just sent the files to the same address."

His cell blasted out "Entry of the Gladiators." He answered, "Farragut." I watched as his face blanched and fell. With a shaky voice, he said, "Are you sure?" then, "Tell Risk Management to get a hold of the family. Red carpet service. We pick up the tab for everything—and I mean everything."

An aggressive knock hammered on the front door. Whoever it was clearly wasn't paying attention to the sign taped to the glass. Farragut clicked a remote, and the bank of television monitors flickered to life. A woman grasping a wad of paper was pounding on the door. He muttered "Crap" under his breath then said into the phone, "Look, I gotta go. I'll be in the office in twenty." He hung up.

I stared at the monitor. "Who's that?"

He heaved himself out of the manager's desk chair and trudged toward the front door. "That's the wicked witch of County Health. She doesn't know her ass from her elbow about the food business. Spends her life pencil-whipping every restaurant in town."

I followed as he turned the ring of keys he'd left dangling from the lock and opened the door. A rapier-thin woman with too much lipstick and a cheap polyester suit shoved a document covered in a blue jacket into his hands. "Mr. Farragut, by order of County Health, I am hereby instructing you to close all of your stores in the San Antonio metropolitan area by noon today pending an investigation into health code violations that may have led to the serious illness of eighteen people." She turned and stalked off. I watched her get in her county car and drive away while Quinten Farragut stood reading the document she had delivered. Sweat ran off his forehead, and his hands shook.

What had started out as a relatively simple case had quickly exploded into a dumpster fire. Farragut was coming undone. I stepped up, pulled him inside, and locked the front door. "We need Addison and Justis to look at that order. Maybe they can get a judge to stop it, at least temporarily."

He slumped down in one of the booths. "That call a minute ago was the guy heading the hospital team. One of the patients at Santa Teresa—the guy with the kidney transplant—just died."

I was struggling to absorb that devastating development when I saw the truck from the evening news pull into the front parking lot. The local reporter who did the tattletale gotcha spot featuring the lowest restaurant sanitation score of the week was setting up to record.

Make that a radioactive dumpster fire.

Farragut followed my gaze and caught sight of the reporter. He mopped his face and neck with the handkerchief again. "Just great. The angel of fucking death is here."

I rushed into the game room and warned Frank not to open the door then handed Farragut his briefcase. "When I pull up to the service entrance, get in the back seat and stay out of sight."

I slipped out the back door and walked to the front parking lot. Without looking up, I unlocked the GV and pulled around to the alley entrance. I took a couple of deep breaths to steady myself as Farragut ducked into the back seat. Resisting the urge to floor it, I pulled quietly out of the service drive onto the side street. In the rearview mirror, I saw the reporter in front of the shuttered restaurant pointing in my direction while her cameraman followed my vehicle with his lens. I merged onto Loop 410 and let out a sigh of relief as I headed to the Hampe Ewald.

A simple vandalism case on Farragut's ranch had immediately escalated to a shootout with a bunch of narco-terrorists. The next night, at least eighteen people had been poisoned in his flagship store, and now one of them was dead. I glanced back at him as he slugged down another Xanax.

All I could think was *What the hell isn't he telling me?*

Chapter 7

Saturday, September 11, 2:30 p.m.

To shield him from the press, Justis and Addison had banished our client to a condo Circus Burgers leased at a high-end complex north of town. I took him groceries and a suitcase his maid had packed, then headed to Sean's to review the surveillance video Farragut had sent.

I found Sean in the kitchen, munching on a chocolate cupcake. He wiped a smudge of icing off his lip with his thumb and gave me a hug. Festus pawed him. "Hey, buddy!" Sean popped the last of the snack in his mouth and ran his fingers under the kitchen faucet. He dried his hands on a towel, dug two cookies out of the jar, and tossed them to Festus.

"What were you eating?"

"It was a keto treat. I got it at the six-thirty meeting. Some concoction of a gluten-free cupcake filled with pudding made of avocado, artificial sweetener, vanilla, and dark chocolate. It sounded hideous, but we're all trying to bring something healthier than coffee and donuts to the meetings. I only tried one to be polite, but it was really good. I brought the leftovers home after I cleaned up. You want one?"

"Avocado, chocolate, vanilla, and fake sugar? Jesus...that sounds like some mess a bunch of kids stirred up when their parents weren't looking. Pass."

He worked the Keurig and made himself a cup of coffee, then waggled a mug, and I nodded. The machine whirred and gurgled, and the aroma of coffee filled the kitchen. "So, what are we doing today?"

I sat down on one of the bar stools at the giant marble-topped kitchen island and told him about Farragut and the files in his email. He opened a drawer and pushed a couple of buttons inside. The floor-to-ceiling shelves of cookbooks made a grinding sound and slid back, exposing the safe room. The space was relatively small, but it had a sleek, ultramodern design. Except for the arsenal of pistols and rifles hanging from a Lucite pegboard along the back wall, the room could have come straight out of *Architectural Digest*. He sat down at the computer. "Let's look at the video first."

"Sounds good." I pulled a green-and-magenta-striped Milo Baughman scoop chair up to his chrome and glass desk and turned it so I could see his monitor. He followed the link Farragut had emailed.

I peered over his shoulder. "How many cameras do we have?"

He studied the directories. "One on the front door and one on the service door. Those are in plain sight to discourage robberies, blatant employee theft, and the like. And...they also have one hidden from view taking a long shot down the alley behind the store."

"Why hide that one?"

"The visible ones are almost like decoys, making bad guys avoid them and thus walk into the trap of the hidden camera. In this setup, thieves taking inventory out the back door won't hide themselves after they clear the building, and vehicles coming up to the service entrance for nefarious purposes won't be scared into parking somewhere they can't be identified."

"Any inside?"

He squinted at the screen. "One, but it's pointed at the exit. Again, to deter primitive robberies and ham-handed employee theft." He pushed back in his office chair. "Standard setup designed to prevent money and inventory from leaving the store, not to monitor what's going on with food service."

I mulled it over. "Let's try the hidden one with the long shot of the alley first. We need to run through the afternoon before the poisoning. As far as we know, all the sick people ate between 6:30 p.m. and closing. Let's start around two that afternoon and see what's cookin'."

We viewed the usual drivel as food purveyors pulled up through the weedy alley, unloaded, and drove away. Employees entered and exited the frame to smoke, sitting on overturned buckets and flicking their ashes onto the cracked asphalt. Around 6:00 p.m. the activity slowed down as the dinner rush picked up.

Then a man in a hoodie came out of the service entrance carrying a small paper bag. He walked down the service drive away from the camera. At the end of the alley, he tossed the bag into a dumpster and disappeared around the corner. I grabbed Sean's arm.

He tapped keys. "On it." He replayed the snippet of video.

"Any chance the camera got a frame of his face?"

Sean replayed it in slow motion. "Nope. See here...he's hiding his face from the visible camera covering the service door. I mean, who needs a hoodie in South Texas in September?"

I fumbled my cell phone out of my purse and called Farragut. "Can you send me a link to the security video from the Tishomingo store? I need it for the day before through the day after the incident with the customer who got sick."

His voice was thick but anxious. Probably the Xanax with Jack chasers. "Yeah, give me a minute." I heard clunking in the background as he muttered, "I've got my laptop with me... Let me check Risk Management's log...here it is. We sent our man up there August 20..." He kept mumbling to himself as he typed. Finally, he said, "I just sent the link to the same address you gave me before." I heard a ding, and Sean nodded that the email had arrived.

"Got it. Thanks."

He stammered, "Iris, I just heard from Risk Management. Three more customers have shown up at Santa Teresa ER."

"Did they eat at the San Pedro store?"

"Yeah, Wednesday night. They just waited longer to go to the hospital. And we pulled the credit card charges. Cheesy fries...all three of 'em. This is a fucking disaster. Please tell me you've found something."

I was almost certain that the stores had been sabotaged. But I didn't trust Farragut, and I wasn't telling him anything more until we worked it all through.

"We'll review that Oklahoma video and see what we can figure out. Also, do you know how often the dumpsters in the alley behind the San Pedro store are emptied?"

"I'll check the schedule." More typing. "Looks like we have two units for that store. One outside the service entrance and one at the end of the alley we split with the Chinese joint down the street. Both are picked up Tuesdays and Saturdays. They should be by around...five for today's pickup. Please, tell me what you've got..."

"Nothing yet, but we'll update you if we get something." I hung up and checked my watch. It was 4:15. I grabbed my purse and briefcase. "I've got forty-five minutes to dive that dumpster before the truck gets there to empty it."

He turned off the monitor. "I'm coming with you. I can't let you hog up all the glamour."

"We need something to secure that sack in if we find it. It probably contains the poison."

Sean nodded. "Gotcha covered." He grabbed a backpack from his hall closet and he, Festus, and I took the elevator to the garage. I pulled on the coveralls and rubber boots I keep in a go-bag in the cargo area of my SUV. I extracted a small plastic box and stuffed it into the pocket of my overalls then dug rubber gloves and a face shield out and set them on the center console as I climbed behind the wheel. Sean loaded Festus in the back and stowed his bag in the cargo section. When he got into the passenger seat, he handed me what looked like a heavy-duty five-gallon Ziploc bag with *Warning—Biohazard* printed in red over a skull and crossbones. I shoved it into my pocket. "What are you doing with biohazard bags?"

He smiled. "Let's just say it's good to be prepared."

I rolled my eyes. "Jesus, Sean. One of these days you're going to get a straight job and write code for Microsoft instead of hacking Caribbean banks, overthrowing banana republics, and blowing up shit in the desert."

He winked at me. "The banks are a bore, but the banana republic thing is way more fun than writing code for Bill. And, I don't know how many times I have to tell you, I don't overthrow—I *undermine*. There's a difference."

I cranked the engine, and we sped up 281 toward San Pedro.

Dumpster diving is best done in the wee hours of the night, but you play the hand you're dealt. I parked the Genesis by the dumpster at the end of the alley and left the engine running to keep Festus cool. Fingering the plastic box in my pocket, I turned to Sean. "Go stand where you can see around the corner and whistle if anyone is coming. If we get made, standard story."

He nodded. "I'm your brother. You think your new engagement ring slipped off in the paper towel when you dried your hands in the ladies' room, and you're desperately trying to find it before your fiancé figures out it's missing. You have the ring?"

I nodded. "Finding" the ring while I was being interrogated by some security guard from the strip mall would validate my story. I pulled the gloves on and fitted the face shield's elastic band around my head, took a deep breath, grabbed the rusty edge of the dumpster, and pulled myself up like a gymnast mounting the parallel bars. I trudged around in the muck, moving bags filled with empty jugs of lemon chicken sauce, fish bones, and plate scrapings of leftover kung pao chicken. As flies buzzed around me, I struggled to keep my mind off of what other life forms might be lurking in the steamy steel box. Then, I saw it—a small brown paper bag sitting between an empty fish sauce container and a crushed foam to-go box. I used my cell phone to photograph my find in place then carefully picked it out of the surrounding detritus and secured it in the biohazard bag.

I crawled out of the dumpster and stripped off my gear before I got into the driver's seat, pulled around the corner, and picked up Sean.

"Did you get it?"

I nodded. "I'll call Cibius and see what they want me to do with it." We had no more than hit the street when the Garbage Gobbler truck pulled into the alley. An inch is as good as a mile.

Chapter 8

Saturday, September 11, 5:15 p.m.

Justis's contact at Cibius gave me directions to their twenty-four-hour lab. The wind whipped through my hair as I drove down 281 with the windows down and the AC blasting full force. Festus stood on his hind legs on the floor of the back seat with his head sticking through the open moon roof. It was his favorite way to ride. The stench of rancid Chinese food clung to me like a creeping vine. When the Cibius tech met me at the door, I caught him sniffing the air, trying to discern the source of the stench.

Back at Sean's apartment, I headed to the shower while he retrieved the video from the store in Oklahoma and queued it up. When I came back to the safe room, drying my hair with one of his monogrammed towels, he inhaled cautiously. "That's much better."

I swatted him with the damp towel and leaned down to peer over his shoulder. His giant monitor displayed a paused shot of a parking lot. I sat down in the scoop chair. "Check the service entrance the night before the illness was reported."

Sean typed and studied the screen. "Date?"

I dug my notes out of my briefcase. "August 19."

Sure as hell, around 7:30 that night, a guy in a hoodie exited the service door carrying a small paper bag. He glanced over his shoulder, tossed the bag in a dumpster, and disappeared from view. "Holy shit! That's our guy."

Sean nodded. "Probably, but we still don't have a face shot."

I shrugged. "But we do have a damn good idea the asshole in the video did the poisonings. And he had to work in the restaurants, or he wouldn't have been coming out of the service doors. That means he's somewhere on the payroll rosters for those stores. That's huge."

He logged off the computer, and I followed him into the kitchen where he rooted around in the stainless steel Sub-Zero. "What sounds good for dinner?"

I laughed. "Not Chinese. That's for damn sure."

He took a pizza out of the freezer and held it up. I nodded.

"We can eat on the roof." We noshed on chips and salsa and drank cold beer while the kitchen filled with the savory aroma of pizza. When the cheese was bubbling and brown, Sean sliced the pie and slipped the pan into an insulated carrier. We rode the elevator up to the roof and headed to the outdoor kitchen. The sun was a giant blood orange slipping behind the San Antonio skyline. Festus took a running leap into the pool, paddled to the wide, shallow steps, and lay down with his belly in the water while Sean and I ate the pizza and talked about the case. When we finished, Sean tossed a piece of crust to Festus then retrieved a plate of chocolate cupcakes from the refrigerator and set them on the bar. I eyed the plate. "Is that the keto crap you were eating before?"

He passed me the cupcake. "Here, just try a bite. You can chuck it if you don't think it's great."

I bit into the cupcake, and it was surprisingly good. "Not bad." I took another bite. "Maybe I'll start attending."

The fleeting expression on his face flashed before me like the strobe lights on a patrol car. I set the half-eaten cupcake on the plate. "She made them."

He frowned. "So? It's not like they're toxic waste just because she baked them. Anyway, I've eaten three. I'm still alive, so just think of me as your food taster."

I caught his eyes. "Sean, this is serious. I am begging you, please tell her you can't see her, block her number, and change meetings. I feel like I'm watching you throw yourself into traffic."

"Iris, this is a GA thing. We're all just there to help each other stay straight. I don't know why you can't accept that."

His phone vibrated on the bar. He snatched it up and walked over to the pool. A couple of minutes later, the chime announced that the private elevator had opened into the rooftop vestibule. Sean cracked the door and slipped into the small area around the elevator, shutting it behind him.

I scooted over to the door and leaned my ear near the crack.

Her voice was venomous and sharp. "Why aren't you letting me in?"

Sean stammered. "I told you. This is not a good time. I'm working."

"I know she's there. She's always been jealous of me. Now, she's poisoning you against me. I can't believe you're letting her do that, just when we're reconnecting."

After some whispering I couldn't make out, Dorinda shrieked, "How dare you turn me away! I'm not going to let her come between us this time." The elevator dinged again, and I dashed back to the kitchen. I was just sitting down on a stool at the bar when Sean walked back onto the roof. For an instant, his eyes were wide like he'd been caught at something, but he screwed on a neutral expression and stalked over to me.

"Iris, don't give me shit over this. I know what I'm doing."

I gazed at the city lights shimmering from the high-rise office buildings of downtown. "Have you talked to X about this? You should run this by him."

When I turned to him, I saw something in his eyes I had never seen before. Sean was angry with me. "What I talk to my sponsor about is my business." He cleared his throat and made a show of checking his watch. "I hate to call it early, but I have a lot of work to do, and I should get on it."

A terrible weight descended over me, carrying with it an odd feeling of disorientation. Sean Galen—my soulmate since he superglued a kid's ass to a toilet seat for taking my lunch in first grade... Sean Galen, who had saved my life when I had been kidnapped two and half years before... Sean Galen was asking me to leave. Too stunned to do anything else, I picked up my purse, whistled for Festus, and stammered, "Sure. I need to head home. Thanks for dinner."

He hugged me like I was some society matron he'd met at a cocktail party. "I'll call you tomorrow."

Festus shook himself off, and we walked into the vestibule and boarded the elevator down to the garage. When the doors closed, I took the Glock out of my purse. Tightening my grip on the pistol, I scanned the garage for threats as we made our way to the truck. I circled the Genesis, checking through the windows for unwanted passengers lurking in the dark. Satisfied we were clear, I unlocked the driver's door. Festus hopped in, and I climbed in the driver's seat, locked the doors, and set the weapon on the console. I let out a deep breath I hadn't realized I'd been holding.

Something felt terribly wrong—like our world was wobbling on its axis. I hoped with all my heart that Sean didn't tumble off the horizon.

Chapter 9

Sunday, September 12, 6:30 a.m.

I was sound asleep, snuggled up against Festus, when my cell rang with Survivor's "Eye of the Tiger." Robbie. It was still dark outside. I fumbled for the phone. "What's wrong?"

"I'm sorry I woke you up. I'm downstairs. Can I come up?"

"Of course." I pulled a robe on and unlocked the dead bolt on the front door. Robbie was climbing the front stairs to my condo, his face knitted into a mask of worry. "Come in here. What's happening?"

He walked in and sat down. Thin and muscular with brown hair and olive skin, Robbie was one of the most handsome men I'd ever known. His gold-flecked tiger eyes grabbed your gaze and wouldn't let it go. His face was so breathtakingly stunning, most people never noticed the thin white line that ran from the corner of his mouth to the top of his left ear. Years of speech and physical therapy had minimized the effects of the paralysis in that side of his face. His crooked smile struck people who didn't know otherwise as just one more feature of his roguish good looks. The damage was a souvenir from the day his Humvee had hit an IED years before. But today, the line was red and angry, and Robbie's normal quiet demeanor was agitated and jumpy. I'd never seen him this way, and he was scaring the hell out of me.

"What's wrong? Is Sean all right?"

He shook his head. "He's not hurt or anything. But, he's not all right." He took a deep breath. "He's gambling again."

I sat down on the couch next to him and forced myself to sound calm. "You suspect or you know?"

He jerked out a shaky nod. "I know. When I got back from Houston last night, Sean was in the shower. His phone rang, and I saw the caller ID. It was a bookie in Vegas. I didn't let on that I saw. When he came out of the bathroom, I went up to my flat, claimed I had to finish a report, but I listened through the door. I heard him placing a bet on the football game today...Seahawks and Colts. He put ten grand on the Colts. The Seahawks are favored by seven."

I leaned back on the sofa. "Jesus. When it starts, he takes safer bets. If he's betting against the odds, then this has been going on for a while." He nodded. "You know Dorinda's in town?" He nodded again. "He doesn't think you know," I said.

"Well, that cat's out of the bag. She showed up at the loft late last night. He tried to get rid of her so I wouldn't see her, but she went ballistic when he wouldn't let her in. I came down this morning, and someone had keyed my car."

I told him about seeing her at Club 12 and about the scene on the roof the evening before after Sean and I finished dinner. "Sean told me she was in town doing some contract job out at Lackland and would be leaving soon. Claimed it was sheer coincidence she showed up at the meeting."

Robbie walked into the kitchen and put a K-cup in the Keurig. I followed him. When the machine spat out the coffee, he tossed the pod.

"He told me the same thing. I don't believe it for a second." Festus ambled up, and Robbie absently scratched his ears. "I called X on my way over here. He's coming to brunch today. We're going to stage an intervention. We need you to join."

"Of course. I wasn't sure we were having brunch today. He was so angry at me last night, he basically asked me to leave. I didn't even know what to say."

Robbie took a swig of the coffee. "I've been up all night." He set the cup down and leaned on the counter. "We got into it after she left. Said a bunch of things I wish we hadn't. I finally went up to my flat around four-thirty. I just couldn't do it anymore. He really raked me over the coals."

"So what's the plan for brunch?"

He swallowed hard. "X is going to show up at 1:00 sharp. We're going to confront Sean about the gambling and tell him he needs to go back to Boston. I'll offer to go with him."

I popped another pod in the Keurig. "When this mess with Farragut clears up, I can come, too. We can take turns. We made it work before. We'll make it work again."

Robbie nodded. "Thanks, Iris." I followed him to the door. He pulled me into a hug and held me for several beats. I was sure I felt him choking back sobs. Robbie was one of the toughest guys I'd ever met. He and Sean had been a sniper team in the Rangers for chrissakes. Robbie could slay an army of terrorists with a pen knife without breaking a sweat. But this had him on the verge of tears. He wasn't alone. Being at odds with Sean for the first time in our lives left me with a weird jangling sensation in my chest like I'd just been in a car wreck. Eventually, he broke the embrace and made his exit. I threw on some shorts and took Festus for a walk just as the sun was coming up. Thoughts of me and Sean floated through my mind as we meandered through the neighborhood and the sun crawled over the horizon.

Sean had been my hero all my life. A year older, he was the big brother I never had. When his addiction overtook him the first time, he had a little money left that he hadn't gambled away, and he, Robbie, and I had moved to Boston. I'd worked a temporary gig at the National Archives, and Robbie was with us when he wasn't off on a job. Together, we'd made enough to pay for a crappy little apartment. We'd even scraped together the balance of the rehab tab after Sean's money ran out.

When a judge had finally gotten sick of Dorinda's relentless stalking and ordered a psych evaluation, she'd disappeared. We hadn't heard from her since, at least not that Robbie or I knew of...until I saw her at the meeting.

I thought of the day two and a half years before, when I'd been running barefoot and half-naked down a deserted caliche road in West Texas after having narrowly escaped a deranged kidnapper. I would surely have died of exposure that day if Sean hadn't come barreling up in his Escalade to save me. Using every skill in his arsenal, he had somehow managed to find me, and the hounds of hell couldn't have kept him from me. I knew for sure that Sean was in that same place now. His caliche road was a phone line to a bookie in Vegas, and it was my turn to do the rescuing.

The difference was that I had run straight into his arms and clung to him for dear life. But Sean was running away from all of us—and straight into hell. I feared the intervention was going to be a shitshow, but I couldn't think of a better option.

Around noon, I called my friend and downstairs neighbor, Ron Forsythe. He answered on the first ring. "I've got potato cakes left over for Festus. You want to come down or shall I deliver?"

"How about I bring him down? I've got a work thing this afternoon. I was hoping he could hang out with you."

"Just grand, my dear. I made extra cakes. You can take them when you pick him up. They're for the freezer because I'll be gone for the next two weeks, and I know how he gets if he doesn't have his treats."

"You're too good to us. Where are you off to?"

"I'm fact-checking a book about the history of the Studebaker Corporation. I'm going to spend two weeks at the Studebaker National Museum archives in South Bend. And, yes, such a thing actually exists. Leaving Friday morning. Meanwhile, come on down..."

At 12:30, I used my key card to ride Sean and Robbie's private elevator up to the loft. Sean met me in the vestibule and gave me a hug. "Where's my goddog?"

"He's spending some quality time with Uncle Ron."

Sean laughed. "So Ron made potato cakes for breakfast."

I nodded. "Festus smelled them when they were in the oven."

Sean fussed around the kitchen, making his usual spread—just like every Sunday, apparently set on pretending nothing had passed between us the evening before. Around five till one, Robbie emerged from his flat and came down the stairs to the kitchen. The tension between them was thicker than the Great Smog of London—and just as toxic. We all managed to play nice for a few minutes until the security phone rang and

X's face appeared on the monitor. Sean's eyes swung between me and Robbie and the screen.

He stared at us for a couple of beats, ignoring the incessant buzz. Then, he calmly removed his apron and tossed it on the kitchen counter. He picked up his keys and wallet from the console table by the door and stuck them in his shorts pocket. Without breaking stride, he said, "Have a nice brunch with X."

Robbie and I followed him into the vestibule and watched in amazement as he walked straight past X onto the elevator and hit the button. I said, "Sean..." but he looked away. The doors closed, and he was gone.

Robbie and I stared gape-mouthed at the elevator doors. X shrugged and said, "So an addict in relapse didn't welcome an intervention. That's a first." When neither of us moved, he said, "You kids need to toughen up." He rubbed his hands together. "I'm hungry. Let's eat."

Robbie, X, and I sat around the kitchen island, working on the cooling breakfast spread Sean had laid out before he ditched us. Robbie seemed heartbroken. My head was throbbing like I'd been up all night drinking cheap booze in a smoke-filled room. We were both just moving the food around on our plates.

X, on the other hand, was an old pro at twelve-stepping. He wore Harley leathers over the sleeves of tattoos crawling up his arms. Once upon a time, X had been Dr. Harold Xavier, a dermatologist with a house in Olmos Park and a wife in the Junior League. Then gambling had taken over his life, and he'd gotten caught up in a Medicare fraud scheme that ultimately landed him in federal prison. Now he's a paramedic riding a hog and living in a doublewide. He sopped up blueberry syrup with the last bites of a golden-brown pancake and dispensed his Big Book wisdom. "There's nothing else we can do. He's taken it out of our hands now."

I dropped the biscuit I was dragging through some gravy. "So that's it? We just sit here and let him ruin his life?" My voice sounded sharper than I had intended.

X shrugged and ate a slice of bacon. "Depends on how you define *ruin his life*. We wait until he wants our help. It took me losing my practice, my medical license, my wife and kids, and every cent I had before I got help. But hitting rock bottom—however hard it was—saved my life. I'm telling you straight, it can be a long way down. Best you buckle your seat belts." He finished his pancakes, tossed his napkin on the table, and stood to leave. We walked him to the door and watched him disappear into the elevator.

Robbie put his arm around me. "I've been up all night. I'm fried. I need to get some sleep."

I gave him a hug and took the elevator down to the garage where the Ferrari was conspicuously absent from its regular space.

I cranked the GV's engine, and Sirius blasted out Springsteen's "Born to Run." I stared out the windshield at the empty parking spot and wondered where Sean had escaped to in the three-hundred-thousand-dollar car. As I listened to the song, a terrible vision flashed through my mind—Sean racing down the highway in the cherry-red F8 Spider with Dorinda riding shotgun, egging him on, demanding he push the powerful machine to its outer limit.

I was just afraid of what might happen when he ran out of road and there was no place left to hide.

Chapter 10

Monday, September 13, 5:00 a.m.

I was dreaming about walking down a black-sand beach in Hawaii when the *Law & Order* ringtone blasted me out of a sound sleep. I groped for the phone.

"Pop? What's wrong?"

"We're all fine," Addison said. "Before I get into it, can you get Sean or Robbie or some of their guys to help us out with something?"

I propped up on one elbow. "When do we need them?"

He cleared his throat. "Like right now?"

"I don't know, but if it's an emergency, they can probably scare somebody up. What's going on?"

"There's more trouble down on the Wind Rose."

I fumbled for the switch and turned on the bedside lamp. "What happened?"

He sighed. "Farragut just got word there's been a fire involving one of the storage buildings in the compound. I can't let go of him today because we've got an emergency hearing at eleven to try to lift that health department order. I need you to get down there ASAP."

"You got it."

"Damn it, Iris, don't *you got it* me. I don't want you down there without backup. That place is a fucking snake pit."

"I'll get somebody. Okay with you if I call Ethon Emmett and have him meet me down there?"

"Absolutely. And Iris?"

"Yes?"

"I wouldn't ask you if we had anyone else. If there's any problem or you are the least bit uncomfortable, you tell me, and we'll get Marvin, or Ethon can handle it on his own."

"Thanks, Pop, but I'll get one of the guys."

"Call me when you get underway. There are some other developments I need to discuss with you, but I want you to get on the road first."

I hit End and dialed Mr. Emmett. One of the top arson investigators in the country, he had bailed us out when the Hampe Ewald burned the year before. Since then, Justis and Addison had formed an alliance of sorts with him. He had a professorial air and spoke in a quiet tone with precise diction, even at five in the morning. He said he'd leave San Antonio in fifteen minutes and meet me at the ranch.

I called Sean, but he was off the grid. I dialed Robbie next.

"What's up?"

"Beats the hell out of me. I've got to go deal with a fire at the Wind Rose. Addison's launched into Daddy mode and insists I not go alone. You think one of the guys could cover me?"

"Well, he's not being unreasonable. Those are bad motherfuckers, whoever they are. I'd go myself, but I've got a gig today I don't think I can juggle. I'll send someone. I just need to think who..." He was quiet for a few seconds. "Okay. It'll be Ansel Highgrove. Tall white guy with a goatee and skull earring. Long hair. Has a full-color tattoo of *The Scream* on his right forearm."

"Oh, boy."

"Oh, boy's right. He won the IPSC championship three years in a row."

"He won the what?"

"Sorry. International Practical Shooting Confederation."

"I have no idea what that means."

He chuckled. "For your purposes, it means he can take out any free-range asshole he wants any time the mood strikes him. And he'll be outside your apartment in twenty. Look for a hunter-green Jeep."

"You sure it's not putting you in a bad way?"

"For you, nothing puts us in a bad way."

I hauled myself out of bed and pulled on some field clothes. Festus gobbled his breakfast while I chowed down a hard-boiled egg, drank a glass of orange juice, and threw together a couple of sandwiches and some bottles of water. The Keurig gurgled as it filled my waiting travel mug. The aroma of Texas pecan-flavored coffee wafted through the air as I dashed around the apartment and rodeoed up my gear. Twenty-two minutes later, we fired up the Genesis. As I pulled out of the driveway, I spotted Ansel in a Jeep across the street, and he fell in behind me.

Once out of town, I hit speed dial and Addison came up. "We just hit 181. One of Robbie's guys is with us. You said you had more news. I assume it's not that you and Papa J won the Powerball."

He snorted. "Hardly. Farragut got word through the grapevine that, come the end of the month, his primary lender is cutting off his main line of credit. Without that credit and with the San Antonio stores closed, he won't have the cash to operate. He's decided to sell the Wind Rose to fund the operation until this mess gets straightened out."

"Does he understand selling one of the biggest ranches in Kenton County isn't going to happen overnight?"

"Apparently not. In fact, Sunday morning he made a cash deal for 13.6 mil with some Mexican mining magnate who's wanted to buy the ranch for years. Simpson from Real Estate is papering up the deal even as we speak. That's why we're so hell-bent you get all over this fire business."

"I'll do what I can."

I could hear him smile. "That's always enough."

I rang off and pushed the speed limit a little harder. With Ansel tight on my tail, we hit the ranch in record time. A dozen firemen milled around the smoking remnants of the storage building, looping hoses and securing equipment in the three fire trucks still in the compound. I parked next to Ethon Emmett's red company truck, and Ansel pulled off beside the ranch road a few yards back. With Festus on my heels, I asked one of the firemen to point me toward the incident commander.

"Chief O'Leary's inspecting the structure for arson." An outstretched hand indicated the charred shell of the largest wooden storage building. The roof had burned through and fallen in. Heading that way, I called out for the fire chief.

Ethon Emmett emerged from the barn followed by a beefy, red-faced man in a bulky fireman's coat and pants. Between his fifties-style lined bifocals and his customary gray suit, starched white shirt, and skinny black tie, Mr. Emmett always reminded me of a midcentury funeral director. Today, he was wearing his customary fire scene duds of red coveralls and rubber boots over his suit.

Mr. Emmett made the introductions. O'Leary pointed to the east wall of the storage building. "The fire definitely started along that side."

Through the burned-out walls, I had a clear view inside of what remained of the structure. Mr. Emmett walked over and pointed to a line more deeply burned than the rest of the wood plank floor. "This is called a fire trail. The extreme charring indicates where the accelerant was poured." He walked to the other end of the wall. "And here's another one. The arsonist set the fire from both corners to be sure it caught."

I pulled my digital camera out of my gear bag and snapped pictures as he pointed. "So it was set intentionally?"

The two men nodded in unison. O'Leary said, "Definitely incendiary." One of the firemen called out for the chief, and he excused himself.

I started reviewing the pictures on the camera's LCD screen. "How'd you get here so fast?"

Mr. Emmett looked on as I scrolled through the shots of the fire trail. "Same way you did. I was just five minutes ahead of you."

My phone chimed with a text from Addison. *The insurance people are sending an adjuster down there this afternoon. We told him to find you.*

Mr. Emmett tipped his head toward the building. "Let's go on inside the remaining structure and start documenting the scene. I'll collect samples to identify the accelerant and look for any trace evidence while you take pictures. Since this is clearly a case of arson, we are going to have to be entirely deliberate in the investigation."

He instructed me on how he wanted me to photograph each of the locations where he selected fragments of the charcoal remnants of the building, placed them in small plastic jars, and carefully labeled each one. His work was slow and painstaking. He would study each spot carefully with a magnifying glass and then direct me to take photographs from different angles before moving on. He was determined to find every bit of evidence that might tell him how the fire was set and by whom. Around one that afternoon, as the day was really heating up, we wound up the small-sample collection phase. Mr. Emmett stored the sample jars in a case in the back of his truck, locked it, and turned to me. "I should review those photos to see if we need any additional documentation."

I handed him the camera just as I spotted Finn Rhodes's truck coming up the driveway. He pulled up next to my SUV, got out, and headed over. I met him in front of the fire-ravaged barn. A smile lit up his handsome face. He said, "What a pleasant surprise. What are you up to in this neck of the woods?"

"Everyone above me in the hierarchy was tied up today, so I'm filling in as the on-scene reporter."

"I thought maybe you just happened to be down here on another 'routine matter.'"

I grinned. "Somebody's been reading the feds' paperwork."

He sloughed off my comment. The awkward silence that followed made me certain he knew about whatever shenanigans the feds were up to in Kenton County. I cleared my throat and said, "So, what brings you to the lovely Wind Rose Ranch where the clues are cold but the crime is hot?"

"I'm just being a good special ranger...flying the association flag and stopping by to see if I can help defend truth, justice, and the American way for our stalwart members who toil tirelessly to feed the world."

"In that case, it's good you're here because this particular one of your stalwart members is ass-deep in trouble. With your vast local knowledge, do you have any inkling about what the hell is happening around here?"

He surveyed the scene. "Not particularly, beyond saying that in my best law enforcement opinion there is some seriously bad shit going down on this ranch."

Ethon Emmett walked up and handed me the digital camera. "I took a few more pictures and then transferred all the shots to my laptop." He introduced himself to Finn then turned back to me. "Iris, I've got my guys coming down to do the gross collection. We'll start after the adjuster releases the site. Any idea on his ETA?"

Just then, a white Ford Taurus came up the drive. "Speak of the devil."

Mr. Emmett followed my gaze. "I'll go walk him through the scene."

"Please stay with him. I don't want anyone traipsing around here messing with this evidence."

Finn surveyed the compound. "Was the damage contained within the burned structure?"

I looped the camera strap around my neck. "Lucky for us, it was. A ranch hand who lives in a trailer over by the eastern gate heard a diesel truck around four-thirty and got up to check it out. He didn't see any vehicles, but he spotted the glow from the flames and called 911."

Finn said, "I need to go talk to O'Leary." He took a few steps, then turned back to me. "Don't get away without saying goodbye."

I couldn't help smiling. "I'm not going anywhere any time soon."

After a brief conversation, the fire chief got in his city vehicle and drove away. Finn joined Mr. Emmett and the adjuster, and they milled around the property for a couple of hours while I returned emails and tried to get Cibius on the phone.

Around 3:30, Mr. Emmett's men arrived with heavy equipment and staged by the burned-out structure. Shortly after the heavy equipment lumbered into position, Mr. Emmett exited what was left of the barn with Finn and the insurance adjuster. Apparently satisfied, the adjuster shook hands with the other men, loaded his equipment into his trunk, and drove away in a cloud of dust.

Mr. Emmett waved his crew ahead. In minutes, they were scooping portions of the charred barn into the bed of a dump truck. Feeling a twinge in my side, I adjusted the pouch on my belt that was concealing my Glock and arched my back to stretch out the muscles. "What'd the adjuster have to say?"

Mr. Emmett shrugged. "Nothing much. Agreed the arson was obvious. He took some pictures, collected some samples from the fire trail, and said they'd be in touch."

I excused myself and called Addison. "How'd it go in court?"

"We're screwed. The judge ruled until we can prove the source of the contamination and show it's been corrected, County Health has the right to close the stores."

"I'm hoping we'll hear from Cibius today. I've called a couple of times, but they haven't gotten back to me yet."

"What's going on at the ranch?"

I brought him up to speed. "When I can get him alone, Mr. Emmett and I will review the video from the game cameras."

"Let me know. And don't mention the video to anybody but Ethon until we get a handle on what it shows. I've got another call. Gotta run."

I put the phone back in my pocket as Finn came walking toward me from Mr. Emmett's truck. "Where's the beast?"

"He was hot." I tipped my head for him to follow me over to the enormous swimming pool where Festus was lounging on the broad first step, his belly and paws fully submerged in the water. He was sopping wet. "He was swimming a few minutes ago."

At the sight of Finn Rhodes, Festus lunged out of the pool and bounded over, standing on his hind legs and putting his wet paws on Finn's shoulders. Ignoring the dripping water, Finn accepted the welcome. Eventually, Festus dropped to all fours, and they tussled and played until Festus shook himself off and lumbered back to his spot in the pool. Finn's shirt was soaked. "Looks like I owe you a trip to the dry cleaner."

He waved me off. "It was a small price to pay for a hug from my favorite big fella." He adjusted his sunglasses. "How much longer will you be tied up here?"

"Probably another couple hours. How come?"

"The Kenton County Junior Livestock Show is going on. I'm judging the Hereford market steers"—he checked his watch—"in about an hour. The judging will be finished around six o'clock. If you want to meet me over there at say...six-thirty, we can check out the exhibits and eat a few thousand empty calories of crappy carnival food. Who knows? I might even win you a stuffed animal."

My mouth seemed to work independently of my brain. "That sounds great. Can Festus come?"

"Absolutely. He can stay in the kennel with Isabella."

I said, "Six-thirty it is."

"Meet me at the main ticket booth."

He strode back to his truck then waved a salute to me as he pulled away. My heart was beating a tad faster than normal. My face was flushed, and I felt kind of fluttery inside. It took me a few seconds to decipher what the sensations were. *Christ, I'm giddy.*

My reverie was interrupted when Ethon Emmett walked over from his post supervising the collection of evidence. I whispered, "I have video surveillance hidden all around the ranch. At least one of the cameras should have captured anyone going into that building."

He motioned toward the pool house, and I followed. Once inside, I pulled out my phone and opened the app for the game cameras and scrolled through the devices until I found the one I had positioned inside a topiary shaped like a dancing bear at the entrance to the barn. I queued up the video for 4:30 a.m.—about the time the ranch hand reported hearing the diesel engine. We watched as a battered pickup truck pulled into the frame. Two men climbed out and hauled large gasoline cans out of the pickup's bed and lugged them into the storage building. A minute later, they came running out *sans* cans, jumped into the truck, and sped away. Flames engulfed the building ninety seconds later.

Mr. Emmett looked at me. "They used a fuse or a timer of some kind to delay the ignition of the fire until they were clear of the building. I didn't see anything like that during my examination this morning. Neither did O'Leary. That means it may have burned up or we just haven't found it yet. We'll keep looking."

We replayed the video several times. No license plate numbers, no face shots. He turned to me. "Let's check the entry cameras. They had to get onto the ranch somehow."

I switched the video feed on the phone. At 4:27 a.m., we saw the pickup come inching through the northeastern ranch gate. I turned to Mr. Emmett. "Let's go check out that gate."

We took his truck over to the entrance. The lock had been cut, and its carcass was lying splayed in the weeds growing up around the barbed wire fence. I checked my watch. Finn would be getting ready to judge the market steers. Mr. Emmett called Chief O'Leary, and he came back over and collected the evidence.

When the fire chief was done, Mr. Emmett dropped me at my car and headed back to San Antonio. It was only 5:45, but I was exhausted. I considered calling Finn and canceling, but it seemed rude. Plus, as much as I hated to admit it, I really wanted to see him. Just thinking of him sent a case of the wiggles running right through my chest.

I cranked the AC and called Cibius again while the steaming-hot car cooled down. My contact told me the cultures should be back the next morning. I sent Addison a text updating him and ruffled Festus's ears. "Mom's got a crush on Finn, buddy. Is that crazy?"

He looked at me with droopy brown eyes then gave me a huge doggie kiss on the face. "Not crazy? Good. You like Finn, huh?"

Another lick.

I nuzzled his huge, wet nose. "So do I, buddy. So do I."

I called Robbie, and he picked up right away. "How's it going?"

"Arson. No doubt about it."

"Crap. You ask me, that ranch is the epicenter of all this trouble. Whatever the problem is, it all seems to be coming from down there."

I buckled my belt and put the car in gear. "Finn Rhodes was here today. Farragut is a member of his association. Anyway, he's asked me to the county livestock show. It's probably okay for Ansel to head on home."

"No chance. You'll be driving home tonight afterward. I don't want you anywhere in that county without one of us. Ansel's staying."

I headed down the ranch road, and Ansel fell in behind me.

My side was aching now. The maniac who'd burned down the Hampe Ewald the year before had shot me when I'd discovered his true identity. The bullet wound had healed, but I must have moved wrong during the long day on the ranch.

I reached for the phone to call Sean and tell him about the day's doings and my upcoming...date? Was it really a date? I hadn't been on one of those since I got shot. Nah...this was just a...casual social outing between colleagues. Something stopped me before I dialed. Sean had his own problems and, anyway, he was pissed at me. To my knowledge, he had never been mad at me before, so I wasn't sure what the rules were. Regardless, I was a big girl, and I could make my own way through a sausage-on-a-stick at the county fair without coaching from my best friend.

I got to the fairgrounds early. Killing time, I replayed the video from the game cameras. The arsonists' faces were hard to make out, but the Bondo on their truck was clear. The men who'd set the fire at 4:30 this morning were driving one of the pickups that had evaded the DEA after the shootout. I stored the videos in the firm's cloud and leaned back in the seat.

What the hell is going on?

Chapter 11

Monday, September 13, 6:00 p.m.

The fairgrounds were packed. From the parking lot, I could hear the screams coming from the Tilt-A-Whirl and the double-looping roller coaster. A brightly lit Ferris wheel sat back from the gate, and the notes of the band organ playing at the carousel were floating across the crowd. I smelled the unmistakable aromas of funnel cake, kettle corn, cotton candy, turkey legs, and sausage-on-a-stick. Festus was sniffing the air and pulling me toward a food cart when Finn came walking toward us.

He greeted Festus with a hearty pat and pointed to a restricted parking area beside the gates. "We're over here."

Festus hopped into the kennel and began nosing the wire partition between his compartment and Isabella's.

Finn checked the climate control, topped off their water bowls, and locked the truck. Pocketing the keys, he said, "Let's go have some fun."

As we walked to the gate, he said, "There's a guy in a green Jeep following you. I made him at the ranch today. I ran the plates, and they came back to some security company that I can't trace. Spotted him again here parked a few slots from your Genesis."

I laughed. "He's a friend of a friend of the family. The clan's a little off their feed about me being in Kenton County after my run-in with the cartel guys."

"Same friends with the armored Escalade?"

I kept my eyes forward. "Pretty much."

He let it ride. We meandered through barns. Finn was a walking encyclopedia about the livestock. He stopped at a pen of wooly white sheep with curved horns where a shearing demonstration was going on. "A single pound of sheep's wool can produce up to ten miles of yarn."

I studied the sea of white faces. "The test subject doesn't look like he's enjoying his haircut. I guess being bald beats being dinner."

He shrugged. "He's a Navajo Churro. They don't make very good meat."

In the bovine barn, we stopped at a row of Charolais cattle. He stroked the side of a giant golden heifer. "Cows have amazing sensory capabilities. They detect odors from up to six miles away, and they see at a three-hundred-and-sixty-degree angle."

I looked at him. "So, either you're the reigning champion on *Barnyard Jeopardy*, or you grew up in agriculture."

He smiled. "My father sells ag equipment—tractors and such. Ranchers, farmers...they have a hard life. They literally work dawn to dusk then get screwed by weather, crop prices—stuff beyond their control. Then to have their stock and their equipment stolen...I've always hated that. I became a special ranger because I wanted to help those hardworking, decent people get a fair shake. What about you? Why did you become a PI?"

"It's kind of a funky story."

We strolled by a tarot reader, who called to us. "See your future, ask me any question."

Finn turned to the woman. "Me?"

The woman shook her head. "No, sir. It's the lady who has the yellow aura, the question's in her mind."

He laughed and produced two tickets. "We can't pass this up."

I reluctantly sat down. The fortune-teller handed me a deck of cards and asked me to shuffle them. A grimace lined her face as she turned down the first card. A drawing of a woman sitting on a bed, her head in her hands. Behind her a row of swords hung on the wall. "The Nine of Swords." Her face lightened as she turned a card showing a revolving wheel with four winged creatures sitting on clouds. "The Wheel of Fortune." She paused before finally turning the third card, revealing a nude woman dancing above a globe. "The World."

The tarot reader drilled into me with her deep blue gaze. "These cards represent the past, the present, and the future." She touched the Nine of Swords. "You are emerging from a time of terrible pain and cruelty. The Wheel of Fortune tells you, in this time of transition, all things are possible—no goal is beyond your reach. And this"—she pointed to the last card—"is the future. You, finally on top of the world. Don't waste this chance. Seize the moment."

I debunk bullshit for a living, so believing a huckster at the Kenton County livestock show could tell my fortune was a bridge way too far. But my hands were a little clammy, and I felt a lump in my throat. The promise—however flimsy and contrived—that I was on my way to the top of the world made me almost euphoric. I swallowed hard and thanked the woman.

Finn gestured to a row of food booths. The savory smell of sausage smoking on barrel grills tantalized my nose. He said, "You want to seize the moment with a sausage-on-a-stick?"

I made a show of doing a double take. "Mr. Egg-White Omelet is going to eat nutrient-free, salt-encrusted, sugar-packed county fair food?"

He smirked. "I'm living on the edge." He winked at me as he approached the sausage booth. "Anyway, I can do penance tomorrow with some more of those kale smoothies."

We got the greasy sausages, doused them with mustard, and carried them to a picnic table. "You want a beer?"

Still riding the high I felt from the tarot reading, I said, "Sounds great." He picked his way through the crowd to the booth and returned with two large plastic glasses of craft beer. He took a big bite of his sausage and wiped a dribble of grease off his chin, then looked at me with those emerald eyes. "So, tell me your funky story."

I took a bite of the juicy sausage. "What would you like to know?"

He wiped his mouth. "I've heard you talking about your fathers. Is that like plural?"

"Yep. Addison and Justis Raines."

"Are they a couple?"

I squeezed more mustard out of one of the little packets. "No. They're brothers."

He sipped his beer. "Even more intriguing." He set the cup back on the table. "How did brothers end up having a child together?"

"As you probably know, every lawyer in Texas has to take their turn defending indigent clients. Most lawyers try to wriggle out of it, but my fathers never fail to do their part. My birth mother was a prostitute who was assigned Addison as her public defender. Addison Raines defending a hooker in county court is kind of like giving pony rides on Secretariat. Anyway, she was pregnant, and when she went into labor late one night, for reasons none of us will ever understand, she snuck into the Hampe Ewald where Addison's office was and gave birth to me in the bathroom. She wrapped me up in an old sweater and stuck me in a cardboard box from the trash with a note asking Addison to decide what to do with me. Nobody ever saw her again."

He stopped chewing. "Jesus."

I wiped my mouth. "Don't worry. Story has a happy ending. Addison and his brother, Justis, found me the next morning and called Child Protective Services. But, in a moment of insanity, when a blasé social worker showed up to take me to a shelter Addison had heard awful things about, they decided to keep me."

"Were either of them married?"

I shook my head. "Addison's never married. Justis married young, but his wife died of cancer two years before I came along. He's never remarried."

"How did they manage raising a kid?"

"They converted an office at the firm into a nursery. Until I started school, a nanny watched me during the day and went home with us at night when my fathers finished work."

He smiled. "Wow. And now you're their investigator?"

I sipped the ice-cold beer. "I started working in the real estate department when I was sixteen, helping find missing landowners they needed to fix land title problems. I majored in real estate at UT, did another year at BYU studying genealogical research, and then spent six months at an internship learning research techniques at the National Archives in Boston. After that, I came home, got my PI license, and started my agency. I do all the work for the firm, plus I have my own clients."

"Now that's a story. If you'll excuse me, I'll be right back. Don't move." I finished my sausage and wiped the remnants of the greasy juice from my face just as Finn returned with a large funnel cake. We shared the sweet pastry as a country band tuned up and started playing. He nodded toward the bandstand. "The Derailers are great." The band was playing "Cold Beer, Hot Women & Cool Country Music." He held out his hand. "Dance?"

I took a last swallow of the beer before he led me to the dance floor. He was a good dancer, and we two-stepped for several songs. His hold was strong but gentle, and he was a confident partner. A warm glow spread through me every time his muscular body pressed into mine. His cologne was a combination of citrus and wood with notes of orange and sage. His breath was warm on my neck. When the band took a break, he said, "You want to try the carnival?"

"Sure, why not?"

We took places on the carousel. I hadn't been on a merry-go-round since I was a kid. Taking a spin on one now with Finn—amid the twinkling colored lights and hypnotic organ music—had a magical, almost ethereal quality. When the ride quit spinning, he hopped off his steed and helped me down from my unicorn. I was light-headed stepping off the platform, and I wondered if it was from the rotation or the company. When I swayed, he put his hand on my shoulder to steady me, and something pleasant unfurled in my chest. Another whiff of the cologne and my pulse picked up. *Jesus...I haven't had a crush like this since sophomore year in high school.*

At a shooting gallery booth, he pulled some tickets from his shirt pocket, and the operator passed him a gun. Ten minutes and fifteen tickets later, he had won the largest stuffed animal on the very top row. He turned to me. "Pick one."

I surveyed the options and settled on a huge kangaroo with a joey in her pouch. The operator used a hooked broomstick to pull the giant stuffed animal down from the overhead rack. It was at least four feet tall. Finn reached up and took the prize. "I'll carry it for you."

I found myself almost overcome with happiness. The last two and a half years had been a long slog through hell. I had eventually gotten to a point where I was just glad not to be in physical and psychic pain anymore. But I had somehow forgotten what it was just to be happy. In that moment, I was giddy...and joyous...and thankful.

The sight of the muscular, bearded man juggling the enormous stuffed animal as he waded through the crowd made me laugh. "We better haul that monster to the car. I've still got to drive back to SA tonight, anyway."

He nodded toward the VIP lot as a furry gray ear flopped into his eye. "My truck's closer. I'll drive you and Festus over to your car."

He pulled up to my Genesis, loaded the kangaroo into the cargo area, then shepherded Festus into my back seat. My heart was doing a little dance in my chest as the moment of truth approached. I wasn't really sure I was ready for a kiss good night. But, on the other hand, kissing this guy didn't seem like a bad idea. I turned to him. "I had a lovely time."

He laughed. "If I'm going to eat junk food, you are the gal to do it with. You just dig in like a champ. Not like those ridiculous women who live on rice cakes and water."

I grinned. "You're going to hate me tomorrow when you're climbing back on the wagon saying ten Hail Celeries and five Our Organics."

He winked at me. "I'll survive." He opened my door and made a sweeping bow. "Madame, your carriage awaits."

I got in the driver's seat and rolled the window down. He rested his hand on the window ledge. "I had a nice time, Iris."

I smiled and put my hand over his. "So did I."

He stood there for a second, just looking at me. The little dance my heart was doing moments before morphed into the kick line in the grand finale of a Broadway show. I wondered if he could hear it pounding from where he was standing.

Maybe he did. He smiled, gave my hand a squeeze, and stepped back. I buckled my belt and drove away. Looking in the rearview, I saw the green Jeep trailing behind.

I pulled onto 181 and headed north. As the shadows of the old live oaks slid by, I thought about Sean. A smoky sadness seeped into my happy state. Normally, I would have already been on the phone with him, dishing all the details of the day's and the night's doings. But now, I was in alien territory with him. We'd never before—not once in the thirty years since I was in first grade—had a cross word. Now, I didn't know where I stood. The lines were as blurry as the moon shadows of the oak trees falling on the road. I wondered where he was now. Was he with Dorinda or, God forbid, off gambling?

I hit the Find My button. A picture of Dick Cheney in reindeer horns and a red Rudolph nose appeared on my screen in a tiny circle. I loved using that photo for Sean's avatar. I thought back to the Christmas Eve he hacked into the White House computer system and changed the screen savers from the presidential seal to his Photoshopped image of the vice president. The memory made me smile. After the dial quit spinning, the words *Location Unavailable* appeared next to Dick's red nose. *Unavailable?* Sean never hid his location from me. If he was off the grid working and security was an issue, he always told me he'd be "out of town" and his phone—at least the one I had a number for—would be staying home. Never *Location Unavailable.*

Current complications be damned. We were Us, come hell or high water, and I was calling him. The phone rang several times before he picked up. "Hey, sugar. What's up?"

I heard what sounded like crowd noises in the background. "Can you hear me?"

He was practically shouting. "Oh, it's just the television. What's up?"

Two *what's ups*? That was politespeak for *tell me why you're calling so I can get off the phone*. Sean hardly ever watched TV. And if it was the TV, why didn't he just turn it down? "I'm on my way back from the Wind Rose." I told him about the events on the ranch. "I've been there with Mr. Emmett since just before seven this morning. I checked the phone before I called, and your location is unavailable."

Still shouting. "Hmm. That's strange. I'll check the phone when we get off. Are you sure you're okay?"

No questions about the fire? And why hadn't he heard about my trip south from Robbie? If he had, he would have surely mentioned it. "Yeah, I'm fine. I was just worried when I couldn't see you on the phone."

"Well, thanks for letting me know. I'll check it out. Let's talk tomorrow."

I didn't know what to say, which wasn't a problem because the line went dead.

Chapter 12

Tuesday, September 14, 9:00 a.m.

I woke at 7:00 a.m. and found Festus asleep on the floor of my bedroom, spooning the kangaroo, his front leg draped over the stuffed animal. I snapped a picture and texted it to Finn with the caption *I had a nice time last night. Thanks.*

Shortly, *I enjoyed it, too. Give the beast my best.* flashed on the screen. I hit the thumbs-up emoji and headed to the kitchen for coffee. The phone rang in my hand.

"Ms. Raines, this is Dr. Jackson with Cibius Forensics. The bacterial growth in the sample exploded overnight. It's definitely *Bacillus cereus.* Not surprising, given the symptoms of the sickened diners."

I scrambled to the desk in my home office and grabbed a pad and pen to take notes. "But I thought *Bacillus cereus* was associated with rice and pasta?"

"That's true. Since our inspection of the store showed not a trace of pasta or rice, and given the contents of the bag, we strongly recommend you consider sabotage."

"I've worried about that all along, but I'd like to hear why you think this was intentional."

"Our inspectors cultured every bit of food in that store, and none was positive for any known culprits of foodborne illness. Additionally, there is a second, more damning piece of evidence. I take it you didn't examine the contents of the sack before you sealed it in the biohazard bag and delivered it to our lab?"

"That's right. It was evidence, and I didn't want to contaminate it. Plus, as you said, I considered it biohazard."

"And you were absolutely correct on both counts. When we opened the bag, we found three two-ounce clear plastic condiment cups with lids containing a shredded cheese product commonly used in restaurants for cheese and queso sauces. We also found a pair of nitrile exam gloves and a three-ounce plastic vial with a stopper. Everything in the bag, including the bag itself, tested positive for a high concentration of the bacteria."

A tingle of glee rippled through my chest. The vial and gloves were proof positive I was on the right track. Nothing in the world revved my motor like that. I forced myself to speak calmly. "Did you take steps to preserve any fingerprints or other forensic evidence in the materials I sent you?"

"Of course. We regularly deal with criminal cases. Our people examined the contents for fibers and other trace evidence and other pathogens. Nothing. There is a smudged partial print on one of the cups, but we don't have access to AFIS to run it. And there's no proof it belonged to the saboteur. We swabbed the gloves for DNA, but got nothing. We believe the perpetrator probably wore another pair of gloves under the ones we found and disposed of them separately. That is a known technique in the espionage community."

What the hell? "The espionage community?"

"Yes, ma'am. In my opinion, whoever did this was a sophisticated operative with substantial biological warfare and tradecraft expertise. We sent a man over to the alley this weekend, and, even knowing where it was, he was unable to see the hidden video camera that recorded the suspect disposing of the bag into the dumpster. We believe your perpetrator was unaware of that camera, or you would have never found the evidence."

"Thank you so much, Dr. Jackson. No written reports for now, and please do not discuss this matter with anyone besides me or Addison or Justis Raines."

"As you wish. And Ms. Raines..."

"Yes?"

"Please be careful. These are potentially very dangerous people."

I rang off, walked back into the kitchen, and cranked up the Keurig. Festus padded in and put his nose in his empty food dish and started pushing it across the kitchen—that's Saint Bernard for *Where's my damn breakfast?* I picked up his bowl and scooped kibble out of the bin. "Mommy is tapdancing in a minefield, buddy." I set his food down, grabbed my coffee, and headed to the shower.

Once dressed, I called Addison and updated him on the information from Cibius.

"Holy shit, Iris."

"And you and Justis go blaming my colorful vocabulary and lack of traditional feminine charms on not sending me to finishing school..."

He chuckled. "We got word from the hospital this morning. *Bacillus cereus.* No big surprise. And the cultures came back today from the samples County Health collected after they shut down all the stores. Zippo. Clean as a whistle."

"Did they just fork that over willingly?"

"Yeah...right after Bernie spent half of yesterday afternoon getting the judge to issue an order demanding they produce the results."

"So where does that get us?"

"Well, we're scheduled for a rehearing on our motion to lift the County Health order. Unfortunately, we couldn't get on the docket until Friday afternoon."

"I bet Farragut is having a fit."

"More than you know. He apparently had an episode around midnight last night. Called 911 and was rushed to the ER with a possible heart attack. The docs diagnosed him with a panic attack and sent him home with some more Xanax. If we get through this without him being hauled off in a long-sleeved jacket that zips up the back, we'll be lucky."

"Well, he better get his act together. I need to meet him at the San Pedro store to see if I can figure out how this poisoner did it."

"Oh, he's up and around. I think he's actually at the store now, meeting with the manager. Payday's coming up."

I called Farragut and told him to stay put and keep the manager handy and filled my travel mug with coffee. Cleaning or no cleaning, there was no way in hell I was eating or drinking anything that came out of that store.

Taking Sunset, I doglegged to Oblate, and followed it to San Pedro to avoid the morning jam on the Loop. I parked in the back lot, and the manager let me in and directed me to his office where I found our client. Quinten Farragut looked like an extra in a zombie movie. The bags under his eyes were swollen and dark, and he was even sweatier than usual. I asked the manager to excuse us, closed the office door, and filled Farragut in on what Dr. Jackson had told me that morning. Then, I explained my plan.

We called the manager back in, told him the broad strokes of the Cibius findings, and asked him to walk us through every single step in the process from bringing the cheese product into the store until it was served to the customer. The man carefully explained each phase of inspecting and accepting the delivery, storing the cheese, prepping the cups, and serving the product. "Looks to me like the contamination most likely took place when the cheese was prepped into the cups or when the cups were poured onto the individual orders of fries. What do you all think?" I asked.

They exchanged glances and nodded in unison. The manager cocked his head, then looked at me. "Can you tell me again what the lab said about the cups they examined?"

I flipped through my notes. "They were two-ounce plastic cups with lids and contained a cheese product used in cheese and queso sauces."

He shook his head. "Not in this restaurant."

I snapped my head to Quinten Farragut. He paused a minute and then slapped his forehead with his palm. "God, I'm so fucked up. I didn't catch that. Good pick up, Mike."

I felt like I was watching a foreign film without subtitles. "Wait a sec, guys. I'm lost."

The manager disappeared into the kitchen and returned a minute later with a giant block of cheese in a vacuum-sealed wrapper and plopped it down on the table. "This is what we use for the cheesy fries. Genuine cheddar cheese. Jacks the food cost by fifteen cents per small order of cheesy fries, a full quarter on jumbos. But the Circus Burgers SOP manual requires the use of the actual food that appears in the name or description of any menu item. If the menu says 'cheese' or 'cheesy' or any variation on that word, the item has to be made of pure cheese. The product you are describing is a commercial version of something like Velveeta. It melts better, doesn't separate oil, and costs about half as much. But it isn't cheese. It's based on a milk protein concentrate—what the food industry calls 'MPC.' I get caught serving an MPC-based product in this store, my CB career is history. It had to have come from outside our operation." He picked up the block of cheese and disappeared into the storage area to return it to the refrigerator.

I nudged Farragut under the table and shook my head as subtly as I could. He took the lead when the manager returned to the office. "This is great news, Mike. I'm so glad you picked up on that." He turned to me. "Iris, do you need anything else from Mike right now?"

I thought of a way to frame my next request. "Why don't we just double-check a list of the employees who would have either prepped the cheese cups or poured the stuff on the fries on Wednesday, September 8."

The manager shrugged. "Sure. You want me to pull their personnel files?"

I nodded. "That'd be great."

In a couple of minutes, he handed me three folders. "These people worked in the prep area where we grate, melt, and cup the cheese." He passed me four more files. "These people worked the service line. Any one of them could have poured the cheese on the fries."

I pulled the files to my side of the table. Farragut heaved himself out of the rolling desk chair and stood. "I hate to keep you any longer than necessary today since you're going to have to handle the paycheck mess Friday, so I think I can take it from here. You've been a huge help, Mike."

"Happy to do anything I can." The manager shook hands with me and his boss and headed out.

When I heard the door close, I looked at Farragut. "So it's definitely sabotage."

He slumped back into the chair, dropped his head into his hands, and massaged his temples. "You don't think Mike's right? That it came from another restaurant?"

Ay yi yi yi yi. "No...I'm sorry, sir, but I don't think there's any reasonable chance it came from another restaurant."

He popped another white tablet and went back to massaging his temples. "Then what's next?"

"I go to work." I held the files up. "May I take these?"

He nodded. "We have electronic copies."

Hmmm. "If you've got them online, can you get me the records for the folks who worked the same positions in the Oklahoma store?"

"Okay, but I thought we decided Oklahoma didn't have anything to do with this."

If I spent much more time with Quinten Farragut, I was going to need to start wearing mouse ears to fit into his Magic Kingdom. I curbed my tongue. "No, sir. I don't think we ever decided that. I have no knowledge of what happened in Oklahoma. That's one thing we are trying to figure out."

His shoulders slumped. "Oh..." He placed a phone call to the manager of the store in Tishomingo. A few minutes later, he hit Enter on the computer keyboard. "I just emailed them to you. But I'm sure that incident was a fluke."

I loaded the folders into my briefcase. I hate whining men, but if we were going to pull this sad sack out of the current riptide, he had to be swimming, not beaching like a killer whale. I sat down and looked him in the eye. "Mr. Farragut, Justis and Addison have national reputations. They wouldn't have taken this job on in return for shares of your stock if they didn't think they could fix this problem. But you have to help us. You can't do that if you don't take care of yourself. I think you should go back to the condo, turn your phone off, and sleep for twelve hours. And you need to lay off the pills and booze. It's not helping you, and it's liable to get you dead."

He looked up at me with Basset Hound eyes. "Sure. You're right."

I waited in my car until I saw him lock the store, stuff himself into his Mercedes, and pull out of the parking lot. I was two lanes over while we both waited at the light at San Pedro and the Loop. I watched as he popped a pill and washed it down with something from a flask while he was waiting for the light to turn green.

So much for the pep talk. I always sucked at that cheerleading crap, anyway.

Back at the office, I was plowing through a tower of mail when Marvin O'Neal called.

Marvin is a retired DEA agent who is *the* go-to guy if you have questions about the drug trade in San Antonio. Marvin knows everyone who's pedaling illegal shit in town, and he's plugged in to all the cops and feds trying to bust them. It's hard to make a move of any size in the local drug trade without registering somewhere on Marvin's radar.

"You livin' out any more *High Noon* fantasies?" he asked.

"It wasn't really *High Noon*. More like an O.K. Corral situation."

"Well then, Ms. Earp, you best be watchin' your ass."

I felt a twinge in my gut. "Uh-oh. What'd you find?"

"Somethin's definitely cookin', but I don't know exactly what. Least not yet. Everybody knows there are a bunch of feds camped down south—King City, Kenedy, that area. What they're up to—that's the mystery. Whatever it is, they've got it shut tighter than a well digger's asshole in mid-December. I can't pry a detail out of anybody. That smells to me like a government corruption investigation—crooked cops or some such. If the locals are bent and the feds are listening in, that would explain why 911 got you federal agents instead of local deputies. Word on the street is that the feds confiscated a shitload of smack in a bust down south, but nobody knows who the dope belonged to or what triggered the raid. Rumors are spreading like a virus on a cruise ship that some *gringa* pumped a bunch of lead into three of the bad guys, but nobody knows who she was or what she was doing there. Not yet, anyway."

"Crap."

"*Crap* is right, so watch yourself. Whoever lost that dope is gonna be looking for payback. Other than that, I haven't found anything solid. I'm still lookin'."

"Stay on it. I've got another problem, though." I told him about the sabotage at the store. "I've got a bunch of personnel files. I need you to see if anyone in the bunch looks good for it."

"Sure. Scan the files and email 'em to me. I'll do a quick background on each of 'em and take a closer look at anyone who seems possible. How confident are you about the list?"

"I think...seventy-five percent chance the doer is on it."

"I'll call you when I have something."

I could feel myself tugging on a thread I thought would unravel the stitching and open up the sugar sack holding the complex secrets of this case. I just hoped to God it really was a thread I was pulling and not the pin on a grenade.

Chapter 13

Wednesday, September 15, 6:30 a.m.

The *Star Trek* warp speed ringtone yanked me awake. While I'll always do what I have to for a case, I've never been a morning person, and I was really wearing thin on these predawn wake-up calls. Today it was Sean. I picked up the phone.

"I know you're still asleep, but I've got something for you."

I forced myself to sit up and adjusted the pillows to lean against the headboard. "Okay. Shoot."

"I had some free time, and I've been going through the video footage from all the cameras for the hour before the ranch hand spotted the fire Monday. I found one brief half-second shot of the arsonist's face. I enhanced it and compared it to the video you got of the guys at the shootout. Matches one of the pickup truck drivers."

That chased away the last vestiges of sleep. "Stick the best version of that face shot in my email while I get dressed. I'll go down to the ranch and see if anybody recognizes this guy."

"No deal. This asshole may work there, or maybe his homies do. I'd rather you let me do it myself, but if you insist on going, I'm going with you."

In the background, I heard Robbie's muffled voice, then shuffling with the phone. Robbie came on. "I'm coming, too, Iris. I hate to miss a good shootout, and lately you've been hoarding all the glory."

I called Addison and let him know where I was heading and why. "I need you to call Farragut and have him let the ranch manager know I'm coming and need to look around."

Addison said, "I'll do it, but you're certain Sean and Robbie are going with you?"

I smiled. "I'm stopping at their place, and we're all going down together."

After a pause, he said, "Okay, I'll call Farragut. You be careful, Iris. You be damn careful."

I threw on my field clothes and gave Festus his breakfast while I scarfed down a smoothie and some toast. I kissed Festus's square, freckled muzzle and headed out. An hour later, I was parking in the garage when Robbie stepped out of the elevator and pointed to a brand-new metallic taupe Toyota Land Cruiser. I slung my gear bag over my shoulder and headed to the new truck. Robbie hit the remote, and the truck's lights flashed. "Look what the insurance bunny put in our basket."

I heaved my bag into the cargo area and was inspecting the windows when I heard Sean's voice. "Yes, it's armored. The insurance company was on the hook for the cost of the modifications, so why not? And with all the trouble you're getting into lately, I figured we might need it."

The vibe between us all was different. It was almost like everything had been before I saw Dorinda at the GA meeting a week ago. I glanced at

Robbie, and he winked at me. He looked almost like his old self. Maybe Sean had come to his senses and climbed back on the wagon.

An hour later, we pulled through the wrought iron main gate of the Wind Rose Ranch and parked behind the Arabian barn. Sean used his thumbprint to open the modified center console and slid his weapon into the specially designed holster he could conceal in the front of his slacks. Robbie checked his gun and stowed it in his shoulder holster. Lifting the hatchback of the Land Cruiser, Sean worked the combination on a trunk in the cargo area and passed me and Robbie bulletproof vests then fitted one over his own head. I lifted the heavy Kevlar and slipped it on. Sean and Robbie were sophisticated operatives who had worked in dicey situations all over the world. If they thought we needed Kevlar, we were in the tall weeds. I tightened the Velcro. Robbie pulled a windbreaker on to conceal, and I did the same.

Sean produced a wad of color prints of the face shot and passed some to me and Robbie. I studied the image. "He doesn't look familiar, but I haven't spent that much time around the staff. We need to take a walk around before we start flashing these pics...see if we recognize him. You two are insurance adjusters, and I'm showing you the damage to the barn. After we look around, I'll go to the ranch manager's office, say we need to ask the staff some questions, and get him to corral everybody up in the stable. Robbie, you drop out and stage for backup while Sean and I check the crowd. If we don't see him, then Sean and I'll start showing the pics."

They nodded.

We walked around the blackened shell of the storage building with Sean and Robbie taking photos and pretending to inspect damage. We ran into several ranch hands and gardeners, but nobody who looked anything like the guy in the picture. In the ranch manager's office, I introduced myself as an investigator working for Mr. Farragut's lawyers and Sean and Robbie as adjusters from the insurance company.

He stood. "I'm Ralph Ellis. Mr. Farragut told me to expect you."

Sean showed the manager the picture. The man shook his head. "I don't know him. He resembles one of the guys on the gardening crew, but he's definitely not the same person."

Robbie said, "What makes you say that?"

The manager shrugged. "Aside from the fact this guy's older, our guy has a tattoo of a spider web on his neck. Can't miss it. Goes all the way up past his jaw."

Sean asked the manager if he would mind gathering the ranch hands up so we could ask them some questions.

Half an hour later, twenty-five men were assembled in the straw-covered runway between the rows of horse stalls. The sound of snuffles and whinnies filled the air along with the earthy scent of the animals. Sean and I watched as Robbie faded away into the tack room next to the manager's office. I felt better knowing he was lying in wait to back us up in case Sean and I ran into the arsonist and all hell broke loose. We milled through the crowd, asking routine, innocuous questions until we were both satisfied the arsonist wasn't there. Sean climbed up onto a hay bail and spoke loudly. "Gentlemen, we're from the insurance company, and we need some help. We have a photo of a man who may know something about the fire. We're going to be in the manager's office and ask each of you to walk through, one at a time. We'll show you the picture, and you can tell us if you have any information about him. We'll never divulge the identity of anyone who helps us, but we will offer anyone with credible information on this man a hundred-dollar bill right there on the spot."

Sean and I situated ourselves in his office, and the manager fed the men to us one at a time. I was beginning to lose hope when the twentieth man walked in and sat down across from us. We showed him the photo. He studied it carefully. Sean prompted, "Sir, have you seen this man before?"

He nodded. "*Sí*. I have seen him. He was working on the crew who trims the plants that look like animals. I heard from some of the workers this man came in place of his brother. His brother went home to Mexico and got caught at the border coming back. The head of the gardening crew allowed this for a part of his wages." He passed the photo back to Sean. "Did this man set the fire?"

"We don't know," I said. "We just want to talk to him. Do you have any idea where we could find him?"

The man studied his hands. His T-shirt clung to his sinewy muscles. His eyes darted back and forth, and his Adam's apple bobbed as he swallowed hard. Sean said, "You don't need to be afraid, sir. We don't even know your name. Who is he?"

The man clasped his hands together between his knees and rested his elbows on his thighs while he jittered his heel up and down. After a few beats, his foot stopped moving, and he looked up at us. "The rumors say he almost killed a man in Kenedy a month ago in a fight at one of the camps for the oil field workers." The man shook his head. "Very bad places."

Sean leaned in to him conspiratorially. "If you happened to be able to help us find him, that one hundred could turn into two hundred dollars."

The man licked his lips nervously. I could see him weighing his options. Finally, he took a deep breath and whispered, "Sometimes, in between clipping the trees shaped like the animals, that crew works at

Mr. Farragut's grain elevator outside of King City. Sometimes I deliver parts to the elevator. I saw this man there last week."

Sean turned and pulled three crisp hundred-dollar bills out of his pocket and subtly passed them to the man. "*Tu secreto está a salvo con nosotros.*" Your secret is safe with us.

The man nodded and walked out. When the door clicked shut behind him, I said to Sean, "We've got to run the last five through...make it look good."

As Sean picked up the photo of our suspect and motioned for the manager to send in the next ranch hand, my phone chimed, announcing a text from Ethon Emmett. *Please call me immediately.*

I held up the phone. "I have to take a call." I slipped through the door as Sean pulled out the flyer and launched into his pitch.

I dialed Mr. Emmett. "Iris, the fire in the storage building was started with a small explosive device. It was not entirely primitive, probably had remote detonation capability. We discovered the remnants of it when we combed through the rubble we hauled up here."

"Okay. What do I need to worry about?"

"Escalation with another bomb. This could have been a practice run. I would call your attention to the pattern. You've had cut fences, then pasture fires, and now a major structure has been destroyed by a fire fused with a small bomb."

I told him the details of our lead about the elevator. Ethon Emmett said, "Oh, dear God."

My pulse picked up. "What?"

"Iris, grain elevators are one of the most explosive places on earth. Grain dust is organic. Elevators are not well ventilated. It's a perfect storm. How big is the elevator?"

My hand was sweating as I white-knuckled the phone. I had driven past the elevator countless times on my way into King City on business for the oil and gas section. I closed my eyes and pictured it. "I don't know... It's maybe...six, seven stories tall."

"Oh, lordy... Okay, Iris, I'm going to call the bomb guys at ATF in San Antonio. You get that elevator shut down and evacuated while I scramble some feds to get down there and take over. And tell the local cops to clear out at least a mile radius from the site until ATF has swept it for explosives."

I was struggling to process the information he was feeding me. When I didn't respond immediately, he said, "Iris, get to it *now*. And don't you dare go anywhere near that elevator. If that silo blows, it will incinerate everything within a hundred yards of it."

Chapter 14

Wednesday, September 15, 9:30 a.m.

As subtly as I could, I motioned for the ranch manager to meet me outside. He headed out the side door while I slipped around the building and joined up with him. "We've got a potentially serious situation." I didn't want to be seen kibbitzing with the head honcho right after we talked to the informant, so I said, "Go open the back door of the main house and meet me inside."

He nodded and walked away without looking back while I ambled past the burned-out structure and stopped to inspect a fallen timber. My heart was thumping in my chest so hard I could barely force myself to squat down and snap a picture of the charred piece of wood. Satisfied the staff was still in the barn and the manager was out of sight, I slipped around the corner of the stable, scampered across the open yard, and ducked inside the house. The manager's brow furrowed, and he was sweating more than the morning heat justified. "Did any of the guys know this man you're looking for?"

"The ranch hands are a dry hole," I lied. "But I just received information from a source in San Antonio that the man we are looking for has been working in his brother's place on the gardening crew and may also work at the elevator."

The manager rubbed his chin with his index finger. "Maybe he's the brother of the guy with the spider web tattoo. Several of the gardeners work over at the elevator when they aren't needed here. Like I said, I don't know specifically about this guy, but it's sure possible."

I took a breath and used my calm-but-no-bullshit voice. "Mr. Ellis, it is possible someone has planted a bomb at the elevator."

His eyes went wide, and his voice boomed. "Jesus Christ. Are you sure? Holy God...a bomb in that elevator could kill everyone in the complex—just for starters."

I cranked my voice up a notch. "Mr. Ellis, please concentrate. We need your help here."

He ran his hand through his mop of brown hair. "Okay... What do you want me to do?"

"Do you know the manager who runs the elevator?"

Sweat was popping out of the pores on his forehead. "He's my brother-in-law. Jud Saxon."

"Great. I need you to call Mr. Saxon right now. Tell him who I am, and put the phone on speaker so I can talk."

He made the call and introduced me. Clearing my throat to steady my voice, I said, "Mr. Saxon, you need to shut down all operations and evacuate the elevator staff immediately. Roll out whatever safety protocols you have in place to protect the surrounding community in case of a fire at the elevator. We are concerned about a possible bomb threat. ATF has been notified. My colleagues and I are on our way over."

I jogged back to the barn just as the last ranch hand was leaving. I joined Sean and Robbie in the manager's office and brought them up to speed.

Robbie pulled the Land Cruiser fob from his pocket, and we ran to the truck and sped off the ranch. Once on the highway, Robbie floored it and headed into town. Half a mile from the elevator, a knot of employees were gathered by the highway. Several King City police cruisers and Kenton County sheriff's cars were parked with lights flashing. Robbie slewed the truck to a stop on the shoulder, and we jumped out. I asked one of the evacuees to point me to Saxon. A stout man in his forties with a buzz cut, wearing a white short-sleeved shirt and khaki pants, he was talking to a deputy. "Mr. Saxon?"

"Are you the woman I just talked to?"

Extending my hand, I dived in. "I'm Iris Raines. Can you tell me where we are with the evacuation?"

"The elevator is shut down, and the staff is assembled over by the highway. I've accounted for everyone who was on the clock at the time you called."

I pulled the color flyer from my pocket. "Do you recognize this man, sir?"

He glanced at the photo. "That's Joel Ramirez. He's substituting for his brother, who is...out sick."

Sean said, "Is Mr. Ramirez working today?"

Saxon shook his head. "He was on the schedule, but the asshole didn't show up. I've called all morning, but he's not answering."

Sean, Robbie, and I exchanged glances. "Can you tell us exactly what Mr. Ramirez does here at the elevator?"

"He's a mechanic. He maintains and repairs the conveyor belts and elevator bucket system."

We all three looked at the elevator then back at Mr. Saxon. "Sir, I don't see any conveyor belts."

Pointing to a stairway descending underground like a subway entrance, he said, "The elevator bucket system starts underground and runs inside the elevator. Those buckets lift the grain up to the distributor floor." Raising his finger to indicate a square enclosure on top of the silos, he went on. "The conveyor belts are inside that enclosure."

Out the corner of my eye, I saw Finn Rhodes talking to one of the locals before he turned and began striding toward us from the road. Isabella was in her harness, tight on his heel.

He walked up to us and shook hands with Saxon. "Jud, I understand you've got a bomb threat."

I said, "Thanks for coming, Finn. ATF is en route from the San Antonio office."

Finn shook his head. "Not right now they aren't. That's who called us, hoping Bella could determine if there is actually a device. The San Antonio response team has been diverted to a bomb threat at the convention center. They're scrambling a crew out of Corpus to come over here, but they're still two hours out. Bring me up to speed."

We told him about Ramirez and the fuse in the barn fire. Sean and Robbie exchanged glances, and Sean said, "I'd plant it underground. Contain and concentrate the blast."

Robbie nodded. "Me, too."

Finn looked around. "Let me guess...Ramirez didn't show up for work today."

Saxon nodded and said, "AWOL."

Finn studied the scene for a few beats. "Bella and I can do a preliminary search...get a better idea of the situation."

Sean and Robbie stepped up. Sean said, "We were Army Rangers. We've both had explosives training. We'll come with you."

A Kenton County deputy who had been listening to our exchange moved into our circle. He was thirtyish and overweight. His uniform shirt gapped open across a gelatinous paunch that oozed over his belt. Taking a toothpick out of his mouth, he said, "We're not trained for this. We'll handle the evacuations, but otherwise, we wait on ATF. If you go in there, you're on your own."

I looked at Finn and Isabella. "Then, let's go."

Sean said, "Everybody empty your pockets. No radios, cell phones...nothing that could accidentally trigger the device." Finn handed his radio to Saxon then said to us, "Just so we're clear... We are making an assessment. Period. We don't have the equipment or protective gear to disarm a bomb. We go in, let the dog search, come out. That's it."

We all muttered our agreement. Saxon walked over to a large, red emergency breaker mounted on the wall by the stairs that descended below the silos. "I'm cutting power to the facility. The emergency lights will come on, but nobody'll be able to activate that belt while you're down there inspecting it." He used both hands to pull the giant switch into the down position.

Finn whistled for Isabella, and they led the way down the stairs. The concrete bowels of the elevator were painted battleship gray. Emergency lights hummed as their beams illuminated tiny particles floating through the hot, stuffy air. The industrial smell of engine grease mixed with a musty odor I assumed was grain and permeated the confined, narrow hallway that was about fifty yards long. At the end sat a bin from which emerged a series of huge buckets connected to a vertical belt that resembled a giant bicycle chain driven by a series of cogs and gears sitting on the cement floor. Isabella sniffed the ground and surveyed every crack and crevice down the hall until she stopped and barked and pawed desperately at the outside of the bin then stood up on her hind legs and tried to climb in. When the chain drive shifted, Finn commanded her to stop and sit. Sean stepped up to the bin, peered over the edge, then gingerly stepped back and said, "Device on a timer. Six minutes left on the counter."

When I turned to see what Finn had to say, he was kneeling on the ground, struggling to remove Isabella's harness, which was caught in the gears of the chain drive. His voice was as tight as a piano wire. "I can't get her loose." He pulled a knife from his utility belt and desperately pulled at the twisted harness. "I can't get the knife under the harness. It's twisted too tight."

Sean said to Robbie, "It looks like a standard setup. I see one trigger running off a basic alarm clock." He peeked over the edge of the bin. "Down to five minutes."

Robbie moved in. "What's the explosive?"

Sean stepped back. "Looks like dynamite."

Finn unhooked his vest. "I have basic bomb squad equipment in here." He shucked the vest and tossed it to Sean then fought to wedge his hand inside the dog's harness and said, "There are wire cutters and batteries in the right pocket. Some extra wire, too." My adrenaline had surged when Bella hit on the bin, giving me the laser-focused concentration that comes from being in survival mode, but the look in the dog's sad brown eyes broke my heart. I wormed my hand underneath the harness and tried to pull it loose so Finn could cut it.

Robbie took Finn's vest. "Iris, Rhodes, clear out. We'll take care of the dog. But you need to leave now."

Finn never took his eyes off the harness. His tone was level and commanding. "I'm not leaving the dog. Get to work."

Robbie pulled the vest on then grabbed the edge of the bin and pulled himself up. Sean stepped up behind him. Without taking his eyes off Robbie, Sean said. "Iris. Go. Now."

Sounded like a grand idea to me, but as I shifted my weight, Isabella yelped and squirmed, and the chain drive rotated another inch, wedging the harness even tighter. I couldn't move. I felt like gerbils were skittering through my chest as neon and black spots floated through my field of vision and sweat poured down my face. I was trapped underground three feet from a ticking bomb.

Robbie disappeared over the edge into the bin.

Sean looked over the side and said to Robbie, "We're going to bypass the current from the clock with Finn's battery."

Robbie's voice echoed from inside the metal box. "I see three wires. Red, green, and black."

Sean mouthed a silent *Damn*. "The colors are probably a decoy." He bit his lip and slapped the heel of his hand against his forehead then exhaled and said in his steadiest voice, "Strip the red one. I'm looking for fiber alloy."

The seconds of silence seemed to stretch for an eternity. I was drenched in sweat. Pain shot up my arm. Bella whined as Finn tugged harder on the vest and the chain shifted again, cinching us in even tighter. I felt like my hand was being twisted right off my wrist. Then Robbie's muffled voice came from the bin, "Bingo."

Sean let out a breath and said, "Attach the battery and run it to the lead."

A couple seconds later, Robbie yelled, "Shit! The clock is racing. We must have tripped a secondary."

Sean pulled himself up on the rim of the bin and shouted, "Attach the lead! It's the only way to stop it."

"Doing it..." Robbie's voice was hard as oak.

The alarm sounded on the clock. My heart jumped into my throat. Finn threw himself over me and Isabella. His weight knocked the wind out of me, and my face was pressed into the dog's wiry coat. I couldn't move, but I could smell Isabella's oily fur tinged with Finn's citrus cologne. My heart was beating a crescendo in my ears. Images of me and my fathers and Festus and Sean and Robbie flashed through my mind. I grabbed the dog, waiting for the explosion.

Then I heard Sean's feet hit the ground followed by Robbie's voice as he climbed out of the bin. "One and done. No sweat, sports fans."

I felt Finn's weight roll off of me. Still caught in the dog's harness, I tried to steady my breathing. Finn groped where his radio should have been. Robbie raced toward the daylight and disappeared up the stairs. Sean squatted down next to me and Isabella. "How you doin', sugar?"

I stared at him. The world in the dank tunnel had morphed into a cross between hyperacute photorealism and something Salvador Dalí might have painted after dropping acid. My wrist was twisted at an odd angle, and it crossed my mind that it might be broken. I shook my head to clear it. All I could think of to say was, "Beats the hell out of me..." Sean tugged on the harness. "We're going to need tools."

Seconds later, Robbie came running, leading a team of firemen and paramedics down the stairs. Using a huge pry bar, two of the men reversed the chain drive and left enough slack in Isabella's harness to free my hand. As a paramedic hustled me up the stairs, I saw the firemen cutting through the harness with what looked like a giant pair of gardening shears. In seconds, Finn was behind me on the stairs, carrying Isabella in his arms with Sean and Robbie right on their tail. I heard Sean yell to the firemen, "We bypassed the detonator, but there's still a live explosive device in the bin!"

Chapter 15

Wednesday, September 15, 2:00 p.m.

Damned if I wasn't back in the frigging federal building. Mercifully, Agent Butler's tone had mellowed since our last meeting. My pals and I had just kept half of King City from being vaporized using wire cutters and a nine-volt battery while Butler's homies tottered around in bomb suits on live television using a robot to "defuse" what turned out to be a shoebox covered in Play-Doh and duct tape. He was almost civil.

We finished our paperwork and headed out. Sean and Robbie loaded into the front seat of the Land Cruiser. As I was climbing into the back, Finn leaned against the truck. He wore stone-washed denim jeans with a white oxford cloth shirt and brown alligator cowboy boots, topped off with a white felt Stetson. The gold star of his badge hung from his shirt pocket in a tan leather case. He rested his hand on his duty belt and said, "You know the Silver Saddle and Brass Spur?"

I nodded. "The country western dance hall north of town on 35?"

"Yeah. They have live bull riding on Wednesday nights. Last year we busted the asshole who supplies the bulls, caught him with fifteen head of stolen Charolais-Brahman crosses. Bastard had some buddies in the sheriff's office. Somehow, a bunch of the evidence disappeared, and he beat the charges. Ever since, one of us special rangers shows up at every gig he works just to check the brands and paperwork on the bucking bulls. Tonight's my turn. I thought you might like to join me. We could get something to eat, take a couple of laps around the dance floor."

I felt a tingle skitter through me, and my stomach went into a slow roll. Was it anxiety about dating again or the thrill of being asked? I felt a stitch in my side and arched my back. I must have pulled something when I was tangled up with the dog in the grain elevator. One wrong move and the remnants of my damn bullet wound could ache for a week. I shook it off. Nothing a little ibuprofen wouldn't fix. I nodded. "Sure. I think I could use a little R&R after today's events. But we'll have to make it an early night. I'm beat."

He nodded. "Pick you up at six?"

We pulled into the underground garage around 4:30. The guys invited me up, but I checked my watch and shook my head. "Sorry, gentlemen, but I've got to hustle if I'm going to get home, change, and walk Festus before Finn picks me up."

Sean walked over and gave me a hug. "Have a good time, sugar." I hugged him back. It felt like things between us were almost back to normal. Over Sean's shoulder, I saw Robbie. He seemed so much happier today. I had no idea what had gone on between them, but whatever it was, it had apparently reset the recent difficulties. Still...there was a trace of something in Robbie's eyes. Sadness? Longing? Worry? It was just a flicker buried deep under the layers of all that had happened during the day. He smiled his crooked smile as Sean and I broke our embrace.

"You guys saved a lot of lives today...mine included," I said. "You know how much I love you both."

Robbie winked and said, "Anything for you, darling."

I hugged him and headed to the Genesis.

With rush hour creeping up, I opted to head north on Broadway and avoid the craziness on 281. Something was definitely up with my side. I kept thinking back to the months after I escaped from the cabin in West Texas where Daniel Kerabos had held me prisoner. The PTSD had manifested itself in a terrible hand tremor. Half the time, I'd felt like a bad verse of Big Joe Turner's "Shake, Rattle and Roll." It was impossible to predict what would trigger it, and it had gone on for over eighteen months until a year ago September 1, when I killed a serial murderer named Gregory Geare who'd shot me and Grover. I'd almost died from the bullet wound that had ripped up my insides and landed me in the ICU for a week.

The past couple of months, the pain in my side had finally faded away. I could bend over without meeting Jesus, and rolling over in bed didn't mean waking up to a hot poker in my gut. But now, my side was twinging again. A nagging voice kept whispering in the back of my consciousness that the renewed pain was a message from my psyche. But for the life of me, I couldn't decipher the memo. My recovery was progressing nicely, but I was still seeing the shrink. I made a note to add the twinging thing to the list of topics for my next mental floss appointment.

Festus bounded through his doggie door to greet me as I got out of the car. He was carrying his leash in his mouth as he ran down the stairs in his lopsided gait. I hooked him up, and we headed down the street. "Not going to be a long one today, champ. Mommy's got a date."

Was it a date? No matter how much I had been kidding myself, any rational person would call this a date. The man was picking me up and taking me out for dinner and dancing. The fact that he was working that night didn't change anything...did it? In the year since I'd killed Geare, I had avoided dating altogether. Getting better was one thing, but I was stuck on the fact that I had been involved with Geare before I'd learned his true identity the night I killed him. Choosing your first lover after a sexual assault is tough enough. But finding out the guy you chose is a serial killer—well, let's just call that a therapeutic setback. I still didn't trust my judgment the way I needed to, the way I had before Kerabos and Geare invaded my life. I was making progress, but feeling so attracted to Finn scared the hell out of me. Was my attraction a sign that meant he was secretly a homicidal maniac? Or did it mean I was recovering? Just turning it over in my mind made my guts roil. But I couldn't quit thinking about Finn at the grain elevator. In the most trying circumstances, he had shown himself to be a real, honest-to-God stand-up guy with guts and character and a selfless sense of duty. Maybe my judgment was better than I thought.

Festus and I rounded the block and headed up the driveway to the Victorian. I glanced at my wrist—5:10. Time to get a move on. After I showered and washed my hair, I chose a new pair of jeans, a houndstooth, drape-necked sleeveless top that fit just right, and a pair of black flats. I was just touching up my lipstick when the doorbell rang.

Finn had changed into a clean, pressed version of his usual jeans and shirt. I invited him in and caught a whiff of citrus and wood as he walked past me into the apartment. When he leaned in for a hug, I felt the smooth skin of his freshly shaved face. He smiled. "You look lovely." Festus danced around and whimpered until Finn squatted down and scratched the dog's chest. Ruffling his ears, he said, "I hate to rush us, but I need to be there when they unload the bulls."

I pulled my purse over my shoulder. "No problem. I'm ready to go." We both gave Festus a goodbye pet before I locked the door. "Where's Bella?"

"She's at a specialty vet place out north of 1604."

"Oh, my God. Is she okay?"

He held up a hand. "She's fine. But policy requires any animal involved in what the department calls a 'crisis situation' to be observed by one of their vets for a minimum of twenty-four hours after the event. In this case, I would have done it anyway. She was sore on her left shoulder where the harness got stuck. Plus, the fireman bruised her right side with those giant shears. The vet looked her over when I brought her in, and he didn't see anything to worry about."

He opened the door of his pickup for me, and I climbed in. Twenty minutes later, we pulled around to the back of the Silver Saddle and Brass Spur. A large cattle trailer with Bill's Bucking Bulls emblazoned on the side was backed up to the gate of a corral. A fortysomething man wearing jeans and a tight-fitting black T-shirt topped off with a black Stetson was leaning on the mesquite pen, his elbows resting on the top rail. Angular features defined a chiseled face pocked with acne scars. A package of cigarettes was rolled up in the sleeve of his T-shirt. He looked up as Finn approached. "Well, what a surprise to find you here."

Finn tipped his hat. "Bill."

The man passed him a clipboard. "Here's the paperwork. I've got ten Charbray bulls. All of 'em branded."

Finn took the paperwork and turned the pages. Apparently satisfied, he tilted his head toward the trailer. "Let's take a look."

The black-clad man turned a handle, and the metal gate of the cattle trailer clanked and squeaked as it swung open. I watched through the metal bars as the light tan bulls filed out of the trailer and down the ramp that led into the corral. The smell of hay and manure hung in the air. Finn watched carefully as the animals paraded past, checking the brand on each bull's left hip. As the last one ambled into the holding pen, Bill closed the gate on the corral.

Finn nodded to Bill and said, "See you around."

Bill glared at him and said, "Can't wait," then strode into the rodeo arena.

Finn grinned at me and said, "Enough of that...let's have some fun. How 'bout some barbecue?"

"I'm starved."

"Well, this will get you fixed right up." He led me out to the side of the building where a long line of people waited for service from a food truck. The smell of smoking beef and pinto beans wafted through the air. As we rounded the corner, a large man in a black apron and a chef's hat was pulling a box out of a fire-engine-red trailer with the flaming Sanderson's Barbecue logo on the side. He spotted us as he put the box down and swung the trailer door shut. "Finneas Rhodes! What's shakin', buddy? Keepin' the world safe for democracy?"

Finn extended his hand, and the barbecue man wiped his on his apron before shaking. "Doing my best."

The embroidery on the man's chef coat read Monroe Sanderson. Finn introduced us.

Sanderson picked up his box and headed toward the food truck. He looked over his shoulder at Finn. "You here giving Bill some shit?"

Finn nodded. "Yeah."

The man laughed. "Good. He needs it." As we walked up to food truck, the smell of pit barbecue intensified and washed over me like a wave. My mouth was watering. "Jesus...that smells fantastic."

Monroe Sanderson put the box down and opened the truck's door. "What can I get you good folks?"

Finn said, "I'll have the rib eye with pinto beans and potato salad."

Monroe nodded and looked at me. "And for the lady?"

I inhaled the smoky aroma of the barbecue. "Just make that two."

Finn pulled bills out of his wallet and passed them to Sanderson. The man pocketed the money and nodded to a table behind the truck. "I saved you a spot. One of the boys'll bring out your plates in a couple of minutes. Beer?"

I nodded. Finn held up two fingers. Sanderson said, "Coming up."

The food was scrumptious. I was afraid I was gobbling like a wild dog, but I was so damn hungry I hardly cared if I was. The rib eye was flavorful and marbled with just the right amount of fat, and the pinto beans had been slow-cooked with hunks of salt pork. "Sanderson's has always been one of my favorite barbecue places. You seem to know him pretty well."

Finn wiped some sauce from his mouth with a thick paper napkin and took a sip of his beer. "He's got a place outside of Seguin where he raises most of the beef he serves in his restaurants. A couple years back, some dipshits helped themselves to some of his stock. I recovered the cattle when Bella and I helped the state guys bust a meth lab over by Corpus. We've been friendly ever since."

He cocked his head at the sounds of the band warming up. Tossing his napkin on his plate, he said, "How 'bout we dance?"

I'd been going full throttle since Sean woke me up at 6:30 that morning. But, instead of feeling worn out, I was relaxed and happy. That seemed particularly odd since I'd almost been blown to bits not six hours before. I smiled. "Sure."

As we boot-scooted around the dance floor, I flashed to the time I had danced with Gregory Geare at the River City Country Club...just a few hours before he almost killed me and I shot him dead. That night dancing with Geare, an inner voice I didn't fully understand at the time was warning me to run for my life—I'd felt it in my bones. Now, dancing with Finn, I searched my psyche for a similar warning. But all I felt was happiness. For the first time since Daniel Kerabos showed up in my life, I was actually having fun.

Around 8:30, Finn checked his watch. "I hate to break up the party, but I need to get moving. I'm supposed to be on a stakeout with a game warden at five tomorrow morning. We're trying to bust some poachers who have branched out into cattle rustling."

I followed him off the dance floor. "You don't have to convince me. I'm having a great time, but I figure I've got about an hour left on my meter before I turn into a pumpkin."

He led the way out of the dance hall and through the parking lot. He opened the truck door and waited for me to climb in. I watched through the windshield as he walked around the front of the truck. He was self-assured and competent without coming across as arrogant or self-satisfied. He had a great face, and all that healthy living had left him with a body that would make an Olympian jealous. I felt a little flutter in my chest as he climbed behind the wheel.

I adjusted my position in the seat, but it didn't help. If I could just get rid of this pain in my side, I'd be batting a thousand.

Chapter 16

Wednesday, September 15, 9:15 pm

When we pulled into my driveway, Finn got out and opened my door then followed me up the front steps to my condo. I was a woman who could open my own door and buy my own dinner, but I also appreciated a guy who made an effort—and Finn was scoring plenty of points in that area. I noticed a prickly sensation in my chest and felt a little edgy as I neared the top of the stairs. Dreading an awkward scene over a good-night kiss, I tapped the combination on the keypad. When the lock clicked, I opened the door and turned to Finn. "I had a great time. Thanks so much for inviting me. I'd ask you to come in, but I know you're in a hurry..."

He was looking over my shoulder. His smile disappeared, and his eyes went wide. Wordlessly, he edged past me into the apartment. I turned and saw Festus stumbling across the living room like he was drunk. Just as Finn reached him, Festus collapsed. Finn rolled him onto his back and searched for injuries. I ran over and knelt down beside the dog's giant head. "There's something brown and sticky around his muzzle." I held my hand up.

Finn sniffed my fingers. "It's chocolate." He put his ear to Festus's chest and listened for a few beats. "Do you have hydrogen peroxide?"

My stomach roiled as I ran into the bathroom and fumbled the cabinet under the sink open. I raked the contents out onto the floor and frantically dug through them until I found the brown plastic bottle. I ran into the living room and handed it to him.

"Get me a funnel," he said.

With shaking hands, I pawed furiously through my utensil drawer and sprinted back with the funnel. While Finn dribbled the hydrogen peroxide through the white plastic cone into Festus's mouth, I dialed our vet, Asa Chiron. My panic worsened when his voice mail announced he was on vacation. "His vet's out of town." Finn scooped the giant dog up into his muscular arms. "Follow me." He carried Festus down the stairs and loaded him into the back seat of his pickup, climbing in beside him. Tossing me the keys, he said, "He's going to start vomiting. I need to be back here with him to keep him from choking. Get on 281 North. Take the Stone Oak exit off 1604 West."

As I pulled out of the driveway, he reached over the seat and hit a switch on the dash activating the truck's lights and sirens. "Drive as fast as you safely can." He pulled his radio from his belt. "Dispatch, Finneas Rhodes en route to Critical Care Vet Hospital with canine medical emergency. Please advise hospital—coming in with a hundred-and-forty-pound neutered male Saint Bernard with acute chocolate poisoning. Cardiac distress. Administered hydrogen peroxide. Need immediate medical assistance upon arrival..." In the rearview, I saw him looking around, presumably for landmarks. "ETA seven minutes."

I was panting. My heart was clanging in my chest like a jack hammer in a coat closet, and I was rubbery with fear. I focused on the road as

I heard Festus retching in the back seat. I took the Stone Oak exit, and Finn directed me through a couple of turns and finally into the hospital emergency entrance. He jumped out of the truck and ran to the back doors where he jammed his finger on a doorbell. Two men in scrubs pushed through double doors with a gurney and raced toward the truck. They expertly pulled Festus out of the back seat and onto the stretcher. I parked the pickup and ran to the entrance where Finn put his arm around me and ushered me through the double doors.

Inside, a vet fell in behind the gurney, and Finn and I jogged to keep up. Finn rattled off the details of what had happened since we returned to the apartment. The vet passed a giant gravy ladle and a plastic basin to Finn. "I need to see what he threw up." Then he turned to me. "You'll need to go to the waiting area. We'll do our best for him." I watched in terror as the doctor and his assistants disappeared into a trauma suite, and I could have sworn I felt my heart breaking in two. *How could I have let this happen to him? What* had *happened to him?*

I turned and walked zombie-like into the waiting area and slumped into a plastic chair. I fumbled my phone out of my purse and dialed Sean. On the seventh ring, his voice mail picked up. I was crying by then. "Sean...something's happened to Festus. Call me."

I tried Robbie. He picked up on the first ring. "What's up?"

I told him about Festus.

"Where are you?"

I grabbed a brochure from a rack on one of the tables and read off the hospital's name and address. His voice was calm like it had been at the grain elevator. "I'm on my way."

"Where's Sean?"

"Just take care of Festus."

Minutes later, Finn pushed through the metal doors and sat down beside me. "He threw up a lot of chocolate in the truck. Maybe a half a cup. That's great. The more he puked the less got into his gut to be absorbed."

"Chocolate..." I was racking my brain, trying to think of what chocolate might have been in the house.

"Looked like dark."

My mind raced. "I..."

Robbie appeared at the locked glass front door. Finn pointed to the emergency entrance and disappeared back through the metal doors. In seconds, Robbie jogged across the waiting room and pulled me into a hug. He turned to Finn. "Thanks so much for your help. Any word on how he's doing?"

I shook my head. Finn said, "The vet is working on him now."

Robbie looked around. "What is this place?"

"It's a veterinary critical-care facility," Finn said. "Dr. Stamper, the guy who's in there with Festus, used to be the head vet for all the armed services."

Just then, the doctor pushed through the metal door. He walked over and shook hands with Finn. "I think you got to him in time. Good work with the hydrogen peroxide." The vet turned to me. "Are you the owner?"

I nodded. He motioned for us to take a chair, and we sat. "I checked the vomitus, and it looks like Festus has ingested a significant amount of dark chocolate."

I was still dumbfounded. "I can't imagine how he could have gotten it... I don't like dark chocolate. All I ever buy is regular."

Dr. Stamper shook his head. "These guys can be pretty sneaky about finding things you don't even remember having. We see it a lot. But the point is, I think you found him in time. We gave him more hydrogen peroxide and a healthy dose of activated charcoal. We've got him on IV fluids to help him flush the poison out of his system. Most importantly, we're getting his heart rate stabilized. So far, he doesn't have any signs of heart failure or seizure. We just need to keep all that up while he metabolizes what was already in his system before we got to him. In addition, when you arrived, Festus was having an episode of acute hypoglycemia. We gave him glucose and resolved the immediate crisis, but it's going to take a while to fully stabilize his blood sugar. We'll know more by morning."

I had a death grip on Robbie's hand, and he put his arm around me. I looked at the vet. "Can I see him?"

Dr. Stamper shook his head. "I don't think that's a good idea right now. Just go on home, get some sleep, and we'll touch base when I go off shift around six-thirty in the morning. I'll be here with him all night. If anything changes, we'll let you know. But now I need to get back in there."

I thanked him, and he disappeared behind the metal doors. Finn turned to Robbie. "Can you stay with Iris, take her home?"

Robbie nodded. "Absolutely."

Then he said to me, "I hate to run out on you, but I'm due for that surveillance job in a few hours. I'll be back here tomorrow afternoon to pick up Bella. I'll call you on my way into town."

I reached over and gave him a hug. "I can't thank you enough. I didn't even think to ask...how is Bella?"

He smiled. "Her usual sassy self. I snuck back and checked on her when I brought the samples in from the truck. She's doing great."

I watched as he disappeared through the metal doors.

"Let's get you home," Robbie said, taking my arm.

I shrugged him off. Tears were brimming in my eyes. "I'm not leaving him. I'll just stay here in the waiting room. Maybe he can smell me...know I'm here."

Robbie's voice was kind but firm. "Iris, you've been at it since the crack of dawn. Hell, by lunchtime, you'd already saved an entire town from being blown to kingdom come. You need rest."

I rolled my eyes. "Says the guy who went all MacGyver on a ticking bomb."

"And I know how tired I am. You've got to be wiped out. I can tell you now—I knew his kind in the army, and there is no chance in hell that vet is going to let you see your dog tonight. Tomorrow, we'll all come see Festus. If anything comes up in the night, then you holler out, and I'll come running."

I shook my head. "There's a Drury Plaza down the block. I'll get a room there and sleep. If they call me, I can be here in five minutes."

Robbie nodded. "It's a deal. I'll leave you my car and have one of my guys come get me." He pulled his cell out of his shirt pocket and made a call. He hung up and said, "Ansel's meeting me at the hotel in twenty."

I slung my purse over my arm, and we headed out to his car. Keyed in the passenger door of his bright red Dodge Challenger Hellcat was a scrawled message. *Fuck you.* My heart sank as it dawned on me Sean had never called me back—let alone shown up to see about Festus. On top of everything else, the specter of Dorinda and Sean's relapse reared its ugly head.

I looked at Robbie over the roof of the car. "The door..."

"Yeah... Can't imagine who did it."

Chapter 17

Thursday, September 16, 6:30 a.m.

Despite being exhausted, I hardly slept. Dr. Stamper called at 6:30 just like he'd promised. He said Festus was stable and beginning to improve. Relief flooded my brain, but it was tempered by disappointment when I learned that I still couldn't see him. I saw a text from Robbie. *Switched cars. I parked your GV where the Hellcat was.* I managed to nod off for a few hours until I dragged myself out of bed and headed home around ten.

Back at the apartment, I crawled around on the floor, digging under furniture and rummaging through every nook and cranny. I couldn't find a trace of chocolate. Had he eaten the package, too? What in the world had I left around that almost killed my dog? Guilt was coursing through my veins like the Colorado River flooding through the spillways of the Hoover Dam when Marvin rang at a little after eleven. "Hey, big guy. What's the word?"

"The word is I think you've got some funky shit goin' on under your circus tent."

I hustled into my home office. "What kind of funky shit?"

"I ran all those personnel files through AccuData. Most of 'em are pretty much what you'd expect—college students, a retired high school coach, a single mother mixed in. I did drive-bys on their locations. Mostly cookie-cutter apartment complexes with $99 move-in specials and free crappy Wi-Fi. I was able to match plates registered to the subjects in the parking lots outside the associated addresses, so I'm not too worried about those."

I grabbed a pen and scribbled notes on a legal pad. "You said *most* of them. You're saving the bad stuff for last. I know you—you're one of those dessert-before-dinner types."

He chuckled. "Yeah. I'm just sittin' in this fuckin' van all day watchin' assholes peddle dope and screw hookers until the summer crowds thin on the Côte d'Azur. Dessert before dinner my ass."

I smiled at his ghetto talk. Besides a graduate degree, Marvin spoke four languages and had lived all over the world while he was doing God knows what in the murky universe of drug-interdicting governmental black ops. "So, what's the funky shit?"

"Two of your guys ain't who they say they are."

"How so?"

"One of the names in the Oklahoma store—Darrin Stephens—comes back to a middle-aged grocer in Tulsa. One of the names in the SA store—Larry Tate—comes back to an eighty-year-old barber in Austin. Socials don't match the dates of birth on the applications."

My mind lurched into overdrive, planning how I was going to chase this lead. But I forced myself to be calm as I had him spell the names and carefully recorded them along with the dates of birth and socials. "Did you pull driver's licenses? I'm going to need photos."

"I can get into the DL database for Texas. So, no sweat on Tate. But Oklahoma's got their DL info locked up like it's the damn Hope Diamond. Good news is the Stephens dude in Tulsa got arrested in a bar fight a couple of years ago, and I found the mug shot. Check your email."

I logged into my account and opened the jpgs. "Got 'em. Thanks."

He laughed. "Darlin', your cases are always a welcome diversion from the same old drug-dealin' shitshow I sit through every day."

"Speaking of drug-dealing shitshows, any new info on the assholes who tried to kill me last week?"

"Not yet, but I'm stirrin' the pot a little. I'll let you know. Meanwhile, you best keep your head low and your powder dry. I'm not liking the vibe."

Uh-oh. "How so?"

"Word is some badass *vatos* tried to blow up a grain silo down south and got short-sheeted by a couple of white guys and a woman and a cop with a dog. I've got my ear to the ground for details about who planted the bomb, but all I can tell you right now—nobody's happy."

I smiled. "Except the four thousand people of King City who didn't get blown to smithereens by an exploding grain elevator."

"Except for them... Oh, crap, there's my guy. I've gotta move. Later."

I called Farragut. He sounded like he might actually be sober...but the day was still young. "I need you to call Mike and have him meet us at the San Pedro store. Then get the Tishomingo manager ready for a Zoom," I said.

"Uh...okay. I can be there in twenty minutes. Mike just lives a couple blocks from the store. What have you got?"

"That's what I'm trying to figure out."

A three-car pileup on the Loop added ten minutes to my trip. While I inched west, the phone rang. I checked the caller ID. Finn. A little zing of excitement followed by a flutter of...happiness?...zipped through me as I hit the green button on my console.

His voice was warm and deep. "I was just calling to check on Festus."

I gave him the latest rundown. "Asa Chiron has talked to Dr. Stamper. When they agree it's safe, Asa will take Festus to his hospital right down the street from the Hampe Ewald. Then, I can see him whenever I want while he recovers."

"I'm so glad to hear that. I heard a talk Dr. Chiron gave at a conference last year. He's top-notch." I sensed genuine relief in his voice.

"He's definitely that. I've known him for years."

"Between him and Dr. Stamper, Festus couldn't be in better hands." He cleared his throat. "I'm sorry for cutting out on you last night, but I didn't have anyone to cover for me on that surveillance gig."

"*Sorry?* Are you out of your mind? If you hadn't been there to give him that hydrogen peroxide and rush us to Dr. Stamper, Asa says Festus probably wouldn't have made it. You are totally our hero, and we both can't thank you enough. How's Isabella?"

"She's great. Dr. Stamper says she's completely street-legal. I'm on my way into town to pick her up."

"Maybe I could buy you dinner to thank you." The offer slipped out before I even thought about it.

"I would love that, but I can't do it tonight. I'm covering District 26 as well as my own since the ranger up there had back surgery. We're heading to a bust just north of Fredericksburg. Some assholes up there are trading crystal meth for stolen Rambouillet sheep. But, I'm hoping I can have a rain check."

I smiled. "You most definitely can have a rain check. While you're in Fredericksburg, be sure to get yourself some giant pretzels at the Old German Bakery. They're my absolute favorites."

He laughed. "Already in my game plan." He rang off just as the traffic broke, and I stepped on it to get to the San Pedro location.

I pulled into the store parking lot as Quinten Farragut was getting out of his Mercedes. Mike let us in the service entrance, led us to his office, and gestured to two empty chairs he'd brought in from the dining room. "What can I do for you folks this morning?"

I pulled out the printouts of the photos Marvin had sent me and passed the picture of the barber to him. "Mike, do you recognize this man?"

He studied the photo and shook his head. "Sorry. I've never seen him." He passed the photo to his boss. "Mr. Farragut?"

Farragut shook his head. "Me, either."

I pulled out the personnel file. "The man in that picture matches the driver's license and Social Security number for this employee."

Mike took the file. "Larry Tate? The guy in the photo's gotta be eighty. Larry's, like, late twenties, early thirties. His DOB should be on the application." He flipped through the folder. "Yeah. Right here. Born 1995." He turned the page to show me.

"Do you keep photos of the employees?"

Farragut shook his head. "No. We used to, but HR and Legal got all worked up about some privacy crap, and we stopped doing it."

I handed the picture of Darrin Stephens to Farragut next. "Okay, can we get the Oklahoma manager on Zoom?"

Farragut pulled out his phone. "I'll just FaceTime him." He tapped keys, and seconds later the man in Tishomingo came on. I held the mug shot of Darrin Stephens up to the camera. The man's face loomed on the screen as he leaned in to study the picture.

"Nope, not the guy who worked for me. Too old."

We told him we'd be back in touch if we needed more help and ended the call.

"The shades are down in the front," Mike said. "We can go get something to drink if you're thirsty." I must not have worked my poker face very well because he chuckled and said, "Everything's already been sanitized, but all we have is bottled, anyway."

I stood. "That sounds great. I could use some tea."

Farragut and I followed Mike into the main part of the store where he pulled bottles of iced tea out of a cooler. I went to the service island and pulled a wad of napkins out of the dispenser to wrap around the sweating glass bottle.

Then I saw it. Above the condiment station. A framed photo on the wall, next to a plaque that read Circus Burgers Center Ring—Store of the Month. Highest Sales. I took the picture off the wall and held it out to Mike. "Is Larry Tate in this photograph?"

He took the picture, pulled his reading glasses out of his shirt pocket, and fumbled them on. "Should be...we just got the award a few weeks ago." He pointed a sausage-like finger at a stocky young man with short, dark hair and generic features on the left edge of the shot. "Yeah. That's Larry. But you can't see his face real good—he was looking away when we took the picture."

I turned to Farragut. "Can you get the Oklahoma manager back on FaceTime?"

He tapped keys, and the man came right up. "Hey, boss. What can I do for you?"

I held the photo up to the camera. "Sir, do you see Darrin Stephens in this photo?"

Again, his eye filled the screen then he pulled back. "Yeah, the guy on the end looks like Darrin, but what's he doing in Mike's Store of the Month picture?"

I stared at the photo and said, "I don't know, but I'm going to find out."

Chapter 18

Thursday, September 16, 3:30 p.m.

I was sitting at my desk studying the award photo. While the guy in the picture was probably the poisoner, I had absolutely no idea about his true identity. But one thing was certain—he was a pro. Accessing Social Security and driver's license numbers post-9/11 was tough. This wasn't some kid who got pissed because he had to work Saturday night. This was a professional with a mission.

But what mission? Was he out to screw Circus Burgers? Or was this more personal...was Quinten Farragut the target? Or was the poisoning a targeted attack on a particular customer, using the other sick diners as a smoke screen to disguise the hit? I started at the sound of my intercom buzzing. I tapped the button. "Yes?"

It was Addison. "Iris, we need to see you now, please. My office."

I picked up a pen and a legal pad and hustled over. I found my fathers and Simpson from Real Estate huddled in Addison's sitting area with Quinten Farragut, who was squirming like a preacher in a whorehouse. Addison motioned to a chair.

"How can I help you gentlemen?"

Justis spoke. "We have just been apprised of a title problem with the Wind Rose." He nodded to Simpson.

A mousy little man with thick, horn-rimmed glasses, Simpson cleared his throat and said, "The 3,122-acre Wind Rose Ranch is comprised of four separate tracts that were aggregated into the current ranch in 1977 when they were all purchased from separate owners by a man named Mathias Albertson. The residential compound is situated on the northwestern-most tract, which contains a total of 1,856 acres. That tract was acquired by Albertson from one Jason Case, who bought it in 1976."

He passed me a plat of the ranch. The four separate tracts were each shaded a different color. "Okay. What's the problem?"

"When the 1,856-acre tract was incorporated into the ranch in 1977, the deed into Albertson was signed by Jason Case."

I was beginning to sketch a title chart on my legal pad. "What was the capacity or style of Jason Case's name on that deed? Married? Single?"

Simpson shook his head. "No capacity was listed." The real estate lawyer took a breath, licked his lips, and continued. "The title company determined yesterday that Jason Case was married at both the time he bought and sold the land. The wife was one Annabelle Case. Under the Texas community property laws, Annabelle Case should have joined in that sale deed. But she didn't."

I considered the possibilities that might make this a nonproblem. "Did they check for a separate deed from the wife?"

Simpson shook his head again. "There isn't one."

I set the plat on the coffee table. "So a one-half interest in 1,856 acres of the Wind Rose Ranch doesn't belong to Mr. Farragut, and the house, stables—all the improvements—are built on real estate half of which is still owned by Jason Case's wife."

Simpson looked like he'd swallowed a frog. "That's the way the title company sees it..." He cleared his throat and adjusted his bow tie. "And I concur."

"So, you need me to find Jason Case's wife?"

Simpson said, "Correct."

I looked over at Quinten Farragut. His eyes were the size of saucers, and he was making a sputtering sound. "What the hell do you mean I don't own half of that tract? How in God's name did that happen?"

Addison said, "Quinten, you told me when you bought this ranch you didn't use a title company. You dealt directly with the owner, correct?"

His head bounced like a fishing bobber. "One of the guys from the real estate department at CB read the deed...said it was fine."

Justis pressed on. "But you didn't have the title examined?"

The color drained from his face as the awful consequences of that screwup years before dawned on Quinten Farragut. "Jesus. The guy I bought it from had owned the ranch for decades... I had hunted down there for ages..."

Justis looked at Addison. "No title insurance."

Addison said, "We got a call from the newspaper an hour ago. Somebody's leaked word that there's a title problem with the sale. And the buyer is making noises he wants out of the deal. We've got him locked in for four more weeks, but come the end of the contract term, I think the sale will collapse if we can't deliver merchantable title."

Farragut dug the little orange pill bottle out of his jacket pocket and knocked back a couple of tablets. I couldn't really blame him. His lifeboat was turning into a wire canoe—and he and my fathers had just handed me the paddle. Much more of this, and *I'd* need one of those pills.

Farragut swallowed hard. "If this deal craters, I lose everything. You guys have got to fix this...please..."

All eyes turned to me. "I'll get on it."

I scurried to my office and cranked up the databases to mine info on Annabelle Case. Before I got into the records, my cell announced a launch into warp speed. Sean. I snatched it up. "Are you okay? I tried to call you last night when Festus was at the hospital."

He said, "Uh, I'm not sure what's up with the phone. I had it with me, but it didn't ring. I was stuck with a client emergency all night. Glad Robbie could come help out. How's Festus?"

"Asa Chiron and Dr. Stamper agreed it would be better for him to stay one more night with Dr. Stamper, then move to Asa's tomorrow. I'm working a crisis here, but when I get done, I'm going to drive out to Stone Oak and see him. You want to come?"

A pause. "Umm...I'm still hung up with my client emergency. I better just plan on seeing him tomorrow. Are you okay? I mean, you must have been worried sick."

Who was I talking to? I felt like I was making small talk with a clerk at the grocery store, not discussing my seriously ill dog with the best friend I'd ever had. "I was out of my mind. I still don't know what he ate. I've combed the house, and I can't find anything."

I heard noises in the background, and he said, "Sugar, I've got to go. Let's talk tomorrow." And he was gone.

I sat staring at my cell phone. I thought of the tarot reader at the livestock show. She said my life was in transition from darkness to light. This sure as hell didn't feel like light.

I turned back to my computer and lost myself in the records of the long-dead Annabelle Morgan Case. When my eyes finally crossed, I shut down the computer and packed it in.

I drove to Stone Oak and rang the bell at the emergency entrance. Dr. Stamper smiled when he opened the door. "I'm so glad you're here. He just ate some dinner. We were thrilled to see him feel like eating." For a dog that usually tore through a bowl of kibble like a tornado through a Kansas wheat field, that spoke volumes to me about the severity of Festus's condition.

Dr. Stamper led me back to a room of adjacent dog runs. Festus wagged his tail and whimpered when he saw me, but he didn't stand up. My heart broke. I forced back tears as I walked up to the run. "Can I get in with him?"

The vet unhooked the latch, and I climbed in the kennel and sat down cross-legged next to Festus. He rested his colossal head on my lap and lethargically moved his tail on the cement floor. I rubbed his ears. "Hey, buddy. I've been missing you something awful. You feeling better?"

Dr. Stamper answered for him. "He's definitely not well yet, but his blood work is normalizing, and his heart rate is much more stable. I think he's going to be just fine."

I dug his favorite plush toy out of my purse. "Piggly Wiggly missed you so much. He's been so sad without you, I brought him to visit." He sniffed the pink stuffed pig and eventually took it in his mouth, set it down, and rested his chin on it. I stroked his soft fur and gave him a hug. I whispered in his huge, velvety ear, "I'm so sorry I let this happen to you. I promise I'll do better." He looked up at me with his droopy brown eyes and mustered the strength to give me a single lap on the chin before he dropped his head back onto Piggly Wiggly and fell asleep.

I've been kidnapped by an erotomaniac, shot by a serial killer, and attacked by a band of raging narco-terrorists, and I swear to God, nothing cut me as deep as seeing Festus that sick and weak and knowing somehow I'd failed to keep him safe. I slipped out of the run and around the corner before I lost control of the tears.

Dr. Stamper led me into his office. "I know he looks really pitiful, but from a clinical standpoint, he's doing a lot better. He's improving by the hour."

I swallowed the block of concrete that had formed in my throat and managed to croak out, "Is he going to be okay? I mean...will he recover fully?"

He passed me a tissue from his credenza. "I think Special Ranger Rhodes got to him just in time with the hydrogen peroxide, and we were able to get him intensive care early enough to prevent any permanent damage. With treatment and a lot of TLC, I think he'll be back to his old self in a few weeks."

I released the breath I'd been holding for what seemed like an hour. I hugged Dr. Stamper, thanked him, and made my way to my car.

I hadn't had a regular night's sleep for...what? Forty-eight hours? I'd almost been blown to smithereens, found my dog poisoned, and spent the last twelve hours swimming in Quinten Farragut's cesspool of problems. I was toast.

I drove home, ate a TV dinner over the sink, and lost consciousness.

Chapter 19

Friday, September 17, 11:30 a.m.

I was staring at my computer screen, hoping the genealogy gods would zap me a clue about Annabelle, when I heard a knock on my office door. Addison stuck his head in and said, "Got lunch plans?"

I swiveled around in my desk chair. "I figured I'd just order in."

He pulled his jacket on. "Let's go next door. I reserved the Orient Express."

"Next door" meant a private lunch club called Rick's that was attached to the Hampe Ewald. The bar was done up like Rick's Cabaret in *Casa Blanca*. The restaurant was comprised of fifteen booths that mimicked private train compartments, each named after a famous rail route and decorated to match. Hampe Ewald tenants could bring clients to the restaurant, close the compartment door, and eat luscious food while they talked business in private.

"Sounds great."

"You can bring me up to speed on Annabelle Case while we eat."

I stuffed some pages into my briefcase and trailed him to the elevator. We followed the oak-shaded sidewalk to the club where the hostess led us to our table. The thick hunter-green carpet complemented the dark mahogany paneling of what looked just like the interior of an old train compartment. Six Art Deco chairs surrounded a table draped with an ivory cloth. Crimson drapes framed a fake window looking out on the skyline of Istanbul. The waiter handed us menus and served iced tea and bread. We ordered, and he slid the compartment door shut behind him.

I looked at the poster of Istanbul. "The feel of this place reminds me of when I was a kid. I loved those rainy Sunday afternoons when you and Papa J and I would pile up on the sofa and eat popcorn and watch old black-and-white movies all day."

"You have Justis to thank for that. He loves those old flicks."

"I always wanted to watch the ones about orphans taken away from their Dickensian beginnings by kindly men who swept them off to happy new lives."

Addison tore a piece of warm bread and smeared butter on it. "I probably still know every damn word of *Heidi* and *Little Orphan Annie*. I finally threw the *Heidi* DVD in the trash while you were at school one day. Every frigging time we watched it, you'd cry your eyes out when that bitch of an aunt would take poor Heidi away from Grandfather."

I smiled. "Yeah, and you and Papa J would insist that couldn't happen to me because you two don't have any sisters. Maybe that was the beginning of my interest in genealogy."

"Speaking of, please tell me you've got something on Annabelle Case." He took a bite.

I pulled my notes from my briefcase. "Annabelle Frazier Morgan Case was married twice. She married a chemist named Harrison Morgan in 1948 in Dallas. In 1949, Harrison and Annabelle moved to Wichita Falls where Harrison took a job with a fertilizer company."

The aroma of the fresh-baked rolls was more than I could stand. I took one, tore it open, heaped a mound of fresh butter on it, and took a giant bite. The bread practically dissolved in my mouth. "Damn these are good."

Addison nodded and kept chewing.

I swallowed and turned the page of my notes. "Between 1950 and 1954, they had three kids—Thelma, Ollie, and Luther. Six years later, in 1960, they had another girl—Rose. Harrison died in 1974. Annabelle remarried in 1975. This time, to Jason Case. Case was a rich guy with a chain of tractor dealerships all across Texas."

Addison stirred sugar and lemon into his iced tea. "Any kids with Case?"

I shook my head. "No. That ship had already sailed. Annabelle was forty-seven when she married him. They divorced in 1979. Case died in 1983. Annabelle died a year later in '84 in Midland. No obit for her anywhere I can find. Death certificate shows the oldest daughter, Thelma, as the informant."

"Well, if the oldest daughter provided all the personal biographical information on the death certificate, you'd think it would be pretty accurate."

I took another bite of the roll. It was like a buttery meltaway. I swallowed and said, "Everything on the certificate checks out fine, it just doesn't help us find Thelma or her siblings. I called the funeral home. They purged a bunch of records, including Annabelle Case's, two years ago when they moved to a new facility. I also checked with the cemetery. Annabelle is buried alone, and they don't have anything besides the name of the funeral home and a copy of the death certificate."

"Did you check for a will in Midland County?"

The waiter opened the sliding compartment door and delivered tiny cups of beef consommé, each accompanied by a petit cheese scone—the appetizing duo that was served with every meal at Rick's. I sipped the consommé. "No probate."

"Crap."

The waiter returned carrying a large round tray with our meals. He set a thick slice of prime rib with au gratin potatoes and steamed asparagus drizzled with cheese sauce in front of me. Addison's Chilean sea bass with rice pilaf and broccolini with garlic butter smelled wonderful. After the waiter exited, Addison said, "What about the kids? Any line on them?"

I handed him a printout from a newspaper archive. He wiped his hands on his linen napkin and studied the article.

In between bites, I summarized the story. "The two oldest sisters were spinsters. Both died in a common disaster when the house they shared burned down due to an electrical problem. Neither one ever married, no kids."

Addison set the printout down and took another bite of the sea bass. "This is absolutely extraordinary. Why don't we do this more often?"

I shrugged. "Because lunch here costs more than a Ford Fiesta?"

My prime rib cut like butter, and the au gratin potatoes had just the right blend of garlic and Gruyère cheese.

Addison said, "Money is overrated. This fish is out of this world. So what about the other kids?"

"I'm working on the boy. But, no luck so far."

"The son have any children?"

"None that I can find. Worse, the youngest sister, Rose, seems to have disappeared into thin air. I'm thinking she may have died as a child."

He sipped some iced tea. "What about hiring Sol to work this in his off hours? I need you to stay on the poisonings and figure out who is behind the trouble at the ranch before they burn that gaudy monstrosity to the ground or blow it into the next county."

Sol was the head librarian for the San Antonio Texana and Genealogy library. He was a talented and sophisticated genealogy researcher who had written several books on local history. "I already called him. He's tied up through the weekend, but he'll start Sunday night. I'll stay on it until then."

The waiter appeared and offered us coffee. We both accepted. Addison stirred sugar and milk into his cup. "What about Case's family? Maybe some of them knew Annabelle's kids."

I set my linen napkin next to my empty plate and said, "Oh, that it were so. I talked to Jason Case, Jr. this morning. The old man married a total of six times, with Annabelle being his last wife. The kids couldn't stand him, so they didn't spend a lot of time with dear old dad and *his harem*—the son's words, not mine. According to Junior, the old man drank and smoked and caroused when he wasn't busy making a zillion dollars. When commodity prices were down, people would come into the dealerships looking to buy a tractor they couldn't get along without. When they wouldn't have the money or credit to buy the equipment, he'd sell them the tractor against a loan on their land. When they couldn't pay, he'd foreclose and lease the land back to them as sharecroppers."

"Robber Baron 101."

"And that's how he ended up with land all over Texas. I asked the son about the property in Kenton County. He said he didn't remember it specifically, but he'd check the records."

Addison pressed a buzzer by the table. "We need dessert."

The compartment door slid open, and the waiter materialized with a tray of pastries. Addison chose a slice of key lime pie, and I selected a thick wedge of black forest cake. Using chilled forks the waiter offered with a napkin-draped hand, we dug into our desserts. Addison swallowed a bite of his pie and said, "Did Case's son have any idea why his father would have sold the land without having his wife join on the deed?"

I sipped some more coffee. "He said the old man knew his marriages were probably going to flame out, so he worked hard to keep his wives from knowing anything about his money."

Addison smiled. "Lest they know where to look when the inevitable ugly end came."

"No doubt. I asked him if he had a master list somewhere of the land his father bought and sold over the years. He said it was in their archives, and he'd pull it and send a copy over later today."

Addison leaned on the table. "So, what's your plan?"

"As much land as Jason Case bought and sold, we're probably not the only people who have run into this issue. I'm hoping someone else from one of those other land deals solved this problem already and I can find the kids that way."

He smiled. "You'll figure it out. You always do."

He refilled his coffee from a sterling pot then took his cup and settled back in his chair. "So, what's going on with you? I mean, when you're not working."

For so long, every time Addison or Justis had queried me about my physical and emotional state, I'd had little positive to report. I knew my fathers had been suffering right along with me, and I hated being such a mess. But, today, it felt great to have some good news to deliver. "Things are finally really looking up. The pain in my side is almost gone. The shrink just said we can cut back to monthly sessions. She thinks I'm recovering nicely from the trauma of being shot. Strangely, she seems to think that me killing Geare in the end was good for me...like I stuck up for myself. It's hard to imagine plugging a serial killer while you're bleeding out as a confidence builder, but the mind is a strange place."

He smiled the fatherly smile that had told me all my life that my fathers' unconditional love for me would forever put them unwaveringly on my side. Sometimes that love enveloped me like a soft, warm blanket, and other times it shielded me like a Kevlar vest. But, either way, it was always there. He sipped his coffee. "How are doing with the Kerabos issue? PTSD is a tough nut to crack."

"I'm a lot better with that. I haven't had a flashback since the night of the shooting. My hand doesn't shake anymore. I think the Geare thing helped me with that, too."

He cocked his head. "How so?"

What I was about to say didn't come easy. I felt a flutter in my chest and took a deep breath to calm it. "Pop, I've never told you this, but I always felt guilty I didn't kill Kerabos. If Sean hadn't found me, I would have died of exposure on that road." I stared at the fake view of Istanbul and gathered my thoughts. "I always thought after I stabbed Kerabos and he was disabled, I should have finished him off, used his phone, and waited inside for help. I didn't trust myself after that... I viewed my decision to run as this colossal failure of judgment."

Addison's eyes went wide at the "failure of judgment" part, and he shot forward in the chair. I held up my hand. "Let me finish..."

He paused, then grudgingly settled back. "Sorry. Go ahead."

"However irrational that thinking may have been, when I shot Geare, it was proof positive I wasn't making that mistake again. Of course, I shot Geare because he had the drop on Sean, but that's somehow beside the point. I finally feel like I can trust myself again."

He swirled the remnants of his coffee in the cup for a few beats. "I'm glad you've sorted out that absurd business about some weakness in your judgment. You survived things a lot of people—hell, most people—would never have made it through, let alone have come back from. And you've fought your way through it like a champ. I'm so glad to hear you're turning the corner."

I was overwhelmed with gratitude for landing on the doorstep of the greatest parents I could have ever dreamed of and for receiving their boundless love. A lump formed in my throat. "I'd never have made it if it hadn't been for you and Papa J. Sean was on that road, but you and Papa J made me the person who survived those days and eventually freed myself. I'll always love you both for that—and for the countless other things you've done for me."

He leaned forward and squeezed my hand. "And you, my dear, have made our lives more than either of us ever dreamed they'd be."

Nuance was one of Addison's special gifts, and he rarely missed even the slightest whiff of trouble. He leaned back in the chair again. "Speaking of Sean, I haven't seen much of him lately. What's he up to these days?"

I poured myself another cup of coffee then told him about Dorinda and the gambling.

"I am so sorry. I know how much you love Sean, and I'm sure it's ripping you up to see him struggling."

I slumped back in the chair and let out an exasperated breath. "I want so much to help him, but he keeps telling me he knows what he's doing."

Addison's voice took on a stronger tone. "Iris, when you were kids, Sean was the big brother Justis and I could never give you. That was great—then. But you're not kids anymore. Yes, Sean saved you on that road in West Texas. But you got him to that rehab in Boston eleven years ago. You are one badass lady. Don't you dare let Sean Galen hornswoggle you into believing his addiction-fueled bullshit. And stay clear of Dorinda Crandall. She is a dangerous, disturbed woman driven by her own addictive impulses. There's no way it's a coincidence she showed up here. And this is one time you absolutely cannot rely on Sean to protect you."

I swallowed hard. "I hear you."

"Good." He signed the check.

Like John and Jackie Kennedy having breakfast in Fort Worth one morning in November of 1963, we went back to the office that afternoon without the slightest inkling of what was awaiting me in the coming days. Ignorance may be bliss...but it rarely ends well.

Chapter 20

Friday, September 17, 3:00 p.m.

Back at the office, I dug into the hunt for Annabelle Case's son, Luther Morgan. Having exhausted all the major databases, I was reduced to searching the pelagic ooze of the genealogy world—tiny, fragmented, local databases like "Partial Register of Burials—Pioneer Rest Cemetery, Iowa Park, Texas" and "Funeral Records of Foster's Mortuary, 1975–1983, Vernon, Texas." I was beginning to think my guy had changed his name to Jimmy Hoffa and caught a ride with Amelia Earhart when Sean called.

"Hey, sugar. What are you up to?"

He sounded like his regular self. I was getting whiplash from the recent pendulum swings between tension and normalcy in our relationship. "I'm struggling with a title problem on the Wind Rose. What's up with you?"

"I've been thinking about our poisoner. You've got a picture of the Larry/Darrin guy. We have every reason to believe he did it. But we've got to ID him to find him."

"Sure, so what's your angle?

"I think we should take that picture and interview every employee who worked in those stores when he was around. Maybe one of them knows something we can use to identify him."

"You may be onto something. When the managers couldn't help us, I quit focusing on the stores."

He said, "Yeah. But a lot goes on between the staff that the boss never knows about."

"I'll call Farragut and set it up."

He picked up on the first ring. "Iris. Have you found anything?"

It was impossible to tell which crisis he was asking about. I soldiered on without clarification. "My associate and I would like to interview all the employees who worked with Larry Tate and Darrin Stephens. How hard is that going to be?"

"Well, as far as San Pedro goes, not very. The whole roster is coming to the store for dinner and a little party while we hand out paychecks tonight. It's an effort to hold the crews together until we can get them working again. So, just show up at the store around five this afternoon."

On my way to Circus Burgers, I stopped at Asa Chiron's office to visit Festus. He was much better than the night before. I was so touched that Asa and Dr. Stamper had gone to the trouble of making sure Piggly Wiggly accompanied Festus on the trip from the emergency hospital to Asa's office. Festus was snuggling the toy when I walked in. He pawed me through the bars and whined until I climbed into the run with him and let him lick my face. I stroked him and sat with him for a few minutes before I kissed him goodbye on his big, square muzzle and tried not to cry as I walked away. I didn't know it was possible to miss a dog so much.

Sean and I rendezvoused at the store at 4:45. He parked the Land Cruiser and walked over to me. "So what's the plan?"

I shrugged. "Mingle around. Say we're investigators hired to try to get the stores open and everyone working again. Show the picture"—I handed him several color printouts of the poisoner's picture I had cropped out of the award photo—"and ask them to tell us anything they remember about him."

He looked at the flyer. "I think we should do it together. One of us might pick up something the other misses."

I opened the door. "Sure."

Manager Mike quit slicing pizza, wiped his hands on a towel, and headed straight over. "Thanks so much for coming. What can I do to help?"

I told him our plan. "Just encourage participation."

"You got it."

The staff filtered in, and by 5:15, the lure of their paychecks and a free meal had rallied a full complement of store employees. We mingled through the crowd and showed our picture to the small army of high school and college-aged kids milling around. We got a litany of "I didn't really know him," "He kept to himself," and "Not a very friendly guy." We worked our way to a man of about thirty with an earring who was eating pizza and talking to an older woman with long, salt-and-pepper hair at a four-top in the game room. I motioned to a couple of empty chairs. "Mind if we join you?"

They both smiled and cleared some space. We sat down and introduced ourselves. The man extended a hand. "I'm Joaquin, and this is

Sally." He wiped some tomato sauce from the corner of his mouth with his napkin. "We're back here in the old folks' section."

I did my pitch.

Joaquin looked at the picture. "You think Larry had something to do with the customers getting sick?"

I kept my voice neutral. "We want to talk to anyone who could help us get the stores back open."

Joaquin shook his head. "This is so TARFU. We're all about to get canned." He nodded to the milling Gen Zers. "These kids live at home, so missing a paycheck won't be a problem for them, but I've got bills. I hate to go work somewhere else, but I can't make it without my check."

I smiled. "What do you do here at CB?"

"Now, I run the kitchen...*ran* the kitchen when the store was open. I'm in the management training program. I'm hoping to have my own store by next year."

"What can you tell us about Larry?"

He bit his lip. "He was quiet. Did his job. He didn't work here long...just a month or so. Mike was pissed he didn't give notice." He looked around the restaurant. "He should be here tonight to get his check, but I don't see him."

Sally chimed in. "I'm the cashier. Larry stood right next to me most of the time. Besides work-related stuff, we never exchanged a word besides *hello* and *goodbye*. Now that I look back on it, that's pretty strange, don't you think?"

I smiled my blandest, noncommittal smile and glanced over at Sean. He said to Joaquin, "Where'd you serve?"

Joaquin's forehead furrowed. "Serve? You mean like in a restaurant? Or like in the army?"

Sean nodded. "I heard you say TARFU. That's army for..."

Joaquin said, "Totally and royally..." He looked over at Sally and shrugged. "Yeah. I didn't know it was an army thing. Funny you should say that, though."

Sean leaned in. "How do you mean?"

"I didn't think about it until you mentioned it, but I picked TARFU up from Larry. One day we were working on the fryer, and the thermostat would not kick on no matter what we did. Larry said it was TARFU. I asked him what that meant and he told me...I loved it. I started using it after that. So many situations where it's right on."

Sean kept his voice casual. "Did Larry ever mention being in the military?"

Joaquin rolled his eyes to the ceiling and chewed his lip again. "No. Not that I recall. Sally?"

She shook her head. "Like I said, we never talked except about work like *here's the guac* or *we're low on ketchup.*"

Sean drummed his fingers on the table then said, "Did Larry have any tattoos?"

More head shaking from Sally. "Not that I noticed."

Joaquin snapped his fingers. "He did have one. I saw it when one of the prep guys accidentally dumped a whole pan of diced tomatoes on him. Larry went in the back to change. I was coming out of Mike's office, and I saw him. It was on his shoulder."

Sean leaned forward. "Do you remember what the tattoo was?"

Joaquin chewed his lip some more. "Yeah, I'd never seen it before, but it was like..." He scrunched his eyes closed. "...like a shield with lightning across it." He opened his eyes and shrugged. "I just saw it for a second."

Sean turned in the chair where Joaquin could see his biceps and pulled up his sleeve. "Did it look anything like this?"

Joaquin's eyes got big. "Just like."

From where I was sitting, I could easily read the writing arcing over the top of the shield draped across Sean's bulging muscle. *Rangers Lead the Way.*

We thanked Joaquin and Sally and milled through the room looking for anyone we hadn't already talked to. Satisfied we'd mined the crowd for all it was worth, we thanked Mike and left.

In the parking lot, Sean walked me to the GV80. "This is bad shit, sugar. If this guy is a ranger, then this is a whole different problem. Robbie and I will kick this around tonight, and I'll call you tomorrow. Don't mess with this until you hear back from us. Okay?"

I hugged him. "Sure."

I watched him pull out of the lot and head west on the Loop. He wasn't going home. The loft was due south.

While we were inside the restaurant questioning Joaquin and Sally, we'd been Us again—on the hunt, playing off each other, ferreting out answers. The two of us together...a whole greater than the sum of its parts. Then, we came outside, and he drove away. No chitchat, no talk about getting something to eat, hanging out, visiting Festus.

He was going to her—and to things that could take him away from me forever. And it broke my heart.

Chapter 21

Friday, September 17, 5:00 p.m.

Back at the Hampe Ewald, I searched for Annabelle Case's son and youngest daughter with exactly zero results until I finally gave up at 8:30 and went home. Out of sorts, I nuked some frozen spaghetti and meat sauce and ate it standing in the kitchen before I took a shower and crawled into bed early.

Just as I dozed off around ten, Finn texted me. *How's my favorite big fella?*

Some part of me felt like I was sixteen again. I replied, *Much better today. Thanks for asking.*

He texted back, *And my favorite PI?*

I laughed and tapped keys. *Wiped out. Going to bed early. Bust any bad guys today?* The three dots of an impending reply made me almost giddy.

Recovered two hundred head of sheep and a stolen tractor and locked three thieving assholes up in the Gillespie County jail. Chalk one up for the good guys. More surveillance tonight. Down south with the game warden again, hoping to bust some rustling poachers. Sleep well. More flashing dots, and a little kissy-face emoji appeared on my screen.

My heart did a staccato drum roll as I typed, *Thanks for checking on us. Happy hunting!* He replied with a thumbs-up. I set the phone on my nightstand and fell asleep.

I woke up at 5:00 a.m. drenched in sweat. Disoriented, I fumbled for a light switch. My left hand was quivering. I grabbed it with my right and forced it steady. I had dreamed of Kerabos. He was at the door, with the rag... Then I was in the cabin chained to the old stove. In some kind of time-warp horror show montage, scenes from the terrible days in the cabin flashed by—the assaults, the blows to my face with his giant fist, the unending fear faded into a herky-jerky scene of me covered in his blood running down the caliche road. Somehow in the dream I knew I'd be rescued when I reached the old dead mesquite tree where Sean had swerved the Escalade over in a cloud of dust, swept me up, and carried me to his warm, safe truck... But when I got to the tree in the dream, Sean wasn't there. I stood in the road, screaming, turning in circles looking for his truck. The blinding, mind-shattering fear woke me up. I was sobbing and gasping for air. My left hand was shaking like a tambourine, my heart was trying to hammer its way out of my chest, and terrible chills racked my body.

I remembered the technique the shrink had taught me in the awful times when I'd had a Kerabos dream every night. I struggled to control my breathing and forced myself to repeat the practiced mantra. "It was only a dream. You are in your apartment. You are safe. Kerabos is in prison. It was only a dream..."

In an effort to separate reality from the nightmare, I dragged myself into the kitchen and forced myself through the ritual of fixing a cup of cinnamon tea. By the time the kettle whistled, I was wide awake and my pulse rate had dropped out of the stratosphere. I carried my tea into the living room and settled onto the couch.

I hadn't had any of the dreams in the past couple of months. The shrink considered this a major development, and I was overjoyed not to be reliving the awful trauma every fucking night. So why were they back now?

The therapist had taught me that during trauma recovery, everyday events could trigger symptoms because somewhere in the victim's mind, that everyday event was linked, however irrationally, to the traumatic event. So what the hell was triggering this? I decided it had to be related to my attraction to Finn Rhodes. Since I'd shot Gregory Geare, I hadn't looked at a member of the opposite sex with even the tiniest bit of interest. Now, I was attracted to a man again, and the PTSD symptoms were flaring up. Then I thought of the recent twinges in my side at the site of the wound from Geare's bullet.

For years now, I had sat in a chair opposite my therapist, Madelyn, and watched her cock her head to the side, scrunch up her face, and say, "Hmm...I wonder where that's coming from."

Madelyn wasn't in my living room at 5:30 that Saturday morning, but I looked at the empty chair opposite me and imagined her sitting there. I decided the messages must have been coming from the unhealthy, terrified, and scarred part of my psyche. Early on, I had concluded that giving in to that fear would leave me psychologically crippled forever. I had promised myself I would go beyond that cabin and be a whole, complete person. Screw Kerabos. He'd taken those three days from me. But I damn well wasn't letting him ruin the rest of my life.

I missed Festus so bad I ached. Out of habit, I picked up the phone and looked for Sean. *Location Unavailable.* Hitting his speed dial icon got me voice mail. I longed to snuggle Festus. To get my mind off the dream—and off Sean and Festus—I turned on Netflix and went to the kitchen to refill my tea. Carrying the empty kettle to the sink, I reached for the faucet. But I froze when I heard a noise come from below.

Ron was out of town. Nobody should be in the carport. My skin prickled, and my pulse throbbed in my ears. I quietly set the kettle on the counter and flipped the light off. Once in the dark, steadying my trembling hand, I pulled the blind back a crack and peeked out the kitchen window. A man was standing in my driveway, his head swiveling back and forth scanning for threats. I yanked my cell out of my robe pocket and called 911. Before the operator answered, another man emerged from the carport and nodded. The pair looked around furtively then skulked down the alley. The operator's monotone voice shattered my concentration. "911. What is the location of your emergency?"

I rattled off my name and address. "Two men were in my driveway. One of them came out of my carport. They left on foot down the alley, walking southbound toward Evans."

"Standby please, Ms. Raines." A few seconds later, the operator's voice came back on. "Officers are en route to your location. Please describe the suspects."

I closed my eyes. "One I only saw from behind... He was in a dark T-shirt and what looked like dark jeans...dark baseball cap. Athletic shoes, maybe." Ron's porch light had afforded me a better look at the man who came out of the carport. "Second suspect was male, shorter than the first, dark T-shirt and knee-length shorts with a toboggan cap.

He had a mustache, and tattoos on his arms. He was carrying a messenger bag slung over his shoulder."

"Stand by..."

Sirens wailed and flashing lights washed through my front window. Other cars were coming down the alley, bathing the kitchen in blue light. The front door shook with a violent banging. "Alamo Heights PD. Open the door, Ms. Raines. We need to know you're okay."

I ran to the door and flung it open. "I'm fine, but the men headed down the alley toward Evans."

Static and gravelly speech rattled through the officer's shoulder mic. He clicked the button and spoke into his collar. "Homeowner secure."

More cars raced down Broadway and screeched to a stop in front of the Victorian. Others swerved around the corner along Lamont as a series of shots rang out from the alley. The cop on the porch slapped his arm around my shoulders and shoved me deeper inside the apartment, dropped on top of me, and kicked the door shut. His shoulder shoved my face into the living room rug, and I smelled his sweat and felt his breath on my neck. The thick Kevlar of his vest pressed against my spine as his shoulder mic spewed a cacophony of traffic in my ear. "Shots fired. Suspects fleeing." More gunfire rang out, and then the mic crackled and a winded voice gasped out, "Two suspects down."

Chapter 22

Saturday, September 18, 6:00 a.m.

The cop peeled himself off of me, stood, and helped me up. He was a large man with a buzz cut and muscular physique, and his name tag read Felan. He looked me up and down. "Are you okay? When I heard those shots, I knew we needed to take cover."

I rotated my shoulders and massaged my neck. "I'm fine. Thanks for your help. You guys are great. If I was in San Antonio, I'd still be waiting for a single officer to respond."

He picked his hat up off the floor. "Response time is one of the chief's top priorities." His radio was alive with traffic. He snugged his hat on and said, "If you'll excuse me, I'm needed downstairs."

When he opened the door to leave, a plainclothes man with a badge hanging from his jacket pocket was standing on my porch. Felan tipped his head to the man. "Detective." He turned to me. "Ms. Raines, this is Detective Cummings." Felan edged past Cummings and jogged down the stairs.

I stammered, "Please, come in." I gestured with a trembling hand to the sofa. "Sit down."

Cummings sat, and I took a chair. The adrenaline rush was fading away, leaving in its wake the jangling feeling that comes from the ugly postcrisis combo of low blood sugar and an outrageous pulse rate. Cummings pulled a small spiral-bound pad and pencil from his coat pocket. "Ms. Raines, did you recognize either of the men you saw in your driveway?"

"I only saw the shorter one's face. But I didn't recognize him."

He flipped a page in the spiral notebook. "Do the names Javier Hernandez or Luis Redondo mean anything to you?"

I shrugged. "They're common Hispanic names, but they're not anyone that I recall."

My front door opened, and Grover Delacourt walked in, his oxygen concentrator hissing from the bag he carried over his shoulder. I felt my eyes go wide. I opened my mouth to speak, but Grover held a finger up to stop me then looked at Cummings. "Detective, may I speak with you outside for a moment?" Cummings flipped the notebook closed and followed Grover out onto the porch.

What the hell is going on?

Through the sidelights by my front door, I saw Grover talking with Cummings for a couple of minutes. Then Cummings nodded, pocketed his notebook, and walked down the stairs.

Grover and I went way back to our days at Churchill High School, when he was the geeky senior star of the debate team and I was his awestruck freshman understudy. While our jobs often made it impossible for us to come completely clean with each other, Grover always did what he could for me. He walked back inside and sat down on the sofa next to me.

"Here's the deal. An AHPD cruiser spotted two male suspects matching the description you gave the 911 operator coming out of the alley at Evans. When he hit them with his roof spots, they took off running back down the alley in this direction. Another car blocked the alley from this end. At that point, the suspects pulled handguns and fired on both of the officers through the windshields of their patrol cars. The officers exited their vehicles and returned fire from behind their doors. Both suspects were killed."

So much for *post* adrenaline anything. My pulse ramped up with record speed. "Jesus. Are the cops okay?"

"The officer on this end was grazed, but the medics patched him up downstairs. They transported him to University, but he's fine."

"Who called you?" I looked at my watch. "And how did you get here so fast?"

"Long story. Right now, I need you to help me. First, where is Ron?"

"He's working up in Indiana for the next two weeks. Left this morning."

Grover nodded. "Festus?"

"At the vet."

"Okay. I want you to come down to the carport and tell me if anything is out of place."

"I need some shoes."

I ran into my closet, pulled on some jeans, and slipped into the first pair of flats I saw, then followed Grover down the stairs into the carport. The motion-sensing security light in the backyard wasn't working. Grover borrowed a Maglite from a patrol officer and shone it around the carport. I noticed an odd shadow around my GV80. I pointed. "What's that?"

Grover focused the beam. We both squatted down and peered under the car. An old-fashioned ladies' train case was sitting underneath the gas tank. Grover grabbed me and damn near yanked my shoulder out of the socket, dragging me out of the carport yelling, "Clear the area! Clear the area!"

Pulling me across Broadway to the parking lot of the high school, he whipped a radio off his belt and issued orders as he jogged. He never slowed down even though he was gasping for breath. "Dispatch... Deputy Chief Delacourt requesting immediate bomb squad response to Broadway and Lamont to assist AHPD. Suspicious device found at location of officer-involved shootings. Respond Code Three. High probability of explosive device."

Cummings was directing AHPD patrol officers who scattered to set up a cordon and move the gawkers away from the scene. Fire trucks showed up and blocked off Broadway four blocks north and south of the Victorian. Patrol cars squealed their tires and sealed off the side streets. The Alamo Heights police chief sped up in his personal vehicle, screeched to a stop, and loped over to us. Grover brought him up to speed. "Bomb squad's seven minutes out."

The chief thanked Grover and tossed him a radio then ran across Broadway to confer with Cummings.

The Alamo Heights officers were evacuating the surrounding buildings when the SAPD bomb squad pulled their massive converted motorhome into the high school parking lot.

Grover pointed to his unmarked car. He was huffing and puffing like the Big Bad Wolf. "Go wait for me in my car. Do *not* leave the car."

"Grover, are you sure you're okay?" I asked. "Maybe we should get the medics over here, have them check you out."

He shook his head. "The bomb squad guy'll take over as soon as I brief him. Then, I'll come wait with you. I'm okay for now. Nick's on his way."

Detective Nick Ballard had come to work as liaison between Grover's investigations division and a network of departments from state and local agencies combating public corruption. Grover had coordinated the network after a scandal involving drugs and murder had rocked the SAPD. Since Grover had been shot, Nick was his near-constant companion. Even over all the commotion, I could still hear the concentrator hissing. "You have enough battery life on that thing?"

Nudging me toward the car, he said, "I've got a backup in the trunk if I need it."

He aimed the fob at the car, and its lights flashed. I headed across the high school parking lot just as the pale precursor to the sunrise was beginning to glow at the horizon. The humidity was high, even by San Antonio standards, and the dawn light mixed with the mist to turn the sky a weird purplish pink. Floodlights and rooftop strobes on the police cars layered over the dawn, giving the whole scene an eerie, surreal cast. My umpteenth adrenaline rush of the past day was ending, and I was as wrung out as laundry run through an extra spin cycle. Waves of queasiness washed over me as I climbed into Grover's Ford Expedition. I settled in the seat and watched him disappear into the motorhome.

Minutes later, the bomb robot rolled on its track down a ramp from the command vehicle. A tech in a bulky bomb suit wobbled fifty feet behind, controlling the robot with a joystick attached to a small laptop he carried on a tray like an old-fashioned cigarette girl. The sun was half-way above the horizon when the robot rounded the corner of my house.

Every muscle in my body was strung as tight as a high wire. I alternated between chills and flashes of heat. *Dear God, please don't let the Victorian get blown up again.* I was clenching my jaw so tight, my temples were throbbing. I glanced at my watch as I waited in terror for everything Ron and I owned to be blown to bits. Twelve agonizing minutes later, the machine emerged from my carport carrying the train case and carefully set it in a bomb box the techs had set up on my driveway. The robot closed the lid to the box, picked the whole package up, and slowly motored to a bomb-proof vault mounted on a trailer pulled behind the command vehicle. The round door to the vault was splayed open like a submarine hatch. After the robot gently slid the bomb box into the vault and retracted its clawlike pincer, the vault hatch closed remotely, its door wheel spinning as though it was being moved by the invisible hand of God. The robot rolled back up its ramp and disappeared inside the back of the command truck. Techs helped their colleague out of the bulky bomb suit, loaded the rest of their gear, and drove away.

Grover walked back to the car. He slid the oxygen concentrator onto the seat and climbed in after it, being careful not to kink the hose. His breathing was ragged.

"You okay?"

He shrugged. "What's okay? The paramedics checked me. My O_2 sats are passable. They ran a strip, and my heart's fine. I just don't have any fucking wind." He looked down at the concentrator. "I swear if you hadn't wasted that asshole Geare, I'd find a way to plug him myself."

We watched as the Alamo Heights cops wound down their operation. "The AH chief asked for San Antonio's help. I've got an investigator from Arson bringing his people out to work this. ATF'll be along later."

"It was really a bomb?"

He looked out the window as the concentrator whooshed. "The bot x-rayed the case before they moved it. Enough dynamite to blow the Victorian halfway to downtown. They're taking it to a site over by the police academy to detonate it inside the vault."

My stomach dropped. "Fused? Timer?"

He shook his head.

My heart was slamming against my chest wall. "What?" Panic was seeping into my voice. "Tell me!"

"Remote detonator. The bomb guys searched the car we found parked at the Evans end of the alley. They found the detonator in the glove box."

My brain locked in a feedback loop. *Ohshitohshitohshit.* "Remote detonator so they could be sure to get me."

Grover stared out the windshield as I struggled against the urge to scream. Then, from the chaotic flood of thoughts and ideas that rampaged through my brain, one question stood out. "I'm going to ask you again. How did you end up here tonight? And so fast?"

Grover turned in the seat and looked me dead in the eye. "Iris, I am very limited in what I can say. So please listen carefully and don't ask me a lot of questions."

Crap. The organized crime task force he's been running since he's been on medical...

"The men who set the bomb—they're part of a drug cartel out of Guadalajara that's moving large quantities of heroin through South Texas. Their names hit the system when the officers checked their pockets for ID after the paramedics pronounced them. They were on a watch list that pings my unit."

"Oh, Jesus. The shootout at the Wind Rose."

He nodded. "The shootout told us the cartel was active in Kenton County and up to no good on the Wind Rose. I've been monitoring the chatter for any trace they had figured out who you were. Nothing. But then I heard the ping tonight and checked with dispatch, and they had your address. I couldn't let that chump Cummings wade into this mess. That idiot can't find his fucking car in the parking lot unless he drops a pin on his phone. Him messing with the Guadalajara cartel makes Bambi versus Godzilla look like an even-money match."

I closed my eyes and tried to sort out the countless ways tonight's revelations were going to fuck up my life. Then, it hit me like a face full of baseball bat. "What about Ron? Oh, Jesus..." Ron had almost died the previous year—an innocent bystander to an attack aimed at me. To make matters worse, his apartment was a total loss when Geare blew up the Victorian. "I can't let anything happen to him again. Oh, God, Grover, we have to keep Ron safe."

Grover and Ron were friends, and I knew Grover was worried, too. "We may have this sorted out before he gets back from Indiana. If we don't, we'll figure it out then."

I fumbled for my phone, but Grover stopped me, putting his hand over mine. "I'll call him when we get done here. Best I talk to him."

I winced at the thought of telling my fathers about this nightmare, but I'd cross that bridge when I came to it...which—I checked my watch—would be pretty damn soon.

The sound of Grover's voice broke into my reverie. "Iris?"

I turned to him. "Yeah...sorry."

"I understand we both work with confidentiality constraints. But you need to get with Justis and Addison and Quinten Farragut and figure out a way to tell me everything going on with the cartel so I can nail these bastards. Promise me you'll talk to them."

The deputy chief of the San Antonio Police Department saying my client's name in the same sentence with the word *cartel* made my already-queasy stomach do handsprings. I said, "Can you come with me while I get some things together? I obviously can't stay here."

He nodded. "We need to talk about your security."

I smiled. "That's a short conversation. I'll pack a bag and call Sean and Robbie."

He chuckled. "Enough said."

Huffing and puffing, Grover spoke into his radio as we headed across the street to the Victorian. His color was dusky, and I was worried sick about him. At the stairs, a tall man in black jeans and a polo shirt with a gold badge around his neck fell in beside us. Grover tipped his head toward Nick. "He's going up with us because I'm not worth a damn for protection if any shit hits the fan."

I greeted Nick as he staged himself on the porch in front of my door. Grover rested on the sofa while I packed. I checked the phone again, but Sean's location was still unavailable. I called Robbie and brought him up to speed.

"Jesus, Iris. I'm on my way. We'll take you up to the lake house. There's as much security there as at the loft, but nobody will link you to the place. You and I will take your car, and Ansel will follow us up and stay with you. One of us will be with you all the time from here on out."

I couldn't help but notice he didn't mention Sean. "Put it on the clock. I'm billing every fucking second of the security time to Farragut."

Through the phone, I heard the Hellcat's engine roar to life.

Chapter 23

Saturday, September 18, 4:00 p.m.

Sean's *Star Trek* ringtone roused me to consciousness a little after four that afternoon. It took me a minute to figure out where I was as I fumbled the phone. "Hey, sugar. You okay? Robbie told me everything. I'm so sorry. I have a missed call from you at three in the morning. Was that before everything went to hell?"

I sat up in bed and leaned back against the headboard. "Yeah. I couldn't sleep. Thank God, though. If I hadn't been awake, I'd probably be history by now." A wave of dread rolled through me.

The pause was a split second too long before he said, "I must not have set the phone in the charger right. It was dead when I found it this morning."

Sean had single-handedly executed a hack that crashed Kazakhstan's entire power grid the year before, so it was a stretch to believe he couldn't work a phone charger. And why hadn't Robbie woken him up when I'd called at sunrise? Because Robbie must not have been able to reach Sean, either... I was torn between pushing the issue and letting it slide when he said, "I called Robbie and just about shit when I heard what had gone on. I can tell from your voice you just woke up. So how about some breakfast?"

"I was up all night. My schedule is all screwed up."

"Well, my dear, I'm about ten minutes out. You sound like a girl who could use some TLC and a few dozen silver dollar pancakes with extra blueberries, no matter what time it is. Plus, I can tell you about the latest dirt I found on your food poisoning mystery."

That perked me up. "What did you find?"

He made a tsking sound. "No dice until I get you fed."

Minutes later, Sean came in the front door carrying an armful of groceries. He kissed me on the cheek and greeted Ansel, then donned a bright red apron and started storing groceries while Ansel retrieved more bags from the car. I had a terrible cortisol/adrenaline hangover piled on top of a good old-fashioned case of exhaustion. "I need a shower."

Sean made a shooing motion with his free hand while he whisked batter.

I stumbled to the bathroom and tried to wash off all that ailed me with hot water and the imported bath gel and shampoo that Sean stocked for guests. When I came back to the kitchen, he was flipping pancakes. He used his free hand to push a glass of fresh-squeezed orange juice across the bar and said, "Almost ready." The security system dinged, and Robbie walked in and joined us as Sean put plates and utensils on the bar along with a pitcher of the fresh juice and a platter piled high with steaming pancakes and crispy strips of apple-wood-smoked bacon. The aroma of the food made my mouth water. Robbie and I took seats at the bar on either side of Ansel. Sean climbed onto his favorite stool and motioned at the food with his fork. "Dig in."

We mowed through the platters in short order. When we were finished, Sean made mocha lattes. He served the coffees then pulled his laptop out of its bag and set it up on the bar.

I looked at the computer. "So what did you find?"

Sean shook his head and exchanged glances with Robbie and Ansel. "Before we get to that, we need to talk about what happened last night and what we're going to do about it."

I held up my hand. "I'm safe here now. Ansel wouldn't even go to bed last night. He sat on the couch until he heard you pull up."

Ansel mopped some syrup up with a piece of pancake. In his thick Liverpool accent, he said, "I tailed the GV up here. Tail was clean. I've had the monitors up on my iPad since we got here. Nothin' moving. I'll be here until you get this sorted."

I smiled. "See...I'm safe as the nuclear launch codes. Let's work some other angle, let me get my mind off of it for a while."

Sean shrugged. "Okay. But you have to promise us you won't go anywhere without Ansel."

Ansel popped the last bite of bacon in his mouth. "She'll be fine."

Sean opened the laptop and typed. "You're gonna love this." He turned the computer where I could see the screen. Three pictures of the San Pedro Circus Burgers store and what looked like the menu photo of their cheesy fries.

I looked from Sean to Robbie. "I'm going to love what?"

Robbie winked at me and said to Sean, "Tell her the rest."

Sean did his smarty-pants grin—the one he's been doing since he was seven and figured out he was the smartest kid at school. "I was bored last night..."

I blew on my latte. "Okay..."

"Since Big Top obviously ripped off their whole store concept from Circus Burgers, I thought it might be interesting to see what's floating around their network."

I said a silent prayer my fathers never got wind of Sean's nocturnal fishing expedition. Justis's reaction would make the hounds of hell look like a litter of Yorkies. "You found these images on Big Top's network?"

He winked. "Yep."

"Could you tell where Big Top got them?"

He shook his head. "Couldn't find a trail."

I sipped my coffee as I stared at the images. Letting out a sigh, I said, "I just don't see how Addison can turn some pictures of the CB store and their cheesy fries into a smoking gun."

Sean did the smarty-pants grin again. "My thinking exactly. So, I dug deeper." He tapped some more keys. "These images are examples of what is called *digital steganography*."

I squinted at the pictures. "Digital what?"

"Steganography." He turned the computer back facing him. "It's a process whereby secret files are hidden inside seemingly innocuous digital images." He tapped more keys and swiveled the screen back where I could see it.

I stared at a series of images of dancers in various poses. Lots of images...at least a thousand. And each one had a series of letters and numbers in the lower left-hand corner. I leaned in for a closer look. "What are these?"

Sean slid the laptop over to Robbie. "You cracked it. You tell her."

Robbie set his cup down. "They're a cipher. It's a variation on what's called the phone code. For example, take the letter *A*. *A* appears on the

Number 2 key on the telephone keypad. It's the first letter of the three assigned to that key. So, in a straight phone code, *A* is 2 1."

I thought about it a minute. "Okay...so these codes are spelling something?"

Robbie shook his head. "Not exactly. It's a system for sequencing the images by labeling these pictures A through Z, then AA and so on—just like the columns in an electronic spreadsheet. That tells us what order to put the pictures in."

I looked at Sean. "Are there other hidden files inside these dancer photos?"

He sampled his mocha latte. "I wrote a routine to check for that and ran the whole lot through the program. No dice. That's where we're stuck."

I stared at the images. Ballerinas in grand jeté and pirouette positions. Jazz dancers in modern poses...Gene Kelly swinging around the lamp post singing in the rain. "Damn..."

Robbie adjusted the computer for me to get a better look. "Come on, Sherlock. Help us out here."

I held my palms up in surrender. "I know nothing about codes, let alone this steganography thing..."

I stared at the images for several minutes while Sean and Robbie discussed various ciphers they encountered in the military. Then it hit me. "Sherlock!"

Both of their heads snapped toward me. Robbie said, "Huh?"

I grabbed my phone. "Sherlock Holmes...what was the name of it? Dancing...Adventure..."

Matter-of-factly, Ansel said, "'The Adventure of the Dancing Men.'"

We all eyed him. "I'm a fuckin' Brit. I's weaned on Sherlock Holmes."

Sean grabbed the laptop, and his fingers flew across the keyboard. In seconds, he produced a screen full of stick figures representing numbers and letters. "It's a simple substitution code."

I stared at the stick figures. "Show me the dancer photos."

He hit a key to split the screen. My eyes darted from the stick figures to the photos. "Look." I pointed to the image of Gene Kelly and used my finger to trace the shape of the first stick figure over Kelly swinging from the lamp post. "That's A."

The men studied the split screen. Robbie said, "I think she's right."

I slumped down in the chair. "There are thousands of these images. It'll take us days to put them in order and translate them all into letters."

Ansel put his dish in the sink and said, "Without characters for spaces or punctuation, it'll take more time to separate the letters into readable text."

Sean swept up the laptop. "I'm going up to the office. I can write a program to sort this out pretty fast. Why don't you all take a swim? I'll be done in an hour or so." Before we could answer, he disappeared up the polished teak plank stairs lined with a floating glass railing that led up to the second floor.

Ansel begged off. "I'm going to take a shower. I'll be out before you blokes leave."

As I headed to the bathroom to change into my swimsuit, Robbie said, "I left my sunglasses in the Hellcat. I'm going to get them. See you in the water."

I was sitting on a lounger on the dock when Robbie came out of the house carrying his Ray Bans. His face was flat, and he was chewing his lip. "What's wrong?"

He shook his head. "Nothing. Let's take a dip."

I stood my ground. "Are you sure you're okay?"

He winked at me. "Right as rain. Race you to the other side of the cove."

We both dived in, but I was only halfway across the inlet before he passed me coming back in the opposite direction. We swam for a few minutes, then sprawled in floating loungers before piling into the hot tub. We were drying off when Sean came out of the house triumphantly waving a sheaf of papers. "Extra. Extra. Read all about it."

Robbie and I joined Sean at a table on the back patio. He grinned. "While the program was running, I took another look at Big Top's network. I still couldn't find where the photos came from, but I did find this." He passed me a printout of an email from the CEO of Big Top Burgers to a gibberish Gmail address.

"'Thanks for the tickets to the ballet. You should keep them and go yourself. We don't have sufficient expertise to enjoy the evening, but we would be thrilled for you to attend in our place.'"

I looked up. "Who's the addressee?"

He shook his head. "Can't tell. I'll give it another shot, but I'm not optimistic we're going to get anywhere with that."

I muttered, "Shit."

He laughed. "But there is some good news. I decoded the dancing man message."

He spread the sheets out for us to read. We stared in horror at what we saw. The first page was titled, "Sabotage with Biologic Agents—The Anarchist's Guide." The second page made my heart skip. "Instructions for Growing *Bacillus cereus*."

I looked up at Sean. Major smarty-pants grin. I mulled over the find. "So, we're certain now that Big Top is behind the poisoning. That's a huge breakthrough. We also know it's a hit-for-hire job because of the email. Also huge. But our only link to the hit man is that gibberish email address."

Sean shrugged. "Absent breaking through that, all we have is the award photo."

Robbie sipped his coffee. "So, where do we go from here?"

"I think I should call Marvin," I said. "Tell him about this steganography thing. After all those years doing cloak-and-dagger shit for the government, maybe some of this will ring a bell with him."

Robbie stood. "I like that. He's definitely got contacts on the government side Sean and I can't get to. Let us know what he says."

That was a signal from Robbie that he was ready to depart. Something had happened during his trip to the car to get his sunglasses that he didn't want to talk about. Being a trained detective, I took the cue. I thanked them for all their help and hugged them both. As we walked to the door, Ansel came down the stairs and wished them good night.

I motioned him into the living room. "Let's see what's on Netflix. I'm too fried to work any more." We settled in front of the giant TV, and Ansel pulled out his tablet and adjusted the security camera views to his satisfaction. "I'm way too tired to pick anything." I handed him the remote. "Dealer's choice."

His selection of *Miss Congeniality 2* told me Ansel was a really considerate guy. Ansel was into buddy-cop rom coms about like he was into pink tutus. He watched the iPad mostly, except for every half hour when he prowled around the house like he was checking a trip-wire along the DMZ. When I nodded off, he gently shook my shoulder and pointed me to the bedroom where I mercifully fell into an exhausted, dreamless sleep.

Ansel's insistence I sleep in an interior bedroom without windows left me in a world as timeless as a Vegas casino. I woke momentarily disoriented in the dark room. Then, the preceding day's events came flooding back, and I lay there and pondered how I could tell my fathers about the bomb in my carport without scaring them to death. I also had to come up with a way to tell them what Sean had found without making them accessories after the fact to a felony. Deciding both were impossible, I forestalled the inevitable by texting Addison I was spending the weekend up at the lake house but to keep it quiet because I was hiding out to concentrate on finding Annabelle's kids. Then I went downstairs to scare up some breakfast.

Ansel was sitting at the kitchen island wearing a T-shirt with Yoko Ono's face enclosed in a red circle with a slash across it. An empty plate sat in front of him, and a savory aroma lingered in the air. He tipped his head to the stove. "I made potato scones with fried tomatoes and mushrooms. Your plate's warming in the oven." He picked up his dish and carried it to the sink.

Starving, I retrieved my meal and dug in. "This is great. I hope you didn't go out of your way on my account."

He shrugged. "Back home, my mum owns a pub. I started working there when I was ten."

I scooped the fried mushrooms onto my fork. "You get any sleep?"

He was studying the tablet. "Enough."

I finished eating and washed the dishes. "I'm going up to the office."

He nodded. "I'll be here."

I had to find Annabelle Case's missing kids before the contract for the sale of the Wind Rose ran out, and the clock was ticking. But first, I dialed Marvin.

"Thanks for calling O'Neal's Sneak-and-Peek Emporium. Whose skirt can we look up for you today?"

I laughed. "You best watch the caller ID before you dole out that banter. You get some feminist hippie chick on the line, and you're liable to find yourself bitch-slapped by cancel culture."

It was his turn to laugh. "Hell, Iris, you're the leftiest feminist hippie chick I'll ever know. I try all that shit out on you first. That's how I stay outta trouble. What's up?"

I told him about the bomb at my apartment, the award photo, the suspect's ranger tattoo, the steganography, and everything else we had figured out. He was quiet for a while then said, "Let me cogitate on it. I'll get back to you."

Cogitate? He knew something...something he couldn't or wouldn't talk about right then. Whatever he knew was probably ensnared in a spider web of security clearances, and God knew what else he was going to have to plow through before he spilled whatever beans he could.

"Great. Give me a call when you have something."

"I'll let you know." The line went dead.

I unloaded the piles of notes and database printouts that had gotten me exactly nowhere on finding Annabelle's kids. I started over on her life story, perusing every document like a jeweler searching for tiny flaws in an uncut diamond. As I studied the records, my cell rang. Finn. I picked up. "How's life on surveillance in South Texas?"

"Are you all right?"

I turned away from the computer. "How'd you hear?"

"Since 9/11, an automatic notification goes out to every law enforcement agency in a two-hundred-mile radius of any incident involving bombs or other explosives. That includes lowly special rangers."

I ran him through the *Reader's Digest* version of the night's events.

"You're not staying at the apartment, are you? I can try to figure out a safe house to borrow..."

"You're sweet, but I'm locked up tighter than the Vatican's secret archives."

"Don't tell me where. These phones may not be secure."

I took a pull off my water bottle. "Gotcha. So tell me about your surveillance."

He laughed. "What a train wreck. We got made and ended up in a chase. Assholes led us through three counties before the state troopers blew their tires with a spike strip. That adventure was followed by a jurisdictional dick-waving contest over which jail to take the bastards to. Sometimes I don't know what's worse—the bad guys or the bureaucracy. How's Festus?"

"I think he'll be able to come home early next week. And we have you to thank for that."

I could almost hear him blushing. "Glad to be of help. We dog people have to stick together."

I found myself about to say something like *Why don't you let me fix you dinner when I get back home?* when, seemingly out of nowhere, flashes of Kerabos holding the chloroform-soaked rag and Geare firing his gun at me surged through my mind. A searing pain stabbed my side. My heart pounded, and my temples throbbed. The phone was vibrating against my cheek, and I realized my hand was shaking. I was having some kind of PTSD episode. I fumbled for an excuse to get off the phone. "Hey, I've got a call coming in. I've been trying to reach this witness for a couple of weeks. I have to take it. I'll call you back." I rang off before I made a complete fool of myself.

What the hell was happening to me? So much for cutting my therapy sessions back to once a month. I emailed Madelyn to schedule an appointment as soon as possible then did deep breathing exercises until my heart rate dropped back down to something that wouldn't reduce an ECG machine to a smoking hunk of burning circuits. Once I herded my cardiovascular system back into the corral, I returned my attention to the Annabelle problem.

I couldn't get rid of Quinten Farragut and his lying bullshit soon enough. He was holding out on me—I could feel it in my PI bones. He knew way more about the problems at the ranch than he was letting on. Maybe he didn't know how or even if the ranch troubles were related to the poisonings, but I was certain the sabotage in the restaurants hadn't just happened as a random event. In any case, finding Annabelle's heirs was key to being rid of him once and for all.

Chapter 24

Monday, September 20, 8:30 a.m.

After a long conversation with my fathers Sunday night, we decided I should stay at the lake house until the problem with the cartel got resolved. Fear that I could draw fire to innocent bystanders at the Hampe Ewald cinched the deal. If you have to be on the lam, doing it in a five-thousand-square-foot ultramodern house with two hundred feet of lake frontage wasn't a bad way to go about it.

Eating yourself silly was also an integral part of the experience. I rummaged through the freezer and found some frozen whole-grain waffles, a package of imported Irish pork sausage, and half a can of orange juice concentrate. In no time, I was whipping up a thousand-calorie breakfast. I laid out the spread and called to Ansel. He materialized in the kitchen almost instantly. "Damn...are you plannin' on feedin' an army?"

I laughed. "Nah...just us. I'm frigging starving."

He slid a waffle and a couple of sausages onto a plate and pulled a barstool up to the marble-topped island. I took three waffles, bathed them in a generous serving of blueberry syrup, and raked four sausages onto my plate, then pulled up a stool opposite him. "Hiding from a bunch of murdering narco-terrorists hell-bent on blowing you to smithereens can sure work up your appetite."

He swallowed a bite of waffle. "You're hungry because the adrenaline rush burned through all your blood glucose. You're craving sugar to combat the hypoglycemia. Now, you'll eat and eat... Then...

I washed another bite of waffle down with the orange juice. "Then...what?"

"Then, at some point, when your body's back to somewhere near normal, it's going to hit you. It may make you crazy mad, may scare the bejesus out of you, may make you cry, or leave you to sleep for hours. Whatever it is, just let it happen. It's part of the deal."

After two and a half years of intensive therapy for PTSD, I could have written a book on those symptoms. While I had no intention of telling Ansel this wasn't my first trauma rodeo, the look in his eyes told me he'd been there, too. While it definitely sucked, the near miss with that bomb the night before was a trip to Maui compared to what I'd already been through. Craving waffles and syrup was child's play... "I'll sleep. But that'll be later...probably hit me tonight."

His dark brown eyes bored into me, then he gave a tiny nod and went back to munching. "Good sausage."

When we finished eating, Ansel conducted his regular check of the doors and windows while I cleaned up the kitchen. In the enormous living room, I sat on a low gray leather and chrome sofa nestled between two sleek, modern black leather chairs and positioned in front of an eighty-inch TV hung above a rectangular in-wall electric fireplace. I was sipping my mocha latte and watching the boats on the lake when Marvin called. "Why didn't you tell me you 'bout got yourself vaporized by those cartel assholes?"

"I'm sorry, Marvin, I just wasn't up to telling it one more time."

"Word's all over the street they tried and missed and two of their guys got dead in the process. 'Least now, we know who we're lookin' for. I'm checkin' my traps."

"I appreciate it. What's up with you otherwise?"

"I've got a gig that's about as exciting as watching paint dry. I thought you might ride along, provide a little comic relief."

"I'm under house arrest with a minder, but I think I can convince him to put a little slack in my rope. Where are we going?"

"Meet me in the parking lot of the Phillips 66 station by the airport in an hour."

"See you there."

I found Ansel downstairs and told him what was up.

He said, "I know Marvin. I'll drive you there. You can get in the van with him, and I'll hang back somewhere close."

I checked my weapon and pulled my shoulder holster on, grabbed my windbreaker, purse, and briefcase, and headed to the driveway. The Land Cruiser was parked next to the GV. I looked at Ansel.

"The armored car fairy popped in overnight." He clicked a fob, and the truck's lights flashed. "Sean and Robbie told me you'd insist on strolling about looking for clues. I fancy having a bit of armor in case we run into our mates from south of the border. Easier if I have some room to get myself arranged before I kill them."

Marvin's dinged-up black Econoline van was idling by the carwash at the Phillips 66 station. Today it was sporting magnetic signs for Ed's

Cleaning Service. "Talk Dirty to Us" was emblazoned above a phone number that was permanently sent to voice mail.

I slung my stuff into the back and climbed into the captain's chair next to Marvin. "So who's talking dirty to us today?"

Marvin is six feet three inches and two hundred forty rock-solid pounds of don't-even-think-about-fucking-with-me huge. His biceps bulged as he wheeled the van out of the parking lot and headed into the airport. "Got a lawyer client over in Houston who handles a lot of the big dope cases in South Texas. Dude buys a shitload of my time. Guy's brother is an oil company exec here in River City. The brother's got some wild idea his wife is playing serve and volley with her tennis coach at the country club."

I rolled my eyes. "And if you want to keep the work on the dope cases coming, as a 'favor' to the client, you're stuck trying to bust the sister-in-law before she makes off with half the brother's worldly goods."

"Game, set, match."

"Been there. Is she really cheating?"

"Like a frustrated housewife at a Chippendales convention. No shit, they do it in the back of the tennis dude's camper van."

He followed the signs to the long-term parking garage and used a card to open a swing arm into the guaranteed parking section. In the side mirror, I watched as Ansel found a spot next to the restricted area. "An oil company exec's wife is having an affair in a parking garage?"

Marvin laughed. "Yeah. Reserved parking runs two hundred forty bucks a month. Designed for frequent flyers who don't want to drive all over hell's half acre looking for a spot. Dude is so damn cheap, he rents one of the reserved spots and brings the wife here in his van."

"No matter how long I do this, shit still amazes me."

He parked in his own reserved spot and killed the engine. Removing his high-res digital video recorder from the storage box built into the van, he extended the tripod, set the camera up looking out the back limo-tinted window, and aimed it at the vacant spot directly opposite our parking place. As he fiddled with the recorder, he said, "No way to wire up a hidden camera with remote feed in here without getting busted by the airport cops, so I'm stuck parking until I get enough footage to convince the brother."

I watched him futz with the tripod. "How much can it take? What else does he think she's doing getting in a camper van at the airport?"

"Beats the hell outta me. I just work here. This is day four, and the brother still doesn't believe it." Satisfied the camera was ready, he sat at the desk in the rear work area of his van, flipped a switch to activate an oscillating fan, and motioned for me to join him.

I sat down. "So, what have you figured out that's going to extract Quinten Farragut from his spinning vortex of crap?"

Marvin removed a folder from the desk drawer and set it in front of him. "We now know that the poisoner is ex–special forces. The ranger tattoo pretty well seals that. So, let's think about what SF guys do when they exit the military. Most end up doing some kind of intelligence or security work. Some are outright mercenaries. Others work in their area of specialization like cybersecurity or hostage recovery. But one damn thing they do *not* do is sling hash in a burger joint—unless it's an assignment. Like from a corporate intelligence outfit."

Five minutes in, and it was already getting hot in the van. I picked up a legal pad from the desk and fanned myself. "But why would Big Top need corporate espionage? The CEO worked for Circus Burgers and stole their playbook when he left."

Marvin shook his head. "Think about it. We know Big Top was behind the poisoning because of the coded messages Sean found on their network describin' how to cultivate the bacteria. Plain as day the email about the ballet tickets was a message tellin' the espionage people to go ahead with the poisoning, probably because those limp dicks over at Big Top didn't have the *huevos* to do their own dirty work."

I thought about it. "Makes sense. So let's assume that Big Top does have some corporate dirty-tricks assholes running this terror campaign against Circus Burgers. Which one is it? There are a ton of those shops operating around the country."

Marvin smiled. "True dat." He held up a finger. "*But* I couldn't get past the steganography thing. Most outfits in this line of work have preferred methods of crypto, but I haven't come across anybody usin' steg since I was doin' some seriously black box shit for Uncle years ago."

Sweat was running down my chest, and I fanned myself some more. "But the government is not running some covert op against frigging Circus Burgers."

Marvin bumped the fan up a notch and made a finger gun. "Right again. But I found some chatter on a couple of merc bulletin boards 'bout what a pain in the ass steganography is. The name of one shop keeps coming up. Allways Security."

"Never heard of them."

He shuffled through the pages in the folder. "I checked the General Services Administration's e-library listing of federal contracts—tryin' to get an idea of what kind of work these boys are really doing." He passed me the pages.

I let out a whistle. "Holy moly! Allways Security has half a billion dollars' worth of federal contracts with the Defense Department?"

Marvin nodded. "Holy moly's right. If our bad guy's one of their operatives, them being publicly linked to a murder during a domestic corporate espionage scheme could be seriously bad news for the company. Congressional oversight'd have a field day with that."

I flipped through the pages. "Like adios federal contracts."

Marvin smiled. "Like adios half a billion buckaroos."

"But what was this big-time mercenary outfit doing poisoning cheesy fries at Circus Burgers? I mean, isn't that a little out of their theater of operations?"

Just then, a silver Winnebago Travato camper van pulled into the reserved spot opposite ours. Marvin leaned over and switched on his recorder. Pointing out the back window, he said, "You gotta see this."

"Too bad we don't have popcorn."

Three minutes later, a tall, leggy blonde in black skinny-legged pants, a tan silk blouse, and leopard-print stilettos carrying an oversized Louis Vuitton purse emerged from an Uber, edged her way around the swing arm into the reserved area, strolled up to the van, and stopped. She looked around the parking garage like a skittish meerkat watching for a jackal. After a few seconds, she opened the side door of the camper van, took another furtive glance over her shoulder, then disappeared inside.

"I need some surveillance—try to link the poisoner to Allways."

Marvin was silent a couple of beats. "Best I set up on their office in Houston."

I looked back at the printouts. "These contracts refer to their offices in Dallas."

He checked his watch and pointed to the van. "Wait for it..."

I watched for a few seconds, then the camper started rocking on its shocks just like a bad cartoon. I laughed out loud. "How'd you know when it would start?"

He shook his head. "Been doing this shit for goin' on a week. Three minutes after Blondie climbs in, the van starts doin' the shake-rattle-and-roll. More regular than a damn Seiko watch. Give it twenty more minutes, she'll be steppin' into another Uber."

I watched the van bounce up and down. "We picked a hell of a way to make a living." I thumbed through more of the pages. "So if their corporate address is Dallas, why watch some place in Houston?"

Keeping one eye on the van, he said, "'Cause the illegal business never gets run out of the corporate office. That'd be shittin' too close to the house. You have a pic of this asshole?"

I dug through my briefcase and passed him the cropped shot from the award photo. He slid it into the folder. "And Iris..."

"Yeah?"

"Don't go messing with these guys. You let me handle it. I don't want you stepping all over my investigation."

It wasn't his investigation. It was mine. But I didn't miss the message. Marvin was warning me to be afraid of these people. That meant he knew the dirt on them. "Okay. It's your deal."

We killed a few minutes with gossip and small talk about my fathers and Sean and Robbie before I gathered my bag to leave.

He cocked his head and raised his eyebrows. "No fucking around on this, Iris. You leave this to me."

I held up my hands in a surrender gesture. "Done. I've already got enough assholes trying to kill me."

Marvin tapped his watch. I followed his gaze to the window. The blonde stepped out of the camper van and walked across the parking lot just as her Uber pulled up. She folded herself into the car and shut the door.

Marvin stood. "And that concludes today's show, folks. Tune in tomorrow for our next installment of *Sandy Does San Antonio International*." He packed up the camera and slid into the driver's seat. I climbed back into the Land Cruiser. My clothes were damp with sweat, and my hair felt like I'd just gotten out of the shower. A cold blast of air from the Toyota's AC washed over me. Ansel was following Marvin out of the parking garage and out onto Airport Boulevard when my cell phone began to bark—the distinctive ringtone for Asa Chiron. I picked up immediately.

"How's my pooch?"

He laughed. "Your *pooch* is bigger than a miniature horse. But, regardless, I'm pleased with his progress. I got some lab results back today, and I wanted to bring you up to speed."

I shucked my purse and briefcase onto the floor of the Land Cruiser. "I'm all ears."

"Dr. Stamper sent the vomitus Festus threw up to A&M for testing. He thought it was important for us to know what he got into."

"Absolutely." I told him about searching my apartment and coming up empty.

"Well, it's a strange combination. Nothing I've ever seen before. It was a mixture of avocado, vanilla extract, xylitol—that's an artificial sweetener—dark chocolate, and cocoa powder."

My heart was pounding. I gripped the phone with my sweaty hand. "You're sure about this?"

"Yeah. I called the lab to double-check." I forced myself to harness my racing thoughts so I could focus on what he was saying. He continued, "While interesting, it hasn't really changed my diagnosis or treatment. Festus's blood sugar is stable. His heart problems from the chocolate are lining out, but we're not quite back to normal in terms of heart rhythm. We're using antiarrhythmic drugs to help him with that. The pancreatitis from all the fat in the avocados is resolving, but his GI situation is still pretty fragile."

I swallowed. My mouth was so dry I could hardly talk. "When will he be well enough to come home?"

"I'd like to keep him until he's got normal cardiac function without any drugs. I'm thinking end of this week or beginning of next is a target date for him going home."

I thanked Asa and assured him I'd be by at closing time for my daily visit. I dropped the phone into my lap then fought to steady my breathing. I was experiencing an almost overwhelming amalgamation of terror and rage. "We've got to go to my apartment. *Now.*"

Ansel shook his head. "No can do, missy. Robbie finds about that, and I'll come to a sticky end. I'll get someone to go pick up whatever you need."

I shook my head. "No deal." I told him about the vet's news. "I need to search the place myself."

Ansel pulled into a gas station at the Loop and Nacogdoches and took out his phone. After a brief conversation, he said, "One of my colleagues is going to the apartment now. He'll make sure the location is not under surveillance, then stay downstairs. I'll come in with you. We're in and out in fifteen minutes—not a second more. And you wear a vest. No debate."

I nodded. The minutes ticked by like hours while we waited for the all clear. Finally, Ansel's phone chimed. He checked the message and typed a brief reply before going to the cargo area and returning with two Kevlar vests. He handed me one and strapped on the other himself, then checked the weapon in his shoulder holster, retrieved extra ammunition from the center console, and stuffed it in his pocket. I checked my Glock while he drove to the Victorian.

Ansel parked in the carport and shuttled me up the stairs while his buddy stood watch in the driveway. Once inside, I ran to the computer and pulled up the log on my alarm system. Nothing. I called the alarm company. No intrusions. I raced from one point of entry to another looking for evidence of the break-in. I found it in the bathroom. Someone had clearly jimmied the window. I'd never noticed because I always kept the bathroom shade down.

How has my alarm not gone off? I checked the outside of the window then examined the alarm wiring all along the exterior of the house. At the control box, the wires supplying power to the alarm had been cut and spliced. The cellular backup must have been jammed electronically.

On my home office computer, I searched the cloud-stored recordings from my video cameras. Sure enough, at 6:12 the evening of September 15, a petite figure wearing a Guy Fawkes mask walked up to the security camera that captured the bathroom window side of the Victorian, pulled out what looked like a small black shower cap, and snapped it over the lens. Fifteen minutes later the same masked figure pulled the cover off and disappeared out of range of the camera. I leaned back in the office chair and tried to regulate my breathing. This bitch had circumvented a state-of-the-art security system, broken into my apartment, and poisoned my dog. If it hadn't been for Sean telling me about her cupcakes, I would have never known it was her. Was she just trying to terrorize me? Or was Festus a practice run? Was I next?

Ansel tapped his watch. "Chivy along. We need to get out of here."

I followed him down to the Toyota, and he waved to his colleague as we pulled out onto Broadway. I needed to call Grover, but I had to be careful about what I said so my report did not lead to a conversation about Sean and his gambling issues. Once I had my story straight in my mind, I dialed.

"J. Edgar Hoover calling for Eliot Ness."

"The hell you say. Wait a minute... Are you wearing a dress?"

I smiled. "Skirt and blouse."

"Close enough. What can I do for you, Mr. Hoover?"

I told him about Festus being poisoned and the window lock and the video camera.

"Crap, Iris. Are you working on a case that's got some psycho riled up? I mean this whole thing sounds *Fatal Attraction* bunny-cooker nuts to me. Way too sophisticated for those cartel assholes. You really need to slow down on the number of homicidal maniacs you're pissing off these days."

"It is pretty...off the rails."

"Whoa...! What are you doing at your apartment, anyway? I understood from Addison you were going to stay...elsewhere."

"I am staying elsewhere. Some of Robbie's guys were with me. We've already been and gone."

Grover cleared his throat. "I assume we defenders of law and order are going to get zippo help from you on possible suspects related to your line of work."

"Sorry, Mr. Ness. I promise I don't have any booze hidden in the basement."

"Fuckin' comedians. The world's full of 'em."

"Seriously, Grover, I really don't think this is about a case."

"Well, whoever did it was ballsy enough to break into a second-story apartment in broad daylight, smart enough to disable a top-notch security system, and crazy enough to try to kill a dog that's bigger than some grown men. Ballsy, smart, and crazy is a bad combination." He sighed. "Call Alamo Heights PD and make a report. Tell them to call me if they need a crime scene crew. If they jerk you around, call me back, and I'll rattle some cages. And, Iris...keep that Glock where you can reach it. This is a no-bullshit deal. The cartels are bad enough, but we can usually see them coming. You know better than any of us, this kind of weird stuff gets out of hand in ways we can't foresee. I know you're holding something back from me on this...you always do. But wherever you think this is coming from, you watch your ass."

Eliot Ness was a really smart cop. And so was Grover Delacourt.

Chapter 25

Monday, September 20, 6:00 p.m.

Sean was my best friend in the world—the brother I'd never had. We would be standing together, back-to-back with pitchforks, fighting off the zombie apocalypse long after the rest of the world had forsaken us. When he got wind of this, I was sure he'd go postal, and Robbie and I would have to hold him off the platinum-blond she-devil for fear he would tear her limb from limb.

As we sped north on 35 toward the lake house, visions of Festus collapsing as he tried to reach me when I came in the door that night morphed into images of Finn carrying my almost-dead Saint Bernard down the stairs. I hit the speed dial for Robbie. He answered and said, "If I'd known you were going to the apartment, I would have met you there myself."

"God almighty. What? You have a satellite locked on me now?"

"My guys stay in touch. What was the emergency?"

I told him about the poisoning and the window and the cameras.

Through clenched teeth, he said, "Fucking bitch. I should throttle her with my bare hands."

"We've got to talk to Sean. It's terrible Festus had to go through this, but it will finally make Sean see the truth."

Silence. "Robbie? Are you there?"

"Sean's on his way to the lake house. The mechanic's coming early tomorrow morning to pick up the boat and take it in for maintenance. He's going to hang with you and spend the night so he'll be there to go over things with the mechanic." I heard him take a deep breath. "I'll be at the lake by the time you get there. But...Iris..."

"What is it?"

More silence. Finally, Robbie said, "I'm worried this may not go the way you're thinking."

"Huh? The bitch broke into my fucking apartment and *poisoned* Festus. I'm just worried it'll take both of us to restrain him."

After a couple of beats, he said, "I'll see you at the house." And he was gone.

I passed the forty minutes it took us to get to Canyon Lake imagining how Sean would go all Lizzie Borden on Dorinda's ass when he was finally confronted with the reality of her wickedness.

When we pulled up, Ansel eyed the Ferrari and said, "I think I'll get some sun on the dock."

I walked up the pathway of concrete squares lined with mondo grass leading to the house. Sean met me at the door, looking puzzled. "Where have you all been?" He motioned to the open door into the house. "I'm just having a sandwich. You want something?"

I shook my head. He looked at me warily. "What's wrong, sugar?"

On the television mounted above the fireplace, a reporter questioned a hedge fund manager about recent fluctuations in the tech market. I looked through the living room's wall of glass out at the water. The sun was a fiery ball slipping below the horizon leaving the sky a deep red reflecting down on the water. Sean hit the Mute button, and the talking heads went silent.

I told him about the lab results and braced myself for the inevitable fallout... But it didn't come. Instead, annoyance crept over his face as Robbie came in the front door carrying two bags from Central Market. Sean looked at his partner then back at me. "What? You two are in on this together? Meeting up for the ambush?"

I stammered, "Ambush? What are you talking about?"

"You hate her. Both of you. You'll take any opportunity to blame something on her. Next I'll be hearing she's the one behind the attacks on 9/11. The whole bin Laden thing was a hoax to cover up the fact that Dorinda did it."

My eyes shifted to Robbie. He set the bags down and put both hands on the kitchen island, leaned on it, and looked down at the ground, shaking his head ever so slightly. I said, "Sean...look. I have video." I pulled my phone out and called up the cameras from my house. I held the screen up where he could see it.

He stared at the recording for a few seconds then said, "So what? That person is wearing a mask. Why say it's Dorinda?"

I felt like Alice falling down the rabbit hole—and Sean was quickly turning into the Mad Hatter. "Sean, look at the hair...the stature, the body shape. It's her. Think about the poison... It's the same list of ingredients in that keto concoction she brought to the meeting."

He turned on his heel and stormed into the kitchen where his half-made sandwich rested on a cutting board. "Jesus, Iris. You are investigating the deliberate sabotage by poisoning of food in a restaurant. You're telling me it never dawned on you that maybe the people behind that are coming after you for investigating them?" He looked at Robbie, who had moved to stand beside me. "So you're on her side now? You all a clique against me and Dorinda?"

I composed myself. It was time to pull out the big guns. I glanced at Robbie, but his face was a stony blank. I walked to where Sean stood angrily slapping mustard on bread and leaned in where he couldn't avoid my eyes. "The day you left rehab in Boston, we took a sacred oath. You promised me if I ever saw you in trouble with your gambling again, I could invoke that promise and you would go straight back to rehab, no questions asked. You said you were trusting me with your life, because you knew I would never fail you. Well, today's the day. I am invoking the deal."

He slammed the lid on his sandwich, started to take a bite then stopped, looked at it, and set it back down. His face was red, and little beads of sweat dotted his skin. Venom dripped from his voice like pus from an infected wound. "Iris, you ran out of that cabin in West Texas in a fucking T-shirt with no shoes in the freezing cold in the middle of nowhere. You would have died if I hadn't found you when I did. You take ridiculous chances every day, and I bail you out, time after time. So don't give me this *invoking the deal* crap. I know what's best for me. I have a Stanford PhD and more money than you'll ever make. Every day, I pull off shit the likes of which you can't fathom. So, I don't need you *invoking* anything. If I need your help—either of you—I'll ask. Otherwise, I would appreciate it if you would respect my personal boundaries."

I fumbled behind me for one of the kitchen stools and sat down. "Sean...someone broke into my apartment and poisoned my dog. If it was anybody but Dorinda, you would take one look at that video and head straight for them."

"No. I would do just what I'm doing now. I would tell you the person in the video is wearing a mask. You don't have the faintest clue who it is. And you need to look in your own bailiwick before you start casting aspersions on mine."

The blank look on Robbie's face reminded me of an old black-and-white casket photograph. With an eerie calm, he said, "You know, Sean, I've had just about enough. Iris and I are a clique—a clique of people who love you. And we are fighting to make you see reality before you screw yourself for good."

Sean's voice was that of a petulant child. "Well, bully for you. What business is it of yours if I screw myself for good? What? No more luxury loft? No more Ferrari? Is that the problem, Robbie?"

Robbie stood in stunned silence. His face was covered by a thin mask of heartbreak, but now his nostrils flared and a vein pulsed in his temple. I chose my words as carefully as my chaotic thoughts would allow, took a deep breath, and said, "Just for the record—I've called Grover, and he's sending a crime scene crew to print the window and check the apartment. If he can prove who did this, I'm going to press charges."

Sean returned the mustard to the refrigerator. "I wouldn't expect anything less."

I gaped at him. Through the wall of glass, I could see the early evening stars twinkling over the lake. The red sky had morphed to a deep royal blue. I thought of the countless nights we'd sat in that gorgeous living room, watching the moon rise over the lake. Now, I felt like a stranger, not welcome here at all.

I was fighting back tears when he said, "Screw the boat mechanic. I'm leaving before we say anything else we're going to regret."

Robbie stood still as Sean stalked out of the kitchen. The sound of his shoes on the marble floor of the foyer echoed through the house and was punctuated by the front door slamming. In seconds, I heard the Ferrari's massive V8 roar to life. Tires squealed, and the engine sounds faded away.

I was terrified Sean and I would never be what we were before I had walked into the house that afternoon. Robbie brushed his hand over my shoulder as he walked past me to the refrigerator. He extracted a beer, carried it into the living room, and dropped onto the sofa. I slumped down next to him as he unscrewed the cap and stared wordlessly out at the inky lake.

We were in the deep water now, a long damn way from the shore.

Chapter 26

Tuesday, September 21, 6:45 a.m.

I carried my coffee upstairs to the high-tech home office and started work early to mine the tedium of Cyndi's List for clues about the Morgan kids. The list is genealogy's largest—and arguably most convoluted—collection of research links and is often referred to as the "genealogical superhighway of the internet." I thought of it more like a rocky, unpaved rut leading to a pick-and-pull junkyard, but you go with what you've got. I was desperately searching for a hit on Annabelle's kids when my cell blared out the distinctive tones of "Bad, Bad Leroy Brown." Today was Marvin's turn to screw up my research plans.

I picked up the phone. "How's the wonderful world of surveillance?"

"Hell, Iris. I sit in this damn van sweatin' my ass off from April to November wonderin' why the hell I didn't set up shop in San Diego instead of South Texas. You free now?"

"Free enough. What's up?"

"Alamodome. Lot B."

"Now? It'll take me an hour to get there."

"Then you best get movin'."

Forty-five minutes later, Ansel and I parked next to Marvin's van. Today, it was outfitted with signs that read "Your wife is hot! Let Jack's Heating and Air cool her down."

Ansel put the truck in Park and said, "I'll wait here."

I climbed through the passenger door of the Econoline to find Marvin huddled around the desk at the workstation in the back with Darnell Washington Carter and his right-hand hatchet-man and cousin of some sort, Omar Washington. Darnell was sporting a lime-green polyester suit and matching pork-pie hat with a rhinestone hat band and a foot-long white ostrich feather. Hanging around his neck was a long gold chain thick enough to anchor an aircraft carrier. I looked him up and down. "Nice suit."

Darnell adjusted his jacket. "Dress for success."

I didn't really pay much attention to what Omar was wearing besides noticing that his ensemble was accessorized by an Uzi draped over his shoulder. Omar didn't talk much, but he always got his message across.

I sat down in one of the swivel chairs screwed into the floor and looked at Darnell. "Those tight-asses up at the UT business school see you in that getup and they're going to want their MBA back."

He ran his thumb under the chartreuse velvet lapel. "The Hugo Boss is at the cleaners. Your daddy makes me wear the damn thing every time we go to court. This here's my work suit."

Disdainful of terms like "pimp" and "gangster," Darnell preferred to think of himself as a "facilitator in the adult entertainment industry" and a "purveyor of recreational substances." Last year, the Bexar County district attorney's office kept Darnell locked up for nine months without bail on drug-trafficking charges until Addison convinced a jury to cut him loose.

The practice of criminal law attracts an...interesting clientele. Unlike most white-shoe law firms that shun any hint of the criminal practice, Addison and Justis have always been firm in their belief that every person accused of a crime deserves the best possible defense. It's strange for outsiders to understand, but I grew up around it, so it was perfectly normal to me that my fathers often represented people a lot of folks found distasteful. Making sure the government respects a client's rights is a long way from agreeing with the client's lifestyle and behavior. But humans are complex creatures who are rarely ever all bad. Darnell certainly wasn't an angel, but we were his defenders—and he never forgot it, either. Marvin cleared his throat. "Darnell and Omar have some information about your run-in down south."

I leaned in. Darnell chewed on the end of a Cuban cigar, not daring to light it around the high-tech gear in Marvin's van. "Heard through the grapevine the gentlemen you encountered down on the Wind Rose and later at your apartment were some...wholesale pharmaceutical reps...out of Guadalajara. The week before the shootout, they were supposed to close a deal with a client who agreed to buy ten keys for half a mill. Turns out, the purchaser had been promised a suitcase full of money to fund the buy by none other than one Quinten Farragut."

The words *fucking liar* ricocheted around my brain like a bullet fired into a rubber box. Rage was rising in my gut. I struggled to maintain a straight face as Darnell continued. "Story goes Mr. Farragut made a down payment to show he was the real deal, but when it came time to ante up the big money, he bitched out. The sellers were...disappointed...about their prospective buyer not making good on his promises. Feeling the pressure, the buyer went back to Mr. Farragut and...renegotiated."

I swallowed what felt like a golf ball in my throat. "By *renegotiated*, you mean the buyer vandalized a bunch of equipment and set fire to two pastures at the Wind Rose to put the fear of Jesus into their errant banker?"

Darnell tipped his head. "The upshot of the renegotiation was that the buyer told Mr. Farragut he had until midnight Tuesday, September 7 to cough up the money."

"Or what?"

Darnell shrugged. "Don't know the details, but apparently the buyers believed they had Farragut back on track, because they told the sellers to meet at the Wind Rose around ten that Tuesday night to close the deal. Of course, that stupid-assed white boy you're working for didn't come across with the cash. Instead, you stumbled into a drug deal gone sideways and almost got yourself wasted while that dipshit Farragut was sittin' around the Cigar Club drinkin' Macallan and playin' cribbage."

I was struggling to absorb this flood of information. The more of it I processed, the more bile rose in my throat. "Well, fuck me."

Darnell smiled. "Somethin' like that."

"Who's the buyer Farragut promised the money to?" Marvin asked.

Darnell shook his head. "Haven't nailed that down yet." He turned to Omar. "Why don't you tell Iris what your guys heard on the street last night?"

Omar's voice was a monotone. "What we've been wonderin' is how did a square white dude like Farragut get hooked up with these serious dealers? And who the fuck was the buyer? One of my guys heard there was a contact who connected the money guy with the buyer and then hooked the buyer up with the seller. But nobody's got the contact's name."

Darnell took up the story. “It’s normally unlikely a deal that size would get set up without us at least getting wind of it, probably without us being asked to fund it. Instead, we’ve been hearing shit on the street about it just like everybody else. This bein’ out of the loop is bad for business. Harmful to my reputation. So, we’re lookin’ into it. When we get something, I’ll call Marvin. I could send some people to watch over you, but”—he eyed the Toyota—“looks like Sean and Robbie’ve already got that covered. They need any extra hands on deck, you have ’em holler out. Meanwhile, we’ve spread the word around that if anyone fucks with the Raines family, Omar here will take it personally.”

Omar didn’t move except for a slight twitch of the corner of his mouth that might have been construed as a smile as he readjusted the sling holding the Uzi over his shoulder. He brushed his finger across the trigger guard like it was his girlfriend’s cheek.

I looked at Darnell. “Well, thanks for that.”

He shifted in his seat. The SIG Sauer 9mm he called Babydoll must have been cutting into his back. “You’re most welcome. Your daddy takes good care of me, so I’m just watching out for my folks.”

“So, bottom line, the buyers Farragut stiffed for the purchase money are vandalizing his ranch?”

Darnell shook his head. “Not that simple. Word is the sellers lost all ten keys of their dope when the feds showed up and one truck rolled over in a ditch during the shootout. Sure, the buyer’s unhappy, but the sellers are out half a mill in dope, and they’ve heard the same thing we have about Farragut backing out on financing the deal. So, nobody’s sure which ones are after your client.”

I looked at Marvin. “Does anyone have any idea why the feds showed up that night when I called 911?”

Marvin shook his head. "Easier to get the recipe for Coke than the lowdown on that. Nobody on my side's sayin' a word." He turned to Darnell.

More head shaking. "Nobody on the street knows a thing about that—unless Farragut played *Let's Make a Deal* with the *federales* without telling his lawyers."

I looked around the table. "If I find out he did, I'll shoot him myself."

Chapter 27

Tuesday, September 21, 10:30 a.m.

I speed-dialed Addison as Ansel pulled out of Lot B. He answered with his usual sunny tone. "Hey, champ, what's up with you this morning?"

I told him about my meeting with Marvin, Darnell, and Omar. When I finished, he said, "You could have been killed. I'm calling that bastard and telling him to get his ass into this office. Are you going back to...where you're staying?"

"Yep. I'll be there in thirty."

"When I get Farragut in here, we'll FaceTime you in." Ansel pushed the speed limit, and we made it to the lake house in record time. Ten minutes later, I saw Quinten Farragut sitting on the love seat in Addison's conversation area flanked on either side by my fathers. His eyes darted around like he was a cornered rat. "Welcome, Iris. Mr. Farragut was just telling us how he didn't mean to almost get you killed by a posse of pissed-off drug dealers."

Farragut turned his jowly face toward the camera. His hang-dog expression emphasized the sagging bags under his rheumy eyes. "Iris, I'm so sorry."

I adjusted my face in the camera view and looked him straight in the eye. "Mr. Farragut"—I leaned forward, resting my forearms on my thighs—"I don't care how much you have fucked up. People who need PIs have always fucked up somehow. While I will never help you break the law, I cannot tell you how little your past escapades, legal or otherwise, will impact the quality of the work I do for you. But you keeping secrets from me can get me killed. I certainly don't speak for my fathers, but unless I am convinced you have come clean with me one hundred percent right here and now, I am out of this deal, and I won't be back."

He swallowed hard, and his head jittered up and down like a bobblehead. "I understand."

I sat back in the chair. "Fine. Then spill it."

He took out his handkerchief and wiped his sweaty face. "The Big Top assholes and their cut-rate prices on that pink slime they call meat were really gouging into our market share. I carry a lot of debt, and the drop in sales was impacting my ability to service the loans and keep the place going. On August 2, I was at River City playing golf with a couple of the financial guys, talking over our options. After we finished our round, we were sitting in the bar by the pro shop having a couple of beers, and the guy who had been my caddy walks by and hands me a note."

"What did it say?" Justis asked.

"That I should meet him at some bar called Elmo's over by SeaWorld at eleven that night if I wanted to hear how he could help me solve all my money problems."

Justis nodded and, in his pre-nuclear-detonation neutral tone, said, "Go on."

Farragut licked his rubbery lips. "That night, I went to the bar. The caddy was in a booth in the back. He got up and motioned for me to follow him back to the men's room. He told me he was going to check me for a wire. He had this gadget looked like a little walkie-talkie...had an antenna and a red light on it with a bunch of switches and dials. He held it close to me and moved it up and down my body."

I searched my phone for images of an RF detector and held the screen up to the camera. "Like this?"

He leaned in and squinted at the image and nodded. "Yeah."

RF detectors were pretty high-tech. This guy wasn't just some schmo off the street.

"Mr. Farragut, can you describe this man?"

He closed his eyes and rubbed the bridge of his nose. "White guy, thirty, thirty-five. Five ten, hundred sixty, brown hair..."

"Any distinguishing marks? Tattoos?"

Farragut shook his head. "Not that I noticed."

"What about the car he was driving?"

More head shaking. "I never saw him come or go. He just sort of appeared when I showed up wherever we were meeting."

I was going to need a fucking crystal ball to find this guy. "Go on."

"Back at the table, he tells me he knows some people who need some short-term financing, and they're paying a handsome interest rate. Come to find out, his pals need five hundred grand, and they'll pay back double that in four weeks."

Justis asked, "How was this arrangement supposed to work?"

Farragut scrubbed his jaw, and his face wiggled like red Jell-O. "I may have been desperate, but I wasn't completely stupid. I told them no way was I starting out with half a mill. We'd have to do a smaller deal first. He said he'd get back to me. The next day, he called and said to meet him at the bar again. We went through the routine with the gizmo, then he said his folks were okay with a trial deal. Ten thousand with eleven back after seven days. I agreed. The next night, I met him behind a bowling alley over off Austin Highway and gave him the cash in a briefcase."

I already knew where this was going, but I asked anyway. "So what happened next?"

He shrugged. "Sure enough, a week later, he calls me. I meet him behind a strip joint off 35, and he gives me back the briefcase with a bunch of cash in it. I fanned the bundles and counted them. Eleven grand. He asked if we were good to go on with the bigger deal, and I said sure. I figure I make half a mill in a month, that's going to take a bunch of the heat off me with those fuckers from Strite, Streckfuss billing me out the ass and leaning on me for payment like a bunch of Vegas knee-breakers."

"And what did this caddy tell you his name was?"

Farragut looked away and said, "Steve Williams...that's what he said, anyway."

I wrote it down, then looked up from my notes. Grover was right—everyone's a fucking comedian. Steve Williams was also the name of Tiger Woods's caddy. "How did the blackmail communication arrive?"

He whipped his head around toward me. "How did you know?"

Because I'm not a complete moron didn't seem like a polite answer. "With the benefit of hindsight, it seems like a setup."

He slumped and let out a deep sigh. "The next night, I get an email. It has video of me giving the briefcase to the caddy and of him giving it back a week later, only the caddy's face is in shadow. There's a clear shot of me fanning out the bills and counting the bundles. My license plate number is readable in the picture. There are audio recordings of everything, only his voice is distorted...like you see on TV shows when the kidnapper calls in the ransom demand. The email says to drop the suit against Big Top in the next twenty-four hours or the recordings go to the cops."

Sean could follow that electronic trail right back to the blackmailer—assuming he was still willing to help me out with the case. I kept my voice steady. "Do you have the email?"

He shook his head. "I deleted it."

Shit. I turned to my fathers. "I'll try to get Sean over there tomorrow to see if he can recover it."

Even before I finished, Farragut was shaking his head some more. "The next day, I had the head IT guy check our systems to be sure it was gone."

"So you told Strite, Streckfuss to settle the suit for whatever you could get and shut it down?" I said.

He nodded like a child admitting to cheating on his spelling test. "I went to River City the next morning after I got the blackmail demand and asked in the pro shop for the caddy. But they said he'd quit, and nobody knew how to reach him. I realized I was totally screwed, so I told Rudolph Streckfuss I just couldn't afford it anymore. That greedy bastard probably bills his kids for telling them bedtime stories, so that's all it took for him to be ready to drop me like a hot rock. It wasn't hard getting the deal done since the Big Top people were obviously in on it... They offered a pittance, and I took it. End of lawsuit."

Addison leaned back. "But the drug dealers weren't so sanguine about your decision to throw in the towel."

Farragut shucked his jacket and headed to Addison's sidebar. He picked up the bottle of Scotch and turned to Addison. "You mind?"

When Addison shrugged, he poured three fingers of Macallan in a lowball glass and waddled back to the love seat. He took a big swallow of the Scotch and continued. "We closed the settlement agreement on Tuesday, the seventeenth of August. That Thursday, I got a call from some asshole saying I owed him half a mill and better pay up. I said what the fuck was he talking about...I settled the lawsuit for nothing. He acted like he didn't know what that meant. I told him to quit playing dumb and hung up. The next night was the first pasture fire at the Wind Rose."

That matched with what I'd learned from Darnell. "Normally, you'd think the blackmailers would have used fake drug dealers in the sting...just have some of their own guys posing as dealers for the extortion pics because they never intended to send them to the cops, anyway. But in this case, the blackmailers actually engineered a drug sting with real dealers." I stopped short of adding *probably to be sure Quinten Farragut would get dead after the suit was settled.*

Farragut slugged back some more of the Scotch. "They kept calling me. These guys I never met, demanding the half mill. They were doing all kinds of crap down on the Wind Rose...vandalizing my equipment, cutting my fences, stealing my stock... Finally, the guy who kept calling—he said some asshole named James Hoffman told him I was the money guy..." Farragut took another healthy dose of the Scotch. "He told me if I didn't have the half mill by midnight Tuesday the seventh of this month, he'd kill me. I didn't know what to do. I couldn't go to the cops. I just hoped you'd somehow figure it out before they... Anyway, I guess he thought I'd sent you down there to bust them somehow."

My fathers were both staring daggers at him. He shifted his eyes between them. "I swear...I didn't have any idea Iris was going to the ranch that night. You didn't say anything about it when you called for the gate combinations."

Justis gave him a look that would have cut glass. "And when my brother asked for those combinations, you never thought to mention you were planning to no-show for a meeting with a gang of angry drug dealers on the ranch that night?"

Farragut fidgeted with the arm of the love seat. "I know... It was stupid. I'm so sorry. Thank God Iris wasn't hurt."

"You better be thankful." Addison's tone made my blood run cold. "If any harm comes to Iris—or any other member of this organization—because you're lying to us..."

Justis cleared his throat. "I think we're all on the same page, Addison." He shifted his laser gaze to Farragut. "We all understand each other, don't we, Quinten?"

He looked sheepishly at me then turned to them. "Yes, we're crystal clear."

Fucking lying clients.

Chapter 28

Wednesday, September 22, 9:00 a.m.

After two fruitless hours of the Morgan kid search, I was beginning to wonder which databases listed alien abductions when the phone rang. I saw Finn Rhodes on the caller ID, and surge of attraction and a tingle of arousal shot through me...and collided head-on with a spasm of pain in my side. There was a slight tremor in my hand as I reached for my phone. I took a deep breath and hit the green icon. "Hey, stranger. What's up with you?"

He laughed. "I love catching bad guys, but I hate the paperwork that comes with it. I'm still wading through an inch-thick stack of forms and reports associated with that three-county chase the other night. Criminals can be so inconsiderate."

"Maybe that's something we should suggest as a prison program. Like charm school for inmates...teach them to use shrimp forks and tie Windsor knots and restrict their evasion efforts to one jurisdiction."

He laughed again. "I'll write my congressman. Now...to the real reason for my call. Ms. Raines, I am calling to invite you out on an actual date where I come and pick you up and take you to dinner like a proper gentleman."

Wowza. That ratcheted up my pulse rate. I rested my elbow on the desk to steady my hand. I couldn't even think of a smart-ass comment to stall with. After what was undoubtedly too long a pause, he said, "If you don't want to go I won't like it, but I'll certainly respect your decision. However, if you'd care to join me, now would be a good time to say something like 'Yes, I'd like that.'"

I forced myself to swallow, recalled my pledge not to give up my future over events from the past, and said, "Yes, I'd like that."

"Well, good, then." I could hear him smiling. "How about I pick you up tomorrow around six?"

"Sounds great."

"I know you're off the grid. Why don't you WhatsApp me a location where I can meet you?"

"I'll do it, but I still have an...escort. The same guy you saw in the Jeep at the livestock show."

He laughed. "I think it's great you've got protection. We'll figure it out."

I hung up and did a series of deep breathing exercises to calm myself. We were going out to dinner, not getting married.

The phone rang again. I shook my head to clear it and picked up. Sol from the library.

"I can take my lunch break in an hour. If you want to come by, I can show you what I've found."

"You *found* something?"

"I think I've found Annabelle's son. But we need to go through the links together and be sure we agree the guy I found is the one you're looking for."

"Sol, that's wonderful! I've been at it since I spoke to you last and have absolutely zippo."

"Well, I was stuck too until I got a break about one this morning. Come on down, and I'll tell you about it."

As I gathered all my notes on Annabelle, I heard violin music coming from downstairs. Bartok's Violin Concerto no. 2 was flowing out of the living room. I hadn't figured Ansel for a classical fan. My jaw dropped when I got down the stairs and rounded the corner. He wasn't listening—he was *playing.* The spiccato, ricochets, and glissandos of the piece poured out of his instrument. When he finished, I applauded. Surprise showed on his face then bled into a blush. He cleared his throat. "I thought you were upstairs."

"Ansel, that was amazing."

He stowed the instrument in the case that lay open on the sofa. "Thanks. It's just a hobby." He shut the lid and closed the latches, then eyed my briefcase. "Are we off somewhere?"

I told him about Sol, and he said, "Great. Let's go."

We got into the truck and headed south. "Where did you learn the violin?"

"I had an uncle who played with a local symphony back in Liverpool. He taught me when I was a tot."

I looked out the window as the sheet metal buildings and industrial businesses along I-35 slid past. "That sure didn't sound like the product of a few lessons as a kid."

He licked his lips. "I attended the Royal Academy in London before I joined...the military."

"What branch did you serve in?"

He fidgeted with the car stereo buttons, and one of the Sirius classical stations came on, then he rolled up his T-shirt sleeve to reveal a tattoo of the words *Légion étrangère* arced over the distinctive emblem featuring the seven-flame grenade.

"The French Foreign Legion? Jesus, Ansel. Robbie didn't tell me he was sending an honest-to-God renaissance man to watch over me."

He laughed. "Bollocks. I'm just an ordinary bloke who can shoot straight and play the fiddle."

I told him about my date with Finn. "I don't know exactly how such things work with...protection."

The San Antonio skyline appeared ahead of us, and he took the Houston Street exit. "You pretend I'm not there, and I make it easy for you by staying out of sight as much as possible. If I can't stay out of sight, then you pretend I'm your dog—because for these purposes, I basically am. Like Festus, I'll happily kill anyone who fucks with you, I make no judgments about what you do in my presence, and I never talk out of school. Trust me...I've done this a million times."

He turned into the underground parking lot. Texana and Genealogy is located on the sixth floor of the Central Library housed in the sprawling scarlet stucco building the locals affectionately call "the red enchilada."

We parked and took the elevator to the sixth floor where I found Sol sitting at his usual spot behind the counter, turned out in his customary razor-creased dress slacks, spotless white shirt, and one of his famous novelty neckties. He picked up a stack of folders and pointed to an area in the back. Ansel pulled a book from a shelving cart, took a chair at one of the library tables, and flipped pages. Sol clocked out then led me past the microfilm readers through row after row of cabinets of US Census film. He set his papers down at a small table, and I pulled out a chair. "Before we get started, what's up with today's tie?"

He held out the end, and I leaned in for a closer look. A dark blue field with a repeating pattern of tiny gold *Zzzzz*s. I cocked my head.

He smiled. "September 22 is World Narcolepsy Day."

I laughed. "You're making this shit up."

He sat and tapped keys on his phone and held it out for me to see. I peered at the screen. The website of national days announced, "World Narcolepsy Day."

I sat. "I should know better than to ever doubt you."

He pocketed the phone and arranged his folders. "First thing, let's run through the basic data."

I scooted my chair next to him. "Sounds good."

He fanned printouts as he reviewed the details of Annabelle's first marriage to Harrison Morgan in 1948, their move to Wichita Falls in 1949, the birth of their four kids between 1950 and 1960, Harrison's death in 1974, her second marriage to Jason Case in 1975, their subsequent divorce in 1979, Annabelle's death without a will in 1984, and the death of the two childless older sisters in 2009.

I scanned the records. "That all matches what I found."

He smoothed his close-cropped, light brown beard. "So, that leaves us with either the son, Luther, or the youngest daughter, Rose. I spent seven hours on Rose and got nowhere."

"I'm thinking alien abduction or time travel."

He pointed a finger at me. "Excellent ideas. But, I think I've found Luther."

I strained to keep my voice down. "Hallelujah!"

He held up a warning palm. "This is where things get a little weird, and I need you to check me."

"Shoot."

After adjusting his half-glasses, he picked up a birth certificate. "Luther Alphus Morgan, born July 5, 1954, in Wichita County, Texas. I last found mention of him by name in Harrison Morgan's obituary in 1974. Then nothing...no death record, marriage records, no listing in the city directories—zip. But, I mined Cyndi's List pretty hard last night. I had to drill deep to get to it, but I found a link to a database of civil court cases from 1960 to 1990 for a smattering of North Texas counties." He handed me a printout of the state district court docket for 1980 for Archer County. I studied the blotchy type Sol had highlighted. *Case #1980-CI-27653. Petition for Name Change by Luther Alphus Morgan.*

I looked up at him. "Why Archer County? Last we know, he was living in Wichita Falls, the next county north."

Sol held up a finger. "Archer County's deed records are available online. I searched the index and found this..." He passed me a printout of a deed.

I scanned the document. "Luther Alphus Morgan purchased a seventy-three-acre tract of land just south of the Wichita County line in 1975."

Sol said, "Do you buy the grantee on this deed is your subject?"

I studied the instrument. "It's styled *Luther Alphus Morgan.*" I flipped to the birth record. "He would have been twenty-three, just starting out. The name is unusual enough... Yeah, I buy it."

"Okay...then check this out." He passed me another deed. As I flipped the pages, he said, "Lawton Alger Meyer sold the same piece of land in 1980." He passed me one more document. "This is the mortgage Luther

Morgan signed when he bought the Archer County property. Check the signatures. Look at the *g*."

I compared the signature on the mortgage to the signature on the sale deed and studied the long, looping descender on his lowercase *g*. "I'm not a handwriting expert, but there can't be two people in the world who make a *g* that way."

Sol nodded. "Couple that with the docket entry for a name change for Luther Alphus Morgan, and I'm convinced. You'll need to order a copy of the original petition and the final order for the name change to be certain, but I'm pretty sure we've found him."

"*You've* found him—because you have the patience of Job to dig through thirty layers of obscure little ragtag databases on Cyndi's List. Now I just have to find this guy."

He smiled. "As an added bonus for today's shoppers, we have this." He produced a printout from the *Fredericksburg Gazette*. The headline read "Local Rancher Lobbies Statehouse Over Water Rights." I skimmed the article which included a quote from "local rancher, Lawton Meyer." "If it's the same Lawton Meyer, your guy's one of the biggest sheep and goat ranchers in Gillespie County."

I couldn't restrain myself. I hugged him. "Sol, you rock!"

He smiled and rubbed his beard. "It was fun."

I gathered the papers. As Sol returned his notes to his file, he said, "Oh, there's one more thing... Not that it matters in your case because Lawton is alive, but he and his wife had two sons." He passed me several newspaper articles paper-clipped together.

I flipped through them. "Had?"

He shook his head. "The oldest boy, Ambrose, died during a storm out sailing with his father off South Padre Island. I couldn't tell a lot about it, but at one point he had been a doctoral candidate in physics up at UT. He apparently never finished. I saw several mentions in the Austin newspaper crime blotter about petty offenses, drug arrests, like that."

I scanned several articles about the boating accident. "They never recovered the body?"

Sol shook his head. "His parents got a court to declare him dead."

"What about the other boy?"

"Maynard. He's famous, at least in the classical music world." He nodded toward the stack of clippings. "I have several articles in there. He was a child violin prodigy. Now, he's apparently a big star. Plays all over the world."

"Good to know. I'll use the son as a backup contact." I slid the newspaper articles into my file. "Thanks so much, Sol. Email your bill to the law firm."

He nodded. "Will do." Then he sat down at his desk and said, "I always love your cases." He scanned his ID card and logged back on to the city's clock.

On the road, I asked Ansel if he'd heard of Maynard Meyer. He looked at me like I'd asked him who was president. "Sure. He's almost as famous as Perlman. I hope you're not looking for him, though."

"He would be plan B if I have trouble reaching his father directly."

He shook his head. "Better find another way. Maynard Meyer's like the Bobby Fischer of the violin world. Nobody knows where he is or how to reach him. Every year or so, he'll release an album of solos recorded in his private studio. The rumor is if he wants to play with a certain orchestra, he just calls and sets it up. He sneaks into town for the rehearsals, the performance is announced a few days beforehand, then he disappears right after the show."

Back at the lake house, Ansel had barely killed the engine before I ran upstairs to the office and yanked the Annabelle Morgan Case file out of my briefcase. My fingers flew across the keyboard as I ran an AccuData report on Lawton Meyer then dialed his number in Fredericksburg. Butterflies fluttered in my stomach as the phone rang. I was almost there... My heart sank as the call clicked over to voice mail. I left a message and hung up. A wave of disappointment that he didn't answer temporarily neutralized the thrill of locating him, but I rallied quickly. I knew who and where he was—the rest was just a mop-up operation.

I spent the remainder of the afternoon finding out what I could about Lawton Meyer. I ordered the name change paperwork from the Archer County district clerk, then turned on my newspaper database and dug in. Mr. Meyer owned over ten thousand acres on which he raised large herds of Rambouillet sheep and Spanish goats. Meyer sat on the tax appraisal board and was a long-time member of the local Rotary. He looked great on paper.

Maybe too good. Why did Mr. Chamber of Commerce change his name all those years ago? He didn't change Moscowictz to Mosher or Humperdink to Humphrey. He changed Morgan to Meyer. Why do that? I'd searched the records and saw no evidence he was running from cops or debt collectors or a string of baby mamas. Far as I could tell, Luther Morgan was just a twenty-something guy trying to eke a living out of seventy-three acres of crappy land in a bleak North Texas county...who got up one day, became Lawton Alger Meyer, and started a completely new life.

I put together a report for Addison and Simpson from Real Estate with a note explaining the name change and assuring them I would call Mr. Morgan/Meyer back the next morning if I didn't hear from him by the end of business.

I had just hit Send on the report when "Eye of the Tiger" rang out from my phone. I tapped the screen. "It's worse than we thought." Robbie's voice was tight and serious.

"That sounds ominous."

"I checked with the airport. Five nights out of the past ten he's taken the Citation out. Flown to Kenner, Louisiana three times and Eagle Pass twice. Only one reason anyone goes to those places—casinos."

I felt like I'd swallowed a rock with a liquid cement chaser. "Does he know you know?"

"He does now. We had a blowup about it."

I flashed back to Saturday afternoon. "What happened when you went to look for your sunglasses?"

"I couldn't find them in the Hellcat. With all the vehicle swapping that's been going on, I thought maybe I'd left them in the Ferrari. When I was digging around under the seat, I found a wad of racing forms from Cenote Park out on 35. They were covered in scribbled computations in Sean's handwriting. He was handicapping horses."

Through the picture window, I watched a white pelican stab at the water with its long, orange beak. "He's never talked to me like he did the other night. He was in deep shit with the gambling back at Stanford, but he never treated me anywhere near the way he did Monday."

"Sean was at rock bottom back then," Robbie said, "and he was scared to death looking down the barrel of expulsion from the doctoral program. He's not at rock bottom this time around—not yet, anyway."

"God help us that it never comes to that."

"But that's exactly where it's headed. I saw one of his bank statements on the desk in the safe room. He's run through over a hundred grand this month alone. The withdrawals are all below the ten-thousand-dollar threshold for a Large Currency Transaction Report, and he's taking them out in odd amounts so they look like they could be for specific purchases in case the accounts are audited in a security clearance renewal."

I was so mad my blood was throbbing in my ears. "As long as Dorinda Crandall is around, the gambling is just going to get worse."

"And she is the one person outside of the family who's aware of the extent of Sean's gambling problem," Robbie said.

I clenched my teeth. "And she fucking knows it. Back in Boston, there was the implicit threat that if we got in her way, she'd leak the information to the government. That happens, and he can kiss his security clearances—and his career—goodbye."

The pelican ducked its head underwater and emerged with a channel catfish in its beak.

Robbie said, "We need to think of this like it's just another case. Right now, we don't know enough about her and her situation to find any leverage."

In a single gulp, the fish disappeared into the bird's giant beak. "You're right. We've got to find a foothold—and use it to knock the bitch off our mountain."

And we would. I'd be sure of it. I watched the pelican spread its huge wings and glide away and wished with all my heart we could get rid of Dorinda Crandall as easily as that bird had dispatched the channel cat.

Chapter 29

Thursday, September 23, 5:00 p.m.

Absent any idea where Finn and I were going for our date, I opted for my standard little black dress and some black, medium-heel pumps Robbie had fetched from my condo. Just as I put the final touches on my lipstick, I got a text from Finn.

I know it sounds crazy, but toss your running shoes in the car.

What the hell? I typed furiously. *I'm wearing a cocktail dress.*

The three flashing dots appeared immediately. *Can't wait to see it. Just bring the shoes. See you soon.*

I slid a pair of black Nikes into a canvas bag as Ansel's footfalls echoed down the stairs. I checked my gun, stuffed extra ammo in my purse, and headed down after him. He leaned on the kitchen island. "So, what's the plan?"

I had thought this through. "He knows you're coming, but I think it's better if I show up in my own car. Otherwise, it's a little like I'm being dropped off at a junior high dance." Ansel nodded. I said, "I decided I should tell him before he figured it out himself. He made you at the livestock show."

Ansel smiled. “He damn well better have. I was more obvious than an Orangemen parade in Belfast.” He extracted a round device about the size of a hockey puck from his backpack.

I took a deep breath and let it out. Putting a GPS tracker on the Genesis was probably overkill, but part of me felt better knowing that, no matter what happened, Ansel could find my car. “Fine. It’s not a bad idea.”

Still not finished, he produced a small black velvet jewelry box from the bag and passed it to me.

“Don’t tell me you’re going to get down on one knee. I like you a lot, but don’t you think it’s too soon to be picking out a china pattern?”

He shook his head. “Not a second too soon. Until Robbie tells me otherwise, you’re my girl. No chance I’m letting some other bloke steal you away from me.”

I opened the hinged lid and removed a gold rose-shaped pin with what looked like a diamond in the center. “You shouldn’t have.”

As I attached it to my dress, Ansel said, “It’s a miniature transmitter.” He held out his hand. “Mobile, please.”

I rolled my eyes but handed him the phone.

“I’m setting us up on Find My.”

I shook my head. “Not even engaged an hour and you’re already getting possessive.”

He finished tapping the keys. “It’s just self-interest.” He passed the phone back to me. “I let those cartel wankers get to you, and Robbie’ll make my days hunting terrorists in the desert look like an afternoon at the King’s garden party.”

Ansel fell in behind me as I steered the GV down the driveway and toward the highway for the short trip to the Comal County special ranger's field office in New Braunfels. As I parked and got out, Finn emerged from a navy blue Lexus ES two spots down. He was wearing a stylish black Zegna suit with slim-fit pants and a double-vented jacket over a black silk tee. A black pocket square and black rubber-soled Cole Haan leather oxford shoes completed the look.

Mesmerized, I may have actually stammered. He looked down at my pumps. I slung my purse over my shoulder and pulled the canvas bag from the passenger seat. "They're right here."

He looked me up and down. "You look spectacular." Over my shoulder, he waved at Ansel at the other end of the parking lot.

"Where are we off to?"

He shook his head. "That's a surprise."

My left hand tingled. I forced myself to banish thoughts of chloroform-soaked rags and cabins in the middle of nowhere. I said, "Well, aren't you mysterious."

He made a gallant gesture for me to go first. "After you, madam." He opened the passenger door of the Lexus for me. Other than Sean, I couldn't remember the last man who'd opened a car door for me...if you didn't count Kerabos sliding the door of his van open before he stuffed me inside.

I pushed the thoughts away and said, "Beautiful car."

He waited for me to buckle my belt. "Thank you. The kennel truck belongs to the association." He closed the door.

The car still smelled new. Between the Zegna suit and the Lexus, either this guy robbed banks in his spare time or special rangering paid a lot better than I imagined. The incongruity tickled my early warning system, but I squelched the message—at least for tonight. I was going to have a nice time on my first real post-Geare date. What could go wrong? I had my own well-armed, violin-playing mercenary hiding in the shadows.

Finn got in the driver's seat and pulled the car onto Highway 46 West.

I was baffled when he turned onto Prince Solms Caverns Road. The caverns were the largest and best developed system of privately owned show caves in the United States. They were stunning and a great way to spend a Saturday afternoon, but they closed at four and the only hot food they served came from a roller grill. Finn pulled into the empty parking lot and killed the engine. Pocketing the fob, he said, "We're here."

He's wearing a three-thousand-dollar suit to eat in the parking lot of a closed tourist attraction? When Ansel pulled in next to us, Finn said, "Could you excuse me a moment?"

Ansel got out, and they spoke briefly. I saw nodding and pointing. Then Finn came around and opened my door. Extending his hand to help me out of the car, he said, "Follow me, please, ma'am."

He led me to the front door of the visitor center where a waiting cavern employee unlocked the door and said, "This way, Mr. Rhodes. Mr. Westerholm is waiting."

Finn held the door for me while Ansel followed discreetly behind. The employee led us into the owner's office and announced us. Ansel stayed back and waited with our escort in the hall. Westerholm was a tall, robust man with weathered skin and a chiseled jaw. His polo shirt and khaki pants showed off a physique that came from hard work. He jumped up and strode across the Persian rug that covered the dark hardwood floor around his massive oak desk. Finn extended his hand. "Bradford...thanks so much for this."

Westerholm pumped Finn's hand. "Nothing's too good for my old roomie." I noticed he was wearing a class ring from Texas A&M. Finn introduced us, and we made small talk for a couple of minutes before Westerholm summoned the staff member from the hall. "Josh, can you take these fine folks down to the south entrance, please?"

The young man nodded. "Certainly, sir."

Josh led us through a maze of hallways to a door marked Employees Only. He indicated a bench along the wall and said, "You might want to change your shoes now." Finn passed me the bag, and I exchanged my pumps for the Nikes. When I was done, Josh slid a key card through the reader and pushed through the door into a small vestibule in front of an elevator. He pressed a button to summon the car that whisked us down to a phone-booth-sized room lit with a humming green fluorescent light. Our guide opened the door into the large cavern and passed Finn a key card. "You can open this door and take the elevator up when you're done. Have a nice evening." As Josh stepped back, Ansel leaned on the wall next to the elevator and silently gave us a little salute. The cave side of the door was faced with limestone, matching the chamber. It disappeared into the cavern wall as it clicked shut—like a magical portal into another world.

Finn took my hand and led me along the path through the beautifully lit chambers of the cave, pointing out features of the limestone structures hanging from the forty-foot ceilings and telling me the story of the Westerholm family's discovery and development of the cavern. It felt good to hold hands with him, and I detected no tremor at all. I started to relax and was surprised to realize I was actually having fun.

After ten minutes of walking, we entered a smaller chamber with a candlelit table set for two in the center. A dining cart was parked next to it along with a standing ice bucket loaded with a bottle of wine. He pulled my chair out and laid a linen napkin across my lap before he opened the heated compartment of the cart and extracted two plates covered with stainless steel domes. He removed the shiny covers to reveal grilled beef tenderloin, corn pudding, roasted broccoli, and crispy plantains—all artfully arranged on our plates. He poured the wine, sat down, and said, "Bon appétit."

I looked at him. "So, something tells me you haven't spent your entire life in a tractor dealership."

He smiled and swirled the wine in the glass before taking a sip. "My father owns an import/export business specializing in agricultural equipment. We lived all over the world but had just landed in San Antonio when I started high school."

I sliced a bite of the tender beef. "Where did you go?"

"Antonian."

"A good Catholic boy."

He laughed. "Not really. We were never churchgoers, but my parents were determined I'd go to a top-notch private school. In San Antonio, that pretty much means Catholic."

"I grew up a few blocks down."

"From Antonian?"

I nodded. "Charles Simpson's old house in Castle Hills at West and Lockhill Selma."

His eyes went wide. "You grew up in the Castle on the Hill? Oh, my God...you're *that* Raines family!"

I nodded. "Guilty as charged. So you know Westerholm from A&M?"

"Yeah. We were roommates my freshman year. Pledged the same fraternity. Been friends ever since."

I studied him. "Interesting pedigree."

He sipped the wine. "And you're dying to ask how a snob from an A&M frat ended up in King City being a cop for the cattle raisers association."

I nibbled a bite of the broccoli. "I absolutely do not think you're a snob...but yes, the question did cross my mind."

He said, "Well, my family's...financial good fortune made it possible for me to do pretty much whatever I chose. I've always loved mysteries and always hated seeing assholes torment good, hardworking people, so I decided law enforcement would be a good fit. I was also interested in ag because of my father's business. So, I double-majored in criminal justice and ranch management. When I was graduating, the association was interviewing at A&M. I signed up, and they hired me."

The food was scrumptious, and we ate with gusto. In between bites, he asked, "How's Grover doing?"

I swallowed and wiped some corn pudding from the corner of my mouth. "How do you know Grover?"

"Couple of years ago, a Shetland pony was stolen from my district as a college football rivalry prank. Spanky ended up in San Antonio for the big game. One thing led to another, and Grover reached out me. We've stayed in touch."

"Grover's fine, but he's chained to a desk as long as he's still on oxygen."

Finn put his fork down. "I heard about the shootout with Geare. Grover's lucky to be alive. I can't imagine what that must have been like for you—and it's none of my business. But I just want you to know, I applaud your courage for shooting him. Fucker had it coming." He picked up his wineglass and took a sip. I fidgeted with my fork, and he said, "I'm sorry I mentioned it. It wasn't polite. But you're the real hero of that story. And however you got there, you're the one who busted him, and the whole South Texas law enforcement community knows it."

However you got there... So he knew I was involved with Geare. Fuck. I clenched my left hand in my lap and managed to say, "Thank you."

While we ate, he asked about my job and my fathers and what it was like growing up with two dads. When we finished, he set the dishes on the cart then poured Kahlua into tiny snifters.

I said, "I feel bad not to have leftovers for Ansel."

Finn smiled. "Ansel and Josh were just served the same meal we had."

I was so touched by this thoughtfulness, a warm wave washed over me. "That was incredibly gracious."

He shrugged. "I've done a lot of surveillance. I knew he was coming, so I considered it a professional courtesy. Josh is a good guy, should have been home hours ago, but he stayed to help out."

We strolled around, exploring a few more nooks and crannies of the caves. On our way back to the elevator, we passed a giant limestone formation reaching from the floor to the ceiling of the enormous chamber. "That's the Prince Solms Throne."

I studied the structure. "It really does look like a chair."

He took my hand in his, and, this time, I felt a warm current flow through my fingers, up my arm, and into my chest.

Then the lights went out, plunging us into a blackness I had never experienced before. Finn gripped my hand. "Hang on. The emergency lights will kick in any second." I felt him fumbling with his free hand and then the light from his phone illuminated the area immediately around us before the beam disappeared, eaten by the infinite blackness. I yanked my hand from his grasp and flipped the clasp on my purse. Before I could reach my gun, the emergency lights flickered on, and a pre-recorded message boomed from speakers hidden in the limestone deposits.

"Please stay calm and remain where you are. Emergency personnel have automatically been alerted about the power outage. The caverns are naturally ventilated. You are perfectly safe. Please follow the instructions provided by your tour guide. We apologize for the inconvenience. Please stay..."

The message was running on a loop, and if it didn't shut up pretty damn soon, I was going to pass the last exit off the express lane to a full-blown panic attack. I was a woman with PTSD trapped underground with a man I hardly knew. How long would the emergency power last? Would the elevators still run? Was this some ruse to get me alone—away from Ansel? Thoughts shot through my brain like laser beams at a Pink Floyd concert.

Finn killed the light on his phone. "It's a recording that's set to autoplay when the emergency power comes on."

"How do you know?"

He slid his phone back into his jacket pocket. "Because I worked here during the summers in college. I was one of the guides visitors were supposed to be listening to."

I forced myself to take a deep, calming breath. "So what happens next?"

"We wait."

"What about the elevator? Isn't it powered by the backup generator that's running the lights?"

He shook his head. "The elevators are automatically disabled to prevent anyone from being stuck in them if the generator goes out. It's going to take a little while for Bradford to get here and start pushing magic buttons."

Like an old vinyl record being played on the wrong speed, the annoying message looping from the hidden speakers ground to a slow-motion halt, then the emergency lights flickered out, submerging us back into the abyssal dark. Finn grabbed my hand and yanked me behind the Prince Solms Throne.

My mouth was dry, and I was fending off panic with a psychological whip and chair. I drew a ragged breath to speak, but I felt a hand clap over my mouth. Panic swallowed the whip and chair and raged through me. I struggled against him. He tightened his grasp on my mouth and whispered in my ear, "We may be under attack. Be quiet."

His grip on me was making me crazy, but I was afraid to scream. Keeping his hand over my mouth, Finn shoved me ahead, grasping me around the waist from behind. I struggled to keep my footing and lurched forward. Another whisper. "Trust me, Iris."

I felt him release his grasp on me and shove past me then start fumbling against the cave wall. I heard a low scraping sound, then he grabbed my arm and yanked me forward. I tripped over something and tumbled into what felt like a pile of ropes. Another grinding sound. Then, Finn's face lit up in the eerie blue light of his phone's lock screen. He held a finger to his lips warning me to remain silent and began tapping on the screen. We were in a closet of some kind, surrounded by ropes and other climbing equipment. He held the phone where I could see. *Do you have your gun?*

I was paralyzed with the decision to confirm or deny. Tell him so he could more easily disarm me? More tapping. *Bad guys may have cut power.*

I swallowed hard, nodded, and pointed to him. He shone the light on his belt where a hidden holster secreted his service weapon beneath his suit pants.

I took the phone and willed my fingers to quit shaking enough for me to type, *Where are we?*

Access point for emergency evacuation. He aimed the phone toward the roof, but the faint light was devoured by the darkness.

Then I smelled it. Onions? Garlic? Mixed with something petrochemical. We both started coughing. My eyes watered, and my throat burned like I was swallowing battery acid. I heard a whoosh, which was followed by a wave of heat that seeped in around the door. Locked in a closet that couldn't be more than five feet by six, there was no way out and nowhere to hide from poisonous gas and a fire that was producing God only knew what kind of toxins. A steel band of icy terror tightened around my chest.

As the temperature in the closet rocketed upward, a beam of brilliant white light shot down from the unseen roof of the closet illuminating a distant vertical hole six feet across. A zipping sound echoed out of the darkness, and Ansel appeared before my eyes, dangling from a rappelling harness. Without a word, he tossed Finn a breathing apparatus, grabbed me, hooked a harness cinching me up to his body, and yanked hard on the rope. I could feel his heart beating against my chest. My face was pressed into his neck, and I smelled the musky scent of sweat and adrenaline mixed with the onion and garlic and smoke that was filling the tiny room. He wrestled a respirator over my face as an unseen force raised us the one hundred eighty feet up to the surface, each foot taking us closer to fresh air. I screamed through the bulky respirator for Finn, left behind in the miasma.

At the surface, Ansel grabbed the edge of the opening, and Josh helped pull us out of the hole before he unhooked the harness and dropped the rope back down into the darkness. I ripped the respirator from my face and gasped, filling my lungs with the night air. Ansel forced me to the ground behind him as he squatted in a shooter's crouch and scanned the area with a gun he had seemingly produced from thin air. Smoke rose from the opening. My eyes burned and coughing spasms racked my chest. I gulped fresh air, and the coughing subsided. Pulling my gun, I positioned my back to Ansel's and covered Josh, who manned the winch. Seconds felt like hours as the rope wiggled and swayed. Then, it snapped taut, and Josh began turning the winch's handle. Maybe two minutes later, Finn emerged from the hole, shucked the harness and breathing apparatus, wiped his tearing eyes with the sleeve of his now-dirty jacket, and pulled his service weapon from its holster. Josh dropped the rope down into the cavern, shoved a manhole cover over the opening, and spun a dial mounted on it resembling a vault lock.

Finn forced the boy behind him and nodded at Ansel, who took the lead, pulling me by the hand. With Finn and Josh behind us, we dashed through the woods to the east of the cavern's visitor center and gift shop. My eyes poured tears, and my lungs burned with every breath. A hundred yards into the trees, we came to a Hummer I had never seen before. Ansel snatched open the back driver-side door and shoved me in. As he leaped into the driver's seat, Finn pushed in behind me, and Josh piled in with us and slammed the door. Ansel fired up the engine, and we bounced through the woods, dodging oaks and mesquites as Josh directed him to a fire road that cut through Westerholm's ranch and out to 3009. We passed state troopers and Comal County sheriffs racing with lights and sirens toward the cavern. As Ansel sped through the night,

Josh and Finn shouted information to Westerholm through the speaker of Finn's phone while Finn and I scanned the horizon for threats, our weapons ready. When we crossed Highway 46, Robbie's Hellcat fell in behind us.

Chapter 30

Thursday, September 23, 11:45 p.m.

Ansel drove straight into the lake house garage, while Robbie hung back on the road, blocking the driveway. Once we were safely inside, Robbie pulled in, and he and two of his guys jumped out of the Hellcat and fanned out around the house, rifles slung over their shoulders. We left Josh waiting in the Hummer while Ansel, Finn, and I cleared the house. When we were satisfied the building was free of bad guys, Josh came into the kitchen. Robbie came through the front door and locked it behind him. His men stayed outside, one in the driveway and the other on the dock protecting the house on the lake side.

Grabbing a remote control, Robbie lowered the shades covering all the windows and turned to Ansel. "Any way they were followed from the ranger station in New Braunfels?"

Ansel checked the load and adjusted the shoulder strap of a rifle he had retrieved from his bedroom. "No chance. I followed Finn, and Leroy and Arlo tailed me."

Robbie pulled a radio from his belt. "Leroy? You sure Ansel was clean when he pulled into the cavern?"

A scratchy reply came through the radio's speaker. "As fucking Scrubbing Bubbles."

Robbie said into the radio, "Arlo?"

Another staticky reply. "Negative tail."

Robbie returned the radio to his belt and took a bottle of water from the refrigerator. He held it up asking if any of us wanted one. We all shook our heads. He took a long pull off the bottle and set it on the kitchen island. "Josh? Could this have been an accident?"

The young man shook his head. "Even if the electrical went haywire on its own...there's nothing for a spark to catch. Had to be some kind of flammable gas. And those backup generators are checked every night. No way they cratered like that without some help."

Robbie turned to Finn. "Could you have been the target?"

Finn leaned back on the kitchen counter. "I'm a cop, so it's possible. But there's no particular threat I'm aware of."

I slumped down on one of the stools around the island. "Ansel? What went on between the time Finn and I went into the cavern and the time you rappelled down the tunnel? And where did the Hummer come from?"

Ansel opened the refrigerator and pulled out a soda and popped the top. "As soon as you told me about the date, I called Finn and found out where he was taking you."

I looked at Finn, and he shrugged. "He asked me not to say anything."

Ansel went on. "Finn arranged with Westerholm for Leroy to come out and do some reconnaissance so we had a response plan if we needed it. After Leroy and Arlo tailed us to the cavern, they staged the Hummer in the woods in case I needed an emergency evac. Josh came down in the elevator to get me when the caterers delivered our meals, courtesy of the special ranger here." He winked at Finn. "Damn fine chow, by the way." Finn gave him a little salute. "Josh and I were eating when the lights went out. We went to the emergency access point nearest where you all were having dinner and came for you—just like we had arranged with Finn. You know the rest."

I looked at Finn. "You knew about all this? And neither of you said anything?"

Finn said, "Standard protection protocol. You know that. I just didn't want to spoil the evening making it seem like we were going to Fort Knox."

Robbie looked at Josh. "How could the attackers have gotten into the cavern?"

Josh shrugged. "I've been racking my brain since we got on the road. We have very strict safety protocols for keeping track of who comes and goes from the caverns. My best guess is they gained access through some undeveloped part of the cave. The system is several miles long. Only a fraction of it has been developed."

I pulled some Milano cookies out of the cabinet, poured them on a plate, and set them on the island.

Finn picked up a cookie. "I need to get back to the cavern. I should be with Bradford...see how I can help. I'm sure Josh needs to get back, too."

Ansel tossed Finn the keys to the Hummer. "Just leave it in the parking lot. We'll sort out all the vehicles tomorrow."

I walked Finn and Josh to the garage, and Josh got in the Hummer. Finn leaned over and kissed me chastely on the cheek. "Other than the poisonous gas and emergency evacuation, I had a lovely evening. But maybe next time, we should just go to McDonald's."

I swallowed hard. "It was great right up until it...blew up."

He brushed his thumb across my cheek and gently tucked my hair behind my ear. "Never a dull moment these days. I'll call you tomorrow."

I went back inside. Ansel was nowhere to be seen. I carried what was left of the cookies into the living room and sat on the gray leather sofa. Leaning my head back on the cushion, I said, "What the fuck is going on, Robbie?"

He grabbed a beer from the refrigerator and joined me, taking pull off the bottle. "Did you hear or smell anything before the fire started?"

I munched on a cookie. "I smelled...garlic and onions. Really strong. But there was an industrial tinge to it...petrochemical, almost. It made me gag. It definitely wasn't food."

He set the beer on the table. "How long after you smelled that until the fire started?"

I closed my eyes and tried to think. "Fifteen seconds...maybe thirty. Why?"

"Acrylonitrile is a highly volatile flammable liquid that smells something like onion or garlic."

I wiped my eyes. They were still watering from the smoke. "What's acrylonitrile?"

"It's used in chemical manufacturing...rubber and plastics. Not too hard to come by."

I cleared my throat. I could still taste the stuff in my mouth. "Who did this, Robbie? How could the guys from the Wind Rose have managed something like this?"

Robbie emptied his beer. "I don't know. But, from now until we get this resolved, we're at DEFCON 1." He picked up the empty cookie plate and his beer bottle and carried them into the kitchen. "I'll be here tonight. Ansel, too. Arlo and Leroy will cover the outside. Go take a shower and get some sleep."

As he went through his ritual of checking locks and alarms, I said, "Thanks for tonight, Robbie. If it hadn't been for you and Ansel..."

He pulled me into a hug, said, "See you in the morning," and settled on the couch with the remote.

I took a long, hot shower and changed into yoga pants and a T-shirt. I nursed the growing ache in my side and wondered if it was coming from my psyche. On the other hand, being winched up twenty stories out of a burning cave could have had something to do with it.

I crawled into the bed and turned on some soft jazz and considered my ambivalence about Finn. On one hand, I was strongly attracted to him. Who wouldn't be? He was gorgeous and charming and kind and capable. But every time I was just about to let my guard down with him, I was hit with fear that he could be a total imposter waiting for a chance to destroy me—like in the B movies where aliens infiltrate the human race, indistinguishable from Earthlings until they bleed yellow goo or morph into monsters when hit with a ray gun. Ambivalence or not, the pleasure of our evening together before the shit hit the fan had been remarkable. I thought of the feel of my hand in his... Then I felt a familiar quiver and my left hand started trembling uncontrollably. The idea of going back to shaking and chills and terror-filled episodes of PTSD made me cry.

Out of habit, I picked up my phone to call Sean. Then it dawned on me that Robbie had mysteriously appeared with Arlo and Leroy, but Sean had never so much as been mentioned during the evening or its aftermath. I hit Find My. *Location Unavailable.* No surprise there. For the first time in my life, I didn't have the unequivocal security Sean Galen had always provided. I had no clue how to fix our relationship, but the idea of a permanent rift between us was unfathomable.

However that eventually worked itself out, though, now was my time to be a grownup and navigate my own way through life's twists and turns. And that included this sea of uncertainty I was sailing through with Finneas Rhodes. I thought back to the support group Madelyn had sent me to after I was kidnapped by Daniel Kerabos. I felt like the women there were in a permanent state of victimhood. Maybe that was just how it looked to me at the time. But surely that wasn't the only such group in town.

I used my phone to search the internet for sexual assault survivor support groups. I spotted a meeting the next morning at 7:00 a.m. "Start your day with the sisterhood of hope." It sure wasn't the same group I had attended before. *Sisterhood* and *hope* were nowhere in their motto.

If I hated it, I never had to go back. I jotted the address down on a pad, set my alarm for 5:30 a.m., and texted Robbie and Ansel we'd be taking a road trip at the crack of dawn. Robbie texted back. *I'll be gone by then. Client's got trouble. Ansel will take you if it's urgent.*

My hand was doing the Saint Vitus's dance. I guessed that qualified as "urgent."

Chapter 31

Friday, September 24, 6:30 a.m.

When I got up, the Genesis had mysteriously appeared in the driveway, the Land Cruiser was in the garage, and the Hummer was gone. Ansel told me the guys had sorted it out after I went to bed. He agreed to drive separately if I wore what we had jokingly taken to calling my "going steady" pin. I couldn't predict what my reaction to the meeting would be, and I had no intention of bawling my eyes out for half an hour while Ansel drove me home. Before we left, I told him he would have to wait outside. He acquiesced without question.

Alamo City Methodist Church occupies a large complex in the upscale bedroom community of Terrell Hills. I parked and watched a steady stream of women cross the lot and disappear into what looked like a chapel. I shouldered my purse and followed them, hoping I wasn't inadvertently walking into a church circle or prayer breakfast where I might get roped into singing hymns or making pancakes shaped like crosses.

I knew I was in the right room when I saw the banner taped on the wall that read "Take responsibility, not blame. Blame the bastard who hurt you. Take responsibility for your choices. Choose to have a great life." Another one read "You saved your own life. Now, live it."

A smorgasbord of donuts and other pastries was artfully arranged on a table draped with a paper cloth and flanked on either side by a Mr. Coffee and a Mrs. Tea. A middle-aged woman with a long, silver braid, wearing a gauzy maxi dress, was stationed next to the buffet, welcoming members. When she saw me, she stepped up and extended her hand. "I'm Evelyn. I'm the moderator. Welcome."

I nodded thanks. She pointed to the table. "Please help yourself to some breakfast. We use first names only here. But we call sisters Jane if they choose not to share their name."

I forced a polite smile and put two chocolate-filled donuts on a foam plate, filled a paper cup with coffee, and took a seat in a metal folding chair. When everyone was settled, Evelyn took her place. "Welcome to the Living Our Best Life support group. For those of you who are new, here we don't call ourselves 'survivors.' That term implies some state of just getting by. To hell with that. Our goal is to help each other thrive and realize our full potential in spite of the tragedies of our pasts."

The women in the circle smiled and nodded. Evelyn continued. "We start by going around the room and sharing the biggest challenge we faced and the biggest success we had during the week."

One woman suffering from agoraphobia after she was raped in an office parking lot joined the meeting via FaceTime through an iPad someone had propped up on a chair. She said her biggest challenge had been leaving her house to go get the mail, a goal the group had apparently helped her set the previous week. Her biggest success was making it halfway down her driveway before she turned and ran back inside.

Evelyn said, "That's wonderful, Grace. Halfway down the drive! Great progress." The circle applauded. "What's the plan for this week, Grace?"

Grace wiped a teary eye. Her chin quivered, but there was determination in her voice. "I'm going to make it all the way to the mailbox this week, come hell or high water."

A woman named Joan said, "I can come walk with you on Tuesday."

Grace's face lit up. "Would you?"

Joan nodded. "See you Tuesday at noon."

When it came to me, Evelyn said, "Jane? Would you like to share?"

I swallowed hard and stood up. The Wind Rose shootout hadn't been this nerve-racking. I took a deep breath and studied the floor. "Almost three years ago, a man I sat next to at jury duty started stalking me. Four months later, he kidnapped and raped me. I got loose after I lured him into untying me by promising him sexual favors. While he was raping me, I stabbed him in the kidney with a broken bottle. He's in prison now. Then, last year, when I finally started dating again, my first lover turned out to be a murderer who wormed his way into my life to derail my investigation into the crimes he had committed. I killed him after he shot me."

A woman named Jackie said, "Good for you!" and the group applauded.

Evelyn cleared her throat. "Jane, while we don't ever advocate vigilante justice here, our sisterhood strongly supports whatever strategy a woman uses to stay alive during the assault. We think anything from total submission to hand grenades is fine as long as you come out alive."

Another round of applause. No one had ever applauded me for stabbing Kerabos or killing Geare. I couldn't believe I had just told a group of strangers that I had submitted to get Kerabos to untie me. Part of me was still ashamed of that. Yet, with these women, there was an unconditional acceptance of any path to survival. I looked around. "Last night, I had my first date since the shooting. Now, I'm having a flare-up of some of my PTSD symptoms, and I keep worrying this perfectly nice, handsome, classy guy is a serial killer or psychopath."

Evelyn looked at me with kind eyes. "We'd all like to remind you that you are alive. Surviving is proof you did the right thing in both situations. Great job on self-preservation!"

The group nodded, and I heard a smattering of "Good job, girl" and "We're behind you" coming from all around me.

I felt a kind of relief I had never experienced before. It was like this group of women had voluntarily stepped up and shouldered a part of the burden I carried, asking for nothing in return. I cleared my throat. "And I don't know if I can...be intimate with him or anyone else."

Louise, a round-faced woman with a soft voice and a mop of curly, red hair, said, "Jane, just remember, you are in control. You can take any relationship as slowly as you want. If the other party doesn't like it, tough shit."

I felt myself smiling. Louise was my kind of gal. "Thanks, Louise." I fiddled with the cuff of my blouse. "I haven't told him anything about the kidnapping. He has some...professional knowledge, I mean he knows through his job about the guy I shot, but I don't know when I should tell him about...the rest of it."

Grace joined in through the iPad. "When the time is right, you'll know it. You shouldn't feel one iota of pressure to do it before then."

A few more women shared, and Evelyn brought the meeting to a close. The group stood and held hands. Together they said, "It is not in the stars to hold our destiny but in ourselves." Gotta love Shakespeare.

One of the women carried the iPad over to the buffet so Grace could visit during the aftermath. I noshed on one more donut and a last sip of coffee. Something about being there made me feel better than I had since Kerabos had shown up outside the door to the Hampe Ewald that fateful night. Evelyn walked up. "We are all so glad you joined us today. We're here three times a week. You're welcome anytime. In between..." She handed me a printed list of first names and phone numbers. "These are members who have volunteered to take calls from sisters who need support outside of a meeting."

Several women walked up and told me how inspiring my story was. I had never imagined anyone calling that nightmare "inspiring." Others stopped by and said they hoped I kept coming back. Evelyn said, "I hope you come back, too. We all deserve a support network of sisters who know what it's like."

I walked out with Louise and Joan. When I stopped at the GV80, Joan bid us goodbye and walked over to her Honda. Louise stepped up and looked me straight in the eye. "I was a doctor's wife playing tennis at River City and going to the Junior League before my rapist pulled me into the back of his van and tied me up. He drove around town, stopping every hour or so to have a go at me. After six hours, I knew he was getting ready to kill me. I gave him a blow job to distract him. Right before he came, he relaxed a little. I bit him while I wrestled the knife out of his hand, then I stabbed him with it six times. He bled out before the ambulance got there. Best decision I ever made." She squeezed my hand. "It's amazing the strength we have inside us—strength we never imagined. Keep coming back, Jane. The support really helps."

I watched her get in her silver Mercedes and drive away. As I buckled my seat belt and steered the Genesis north on Broadway, I thought about how these kick-ass women were reclaiming their lives with a ferocity I'd never seen before. I took a picture of the list of volunteers with my phone before I tucked it into my wallet and headed north.

Chapter 32

Friday, September 24, 10:30 a.m.

I was rummaging through my briefcase for the Lawton Meyer file when Finn Rhodes called. My fingers tingled—I hoped in a good way, not a PTSD way. I answered. "I had a really nice time last night—at least before the apocalypse. I've been on the regular tours of the cave, but that's nothing compared to last night. And the food was fantastic. Thank you so much."

"I'm so sorry I grabbed you and shoved you into that closet. It dawned on me late last night how terrible that must have been for you. I wanted to apologize."

A lump formed in my throat. "Finn, you did that to protect us. You were great through the whole thing. Please don't worry about it."

"Thank you, but just so you know...I'm sorry. I didn't think I had a choice."

There was something in his voice that told me there was more. He cleared his throat. "Iris, I'm just up the road in Fredericksburg for the next few days... I was wondering if I could bring you a late lunch, say around two? There's something I'd like to talk to you about. It won't take long."

Curious, I said, "Sure. Best we do it here. The guys are trying to keep me out of sight."

We rang off, and I realized I was oddly anxious about what the afternoon would hold. We'd had only one official date, so what was I nervous about? I just wanted Finn to be a good guy. I needed to know I could be attracted to a normal, decent man who wasn't a serial killer or some other variety of asshole in disguise. I hated to think of myself like a drug-sniffing dog, prowling through the world singling out killers and psychopaths based on how attractive I found them.

I opened the file containing the research on Lawton Meyer that Sol and I had amassed. I kept coming back to that land in Archer County. Bought under the birth name, sold under the new name. Same acreage, same signatures, same funky *g*.

One thing you learn in the investigative business: before you invest thousands of dollars' worth of time and resources on in-depth investigations about why people do things, it generally pays to just ask them first.

Since Lawton Meyer hadn't called me back, I doubted he would answer when I called again. So I set my phone to spoof a caller ID report from a number in Fredericksburg, and he picked up right away. "This is Lawton."

"Mr. Meyer, I hate to bother you again, but this is Iris Raines. I left a message for you yesterday. I just have a couple of questions if you have a second to help me out."

Good ole boy pseudo-politeness coating a core of exasperation oozed out of the phone. "Sorry about not calling you back, but we're getting ready to breed up here, and things are pretty hectic."

I told him why I was calling.

"Ms. Raines, that's not me. I've never heard of the people you're talking about."

I've made these calls my whole career. When you get the wrong person, they always sound confused. But this guy's answer rolled right off his tongue. I pressed. "I just need to be sure I'm covering all my bases here. I am looking for the son of Annabelle Frazier Morgan Case and her first husband, Harrison Morgan. Everything I find in the genealogical record is pointing to you."

He sounded like he was dipping snuff. "Darlin', I'm just not that guy. You seem like a nice lady, and I wish I could help you, but those are just not my people."

So, out of the seven thousand two hundred and seventy-six folks the Census Bureau counted living in Archer County, Texas, in 1980, there were two Luther Alphus Morgans who didn't know each other and weren't related? Since experience had taught me "Bullshit, you big fat liar" is not a great way to keep a subject talking, I held the sarcasm and soldiered on. "Mr. Meyer, I found an entry in the Archer County district court docket of a legal name change from Luther Alphus Morgan to Lawton Alger Meyer. Are you the person mentioned in that petition?"

He laughed. "I am. When I was a kid, my mother scraped together a little money and took me to see *The Sun Also Rises* with Tyrone Power and Ava Gardner. I decided I wanted to be a writer, so I wrote a story about a kid in a crappy little nowhere town who wanted to be a writer and see the world. Wrote it in pencil on notebook paper and mailed it in to a contest advertised in the back of my mother's *Ladies' Home Journal*. I won a picture of Ernest Hemingway in a plastic frame." He chuckled. "Convinced me I was going to be famous. I changed my name because I thought 'Lawton Alger Meyer' made me sound more like a writer and less like a dumbass loser with a seventy-three-acre dirt farm in Archer County, Texas."

The story was touching and self-deprecating. It also was rehearsed, contained way too much detail, and struck me as unadulterated malarkey. "Well, I'm in a pretty bad way here, sir. We need to find Annabelle Morgan Case's kids because they own an interest in a tract of land in Kenton County that Annabelle acquired during her second marriage. Is there anything you can tell me about these folks or how I might find them?"

"No, darlin', I haven't a clue. And you aren't the first person to make this mistake. I've had calls about her ranch land from Pecos to Tyler." Funny. A minute ago he'd never heard of Annabelle Morgan Case. Now, he got calls about her on a regular basis.

"I wish I could help you," he continued, "but I just don't know anything. You have a good day, darlin', and if you're ever in Fredericksburg, I own Big Daddy M's Barbecue. Best brisket around. You're welcome to drop by and have lunch on me."

Fat chance. I'd been there before. His barbecue tasted like shoe leather. And I hate it when men call me "darlin'."

Chapter 33

Friday, September 24, 2:30 p.m.

Ansel answered the door and welcomed Finn, then disappeared upstairs. We went into the kitchen, and Finn juggled a large brown grocery bag and a white bakery box onto the marble island. He presented me with the white box. "For you."

The warm, yeasty aroma of the pretzels wafted through the air. "The Old German Bakery! These are my favorites!"

He smiled. "You mentioned that. They just came out of the oven."

Wow. I felt an ache in my side, then I remembered the banner at the support group. *You saved your own life. Now, live it.* "Thank you, Finn. You really know how to spoil a girl."

He began unloading our lunch from the brown grocery bag marked with the logo of the Welfare Cafe. The aroma of chicken-fried steak filled the kitchen. Mashed potatoes, cream gravy, and a box of fresh corn bread topped off the spread. My mouth watered at the sight of the food while I put plates and utensils out on the island. "With all the carbs and fat on this table, you're liable to break your arm falling off the healthy wagon."

"I'll repent tomorrow." He scooped mashed potatoes onto his plate. "When the sun came up, Bradford and I found the access point."

I set my fork down. "Where?"

"There are multiple natural openings to the cave system. They obviously don't advertise them, but they can't block them all. There's one not far from the Prince Solms Throne. We found a homemade contraption, something like a giant bubble machine with a hose on it beside that entrance. Empty bottles of acrylonitrile were scattered around the site, along with wrappers from some Fourth of July sparklers."

I felt an evil force crawling up my spine. "Someone pumped the chemical down through the opening and then set it on fire."

He nodded. "State Troopers picked the evidence up this morning and took it to the state crime lab for processing."

This was something way more sinister than a bunch of cartel thugs pissed off about money and drugs. A cold fear was running through me, but in case all this might have something to do with Farragut's difficulties, I couldn't discuss it with anyone outside the firm. "It's a lot to take in," I said.

He smiled. "It is. So...what do you say we talk about more pleasant things?"

I shook my head to clear it. "Sounds good to me."

We visited about his latest exploits chasing cattle rustlers while we inhaled the wonderful food. When I finished the last bite of my chicken fried steak and mopped the remaining gravy up with a roll, he dug around in the bag and held up two white Styrofoam containers. "I have pecan or cherry pie. Your choice."

"Can't beat pecan. You want coffee?"

He perused the Keurig selections and popped a cup in the machine while I dug into the rich, gooey slice of pie. When he settled back onto a stool, the drawn look on Finn's face told me we had reached the main event. He took a sip of the coffee and carefully set the mug on the marble countertop then cleared his throat. "I need to tell you some things before you discover them for yourself. I'm sure more complicated crap is the last thing you want to deal with, but I want you to hear this from me."

Uh-oh. I nodded and forced myself to be calm—or at least act that way. I reminded myself I wasn't too deep into this to get out. I swallowed my bite of pie. "Go ahead."

"My soon-to-be ex-wife was a game warden who got caught up in a ring of law enforcement corruption involving game wardens and cops taking kickbacks for turning a blind eye to poachers and drug runners. The scheme reaches across much of South Texas. I was thoroughly investigated because of my marriage, and I was cleared. But I want you to know there is still talk about me because certain findings that cleared me can't be made public as long as the overall investigation is still ongoing."

My mind was reeling. "Does this have something to do with why the feds showed up at the Wind Rose instead of the sheriff's department the night of the shootout?"

He licked his lips. "I can't go into that, but..." He let it hang.

I nodded dumbly. The whole official corruption thing had morphed into a kind of background noise when my mind locked on to the *soon-to-be* part of *ex-wife*. "So you're telling me you are currently married?" The words tasted like bitters.

"Yes. I'm in the midst of divorcing her, but her legal problems are complicating the process. It's hardly like we're still together. She's in prison and not getting out anytime soon."

I busied myself with the Keurig. I needed a shot of caffeine to clear my head. Taking a breath, I willed my voice to stay even.

"Exactly what's complicating the divorce?"

He wiped a dribble of coffee off the island with his napkin then carefully adjusted the placement of his mug. "At trial, my wife used a defense of mental illness, but the jury didn't buy it. She's no more crazy than I'm the director of the FBI. But it's one of the grounds for her criminal appeal, and her attorney is fighting the divorce, claiming she's not competent to understand the proceedings. If the attorney lets her get the divorce, it would undermine their claims of her mental incompetence. So my divorce has gotten tangled up in a key element of her appeal." Now it was my turn to fidget with my coffee mug. After a few beats, he said, "It's a lot to digest, and we don't need to talk about it now. But, if you have questions, I'll tell you anything I'm allowed to discuss."

I stalled for time, fiddling with the cup some more. As I struggled to formulate a response, I remembered Louise saying at the meeting that I needed to take things at the pace I found comfortable. "I need to think about it for a while."

He bored into me with those green eyes. "It's not like the money went into our household account. She was stashing the cash in a safe deposit box I never had access to and never even knew about. I know it's hard to understand, but I swear I didn't know anything about what she was doing."

I shrugged. "I'm in no position to criticize... I was sleeping with a serial killer and didn't know it."

He put the foam containers in the trash, then stood to leave. "I'm sorry, Iris. About all of it."

At his car, he leaned forward and kissed me gently on the cheek. I said, "Thank you so much for lunch. And for the pretzels. I really appreciate it."

He smiled softly and said, "Goodbye, Iris."

Chapter 34

Friday, September 24, 3:30 p.m.

I watched him drive away. Visions flashed through my mind of an afternoon a year earlier when Gregory Geare had stood in my apartment and spun a tale about his dead wife and all the trouble he was having sorting out his feelings about me. Of course, Geare had left out the part about his wife being dead because he murdered her. He seemed to have his conflicting feelings pretty well straightened out twelve days later when he shot Grover at point blank range and unloaded a .40 S&W slug into my left side, ripping up half of my vital organs before I used my last conscious moment to shoot him dead.

I called to Ansel. "I've got to go out. You'll have to follow behind."

He pulled a fob from his pocket and said, "Let's go."

I sailed west on Highway 46 to 281 South with Ansel right on my tail. I told Siri to send him a text—*Thanks for not asking questions*—then turned on Sirius, desperately trying to distract myself from the rapid-fire slideshow of images of Gregory Geare flashing through my mind's eye. My left hand shook. The chills were coming on as I teetered on the precipice of a full-blown PTSD episode.

Just north of downtown San Antonio, I exited onto 35 South. At the little town of Von Ormy, I followed the signs to the back of the Sunset Haven Cemetery and pulled to a stop by a placard that read Common Burials. Ansel stopped fifty yards back and stayed put. I walked through the paupers' graves until I found the small, flat concrete marker for Gregory Geare.

I stared at the stone. Unlike my kidnapper, Kerabos, who was alive in an isolation cell in Huntsville, Geare was dead. And I was the one who'd killed him. I sat down by the stone and traced the letters with my trembling index finger. I fumbled for my phone and called the first number on the list of support group volunteers. A slow, deep voice answered, "This is Rebecca."

The sound calmed me. "This is...Jane... I'm from the support group..."

"I understand. Are you safe right now, Jane?"

I looked around. "I think so. I'm sitting in a cemetery...at the grave of my attacker."

Rebecca's voice was soft and reassuring. "The best place for an attacker to be. What's happening with you right now, Jane? How'd you end up at the cemetery today?"

I stammered. "I don't know... I met a man... He seems kind and decent, but ever since I've been seeing him, I'm having these flashes of the monster..."

Rebecca said, "Like you see him in your mind?"

"Yes."

Rebecca was quiet for a couple of beats. Then she said, "Were you close to this man, Jane? The monster?"

Tears flowed down my face. "Yes."

Rebecca was so kind, and there was a hypnotic quality to her voice. "I'm so sorry about that, Jane. Sometimes we're tricked by monsters. It's not our fault."

I sniffled. "Thank you."

Rebecca seemed to be considering her next question. Finally, she said, "I'm wondering, how'd this monster die, Jane?"

I wiped tears away with the palm of my hand. "I killed him."

A touch of animation lilted through Rebecca's voice. "Well, good for you, Jane. Are you seeing the scene where he died?"

"No. I'm seeing all the times before that..."

"Images from when you thought you were happy with him?"

I whispered, "Yes."

"Well, let's try to substitute some different mind pictures for those images that are making you so sad."

I was still shaking, but Rebecca's voice was anchoring me, comforting me. "Okay. Like what?"

I could hear her smiling through the phone. "How about when you killed him?"

Stunned, I wiped my nose with the back of my hand. "What? I thought you were going to tell me to think about puppies and kittens and days at the beach."

Rebecca said, "What a load of crap, Jane. Only idiots who have never lived through what we have would come up with that puppy and kitten bullshit. I'm interested in the moment you killed him. Can you visualize that now, Jane?" I thought back on that night. I could feel the searing, white-hot pain ripping through my body as I lay on the floor of the loft...as I saw Geare turning the gun on Sean. I felt the agony that tore through me as I forced myself up on my left elbow and fired into his center mass until the gun was empty.

I was still weeping. "I can see it."

Rebecca's voice was rhythmic and steady. "What does that make you feel, Jane?"

"I don't know..."

"Think about it, Jane."

Then a lightning bolt of realization shot straight through my mind, searing its way through all the suffering and confusion and doubt. "Relief."

"Damn straight. Jane, killing your attacker was your Neil Armstrong moment—the instant when you planted your flag on the moon. You transcended the boundaries of the life you lived before and made your stand. You're alive. You can be whole and complete and happy. And you deserve that, Jane."

As I hung up from Rebecca and sat staring at Geare's headstone, thoughts of Kerabos shot through my mind. For the first time since I'd climbed into Sean's Escalade that fateful night, I realized I had saved myself from Kerabos. I'd always assumed I would have frozen to death on that road if Sean hadn't found me. I had never before considered that the same courage and ingenuity and cunning I had used to escape Kerabos's cabin might have saved me on that road if Sean hadn't come along.

The chills were gone, and my hand wasn't shaking anymore. The pain in my side had disappeared. I fired up the Genesis and drove home as the sun was setting in a bloodred sky.

When Ansel and I pulled up to the lake house, Robbie's Hellcat was parked in the turnaround outside the garage. At the front door, I heard the unmistakable sound of my Saint Bernard's chesty bark. It was not as loud as usual, but it was definitely my boy. I ran into the living room and found Robbie and Festus stretched out on the couch watching *The Dirty Dozen*.

Just the sight of Festus sent a river of happiness flowing through me. When he looked up at me with his sad, droopy eyes then dropped his head back onto Robbie's chest, I was overcome with guilt and soul-crushing sadness that I had let him get so sick. I dashed to the sofa and scratched his ears.

"Did you two stage a jailbreak at Asa's office?"

Robbie sat up, gently rearranging Festus's head on a pillow. "When I called around three to check on him, Asa told me Festus could come home today, and we cooked up a plan to surprise you."

I crawled onto the couch and lay down beside Festus. His thick, wooly coat was soft and comforting. I stroked his massive head.

Robbie said, "He ate his dinner and drank a little water, and he's been outside. I thought he might enjoy checking out his domain. But he just did his business and came straight back inside."

As I rubbed Festus's silky ears, Ansel carried an armload of sheets out of the downstairs bedroom he'd been using. "I'm going to switch rooms with you. Doesn't look like the canine is up to the stairs."

Robbie stood. "I'm going to hang here tonight, so why don't you take a break?"

Ansel glanced at the wall clock. "I do have tickets to the symphony tonight. My clothes are in the car. If I hustle, I can still make the second half."

Robbie checked the load in the gun he had hidden in a belt holster then replaced the weapon, walked to Ansel, and took the bedding. "I'm on it. Have fun."

He carried the sheets to the laundry room while I cuddled with Festus. Ansel hustled out to his car then rushed through the foyer carrying a suit bag and disappeared up the stairs, only to emerge ten minutes later freshly shaved and dressed in a stunning black tux. The skull earring was nowhere to be seen, and the Munch tattoo was hidden under his shirt. Robbie tossed him a fob. "Take the Hellcat. I better have the Toyota in case we have to go out."

Ansel waved good night as Robbie piled on the couch with me and my dog.

Nobody said anything about Sean.

Chapter 35

Saturday, September 25, 8:45 a.m.

Carmine Pagano was a commercial real estate developer and the majority owner of the Hampe Ewald, making him Raines & Raines's real estate partner. After the Hampe Ewald had gone up in flames the year before, Justis had evicted Carmine and his Sansabelt pants and Doral cigarettes from the R&R client list, fearing a conflict of interest. Now that the Hampe Ewald was rebuilt and making good money, Carmine had wormed his way back into my fathers' practice.

Since Justis and Addison shunned the River City Country Club as a bastion of self-aggrandizing, status-signaling vanity nearly devoid of diversity, nobody in our shop had an inside track there. But Carmine had married the unpleasant great-granddaughter of one of the founding members. He was River City royalty.

After all the trouble my fathers and I had bailed him out of over the years, Carmine was happy to make a couple of phone calls to get me some help locating the caddy. When Robbie and I pulled into the club parking lot for my nine-o'clock meeting with the head of security, Carmine was waiting for us by the main entrance of the massive tan stucco building with its peaked red-tile roof and trademark cupola.

"Hey, Iris."

I greeted him and introduced Robbie.

He pulled open one of the massive front doors carved out of Texas oak and motioned me through. A bulky man descended a grand staircase covered in rich, red carpet and walked toward us. The man's navy blazer strained across his massive chest and bulging biceps as he extended his hand. "Mr. Pagano."

Carmine shook and introduced us to Elwood Johnson, head of security. "I'd love to stay, but I've got a tee time in..." Carmine checked his chunky, gold watch. "Now." He turned and hustled out.

"I really appreciate this," I said to Mr. Johnson.

He dipped his head slightly. "Happy to be of assistance to Mr. Pagano."

I smiled sweetly at this not-so-subtle reminder of how not happy he was to be of assistance to me. You take it where you can get it.

Johnson led us through a maze of fluorescent-lit corridors traversing administrative parts of the club until he swiped a key card through a reader by a door marked Security. Inside, a tattooed, thirtyish man in faded jeans and a Lollapalooza T-shirt sat at a keyboard behind a bank of monitors. Johnson looked over the man's shoulder. "Anything interesting?"

The tattooed man tapped some keys and one of the monitors flickered. "A waiter tried to take a ham out the kitchen delivery entrance, but the chef busted him and fired him on the spot." He sipped black cherry soda out of a can. "I grabbed the video for HR in case there's any shit over the firing."

Johnson cleared his throat over the profanity. Tattoo guy flinched and said, "Sorry, ma'am."

Johnson said, "Ms. Raines, Mr. Hazelwood, this is Tye Henderson. He's going to be assisting you today."

Tye stood and extended his hand. We all shook.

Robbie said, "Thanks for helping."

He smiled. "Sure."

Johnson excused himself and slid out the door.

"I've got you set up over here," Tye said, indicating two desk chairs at another station of monitors. We sat, and he pointed to a manila folder positioned to the left of the keyboard. "That's the personnel file you requested for Steve Williams."

I picked up the folder and glanced through it.

"I'm sorry, but Elwood said I can't make you any copies. You're free to look through it, though. Let me know when you're ready to start the video." He returned to his station and studied the monitors.

I passed pages to Robbie as I read. Steve Williams had applied to River City via their online portal July 10. He was interviewed July 14 and started at the club the next day, July 15, and he'd worked steadily until August 13 when he'd called and said he was quitting because his mother'd had a stroke and he had to go tend to her. I pulled out my legal pad and noted the location and identification information listed on his application.

I used my phone to log into a service called SSNVER. I typed in the Social Security number Steve Williams had listed on his job application and discovered the number had been issued in Alabama sometime between 1936 and 1938. Unless this guy was the oldest caddy in the history of golf, the application was a total fraud. The story about his mother was complete fiction, too. A guy with that social would have a mother at least 120 years old. He listed four references, whose names I didn't recognize, and I copied down their contact information as well. Someone in HR named Ronald noted that he had checked all the references, and they had all responded with glowing reports. I put the pad back in my briefcase and handed the file to Tye. "Thanks."

He pulled his rolling office chair over and sat down. "After Mr. Pagano called, I searched a bunch of archived video and came up with only one clip I thought might be interesting to you."

He pulled the keyboard in front of him. As he typed, the monitors above us came to life. "The facial image in the first part of the clip is pretty decent." A shot of a back door facing into an alley filled one of the screens. "This is the service drive behind the kitchen. It's where all the food deliveries are unloaded. That's a prime area for theft, so we have good IR lighting there on a top-flight hidden camera. Nobody but the general manager, Elwood, and I knows it's there."

He hit a key, and the video began to play. After a few seconds, the door opened, and a man stepped out. Tye froze the video. "This is August 11 at 2:33 p.m. That's Steve Williams." I studied the image. The face shot was very clear, but I'd never seen the man before. I got a head shake from Robbie.

I turned to Tye. "Can you grab me a still of that?"

He hit a key. "Sure. You want it emailed?"

I nodded and rattled off my address. Once he dispatched the image, he tapped the space bar on the keyboard, and the video resumed. The caddy checked his watch and looked up and down the service drive then lit a cigarette and leaned up against a wall to smoke it. He checked his watch a couple more times before a man in a hoodie entered the frame on foot. The caddy stood up and thumped his cigarette away, exhaling a cloud of smoke as he greeted the man in the hoodie. The men spoke briefly, then the second man passed Williams a briefcase and turned to leave. For a split second, Hoodie was facing the hidden camera. I lurched forward. "Can you freeze frame on that shot of the second man's face?"

Tye slid the cursor back and forth until the face shot came into view. My fingers prickled as I leaned in for a closer look. "Could you email me a shot of that, also, please?" I glanced at Robbie, who tipped his head. He saw it, too.

As Tye typed, I felt like a rock climber stuck on a cliff face finally spotting a handhold. Parts of the case started falling into place in my mind as I stared at the face of the man we had come to call "the poisoner."

Chapter 36

Saturday, September 25, 11:00 a.m.

My fathers usually worked until noon on Saturday, and I was relieved when I saw both of their cars in the parking lot. Robbie made two full trips around the block and cruised the neighborhood for another five minutes before he agreed to stop at the Hampe Ewald. A mile south of the building, he parked on a residential street and retrieved the Kevlar vests and strapped his on. He stuffed extra ammunition into his pockets while I tugged the heavy body armor over my head and pulled the Velcro straps tight. Satisfied mine was fitted properly, he got into the driver's seat. I called Addison and told him we were coming up. Once Robbie had parked, we made a beeline to the fourth floor. My father's face lit up with a smile when I knocked on the door frame, and he set his gold pen on the desk and leaned back in his chair. "I have breakfast tacos left by the coffee maker."

I said, "You better call Justis. We need to have a chat."

We poured coffee and brought it and the breakfast tacos back to Addison's desk and sat down as Justis walked through the door. He greeted us, poured himself some coffee, and sat down in the remaining client chair. "What's on your mind?"

I told them about the caddy and the poisoner meeting in the River City service alley. Skipping over any unseemly details of Sean's "research" into Big Top's network, I simply said Marvin had checked into it and thought maybe the poisoner worked for Allways Security and I had Marvin and his crew sitting on Allways to try to pick up the poisoner's trail.

Justis sipped his coffee. "So where's the link between this Allways Security and Big Top Burgers?"

It's hard to finagle legal geniuses who cross-examine witnesses for a living. When I didn't answer, Justis got up and closed the door. "Remembering we are officers of the court, tell us what you can about the connection between these entities."

Robbie cleared his throat and said, "Sean has reason to believe the Big Top organization has been in possession of peculiarly encrypted information about growing *B. cereus* for use in biological warfare. Marvin located some chatter on the dark web linking Allways Security to that peculiar type of encryption."

Addison leaned forward and rested his forearms on his desk while he slid his pen through his fingers, turning it end over end. "And now, courtesy of the country club's security video, you can link the poisoner in the award photo to the caddy who set up the drug sting involving our client."

Robbie and I nodded. I said, "That's correct, but all the identities we have for the two men are fakes." My cell barked out a chorus of "Bad, Bad Leroy Brown." I fished it out of my briefcase and hit the speaker button. "Marvin, you're on speaker here with Robbie and Justis and Addison."

"Good. I just heard from my guys sitting on the Allways Security office in Houston. An hour ago, the dude in the award photo went in the back door."

A buzz of excitement hummed in my chest. "Are you sure it's the same guy?"

"That's affirmative. My guy took a pic and texted it to me. I compared it to the award photo. Plus, in our pic, the guy's got on a sleeveless T-shirt, and his biceps is exposed. He's got the ranger tattoo you described."

Addison leaned in closer to the phone. "Marvin, it is critical you all stay on this man."

Marvin said, "I'm already on my way to Houston to manage the surveillance myself."

"We have some new information for you." I told him about the video of the caddy in the service drive.

Marvin said, "Okay... So Big Top hired Allways to run a dirty-tricks op against your Circus Burgers guy. They poisoned the food to get his stores shut down and entrapped him into the drug deal to pressure him into dropping his lawsuit against them."

Justis and Addison exchanged looks. "So it seems."

"These are bad boys, Iris," Marvin said. "I'm serious as a heart attack when I say leave dealing with them to me and my team."

Justis eyed me with the same I-mean-business look he'd used when he would tell me to practice my piano or finish my homework and said, "We agree completely. Whatever resources you need, we'll pay for."

"Roger that." And Marvin was gone.

Addison looked at his brother. "Jesus H. Christ." He got up and poured himself some more coffee. "This is like a Chinese finger trap. We pull the poisoning thread and the drug deal story pops out."

Justis shook his head. "As far as Quinten is concerned, the drug deal sting was clearly entrapment. Quinten didn't go looking for them. They sought him out as part of a blackmail scheme."

"Narcotics version of a honey trap," I said.

Justis went on. "I can't see how charges against Quinten for his role in this drug business could stick, so I don't think, from a legal standpoint, we need to worry too much about that coming out. As far as we can tell, there's no proof the money Quinten gave this Williams man was ever used for any illegal purpose. For all we know, they just added a grand and gave him his own cash back."

Addison leaned forward. "One of the CB patrons died. If the poisoning was intentional, that makes the contamination scheme felony murder for everyone involved in it. We could probably get Grover interested in that." He turned to Robbie. "You think Sean can provide any evidence of his discovery of the biological warfare thing on Big Top's computers?"

Robbie shook his head. "That would be...tricky."

Justis looked at Addison. "We need that poisoner locked up so we can point to him as the source of the illness instead of some food sanitation error on CB's part."

Addison nodded. "With any luck, we get the San Antonio stores open before Circus Burgers has to fold up its tent." He turned to me and Robbie and said, "Okay. You clean up the story best you can. Obviously no mention of the drug deal thing or whatever Sean was up to."

I made some notes. "I'll just go with the security video of the hooded guy tossing the bag in the dumpster and the Cibius report, emphasizing the part about the poison being in a cheese product not used at CB. Then I'll hit the Darrin Stephens/Larry Tate aliases and the award photo bit hard, and finally wind up with Marvin finding the guy in Houston coming out of a building we have traced to Allways Security."

"Sounds good. When you've got it all ironed out, run through it with me. Then, you can go downtown and try to convince Grover to arrange for Houston PD or some state troopers to arrest this guy on the poisoning charge and have him brought back here. The poisoning and the death took place inside the San Antonio city limits so it's Grover's jurisdiction."

I gathered my briefcase. "It shouldn't be that hard. It *is* murder."

Chapter 37

Monday, September 27, 8:00 a.m.

I woke up with Festus plastered against me. He was warm, and I rolled onto my side and stroked his head. He made the *yow-wow-wow* sound that means *scratch my belly* and rolled over onto his back. When I obliged, he rewarded me with a slobbery kiss. I took him into the backyard so he could take care of business. Back inside, he headed to the kitchen and assumed his feed-me position by the refrigerator. It was great to see him getting his appetite back, but he wasn't a fan of the GI-friendly canned food Asa had prescribed. He sniffed the chow then looked up at me and whined.

"Sorry, bud. That's what we have. Dr. C has put the kibosh on the good stuff. I know it sucks, but it's gruel for a couple more weeks."

He dropped his head and ate the bland dog food with the enthusiasm of a factory worker at the end of a long shift. When he finished, he wandered into the living room and curled up for a nap. Robbie and Ansel walked in as I poured cereal into a bowl. "You boys want some breakfast?"

Ansel pulled up a stool and eyed the box of Cocoa Krispies. "You eat that rubbish?"

Robbie pulled eggs out of the refrigerator. "She's loved them since any of us can remember. I'm making eggs. Anybody?"

Ansel held up three fingers. Robbie scrambled the eggs, and we all ate together. I looked over at Ansel. "How was the symphony?"

He swallowed a bite of eggs. "Beethoven's Violin Sonata no. 9 was superb. The Alamo City Symphony has an amazing violin section."

Addison FaceTimed just as I put the last bite of cereal in my mouth. "Farragut's gotten wind that one of Circus Burgers's largest creditors is getting ready to call a note that would foreclose all the stores in Fort Worth. If we don't get this ranch sale closed soon, I'm going to have to put Circus Burgers into bankruptcy to protect the assets."

I told them about my conversation with Lawton Meyer.

Addison leaned forward on his desk. "So you're convinced this Meyer man is Annabelle's son?"

I shrugged. "He's adamant in his denial, but his story has more holes than the course at Pebble Beach."

Addison rocked back in his chair and drummed his fingers on his rosewood desk, then said, "So what are you going to do about Mr. Meyer?"

I checked my watch. "Robbie and I can drive up to his ranch. Maybe we can shake something loose in person."

Ansel picked up the dishes off the bar and set them in the sink. "You kids go on about your business. I'll take care of Festus."

While Robbie drove, I spent half of the forty-five-minute trip to Fredericksburg on a three-way call with Sol and Cheralyn Cunningham, one of the top genealogists in the state, brainstorming research techniques.

Sol was inclined to think Rose Morgan had died as a child, while Cheralyn was considering an elopement in a place we'd never think to search. Both had a high degree of confidence that Lawton Meyer was Annabelle Morgan Case's son.

We pulled into Big Daddy M's Barbecue and crossed the gravel parking lot to the front door. I asked the hostess if Mr. Meyer was there.

She stuck a pencil behind her ear and said, "He doesn't come in until after the lunch rush. Usually around three. He's probably at the ranch."

I got directions from her, and we drove the twenty minutes out into the Gillespie County countryside.

The ranch house was a massive redbrick affair with a black wrought iron fence set into matching redbrick columnar posts. A cobblestoned walkway led to the boxy two-story Federal-style house with its symmetrically placed windows surrounded by classic black shutters and topped by three evenly spaced dormers. The house sat next to a three-car garage and a large swimming pool with a grotto and waterfall. Robbie parked in the roundabout at the end of the driveway.

I pulled on my suit jacket to conceal my shoulder holster, and we walked to the shiny, black double front doors. I pressed the doorbell and heard the tones of Beethoven's Fifth echo through the giant house. A beautiful older woman opened the door with a socialite smile and a vacant look in her eyes. "May I help you?"

I showed her my pocket card, introduced Robbie as "my associate," and told her we needed to talk to Mr. Meyer about Annabelle Case. For a second, the vacant look was replaced by a flash of what I thought might be recognition. But it came and went in a microsecond. Maybe he'd told her about our earlier conversation. She nodded. "I'll call my husband. Please come in."

She called for Meyer as she led us past a mahogany staircase into an old-fashioned parlor filled with red brocade Victorian-styled furniture and an ebony Steinway grand piano. She offered us chairs and sat down. When she pressed a button on the side table, the bells of Notre Dame chimed through the entry hall.

Just then, Meyer came through the parlor door and shot his wife a questioning look. Robbie and I stood and introduced ourselves. I saw a flicker of something—fear or anger, maybe?—lurking behind his boisterous greeting. Something about the couple set me on edge. The Glock felt good under my arm, and I was glad Robbie was there. Before we sat, a maid in a black-and-white uniform, complete with a lace-trimmed apron, entered. "You rang, Mrs. Meyer?"

I felt like we were Brad and Janet in the opening scene of *The Rocky Horror Picture Show*. Mrs. Meyer turned to us. "Could we offer you something to drink?"

Lawton Meyer was smiling like a car salesman, but his eyes said the only thing he'd like to offer us was a route out of his house. I said, "Water would be great." When the maid looked at Robbie, he said, "Nothing for me, thanks."

The woman disappeared through the door, and Lawton Meyer turned to his wife. "Darlin', could you go see about the gardeners? I've been round and round with John about trimming the ligustrums. If one of us isn't there, he's liable to cut them to the ground."

She smiled primly and said, "Nice meeting you, Ms. Raines, Mr. Hazelwood."

With his wife out of the way, Meyer said, "So what can I do for you today?"

Opting for the face-saving approach, I said, "I hate to keep pestering you folks, but it's come to me that I may not be asking the right questions." I told him about the ranch in Kenton County and the title problem.

Robbie said, "We're really up against it. Our client is very unhappy with us for not getting this straightened out. We wouldn't have bothered you today, but the client insisted we come up here and meet with you in person. I'm sure you know how lawyers can be."

Meyer said, "Well, I'm sure sorry to hear those old boys are on your case, but I can't just wave a magic wand and make this Annabelle woman my mother."

I smiled. She was already his damn mother, and the longer I sat here with him, the more certain I was of it. "Could I go through the list of Annabelle's children and see if any of the names ring a bell?"

His façade showed a tiny crack. He compensated quickly, but I was sure I saw it. If he was going to keep lying to me, I might learn something from what made him the most nervous. I pulled a legal pad out of my briefcase and flipped through my notes. "Annabelle and Harrison had four children—two older girls, Thelma and Ollie, a boy, Luther Alphus, and a younger daughter, Rose." I pretended to study the legal pad while I watched his face in my peripheral vision. "The older sisters, Thelma and Ollie, never married or had kids." I looked up. "Do either of those names ring any bells with you?"

He shook his head. "Never heard of them."

I pressed on, positioning the legal pad where I could see him clearly out of the corner of my eye. I was glad Robbie could watch body language while I volleyed questions. "Then there was a younger daughter, Rose." His face remained steady, but his eyes showed fear. No doubt about it. His pupils shrank to pinholes when I mentioned Rose. Then, that fear morphed into anger. I set the pad on my lap and said, "I think I'm out of luck on those two older girls, but that youngest one"—I busied myself putting the pad back in my briefcase, muttering just loud enough for him to hear—"that's who I'm going to focus on..." I looked up at him as I shouldered my satchel. "I don't suppose Rose's name means anything to you, does it?"

He shook his head and cleared his throat before he stood. I could see little beads of sweat forming on his forehead, and his ears had turned crimson. "I'm so sorry I can't help you." He checked his watch. "I've got to run... I need to get to the restaurant, check on the lunch crowd." Now I was sure he was lying.

When we didn't start walking toward the door, he made an after-you gesture. I smiled and led the way out of the parlor. As we exited, I stopped at a gallery wall of photos. I spotted a picture of him and his wife in front of the Sphinx. I stopped. "Wow! You've been to Egypt?"

Impatiently, he said, "Yep, three years ago."

I kept studying the wall. There were at least twenty framed pictures of Maynard with his violin. "Is this your son?"

Meyer said, "Yes. He's a famous violinist. Been playing since he was a little tyke."

I scanned the wall again. Impatience was rising off him like a heat mirage wavering up from a West Texas highway in August. I turned and said, "Amazing. You must be so proud."

He nudged me forward by invading my space, plastered on a smile, and said, "He's really something."

As we exited the parlor, the maid approached carrying a silver tray with my water. Lawton Meyer said, "Doreen, would you show Ms. Raines and her friend out? I'm late for the restaurant."

The maid nodded and led us to the front door. On the way, we passed Mrs. Meyer. When I bid her goodbye, she was still wearing the blank stare like it was a hat from Neiman's.

Robbie checked his phone as we crossed the wide expanse of the cobblestoned parking area. When we got to the Land Cruiser, he headed to the passenger door. "You mind driving back?" He held the phone up. "Something came up I need to deal with pronto."

I opened the driver's door and hopped in. "Absolutely. I'm beginning to feel like Miss Daisy, being driven around all the time."

While we bumped down the cobblestoned driveway, Robbie pulled out his laptop, tethered it to his phone's hotspot, and went to work. As the scrub brush of the Texas Hill Country slid by, I mulled over how I had pushed Lawton Meyer's buttons like I was banging the keys on that Steinway when I'd talked about Rose Morgan. I called Sol and Cheralyn and told them something was up with the sister. They agreed to keep up a full court press.

When we pulled from the county road onto 87 South, it occurred to me that the Meyers had an entire wall paved in framed family photos, yet there was not one single image of their oldest boy.

That was taking "dead and gone" to a whole new level.

Chapter 38

Monday, September 27, 11:00 a.m.

The sun was burning bright in the cloudless blue sky, making for the flawless beginning of an eighty-five-degree fall day in Texas. I called Addison and gave him a brief report, then tuned into some soft jazz on the satellite radio while Robbie typed on his laptop. The traffic on the once-sleepy rural road had turned nasty with the building craze that was sweeping across central Texas like a tsunami. Today, I was stuck behind a flatbed truck stacked high with thirty-foot lengths of steel pipe held in place by a series of chains stretched across the width of the flatbed.

I was thinking about Quinten Farragut and his litany of troubles when the pipe truck hit an oil slick and began to jackknife across the road. A slow-motion disaster unfurled as a pickup speeding toward us in the opposite lane swerved to avoid the tractor, hit it broadside, and skidded into the bar ditch. The truck's trailer slid perpendicular to the highway, and the chains snapped, unleashing a clanking metallic cacophony as the joints of falling pipe crashed into each other and tumbled to the ground. Hundreds of the lengths of pipe flew off the truck and rolled across the road, heading straight for me. I swerved onto the shoulder and slammed on the brakes.

Instead of stopping, the Toyota swung off the highway and lurched across the shoulder onto the dirt and rocks, gaining momentum as it sailed down the hardscrabble ranchland that sloped steeply away from the road. I pumped the brakes harder, but the giant SUV didn't slow.

Robbie's laptop flew onto the floor. He braced himself on the dash and shouted, "Hold on to the wheel. I'm going to downshift!"

Heart pounding, I gripped the steering wheel with both hands while Robbie grabbed the shifter and jerked it back into the lowest gear. Still the Land Cruiser hurtled across the rough limestone terrain. The hammering sound of rocks kicking up into the undercarriage reverberated around us as I careened straight for a giant oak tree. Joints of the pipe were scattering everywhere like a lethal game of pick-up sticks. One rolled in front of me, and I jerked the wheel to the right. The truck lunged to the passenger side, and the center console jammed into my ribs as the SUV's left wheels came off the ground then slammed back down. I missed the pipe, but the truck was still racing headlong toward a thick copse of gnarled mesquites and towering oaks.

Robbie yelled, "Try the emergency brake." I pulled the release and pumped the parking brake pedal as I sideswiped a mesquite tree. The Land Cruiser swerved and sailed into a barbed wire fence. The airbag blasted out of the steering wheel with an explosive *pop*. I felt like someone had hit me in the face with a cast-iron skillet as the big SUV yanked up several mesquite posts before plowing into a large patch of giant prickly pear and finally coming to a stop.

I took a moment to clear the cobwebs in my addled brain. There was blood spattered across the deflated silver airbag. A voice blasted through the truck's speakers. "This is a Toyota emergency agent. Mr. Galen? Mr. Hazelwood? Do you need emergency responders?"

Robbie spat out blood. "This is Robert Hazelwood. That is affirmative. We need emergency assistance."

I struggled to look out the driver's window to see the other vehicles. "There's a pipe truck and a pickup that are also involved. There's pipe all over the road."

"Highway patrol is en route. Do you need medical assistance?"

I wiped my face and looked at my hand. "I don't know...there's blood..."

Robbie said, "Affirmative. Send medical."

"Stand by, Mr. Hazelwood, I'm dispatching ambulances to your coordinates."

I tried the driver's door, but the crumpled front quarter panel had wedged it shut. I took several deep breaths and tried to steady my trembling as I tested for damage. I wiggled my fingers and moved up to my wrists and shoulders then my toes and feet and up through my knees and hips. All my parts were working, but blood poured from my nose, and my right ribs felt like someone had hit me with a baseball bat. I fumbled for my seat belt, but it wouldn't unlatch. Robbie had just managed to get his belt off as a rail-thin young man with long, dark hair and a tire tool in his hand rapped on my window and shouted, "How badly are you hurt?"

Dazed, I managed to say, "I think I'm okay."

Robbie strained against his own jammed door. I heard the sound of bending metal as he forced it open then leaned back across the front seat. "Do you think you can make it out my side?" Trying to formulate a response felt like the cognitive equivalent of trying to break-dance in lead boots.

As I sluggishly fought to shift mental gears, the young man opened the back passenger door and crawled across the back seat. In a high voice, he said, "I'm Andy. I'm going to help you out."

I stammered, "My belt won't unlatch."

Andy produced a knife and leaned over the seat just as three sheriff's deputies and two ambulances rolled up on the scene. One ambulance stopped at the jackknifed pipe truck, and the other swerved onto the shoulder parked next to us.

The paramedics leaped out of their rig and yanked their cases from the side compartments of the ambulance. The horizon got wavy and started to spin, and I slumped back down into the seat of the mangled Toyota. Andy slid out of the back seat and stepped out of the way while one of the medics cut my seat belt and helped his partner check me over. Robbie shook off the other man and said, "I'm fine. Concentrate on her."

The EMTs helped me to the ambulance where I sat in the open back doors. I looked for Andy, but he was already across the highway getting into a white car. Hoping I could track him down later and thank him, I squinted to get his plate number, but the car was at a bad angle, and the swelling in my face was blurring my vision.

When no amount of pinching and icing would stop the bleeding, I cried out in pain as they packed my nose with what must have been ten yards of gauze while Robbie stood by holding my hand and promising they were almost finished.

I held an ice pack to my face as a tow truck hooked up the crumpled SUV. As the tow driver pulled off his gloves and tossed his metal clipboard into the front seat of his cab, Robbie let go of my hand, jogged over to the truck, retrieved my purse and briefcase along with his laptop and our phones, and handed the driver a piece of paper. The man nodded and got in his truck, and Robbie climbed back into the ambulance. "How're you doing?"

"I feel like I've got a block of concrete in my nose. My ribs hurt like a sonofabitch every time I breathe, but the ambulance guys say nothing's broken. What were you doing with the tow driver?"

"I'm having the Land Cruiser taken to a friend of Marvin's who used to be a forensic tech with the DEA. I want to know why the fuck a brand-new truck didn't stop when you slammed on the brakes. But, right now, let's worry about getting you home." He pulled his phone out of his pocket and tapped keys. After a brief conversation, he hung up. "Ansel's on his way."

Thirty minutes later, Ansel reined the Hellcat to a stop on the gravel shoulder. Robbie helped me out of the ambulance and over to the car. A band of primer now covered the *Fuck you* message previously scrawled on the side of the Dodge. Ansel opened the passenger door, and Robbie helped me ease into the seat then popped the glove compartment and retrieved a bottle of Extra Strength Tylenol. He handed me two capsules and a bottle of water from the drink holder. I slugged them back and handed him the bottle. He shook his head. "Drink it all. You need fluids." He reclined the seat back a little. "You comfortable?"

"I'm fine."

Robbie folded the driver's seat forward and climbed into the back. I swallowed the rest of the water and draped the cold pack over my face while I felt Ansel pull onto the highway.

What a fucking day.

Chapter 39

Monday, September 27, 10:30 p.m.

I woke up as Ansel pulled the Hellcat into the driveway of the lake house. He helped me out, and we walked up the sidewalk. Robbie unlocked the front door and motioned me inside while he and Ansel stayed on the porch. Festus walked up and whimpered. I was too stiff to squat down, but I petted his giant head, and he licked my hand. "Hey, buddy." He kept whining. "I'm okay, pal. It's just a few bruises."

Through the window, I watched as Ansel got back in the Hellcat and drove away.

Robbie took Festus out while I showered, pulled on a loose T-shirt and some yoga pants, and stretched out on the couch. When Robbie brought Festus inside, the Saint Bernard gently climbed up onto the sofa next to me and rested his head on my thigh.

I heard Robbie rummaging around in the refrigerator. Then the microwave dinged, and he emerged with a tray loaded with a bowl of tomato soup and a grilled cheese sandwich. I sat up. "I didn't even know how hungry I was until I got a whiff of the food." I sipped the soup and munched on the sandwich.

When I finished, Robbie returned the tray to the kitchen then came and sat on one of the black leather chairs beside the sofa. "How're you feeling?"

"A lot better. Those Tylenol really helped." I leaned my head back on the soft gray leather. "We better call Sean and let him know about the accident."

Robbie looked out the wall of glass at the shimmering lake. "I've tried him several times. He's not picking up."

"I can't believe he's not up here with us...knowing you've been coming and going with me for days now..."

Robbie cleared his throat. "He probably doesn't know about that... I've been staying with one of my guys."

"I'm so sorry, Robbie. He didn't tell me."

He fiddled with the arm of the chair. "Lot of that going on lately."

I massaged my neck. "He doesn't even acknowledge the evidence I showed him of Dorinda poisoning Festus. All I get is the party line. He and Dorinda are just members of the same GA group and her showing up there is purely coincidental. I know that's complete nonsense, but I just can't fathom he'd flat-out lie to me."

Robbie was quiet, but his jaw was clenching like he was chewing on a squash ball.

"What?"

He walked back into the kitchen and made us cups of tea. Since he didn't ask me if I'd like one, I assumed he was just stalling for time and let him do what he wanted. He set a cup down in front of me and resumed his position in the chair. He sipped the tea and then placed the mug on a coaster. Very deliberately, he said, "But he would lie to you, Iris."

Robbie was fiercely loyal, particularly to Sean. He would never gossip about his partner. I sat up. "What makes you say that?"

He fiddled with the coaster then said, "Because Sean has lied to you before."

My mouth went dry, and my stomach rolled over as I sat speechless. Robbie looked solemnly into my eyes. "Iris, you have to swear not a word of what I am about to tell you will ever leave this room. If you ever confront him about it, it could destroy my relationship with him. I love Sean, but I believe this needs to be said."

I nodded and croaked out, "You have my word."

"Sean's version of our breakup and the origins of his gambling problems that you know are not accurate."

I felt weak and jittery inside. "How do you know this?"

"Because Sean told me how he pitched it to you, and I agreed not to contradict his version of events if it ever came up."

Had Robbie fallen down the rabbit hole with me and Sean? I struggled to find the horizon. "Why have you decided to do that now?"

He sipped the tea again. "Because if we don't stop what's happening, we're both going to lose him forever."

I leaned forward. "I'm listening."

Robbie set the mug down. His beautiful golden eyes were glistening, and he had a faraway stare. "Sean came undone after I got hit by the IED. That's why he left the military. He blamed the army, the enemy, the government... I think most of all, he blamed himself—like somehow he should have prevented it, which was absurd. He felt like me getting hurt was a personal thing—when I was just one more guy who got fucked up in the desert.

"When the army shipped me to Germany, Sean got a little apartment in Ramstein. He stayed at the hospital as long as they would let him. When I was asleep, he wrote code for some defense contractors, cranked out a couple of video games that did pretty well. During that time, I had fifteen plastic surgeries to reconstruct my face—three major ones and twelve touchups. You don't notice now because the surgical incisions were placed in my hairline and in the natural lines of my face, but while it was going on, I looked like Frankenstein's monster. I was a total mess—physically, emotionally, and psychologically. That's when Sean started gambling."

He must have seen my jaw drop. This was where the story veered off the rails that had defined the tale as I had heard it from five thousand miles away. "In the version he told me, you two had taken a break because you wanted to convalesce in solitude while you adjusted to your new appearance. There was no mention of the gambling."

He said evenly, "I know what you heard. Now, I'm telling you what actually happened."

I took a deep breath. The pain that stabbed the right side of my chest reminded me of the wreck and what a lousy day it had been, but I was transfixed by Robbie's story...and terrified about what it meant for the life I thought I had lived with Sean Galen. "Go on."

Robbie took another sip of the tea. "Sean wasn't rich then. He had a decent income from the code and the video games, and I was still getting my military pay, but that sure wasn't putting us on the Forbes list. The gambling got worse, and he got in over his head. At one point, some loan sharks showed up at the apartment and tore the place up."

This story was so surrealistic, it was like listening to H. G. Wells telling me about the War of the Worlds. "How did he dig himself out of that?"

"He hacked into the house side of an online poker site. Once inside the site where he could see the other players' hands, he gambled back enough money to pay off the debts."

"He cheated? Basically just stole the money?"

Robbie shrugged. "Desperate times..."

My heart ached for Robbie. "I can't imagine. To be so injured, so traumatized, and have your partner come unsewn. What a nightmare for you. I'm so sorry."

He leaned forward. Resting his elbows on his knees, he massaged his temples. "Iris, all my life things had gone my way because I was...well, because I looked the way I did. In a split second, that was gone. You didn't see me then."

I bit back the pain that shot through my ribs. "I wanted to come, but Sean told me you didn't want visitors."

He looked out at the lake. "You were family. I wanted you to come. I needed some smart-ass banter. But Sean refused. He didn't want you to know about the gambling."

That was a gut punch. I remembered countless telephone calls where Sean was lost in his worry about Robbie and his suffering. I said a hundred times I'd be on the next plane, but he always insisted Robbie didn't want me or anyone else to see him.

"Eventually, they released me from the hospital, and I stayed at the apartment with Sean in between doctor's appointments and therapy sessions. I was exhausted and weak and not in any shape to cope with a bunch of German gangsters showing up to collect money at all hours of the night. I just couldn't deal with the gambling and the lying and the chaos that was coming with it. Sean was eager to put some distance between him and the loan sharks. He went to Stanford, and I stayed in Germany in treatment until I got a medical discharge the next year."

I did some math. "But he managed to keep it together for the first three years. I didn't hear about the gambling until after he took his comps and was well into writing his dissertation."

"We weren't together, but we stayed in touch every month or so. I got the impression it came and went in waves. But, by then, he'd written several software packages and was making a good wad of money, so he could take some financial hits. Plus, he's a mathematical genius, so as long as he sticks to the odds, he can usually stay ahead. But when he's not getting the thrill from the risk of playing because he wins all the time, he starts making crazy wagers, and the shit gets pretty deep pretty fast. That's what happened right before his defense."

"And that's when he told me about it."

Robbie nodded. "When he wasn't getting it done in terms of the final lap on his dissertation and his advisor got on him, he swore he was going to buckle down. But he and Dorinda were running over to Tahoe all the time, tearing the place up. One weekend he got into a fight with some bad dudes in a dive in Reno. One of them hit him in the face with a pool cue, and he showed up back at school with two black eyes."

This wasn't me and the Mad Hatter anymore. This was Auntie Em's house spinning right off its foundation, sailing into a bizarre new world. "Sean Galen let an asshole in a bar hit him in the face with a pool cue?"

Robbie let out a sigh. "He was drinking pretty heavily then. Meanwhile, Dorinda got caught in some cheating scheme and was booted out of the program. She was hacking into university computers and getting copies of exams before they were administered then selling the tests to undergrads."

I swallowed hard. "But Sean wasn't involved in that."

Robbie walked to the wall of glass and looked out at the night sky. "If he was, he didn't get caught. My take was they suspected him of being in on it but couldn't prove it. The advisor was Sean's staunchest advocate, and I got the feeling he wanted Sean done and gone before any link to the cheating scandal could be proven." He came back to the chair and sat. "I knew he wasn't going to be able to make it without you. I told him if he didn't call you and get you to come out, I would."

I could barely speak. "So he called me himself to control the narrative?"

Robbie looked away and sighed. "Yeah."

I'd always loved Robbie and thought he was good for Sean. I'd just never known how good. "And even after all you'd been through with him, when I called you and told you I couldn't do it alone, you came to help us."

He looked at me. "Iris, I've loved Sean since the first day I met him. I've loved you not only because you're you, but also because you are as much a part of him as his mind or his soul." He came over and sat on the couch next to me and looked straight into my eyes. The gold flecks in his brown irises shimmered in the light reflecting off the lake. "Dorinda will destroy him. If she will break into your apartment and poison your dog, she's capable of anything. We have got to stop her."

I chewed my lip and forced myself to think. "We don't really know what we're up against with her. That's likely our biggest problem."

Robbie leaned back on the couch. "I only know what Sean has told me. In that version of events, her mother ran off when Dorinda was in junior high. The dad was a fuckup with a gambling problem. The story goes by the time she was twelve, she was already a math genius, and her father co-opted her into helping him handicap horses. That's supposedly how they supported themselves until she was sixteen when the old man died of cirrhosis. She hid from social services and supported herself with online gambling until she was eighteen. In college, she was a full-fledged gambling addict. During grad school, she spiraled down into severe mental illness by the time we showed up at Stanford to get Sean through his defense."

I shook my head. "I knew she had left the graduate program, but I had no idea she'd been kicked out over a cheating scandal. I never actually laid eyes on her until we saw her in court when she broke into the rehab in Boston."

Robbie closed his eyes and took a breath. "We have to get Sean away from her before he's so far gone we can't get him back."

Pain stabbed my chest every time I took a breath. I winced and clutched my side.

Robbie stood up and held out his hand. "Come on. It's time for you to get some rest."

He helped me up. "Thanks for everything, Robbie."

He laughed. "You act like I'm going somewhere."

I cocked my head. "What about the work emergency you were dealing with in the car before we had the wreck?"

"Ansel's all over it. You get some sleep. Festus and I will be right here, holding down the fort."

I hugged him. "You know, I've always loved you, too. Like you said, not just because you're you, but because you're part of him."

He turned me toward the bedroom and patted my back. "Get some sleep."

I trudged up the stairs thinking about how Madelyn and I were going to have a lot of sorting out to do on the topic of my past with Sean. But, for now, I needed rest. I crawled into bed, and Festus lumbered in, stepped up onto the mattress, and cuddled up next to me. I buried my face in his soft fur and fell into a deep, dreamless sleep.

Chapter 40

Tuesday, September 28, 6:00 a.m.

Feeling like I'd been pummeled by a gang of angry men, I stumbled into the bathroom and examined my face in the mirror. Two black eyes topped off swelling that spread from my nose across my cheeks. Robbie came in and leaned on the bathroom door frame as I rummaged in the medicine cabinet. "I need Tylenol."

He pulled a bottle out of his shirt pocket and offered me two pills. Gently tipping my face up to the vanity light, he said. "I think we can take that packing out." He motioned to the toilet. "You better sit down."

I sat and leaned my head back while he slowly pulled what seemed like miles of gauze out of my nose. He tossed the bloody wad in the trash can and said, "You take it easy while I fix some breakfast."

I got dressed and ambled into the kitchen as Robbie served up scrambled eggs and toast with coffee. "It's not Chef Sean's Sunday brunch, but it'll do."

I took a bite. "This is great. Thanks."

When my cell rang, he retrieved the phone from the bedroom and handed it to me. "It's Marvin."

I hit the speaker button and said, "Hey, big guy. How's our poisoning suspect?"

"He's fine. I've got two of my best guys on him. You sound like hell."

"I feel like hell, so that fits."

He chuckled. "Touché. My pal'll get started on the Toyota later today. Meanwhile, you up for a little road trip?"

Robbie said, "Hey, Marvin. I'm here. Where're we going?"

"The Mount Zion AME Church across from the Lincoln Courts." Lincoln Courts was one of the most dangerous housing projects in the state.

"Yikes. You in a bunker somewhere?" I asked.

Marvin chuckled again. "I'll be in the church. Omar's folks'll be outside providing security. If you feel up to it, head over there."

Robbie scooped the last bite of his eggs into his mouth. "We're on our way. See you in forty."

I pulled on some jeans and a T-shirt and slid my Glock into my shoulder holster. Robbie served Festus his gruel and walked him over to the guest house where Ansel was hanging out before we got into the Hellcat and drove south.

Forty-five minutes later, we pulled up to Mount Zion and parked next to Marvin's van. A parade of church ladies all dressed in white was making its way into the fellowship hall as a phalanx of armed men from Darnell's crew surrounded the church. Omar Washington was guarding the front door. I winced as I pulled a windbreaker on to conceal my weapon.

I was getting ready to call Marvin when a tall, thin Black man with an AR slung over his shoulder tapped on the car window. We got out and followed him up the sidewalk where he took over his boss's position.

Omar tipped his head toward the back of the church. "Darnell's this way."

Omar led us down a hallway past the sanctuary to a Sunday school classroom. He opened the door and motioned for us to go inside, following us in and pulling the door shut behind us. Marvin was sitting with Darnell at a chipped laminate-topped table surrounded by folding chairs. Framed drawings of the headquarters of the Free African Society in Philadelphia shared the walls with photographs of Dr. King and all the pastors who had ministered at Mount Zion. Next to Darnell sat a thirty-something guy with a medium build and short brown hair. His leg bounced up and down, tapping his heel, as his dark eyes darted around the room. He was biting one of his nails to the quick. Marvin nodded toward two empty metal chairs. "Have a seat."

Robbie and I sat down. Darnell was decked out in his pimp duds, only today's ensemble was lavender instead of lime green. He smiled at me and said, "Iris Raines, I'd like you to meet Matthew Tarleton. I believe you know Mr. Tarleton as 'Steve Williams.' Mr. Tarleton hooked Quinten Farragut up with those nice men looking for an investor to finance their inventory acquisition program."

Now we were getting somewhere. Instead of saying *So you're the asshole who baited my client into a blackmail scheme*, I smiled sweetly and said, "Thanks for agreeing to talk to me today, Mr. Tarleton."

He eyed my face. I said, "You should see the other guy," and produced the award photo. "Do you know this man?"

Tarleton's head bobbed up and down. "That's the dude who hired me to set up the guy from the burger joints."

I set the picture on the table. "Could you just tell me in your own words what happened?"

He swallowed hard and looked at Darnell, who nodded for him to proceed. "I met the dude in the picture in a bar one night in early July. He came up and took the stool next to me. He mentioned the name of a friend of a friend and said he'd heard I could fix him up. The name was solid, but I didn't know the man, so I checked him for a wire. Everything seemed okay, so I sold him a gram."

Robbie leaned in. "Of heroin?"

He jittered a nod and wrung his hands. "After that, he'd show up at the bar every couple of days and make a buy. He didn't have any tracks I could see, didn't strike me as a junkie. I figured maybe he had a woman with a problem. But there was something about him...like he was a regular guy on the surface, but a seriously scary motherfucker underneath."

I cocked my head. "Can you tell me what gave you that feeling?"

He chewed his lip. "I can't say except there was something wound real tight about him."

Robbie said, "Like a cop?"

"Not exactly...this was like...maybe he was a mercenary or some seriously badass security guy." He tipped his head and looked up at Robbie. "No offense, but kind of like the vibe I get from you." Robbie cracked the tiniest hint of a smile, and Tarleton licked his lips and continued. "One night he comes in and asks me could I get him ten grams. We worked out the price and did the deal the next night. No problem. So after a couple of weeks of this, he comes in one Saturday night and says could we get a booth, he wants to talk business. We take our beers to a booth, and he asks me did I ever play golf. Alarm bells are blaring in my head now."

I wrinkled my brow. "Why?"

He looked at me like I was asking him why it was bad to live in Nagasaki in 1945. "Well, lady, golf is hardly what anyone is talking about in a badass bar on South Presa. What day the welfare checks come and who got busted and what the bangers are up to—that gets talked about. But golf? Not so much. But that's not the thing that got me..." He caught himself, biting his lip like he'd said too much already.

I said in my everything's-just-fine voice, "What was the thing that got you?"

He looked at Darnell, who nodded at him again. "I was the Texas Junior Golf champion my senior year in high school. Like fifteen years ago. Nobody besides my dad gives a damn about that or might even know about it. I went to a two-bit high school in the middle of nowhere. I peaked early and got the shanks and never got over it. But this guy had to know. Why else would he be asking me about golf in a South Side pool hall?"

I nodded. "Good question. So what was the business he wanted to discuss?"

"He said he had a job for me. The scam was he would get me a gig as a caddy at this country club so I could get close to this rich dude from the burger places who played there all the time. I was supposed to set up a deal between the hamburger guy and the bar guy because the bar guy's contacts were looking for the bank to move some major weight. Said he was in the deal like a matchmaker. He'd be getting a finder's fee he'd split with me."

I studied him. "So what did you think about that?"

He scoffed. "Scared me shitless. I didn't answer right away. Said I had to take a piss. Once I got to the can, I bailed. When I crawled out the men's room window, the dude came out of fucking nowhere. He was waiting for me. He had a nasty-assed blade, and, quicker than shit, he had me up against the wall with the knife at my throat. He said I better never try to split on him again...told me to go on home, and he'd be in touch with the instructions. Then he disappeared around the corner."

Marvin leaned forward. "What happened then?"

"The next day, I'm sleeping it off at my apartment and wake up to find the dude from the bar sitting on the foot of my bed...not a care in the world. My blood ran cold. He told me I had already filled out an online application for me to caddy at the club. He passed me a copy of the application and this résumé, both for somebody named Steve Williams. When I asked him how would I pass for this Steve Williams, he said, 'We've taken care of that,' and handed me a driver's license for Steve Williams with my picture. He told me I had an interview the next afternoon at three at the club then set a bag down by my bed and told me to wear the clothes in the sack and make sure I memorized the résumé."

I was hoping to God the "fountain pen" clipped in the pocket of my T-shirt was recording this. I tried to sound casual, as if I heard stories like this every day. "So, what happened at the interview?"

He tapped his heel so fast, his whole body shook with the rhythm. "I showed up at the club that Wednesday, and the golf course manager almost tripped over himself rushing to hire me, said my references were world-class and wondered if I could start the next day. That was it. Then all I had to do was watch the tee time reservation book and be available to work for the burger guy."

The complexity of this scheme was impressive. "So how'd you set up the deal?"

The metal folding chair squeaked as he shifted his weight and took a ragged breath. "I heard the burger guy talking to a couple of money types about how he was in deep shit with this other chain cutting into his business, so after the round I passed him a note to meet me at a bar over by SeaWorld. At the meet, I told him I might know a guy who was looking for some short-term financing with a ROI way above market. I wasn't sure what all that meant, but that's what the guy in the picture told me to say. It worked." He went on to tell the same story as Farragut about the smaller trial deal they'd worked out. "The next night, I show up at the bar and the guy in your picture there gave me $500 and told me there was more where that came from when the big deal got done."

"But that didn't work out, did it?" Marvin said.

The man's eyes were wide, and his head jerked from side to side. He told us about Farragut ghosting him. "I called the guy in the picture from the bar and told him the burger dude was a no-show. He sounded cool about it. So I had a few beers and headed home. On my way out to the parking lot, a...client...stopped me. He wanted some blow. I kept a little stash locked in a box hidden under the carpet in the floorboard of my car for impulse-buy type situations just like that. I went to the car, and when I pulled the rug up to get into the box, I saw a fucking bomb under the driver's seat. A bunch of dynamite taped together with the wires running under the mat and up behind the dash. I about shit myself. I grabbed the box and told the guy he could have all the coke in it if he'd give me his car keys. It was a beat-up '92 Trans Am covered in Bondo, but who gave a fuck, right? I got in the car and drove to my cousin's house a hundred miles away. Next day, I called the club and quit...told them some shit about my mother being sick. I didn't want those rich assholes out looking for me. I've been hiding out ever since."

I tapped my finger on the photo of the poisoner. "Did this man ever tell you his name?"

The caddy gave me the look again. "Yeah...sure. I never asked, but he told me to just call him James...James Hoffman."

I slumped back in the folding chair. "Jesus wept."

Out the window, I saw the first of the church ladies exit the fellowship hall and walk down the sidewalk. Omar checked his diamond-encrusted Rolex. Darnell nodded at him, and Omar left. I watched through the window as he assumed his position by the front door of the church, his AR still slung over his shoulder.

Darnell looked at the caddy. "Mr. Tarleton, I'd appreciate it if you would give this nice lady a number where she can reach you, and I would consider it a personal favor if you would do whatever she needs. Do we understand each other?"

Tarleton's head bounced like a ping-pong ball. He picked up an old church program, scribbled a number on it, and passed it to me before he skittered out the door.

As the last of the church ladies dispersed through the neighborhood, Darnell cleared his throat and said, "Duty calls." He turned to me. "Give your daddies my best." He nodded to Marvin and said, "Later," as he walked out of the room. At the Hummer, Omar opened the door for Darnell then climbed into the driver's seat and drove away.

I looked at Marvin. "Please tell me you still have the guy in the award photo?"

Marvin smiled. "Three men on him at all times."

"Thank God for that. And since when are Darnell and Omar in the church security business?"

Marvin leaned his elbows on the worn gray tabletop. "Mount Zion is in a free-fire zone between two rival gangs with crack houses on either side of the church. Darnell's granny is a member here. He and Omar show up every fourth Tuesday to ensure Darnell's grandmother enjoys her Women's Missionary Society meeting in safety."

I drummed my fingers on the table. "Speaking of safety, I'm worried about Tarleton's. The bomb thing means he's on the bad guys' list of loose ends."

Marvin laughed. "Iris, that boy is bein' watched over by the Omar Washington Executive Protection Agency, where the company motto is *Think about fucking with my guy, and they'll never find your body.*"

"Catchy." I shook my head. "Not very good for media, though."

Chapter 41

Tuesday, September 28, 11:30 a.m.

Robbie and I had just pulled onto Broadway when Marvin rang. I hit the speaker icon and said, "Long time, no talk."

"We've got a problem."

"What kind?" Robbie asked.

"Somebody tampered with the brakes on the Land Cruiser. And it was a pretty sophisticated attack. Whoever it was punctured a small hole in the brake fluid line."

My nose was throbbing, and I wasn't in the mood to hear about more people trying to kill me. I said, "Couldn't that have occurred without malicious intent?"

"My guy says no," Marvin said. "The puncture was in a place you'd have to try to get to. The hole was positioned so the fluid wouldn't leak much until the truck was being driven."

Robbie said, "Did your guy find any tracking devices?"

"Nope. He searched from stem to stern." I heard a click on the line. "That's a client," Marvin said. "Gotta run."

Robbie exited 35N for Canyon Lake as my cell rang again. The *Enterprise* engaging warp speed. I hit the speaker icon. "Mr. Galen...I feel like D. B. Cooper just landed at San Antonio International."

"I'm so sorry I've been in the wind. I was on a job. Are you okay?"

"I'm in the car with Robbie." I told him about the wreck and what Marvin's friend found out about the brakes.

"Holy crap, sugar. Are you sure you're all right?"

"I look like a cross between Rocky Raccoon and Jimmy Durante, but otherwise I'm fine."

Robbie chimed in. "We're on our way back to the lake. We'll be having a FaceTime to chat this up with Addison and Justis. You want to join us?"

After a fraction of a second's pause, Sean said, "Sure. I'll see you there." I ended the call.

Robbie said, "I was curious if he was really in town." He white-knuckled the steering wheel.

"Why?"

"One of his biggest clients called while you were asleep last night and needed something handled. They called me after they couldn't reach Sean."

I turned to him. "You should have gone. I would have been fine."

He shook his head. "I sent one of the guys. He got it taken care of inside of an hour. But Sean went off the grid without even bothering to tell me to cover his people. It's not like the folks who hire us need their sinks unclogged. If they're calling in the middle of the night, someone's in deep shit. They expect us to be there to get it handled."

Robbie pulled the Hellcat into the driveway. As we walked up to the house, he said, "Do your fathers know about the wreck?"

I nodded as I unlocked the front door. "I called them before I checked out last night."

Ansel and Festus were on the sofa watching *Beethoven*. Ansel muted the TV. "He seemed a bit down in the dumps this morning. I thought this might cheer him up." I sat down next to Festus and petted him. He nosed me and rested his head on my thigh.

Robbie pulled bottles of water from the refrigerator and sat down in one of the black leather chairs just as Sean walked in the door. He took one look at my face, and his eyes went wide. "Jesus, sugar. I am so sorry I wasn't there."

Robbie shot him a killer look. "We're getting used to it."

Festus climbed down from the sofa, lumbered over to his water bowl, and took several big laps. Sean squatted down to scratch his ears, but Festus spurned the gesture, wandered back to the sofa, and snuggled back up to Ansel.

The air crackled with tension. I cleared my throat and said, "I'm fine. Robbie was great."

FaceTime tones announced my fathers' call, and I braced myself for another round of *ohmyGods*. When Addison saw my face, he said, "When I find out who's responsible for this, he's going be one sorry sonofabitch."

I tipped my head toward Robbie and Sean. "You'll have to get in line. Rambo and Dirty Harry here are pretty pissed, too."

Robbie and I brought everyone up to speed on the caddy and "James Hoffman" and the brakes. Addison stared out his window for a while, tapping his pen on the desk. Finally, he said, "Let's boil this down to brass tacks. Allways Security sends this asshole who calls himself James Hoffman to poison food in the stores and to hire Matthew Tarleton to entrap Quinten Farragut into the drug sting, which Allways then uses to blackmail Farragut into dropping the suit against Big Top Burgers. Do we all agree this is a strong enough series of links for us to conclude Big Top Burgers hired Allways Security to run a dirty-tricks campaign against Circus Burgers?"

We all nodded. I said, "They used Matthew Tarleton to play Steve Williams because Farragut might have recognized Hoffman from him working in the stores."

Sean said, "And they set up a real drug deal instead of using fake operatives because they wanted the real pissed-off drug dealers to wage war on Farragut, maybe kill him. These are the guys tearing up the Wind Rose."

Justis said, "Well, it was a good plan. As it stands, half the Circus Burgers stores are closed, the Wind Rose Ranch has sustained extensive damage and is on the block, and CB's financing is falling apart." He peered over the edge of his reading glasses. "Tell me again what we know about this Allways Security."

I shrugged. "Bottom line, they have hundreds of millions of dollars in defense contracts, are a major supplier of mercenaries, and have a nice-sized corporate espionage department."

Addison looked at Justis. "An outfit that size is a formidable target. I'm thinking go to the US attorney, but what's the claim?"

Justis said, "The targeted stores were in two different states. That makes the poisoning scheme federal."

Addison jotted a note on his legal pad. "That should work. Meanwhile, we need to get Mr. Tarleton a lawyer. I'll make some calls and have Marvin get him over to whoever I line up. Once he has representation, I'll get a court reporter and take his statement under oath."

Justis said, "Tomorrow, I think Iris should proceed with the plan to persuade Grover to have this James Hoffman arrested on the murder charge resulting from the poisonings at the San Pedro store. If she's successful, the arrest should be enough to convince the health department to allow Farragut to reopen the restaurants. If they refuse, the arrest gives us something to take to a judge to overturn the health department's order."

I pulled a folder out of my briefcase. "I have the pitch and all the supporting documents ready. I can run you through it whenever you want."

"We have enough for an arrest," Addison said. "It being murder should get Grover's attention. Allways will send a team of legal heavy hitters down to represent Hoffman and be sure he keeps his mouth shut. That should keep a lid on the drug story for a few days. Justis and I can use the time to refine our strategy on dealing with that issue."

Justis flipped pages of his yellow legal pad. "Iris, where are we on the title problem on the Wind Rose?"

I shook my head. The motion made my nose feel like someone was playing a Led Zeppelin drum solo on my face. "Nowhere. Me, Cheralyn, Sol...no matter where we look, we keep coming back to Lawton Meyer. I'm going to spend the rest of today on it."

Addison said, "Please do. The judge granted our motion for the temporary restraining order, but we've only got a little over two weeks before the creditor can begin foreclosure proceedings up in Fort Worth. Come October 15, the creditor is free to proceed. I'm having the bankruptcy guys draw up the filings now just in case we need them."

When we said our goodbyes and the screen turned black, Sean checked his watch. Robbie sniped, "You need to be somewhere?"

Sean stood and tucked the phone into his pocket. "Yeah. Sorry. Client's got trouble."

We followed him through the foyer to the front door. He hugged me. "Call me if you need anything."

He stepped out onto the front porch and nodded at Robbie, who stayed inside with me. "Thanks for covering that thing last night."

Robbie gave a barely perceptible nod, and we watched Sean get into the Ferrari and drive away. Once back in the living room, Robbie handed me a bottle of Tylenol. "You're gonna need these."

I took the bottle, plopped down on the sofa, and knocked back two of the capsules. My face throbbed as I thought about the pile of Annabelle Morgan Case research on the desk upstairs. The sooner I broke the logjam on that problem, the sooner I would be rid of Farragut and his spinning vortex of bullshit. I climbed the stairs up to the office, sat down at the desk, and began to flip the pages.

About an hour in, as I scanned the Bible-sized print of a Wichita Falls city directory, it occurred to me some of Annabelle and Harrison's neighbors might have known something about the Morgan kids. I studied the pages and found a widow named Inez Crain who'd lived next door to the Morgans on Pearl Avenue from the time the Morgans bought their house until Annabelle moved away. I tracked Inez to a high-end retirement community in Austin and called to set up an appointment to see her the next day. Then, I called Addison and ran him through my pitch to Grover.

Robbie put a frozen pizza in the oven, and he and Ansel and I kicked the case around the table while we ate dinner. Exhausted, I put my plate in the dishwasher and flopped down on my bed where I put an ice pack on my face and fell asleep spooning my Saint Bernard.

Chapter 42

Tuesday, September 28, 11:30 p.m.

I woke up to darkness. Disoriented, I fumbled for the light and stared at the clock. I'd slept for the better part of six hours. Festus looked at me with sad, droopy eyes. "You hungry, boy?"

We padded out of the bedroom and found Robbie streaming *August: Osage County*. He paused the movie, stood, and hugged me then scratched Festus's ears. "How are you feeling?"

I massaged my shoulder. "Now I know how Ali felt after fifteen rounds with Joe Frazier. Those airbags really pack a punch."

He perused my face. "Swelling's a little better."

I dished Festus up a bowl of his prescription kibble. He was eating better and had more energy every day, but he still wasn't his regular self. When he finished with his chow, he ambled into the living room, climbed onto the sofa where Robbie was finishing his movie, and settled in for a nap. Not wanting to interrupt Robbie again, I climbed the stairs to the office and started digging into Dorinda Crandall's past. I'd been so focused on the Farragut case, and trying to stay alive, that I hadn't had a chance to work the Dorinda problem. But if Sean was in a full-on death spiral, I couldn't delay any longer.

It didn't take long. I found the magic bullet in the federal court case index. I watched wide-eyed as the printer disgorged page after page of court records. When it stopped, I grabbed the printouts and hustled down the stairs. The credits were running on the movie as I walked into the living room carrying my bounty. Robbie used the remote to kill the TV. "What?"

I handed him the printouts. While he read, I made tea and carried the mugs to the living room. Still flipping pages, he said, "We should be able to get her locked back up."

I put my feet up on the ottoman and sipped my tea. "As I understand it, conditional release of inmates from federal prison psychiatric hospitals is at the sentencing judge's discretion based on recommendations from the Bureau of Prisons' doctors."

Robbie pointed to one of the court records. "It says right here she is 'not to have any contact with Sean Galen and is specifically prohibited from interacting with any gaming establishments, including but not limited to physical, online, or telephonic gambling businesses. Placing wagers of any type, whether legal or illegal, is absolutely forbidden...'"

"Did you see what she did to get locked up in the first place?"

Robbie shook his head. "I didn't get that far."

"She got caught counting cards in a casino up in Maine. They busted her and threw her out. She raced home, mixed up a Molotov cocktail, drove back, and tossed it through the front door. Almost burned the place to the ground. Six patrons were hospitalized. One ended up blind."

Robbie clenched his jaw. "Fucking bitch. I think she's basically staying at the loft since I split. After the meeting with your fathers today, I checked the security cameras in the garage. Her car was there. I had one of my guys sneak in and stick a GPS tracker on it." He tapped the screen on his phone and held it out for me to see. "She and Sean are at the casino in Eagle Pass."

I stared at the flashing dot on the map. "We need pictures."

Robbie nodded. "I'll go now. They'll be there all night."

He pulled his keys from his pocket. "I'll text Ansel to come inside and take over until I get back."

I walked him to the door. "When you get the pics, I'll take them to the doctors at the prison psych hospital. Maybe we can get her locked back up before she kills someone."

Chapter 43

Wednesday, September 29, 6:00 a.m.

Robbie called at 6:13 a.m. "I got the pics. Great face shots of her coming out of the casino. Even got the sign in the frame. And they don't have Sean's face in them."

"Send them to me, and I'll try to get the shrinks on the phone when they open up."

"Thanks for doing it, Iris. If I was the one to call...well, I think it might be the end of me and Sean forever. I've got some things to take care of. I'll check in later this afternoon."

A shot of fear tumbled through my gut. "It may be the end of me and Sean, too. Hell, he and I may already be past that point. But I'd rather have him pissed at me forever than dead. You've done your part. Now's my turn."

The phone dinged as the pictures landed. The time and date stamp was displayed in the lower right corner of each shot. There was a newspaper stand by the door she was coming out of, and a copy of the local newspaper was visible in the images. Robbie was a pro.

I made a cup of coffee and checked Google for the psychiatric hospital's number. When the clock turned over to 8:00 a.m., I called, introduced myself, and asked for the psychiatrist whose name was listed in the court files. The clerk identified herself as Mrs. Jones and took an officious tone. "And the purpose of your call, please?"

"It's confidential."

"I'm sorry, ma'am. We don't forward messages to the doctors without the purpose of the call."

I took a deep breath and said, "It's about a patient. Dorinda Crandall."

"Do you have a medical power of attorney for the subject of the call?" She sounded like she was reading from a script.

I struggled to keep my voice even. "Mrs. Jones, I am a licensed private investigator. I have an urgent matter I need to discuss with Dr. Robinson. Please give him my message and ask him to call me at his earliest convenience."

I could almost hear her sneer through the line. "I'm sorry. I won't be able to relay your message until you explain the purpose of your call and provide a certified copy of a medical power of attorney. I can give you the mailing address, if you'd like."

I cleared my throat. "Mrs. Jones, could you please transfer me to your supervisor?"

"I'm sorry. My supervisor is unavailable to take calls of this nature. Please call back when you are prepared to provide proper documentation to support your request to speak with the doctor. Good day."

Why does it always have to be the hard way? I logged onto AccuData and drilled down until I found the psychiatrist's mobile number and email address. Doctors are pretty touchy about their cell phone numbers, so I opted for email.

I got another cup of coffee and composed a message to Dr. Edward Robinson, who had signed off on Dorinda's conditional release. I identified myself then detailed the date and time of her visit to the Eagle Pass casino. I included the photos of her Robbie had taken.

A drum roll reverberated in my gut, and my pulse thumped in my ears as I stared at the screen. I was about to launch a message out into cyberspace that I knew would infuriate Sean and could change both our lives forever.

I hit Send then trudged into the kitchen and fixed breakfast. It tasted like glue, but I ate it anyway. As I was putting the dishes in the sink, my phone chimed an incoming text.

Are you okay? Just saw the accident report.

A quiet warmth spread through me as I picked up the phone. As much as I was trying to play it cool with Finn, there was no denying I was strongly attracted to him. I often daydreamed about him, but the romantic fantasies were always quashed by the fear that he might somehow be dangerous. Ambivalence be damned. I hit the Call button. When he answered, I said, "This is Iris Raines from the Raines Detective Agency and Stunt Driving School. May I speak with Ranger Rhodes?"

He laughed. "It's great to hear you being a smart-ass. The accident report sounded like you took a hell of a ride."

"I took a standing eight count, but everything still works, and I'm ready for the next round. How'd you hear about it?"

"Robbie called to follow up on the investigation into the attack at the cave. He thought maybe the same folks could have tampered with the brakes. How are you? I mean really."

"The airbag is what got me. It feels like someone hit in the face with a shovel."

"Yep, but better that than the steering wheel or windshield."

"True. I appreciate you checking on me."

"My pleasure. How's Festus?"

"He's still a little slow out of the gate, but he improves every day."

"Well...I'd love to see you, but I don't know how you feel about that..."

I considered my reply. The sound of his voice was comforting, and I was touched he'd called to check on me. But the ambivalence was creeping back up my consciousness like an evil, clinging vine. The thought of being dragged into a soap-opera-style divorce between him and his incarcerated, pseudo-mentally-ill wife was a real buzzkill.

"I don't know, either, Finn. But I'll figure it out. Meanwhile, I think we probably shouldn't be parading around in public while you're still legally married."

After a beat, he said, "I certainly understand. May I check in with you from time to time?"

"I'd like that, but don't say anything over this phone or in an email or text message either of us wouldn't want read out loud in open court."

"Fair enough."

After an awkward pause, I said, "I need to go, but thanks for checking on me."

He sounded almost wistful when he said, "Take care," and the line went dead.

I forced myself to shove the issue of Finn Rhodes and all the drama it evoked into a neat little box and shelve it in the back of my mind. I had a lot of plates in the air, and letting my concentration slip could send the whole spinning mess crashing down.

I threw on a suit, and Ansel and I headed downtown in my Genesis. At the police department, he opted to stay in the car. "You should be safe in there. Better you tell this story your own way."

At the bullet-resistant glass booth in the lobby of SAPD headquarters, the duty officer called Grover then directed me to a conference room on the second floor. When I got off the elevator, I found him sitting at an oblong woodgrain Formica table reading a file. The room was barely large enough to pull the cheap rolling desk chairs out to sit down. The white acoustic ceiling tiles and gray vinyl floor screamed "government office," and a blank whiteboard covered the wall on one end of the room. Grover was wearing his customary khaki pants and polyester short-sleeved white shirt accessorized with his ever-present clip-on tie. But his clothes hung on him like a scarecrow's since he'd lost the extra forty pounds he'd been carrying for the last few years. For months, I'd been telling myself he was just too frugal or too busy to buy new duds. But, deep down, I worried Grover hadn't wrapped his head around the possibility that some things might have changed forever. His face had the same sickly pallor I'd seen during the escapade at my apartment, and the omnipresent hissing of his O_2 concentrator was a sad reminder that things in our world were a damn long way from how they had been before the shootout with Geare. We all hoped someday soon the supplemental oxygen would be nothing but a bad memory.

I knocked on the door frame. "I saw the Batsignal flashing over Gotham...so I hopped in the Batmobile and zipped over to see what's doing."

He didn't look up. "There's a short in that damn thing. I keep telling the mayor to get it fixed. False alarm, Batgirl. Go back to your cave."

I sank down in a chair and set my briefcase on the conference table. "How ya doin'?"

He kept reading. "I can't breathe worth a damn when I'm not sucking on the ball and chain here. I hate admin, and I'd give my left nut to go chase some bad guys. The only good news is my mother-in-law's talk about moving in with us dropped off since she realized she can't smoke in our house."

"Every cloud..."

He closed the folder and looked up. "What can I..." His eyes went wide. "What the hell happened to your face?"

"I was coming back from a meeting in Fredericksburg Monday when a pipe truck lost its load. I went a couple of rounds with the airbag." I pulled my file out of my briefcase and slid the award photo across the desk along with a blowup of the poisoner I had cropped out.

He looked down at the pictures. "Who's this asshole?"

"The guy who poisoned the diners at the San Pedro Circus Burgers store."

I took him through us using the credit cards to figure out the poisoning came from the grated cheese, Marvin's discovery that Darrin Stephens and Larry Tate were aliases, me finding the award photo, and both managers picking out the subject as Darrin and Larry. He looked up from the pictures. "But what makes you think this is the guy who poisoned the cheese?"

I told him about our experts not finding any contaminants in the stores but finding the bacteria in a cheese product not ever purchased or served by CB. Then I held out my phone and played the security videos of the hooded man tossing the bags in the garbage bins. "I was able to retrieve the bag from the San Pedro dumpster before it was picked up. Our experts tested it and found *B. cereus*." I slid him the report.

He studied it. "So how do you suggest I find this guy?"

I shrugged. "You don't have to. Marvin's got him under surveillance in Houston."

He eyed me. "I can hardly wait to hear how that came about."

"Marvin caught him coming out of the Houston offices of a corporate intel outfit called Allways Security."

He lowered his chin and looked at me over his reading glasses. "And I assume it was an amazing coincidence that Marvin just happened to be driving by when he spotted this guy."

I did a beats-me gesture and said, "Marvin's lucky that way."

He picked up the photos and studied them. "So we don't have an ID on this asshole?"

I shook my head. "Except that he's definitely not a grocer in Tulsa named Darrin Stephens or a barber in Austin named Larry Tate."

"That's for damn sure. What about vehicle registrations, addresses picked up while Marvin's been watching this guy—who do those come back to?"

"More aliases. All dead ends." I passed him a sheaf of printouts showing the AccuData results Marvin had gotten during the ongoing surveillance.

Grover stared down at the photo and shook his head, chuckling.

I cocked my head. "Am I missing something?"

He rolled his eyes. "Iris, Darrin Stephens was the husband on the old sitcom *Bewitched*. Larry Tate was his boss...talk about getting punked."

He tossed the printouts on the conference table and pulled off his glasses, letting them dangle from the string around his neck. "Absent a face shot, we can't prove the guy in the video dumping the bags is the same guy in the award photo. And the chain of evidence on the bag from the San Pedro dumpster is for shit. Some defense attorney will go nuts on that. Hell, there's not even any proof the bag you pulled out of the dumpster is the same one our mystery man threw in."

I gathered the pictures back into the folder. "Nothing's perfect. But the lab guys at Cibius preserved the bag and the containers inside it. They don't have access to AFIS, but they did say there is a partial print on one of the condiment cups containing the cheese product. If you pick up the guy Marvin's watching, and the print on the container is a match to his, we're in business. Plus, Mr. Bewitched there worked in both stores the week before the food poisonings showed up and disappeared the day they were reported—both times. And both times, he was using an alias." I handed him copies of the personnel files.

"The timing thing has some teeth, and the aliases...that should help with the warrant." He pulled on his half-glasses again and thumbed through the folders then tossed them onto the pile of papers in front of him. "Fill in the gaps, please." When I screwed on my best confused expression he said, "Don't make me call Marvin."

I took a deep breath. "We talked to a bunch of 'Larry Tate's coworkers at CB. Turns out, the man in the award photo had an Army Ranger tattoo. Marvin found some chatter on the dark web about Allways that made him suspicious then set up on their offices and caught this guy coming out."

"'Some chatter that made him suspicious.'" He looked straight at me. "Iris, when are you going to realize I can spot bullshit faster than A. J. Foyt could take a lap at Indy? I didn't get my detective's shield by mailing in a bunch of fucking cereal box tops."

I chose my next words carefully. "We came into possession of some peculiarly encrypted intel that indicated Big Top Burgers, the company recently involved in serious litigation with CB, was communicating with an unidentified party about weaponizing *B. cereus.*"

He rolled his eyes. "Fucking Sean." He held up his hand. "I don't want to know... Just tell me how that led you to Allways."

"There was talk on the dark web about Allways using that particular type of encryption. Marvin set up on the Allways office, and the mystery man in the award photo showed up there."

He rested his elbows on the conference table and massaged his temples. "Since I'm going to have to leave out the parts of this story that probably involve you and your cohorts committing felonies—of which I have zero knowledge—I don't know if I can get the DA to go for it." He dropped his hands to the table and looked up. "But there is a dead guy who didn't do anything but pick the wrong day to eat French fries, never mind twenty other poor bastards who ended up in the hospital, so maybe that'll help him...overlook some gaps in the story." He gathered the documents I had given him. "And quit driving so fast in the Batmobile."

Chapter 44

Wednesday, September 29, 2:00 p.m.

Ansel took a seat in the lobby of the assisted-living section of the Hill Country Estates Retirement Community while I checked in with the "concierge" at the front desk. She directed me through a maze of carpeted hallways to Inez Crain's "suite."

I knocked on the door and stuck my head in. "Mrs. Crain?"

Inez was sitting in a recliner next to a twin bed watching a game show. She muted the television with a remote and motioned me in. I introduced myself, and she pointed to a dorm-sized refrigerator with a jar of Sanka and a cup boiler sitting on top of it. "Help yourself if you'd like coffee or a soda."

I smiled. "Thank you, but I just finished lunch."

She tipped her head to a straight chair with a worn gold brocade cushion, probably left over from a dining set she'd enjoyed in happier days. "Take a seat. Sorry I don't have a proper chair."

I settled in. "This is fine. Thanks."

She looked at me with dark blue eyes. "You're here about the Morgans?"

I nodded. "Yes, ma'am." I told her about the Wind Rose and why I was looking for Annabell's children.

She shrugged. "I'd already lived in the neighborhood for on to three years before they moved in. I liked them fine when they first got there. Seemed like a nice young couple. You know, I never had children myself. We didn't have a chance before my husband died, so some people might say I'm not in a position to talk. But the way those people did...well, I never could accept it."

"How so?"

"I'm talking about that youngest girl...sending her away like that. It just wasn't right."

My heart skipped a beat. "You have any idea where they sent her when she went...away?"

"Well, you know it's all so secret... Talk in the neighborhood was that they put her up for adoption. And the lady who came for the child was in a car with something about Catholic Charities written on the door."

"So Rose Morgan left with the woman from Catholic Charities and never came back?"

When she shook her head, her cap of gray pin curls moved like a helmet. "It was horrible...just broke my heart. Poor little thing was crying and screaming while the woman carried her out with nothing but a little blue suitcase and her teddy bear. Annabelle and Harrison just stood on the porch and watched the woman drive off. I can still see that child's face pressed up against the car window of that old black Ford."

"And that's the last time you saw her?"

Inez nodded. "Never laid eyes on her again."

"How old was the child when the woman from Catholic Charities took her away?"

"Let me see..." Inez looked up at the ceiling and ticked the years off on her fingers. "It was about three years after Irwin died, so that would have made it 1968. She must have been...seven or eight. Something like that."

"The Morgans had four children, right?"

"That's right. The two older girls and that terrible boy and the little girl we're talking about. The boy was the one they should have sent away. He was the problem, after all. But a woman down the street told me they gave the girl away instead because nobody'd take that little monster."

I struggled to maintain a neutral tone so as not to slow the torrent of information spilling out of Inez's memory. "What was the problem with the boy?"

She leaned in and whispered, "Word was they sent that poor, precious girl away because that little bastard was doing things to her. It was shameful—especially with her being...the way she was."

I wrinkled my brow. "The way she was?"

Inez pulled a lace handkerchief from the sleeve of her blouse and wiped her nose. "Well, you know people didn't understand things back then the way they do now. Didn't have a fancy name for everything, so I don't know what you'd call it. Truth be told, I never really understood what was wrong. But, God bless her heart, the poor little thing was just never right."

"Never right how?"

"It's hard to explain. It wasn't like she was slow, exactly. She went to regular school, but she never knew who anyone was. No matter how many times I introduced myself, she never could recognize me. Poor child, every time I saw her, she'd smile and say, 'Hello, ma'am. My name is Rose. What's your name?' Did the same thing with everyone in the neighborhood. Annabelle just said she had 'problems.' You ask me, that family was the problem."

"We haven't found the son yet, but the older sisters moved to Florida and passed away several years ago when their house burned."

She chuckled. "*Their* house? They were living together, huh?"

"Yes, ma'am."

Inez leaned forward and said in a low voice, "Back in my day, we called women like that *sapphists*. More polite talk was just *spinster*, but that didn't paint the whole picture, if you get my drift."

I smiled and gave her a little wink. "I think I do, Mrs. Crain. That would explain why neither of the older girls married or had children."

She nodded. "Harrison got the cancer, and it took him fast. Annabelle sure didn't let any grass grow under her feet after he was gone. That Case man started sniffing around, showing up at the house not a month after Harrison's funeral. Case had tractor dealerships. Word was he knew Harrison from business, Harrison working for the fertilizer company and all. Between you and me, I always thought Annabelle and Case were carrying on before Harrison died."

"Do you have any idea what happened to the boy?"

She took a sip from a chipped china cup and returned it to a wobbly TV tray crowded with orange medicine bottles and wedged between her recliner and the bed. "Luther was grown when his daddy died. Last I heard, when Annabelle married Case and moved to wherever, Luther bought some land somewhere not far from Wichita and took up farming. He always scared me, so I was glad to see him go."

I stood and thanked Mrs. Crain. She let out a deep sigh, and her voice was wistful. "I've always wondered what ever happened to that sweet little girl. If you ever find her, you tell her I called the Catholics after I saw her leave in the Ford—I was trying to find her, see if they'd let me take her in. But they wouldn't tell me where she was, and I didn't have any way to look. I've often wondered what would have happened if I'd gotten her... We could have moved back to Tennessee with my people. Maybe she could have had a nice life... Maybe I wouldn't be dying alone in this place, drinking instant coffee and watching *The Price Is Right*."

I walked back to the Genesis, and Ansel pulled out of the circuitous driveway. I couldn't get away from Hill County Estates and Inez's suffering and loneliness fast enough. With my relationship with Sean on life support, I was finding it harder and harder to think about an old age spent facing the vagaries of time alone.

Once back on Lamar, we pulled through a Burger King, got some fries and shakes, and sat in the parking lot. As I sucked down carbs, I processed Inez's terrible story. Finding adoptees who passed through the Texas court system is not an easy task. The state health department is brutal in the defense of their records, and most Texas judges won't even consider opening an adoption file for land title purposes. However, many years ago, Cheralyn had taught me about a little leak in the system... We finished carb-loading and headed to the Legislative Library next door to the capitol.

Cheralyn's technique was a solution for identifying the new name of a child placed for adoption after the child's original birth certificate was issued—like Rose Morgan was. It involved a tedious process of comparing an old printed index stored in the state archives to a modern online index that will show only the child's new name and parentage.

I checked my watch. The library would close in two hours. Ansel rolled the wooden ladder around in its track to the towering shelves of old indexes and retrieved the dusty cardboard binder that held the fan-folded printouts of the original 1960 birth index while I logged my laptop into a modern online version. With Ansel helping, the comparison process moved faster than I had imagined, but as we got to the last of the printouts, I was beginning to wonder if I had missed something. We rushed to finish as the librarian circulated through the reading room, pushing in chairs and gathering reference materials left on tables. At the bottom of the last page, my heart leaped. Rose Belle Morgan born June 5, 1960, in Wichita County to Annabelle Frazier and Harrison Morgan became Roslynn Hunter, child of Linda and Herbert Hunter. I saved a screenshot from my laptop and snuck a cell phone pic of the relevant entry in the old index when the librarian wasn't looking. I stuffed my research materials into my briefcase, and we hurried to the parking lot and headed home.

I was in business.

Chapter 45

Wednesday, September 29, 7:00 p.m.

Back at the lake, I unlocked the front door to find Festus growling and barking like we were strangers. He stayed under my feet and almost tripped me twice as I headed across the foyer. "You need to go outside, buddy?"

When I took him out to the front yard, he did his business and then sat in the grass, refusing to go back inside. I practically had to drag him back into the house.

When we got to the door, Ansel stepped up to block our path. He had his gun in his hand. "There's something wrong with Festus. I'm going to clear the house. You stay out on the road until I call you."

That amped up my pulse a couple of notches, but Ansel's tone told me not to waste time asking questions. I led Festus down the walkway to the street.

I fidgeted with his leash as I paced back and forth across the driveway while Festus lay on the lush lawn a few feet away, never taking his eyes off me. *What the fuck is wrong now?* I needed to be inside looking for Roslynn Hunter, not cooling my heels waiting for the other shoe to drop in the devolving state of my personal security. Ten minutes later, Ansel opened the front door and waved us inside. "I checked the house. Nothing."

Festus still didn't want to come in but eventually acquiesced when I lured him with a treat. I slipped out of my suit and into some shorts, then Ansel and I whipped up some spaghetti and covered it with meat sauce I found in the freezer. Festus paced the floor and finally sat in the door to the living room and stared at me while we ate at the bar in the kitchen. After dinner, Ansel flopped down on the sofa, picked up the remote, and started channel surfing. I stuck the dishes in the dishwasher and decided to head upstairs to the office to look for Roslynn. As I crossed the kitchen to cut through the living room, Festus pushed ahead, almost tripping me. When I tried to edge past him, he turned on me, growling and snarling. He advanced on me, forcing me back into the kitchen.

Ansel shot off the couch. Dread welled up inside me. I stumbled back into the counter, and Festus assumed his position in the doorway to the living room, barking. Ansel pulled his gun and scanned for threats.

Then I saw it.

A rattlesnake slithered out from under the sofa and coiled, ready to strike. It was four feet long, and an awful brown and white diamond pattern covered its rubbery skin. Moments later, an even bigger one appeared from underneath one of the chairs and raised its rattler. The sound sent a lightning bolt of terror through me. I screamed for Festus, and he bounded toward me. Ansel must have spotted the snakes a second after I did and shouted, "Get out! Cut through the garage!"

I called Festus and turned to run as another snake came out from under the refrigerator and slithered toward me.

Ansel yelled, "Get on the island!" as he jumped up onto the coffee table.

I lifted my hips onto the marble, jerked my legs up, and got up on my hands and knees. Festus, still weak from the poisoning, barely managed to scramble up alongside me just as the snake coiled to strike. I heard another rattle and watched in horror as a fourth snake emerged from under the stove. The rattler closest to the sofa hissed and prepared to strike. Ansel fired. The snake's head disappeared in a cloud of blood, and its body danced across the marble floor as the bullet ricocheted off the stone fireplace and zipped across the room, lodging in one of the black leather chairs. Ansel fired again, and the first snake we'd seen joined its comrade in a headless tarantella as the bullet disappeared into the white plaster wall. Ansel jumped off the coffee table, ran through the patio door, tucked the gun in his shoulder holster, and grabbed a hoe from a rack at the corner of the house. He raced into the kitchen and swung the implement in a deadly arc, cutting the snake closest to the island in two, severing it a few inches behind the head. He jumped up onto the island and leaped to the other end where the last snake lay beneath him coiled and hissing on the tile floor. Kneeling on the island, he struck the snake with the hoe then climbed off the counter and hacked the rattler with the blade until it quit moving.

Motioning for me to stay put, he threw the kitchen door open and hit the button for the garage door. As it clattered overhead in its tracks, he yelled, "You and the dog get in the yard."

Festus and I ran through the garage into the driveway as Ansel came out and slammed the kitchen door behind him then squatted down and used his phone's flashlight to check under the SUV. He threw open the doors to the Genesis and checked under all the seats and the cargo and engine compartments. Apparently satisfied it was clear, he rocketed the GV backward out of the garage, tires squealing, fishtailed the car up to where Festus and I were standing, and yelled out the window, "Get in."

Chapter 46

Thursday, September 30, 1:00 p.m.

After extensive discussion, Addison, Justis, Robbie, Ansel, and I had finally agreed that, now that the lake house had apparently been compromised, hiding out at the Raines mansion wouldn't be much safer than going back to my apartment. Since Sean was taking a walk on the wild side with Dorinda, the loft was not a viable option. With few other choices presenting themselves, I called Carmine Pagano, who was more than willing to set me up in one of his "executive rentals"—for a hefty fee, of course. So, yet once more, I found myself and my dog sleeping in a strange bed flanked by a bodyguard.

What Carmine called an "executive rental" was really a bargain-basement tract home outfitted by a hotel-furniture liquidator. Four place settings of Corelle dishes, some cheap flatware, a few mismatched plastic glasses, three nonstick pans, and a spatula from Walmart were apparently Carmine's idea of a "fully equipped kitchen."

While far from the luxury of Sean and Robbie's lake house, the tacky rental beat the hell out of being blown to bits or killed by venomous reptiles. I stuffed a stack of paper napkins under one leg of the wobbly dining table, set my computer up, and got to work. The sooner I hauled Farragut's ox out of the ditch, the sooner my life would return to normal. I had only a few days to solve his title problem before the ranch sale circled the drain and his operation tumbled into bankruptcy. If that happened, we might be stuck with him for years.

I was deep in the search for Roslynn Hunter when my cell rang. I picked it up without taking my eyes off the city directory page I was searching for her name. Without preamble, Grover said, "Iris, I need you to come to my office...now."

Skipping the ritual smart-ass banter meant some seriously bad shit was cooking. "On my way. Leave word with the guard dogs behind the bulletproof glass."

"Will do."

Ansel was minding me while Robbie tended to a client. He cranked up the GV, and we drove downtown. When I showed my ID to the duty officer, he waved me straight back to a meeting room where I found Grover sitting at a conference table reading some printouts. I knocked on the door frame, and he waved me in.

"What's up?"

He indicated a seat. "How's Festus?"

"He's still weak, but he's improving. God love him, he was well enough to save my life last night." I told him about the snakes.

He stared at me. "Four rattlesnakes in that multimillion-dollar glass box of Sean's?"

I shook my head. "Eight, actually. We had some pest control guys go over there this morning. They found four more."

He leaned back in his chair. "I know you're not telling me the whole story about all this, Iris. But this business with the snakes means you're in serious trouble. You better get with your daddies and come clean with me before something happens we can't fix."

My silence and a barely perceptible nod was the loudest message I could shout at him. He tapped the desk with his hand. "Okay, then."

He leaned forward and picked up a folder off the table. "We got the state troopers to arrest the asshole in the award photo last night. Marvin led them right to him. We're holding him in the jail here. Prints come back to a former army ranger named Bart Harkenson. Got booted out of the army on a psych discharge. The troopers took him to the Harris County jail to meet our guys for the exchange. Before my officers got him in their patrol car, the esteemed firm of Jones & MacManara already had a full partner from their criminal section on the scene. Damn lawyer followed the patrol car here. My guys said the fucker was on their bumper every mile of the trip."

"So Allways is scared shitless Harkenson'll talk."

Grover leaned back. "Looks that way to us. I wondered about the Big Top outfit being behind it, but I don't think a guy with four burger joints has the juice to mobilize that kind of legal muscle. Had to be Allways."

"So what's going on with Harkenson now?"

He shrugged. "'Bout what you'd expect. Won't answer questions, blah blah. The DA formally charged him this morning, and the judge denied bail. So, for now, we've got him locked up, but the ADA says a guilty verdict is iffy if we can't fill in those holes in the case you and I talked about yesterday. Good news is the partial print on the cheese cup matched Harkenson, so that will go a long way toward quashing crap about the chain of evidence on the bag you pulled out of the dumpster."

"Thank God. Now there's a good chance the health department will let Quinten Farragut reopen his stores. That could save his business. I can't tell you how much I appreciate you cutting through the red tape on this."

"Hell, Iris, those bastards killed someone in this city. That makes it our problem." Grover drummed his fingers on the table and looked around the room, then made a show of checking his watch. "It's almost lunchtime. I'm starving, Iris. I'm going to get a taco. You want one?"

There were messages flashed on the Jumbotron at the Super Bowl that were less obvious than the one he'd just sent me. I nodded. "Sounds great."

We walked down the block to a food cart and bought a couple of chicken tacos. As we headed back toward the PD, Grover motioned to a bench in a small park across from his office. He took a bite of his taco and chewed way longer than he needed to. Looking straight ahead, he said, "Iris, what I'm about to tell you can never leave this bench. You can't tell Addison, Justis, Sean...not anybody. I could end up in jail if it ever comes out I leaked this."

A sick feeling in the pit of my stomach rose up into my throat like mercury on a scorching summer day. "You have my word."

We sat in silence as I waited for what he had to say. My heart hammered in my chest as I desperately tried to imagine what the hell was going on. After a couple of minutes, he swallowed the last bite of his taco, balled up the tin foil wrapper, and turned to look at me. "You know I've been running this task force since I'm still on medical restriction."

I nodded.

He looked off into the distance, staring at the looming white limestone building that housed the police department where he'd made his career. "A lot of intel comes through my office. Organized crime, drug cartels, public corruption..." He let the "public corruption" thing hang in the air like fog over the Golden Gate. He turned back to me and licked his lips. "I know you're seeing Finneas Rhodes."

My mind raced to figure out how that information came through Grover's shop. My mouth guppied open and closed as I fumbled for a response.

Grover took a wheezy breath and said, "Finneas Rhodes is under surveillance, and you're in some of the pictures. There were some shots of him carrying Festus out of your apartment, a couple of the two of you at the Kenton County livestock show."

I let out a sigh of relief. "Grover, he told me about all of this—about his wife, the crooked game warden, about him being investigated...all of it. Word must not have trickled down to your unit yet, but he was completely cleared. He's just waiting for his divorce to be final. It's hung up in some legal crap about her appeal."

Grover shook his head. "No, Iris. He *hasn't* been exonerated. He may think so. They may have told him that so he would let his guard down. But he's still in the crosshairs." He took a sip from his water bottle and turned back to me. "I'm telling you this because I watched you go through hell with Kerabos. You had just started to get back on your feet when Geare came along. I can't stand to see you get dragged down again by some asshole. Iris, trust me on this. Do not let this guy into your life."

The stabbing pain in my side felt like someone had jabbed me with a red-hot poker. I grabbed my left hand in my right to keep it from shaking as I set my jaw and steadied my breathing. It was happening again. Of all the men I could be attracted to, why did it have to be a married, crooked cop? What was wrong with me? When I found my voice, I said, "What should I do?"

He returned his gaze to the police headquarters. "Where are you with him now?"

I shifted on the bench to try to ease the pain in my side. "I talked to him yesterday. I told him no more dating until his divorce is final. I didn't want to get caught up in some domestic litigation drama. I said we could see what's what after the final decree is entered. But from what I gather, that won't be happening anytime soon."

Grover was quiet for a few long beats then said, "Good. The investigation'll probably be over within the month, and he'll either have been cleared or arrested by then. Just stick with where you're at. Casual conversation over the phone...I think that's fine. Just remember—somebody's probably listening. Don't make a stink, don't tell him to screw off. Just maintain the status quo. And, for godsakes, Iris, under no conditions are you to ask him about this. Do you understand?"

I nodded. "I understand."

He picked up his concentrator and slung the strap over his shoulder. "I've got to get back to work. You take care."

I said, "Thank you, Grover."

He nodded wordlessly and headed back to his office. I stood on Santa Rosa and watched him walk away. What the hell was wrong with me? Visions of my hooker birth mother dumping me at the Hampe Ewald flashed through my mind. Maybe I was damaged from the start...maybe all of this—Kerabos, Geare...now Finn Rhodes—had happened because I was inherently defective, genetically unable to have a normal, healthy relationship with a man. Maybe that was what had finally ruined my relationship with Sean. Was I no better than the woman who had abandoned me?

I sat on the bench while the bottom dropped out of my life.

Chapter 47

Thursday, September 30, 2:00 p.m.

Ansel pulled up and tapped the horn. I took a deep breath and forced a façade of normalcy as I climbed into the GV. After a couple of minutes, he said, "You okay? You want me to call Robbie?"

I shook my head and prayed my voice didn't sound as quivery as it felt. I struggled to control the shaking in my left hand. "I'm fine. Grover just wanted to tell me about them arresting the guy from Allways."

He nodded and kept his eyes on the road. When we got to the house, I took Festus outside then went to work at the dining table, but images of Geare and Kerabos swam through my head along with the imaginings of my birth mother and flashes of my experiences with Finn Rhodes. My attraction to him felt like the symptom of a fatal disease—a psychic cancer returning after the delusion of a momentary remission. A tremor was spreading through my world like an earthquake in the middle of the sea, stirring up a seemingly innocuous wave that builds on itself as it crosses thousands of miles of ocean.

Trouble in our relationship or not, I needed Sean. I dialed. The call rang twice before his voice mail kicked in. I stared at the phone. Sean

Galen had just declined my call. I could feel the tsunami approaching the shoreline of my mind.

When I heard Ansel get in the shower, I scribbled a note, grabbed the keys off the counter, and left through the front door.

I turned off my phone, pointed my car west, and headed to hell.

As the beautiful Texas Hill Country gave way to the stark desert of West Texas, I remembered the night Daniel Kerabos had driven me down this road. I had only sat next to him at jury duty for a few hours. The judge had released me early because I knew one of the lawyers in the case. I never even remembered hearing his name, but he'd learned mine from the roll call and had developed a bizarre erotomaniacal obsession with me that had climaxed after four months of stalking, when he'd drugged me, tied me up, and thrown me in the back of his Chrysler minivan. Groggy and nauseous from the chloroform, I drifted in and out of consciousness as we drove west.

When we finally stopped, it must have been late in the night. I had no idea where we were. The moon was full, and the inky black sky was punctuated with a million shimmering stars. A cold wind howled across the desert as Kerabos grabbed a fistful of my hair and dragged me out of the van. He yanked my head back then held a knife to my throat and frog-marched me into his cabin.

When the creaky door slammed and the lock snapped shut that night, I imagined I might die there. But I had no inkling of the horrors that awaited me in the coming days.

I signaled to exit onto a remote farm-to-market road between Fort Stockton and Pecos. Twenty-seven miles north of Fort Stockton, I cut down an unpaved road and drove until I spotted the clearing. My heart pounded when I saw it, and I staunched a searing wave of nausea. This was only the second time I'd been back to the place since my escape. I parked the car and got out. The sun was setting, turning the clouds orange like burning coals. The scorched earth where the cabin had burned was all that remained of Kerabos's house of horrors.

I sat down on the ground and watched the sun set across the clearing. The second day in the cabin, when Kerabos was outside getting firewood, I'd managed to slide a broken bottle I'd spotted under the stove forward to where it was still not visible but was within my reach.

I became obsessed with the bottle. I imagined a million ways it could save me, but I knew they were all sheer fantasy. On the third night of my captivity, Kerabos announced he was going to kill me at sunrise. In the silvery moonlight seeping through the tattered curtains of the cabin, I saw him gathering his things and wiping down the surfaces for fingerprints. I was starving and dehydrated and broken. Unable to withstand another day of the assaults, in some perverse way, I felt relieved. A calm washed over me as I relinquished my struggle to survive.

Then, in my peripheral vision, I caught a glimpse of the bottle. In that moment, I learned the strength that comes from total surrender. I'd made my peace with dying—but the prospect that I could use the bottle to take him with me gave me purpose.

I zipped up my windbreaker as I walked through the clearing to the spot where the mattress had been. Tears streamed silently down my face as, in my mind's eye, I saw myself seducing him, begging him to unchain my hands...offering him anything he wanted. Unable to suppress his insatiable appetite for sexual violence, he said he would do it...so he could slit my throat and feel me die while he was inside me. I gave over to his every sick desire until he closed his eyes in twisted ecstasy.

Then I shoved the broken bottle into his kidney. I felt the pointed shard of glass slice through the skin and muscle. As he screamed and writhed, I jammed the glass deeper into his body. Blood poured out of the wound, saturating the mattress and spraying all over me. I ran for my life. Adrenaline was driving a will to survive I had never imagined possible.

I raced out of the cabin and into the night, naked except for a filthy white T-shirt. The rocks on the caliche road were cutting my feet, and the freezing air was making me shiver so hard I could barely stay upright. I was so weak, I stumbled every few steps, but I ran on through the moonlit darkness. With no clue where to go, some unseen force drove me onward. I feared I was hallucinating when a glowing dust cloud in the distance seemed to be billowing in my direction. Then, the light shone brighter, and a black Escalade skidded to a stop next to me. Sean poured out the door and ran to me, scooped me up in his arms, and carried me to the warm safety of the truck.

During the investigation, we learned Kerabos had been squatting in the cabin, a distant relative of the old West Texas hermit who'd owned it and died years before. Unbeknownst to me, after Kerabos went to prison, Sean found the people who actually owned it and bought the cabin and the land it sat on from them.

One bright, sunny day that next June, he picked me up at work and said he was taking me on a trip. To my horror, he drove me to the cabin. It looked the same—except a wide swath of the brush and mesquite around it had been cleared, leaving the shack sitting on a plateau of naked limestone.

Shaking and crying, I couldn't imagine why Sean would have brought me to this terrible place, but I trusted him with every fiber of my being.

He pulled two large red gas cans out of the back of the truck and handed one to me. Together, we doused every inch of the place in gasoline. He took my hand and led me back to the Escalade where he lit a road flare. He passed it to me wordlessly, and I hurled it through the open front door and watched as the cabin exploded into an orange ball of fire.

We stood in silence as the flames devoured the place where I had met the devil.

And now, over two years later, I was back there. I noticed shoots of green emerging from a scorched oak stump near where the cabin had once stood, and I thought about how it wasn't really a terrible place anymore. It was just a charred spot in the desert of West Texas, coming back to life in a new incarnation. The cabin was long gone, and Kerabos was rotting in solitary confinement five hundred miles away.

It was getting dark when it hit me that I wasn't afraid anymore. The crying stopped. I climbed back into the GV and turned on the heater. I stared out the windshield and wondered if Kerabos had fixated on me instead of any other woman in the world because of some silent signal I transmitted like a psychic dog whistle. Like a homing beacon for disturbed, evil men looking for someone to abuse. It was a matter I'd sort out with Madelyn, with my new friends in the support group...somehow.

But that was for later. Here, Sean had saved me. Through a complex series of computer hacks that could have landed him in prison for years, Sean had found me. He'd saved me that night, and he'd helped heal me the day we burned the cabin to the ground... Just like he had been there for me every day since I was six years old.

He was in the worst trouble of his life now. It was time for me to step up, no matter how hard he was to love right now or how little he wanted my help.

I put the GV in gear and headed home, leaving the burned-out cabin behind in the dark. As I pulled onto the farm-to-market road, I noticed Robbie was parked there in his Hellcat and silently fell in behind me.

Chapter 48

Friday, October 1, 1:30 a.m.

Robbie was still on my tail when I parked the GV in the garage of the rental. Inside, he pulled a beer out of the refrigerator and leaned on the counter. "You want to talk about it?"

I poured myself a glass of wine. "I had to go there. I can't describe it... It was like one of those postapocalyptic movies where the survivors just *know* they have to gather at some particular place to begin their new society. I had to do it alone."

Robbie nodded. "Fair enough. You okay?"

"Yeah. I'm okay." I took a small chunk of Muenster cheese out of the refrigerator and pulled the cutting board out of the rack. "How'd you find me?"

Robbie sat on a stool. "Ansel called me as soon as he found your note. He'd tied the GPS into my phone, so I could be backup in case both of you got swept up by the bad guys. Standard procedure during protection gigs."

I finished slicing the cheese and turned the cutting board to share with Robbie. "So where's Ansel now?"

He took a slice of the Muenster. "I told him I'd handle things here until tomorrow. He's at the symphony."

"I hope you didn't give him a ration of shit for letting me get away."

He took a pull off the beer and gave me his crooked smile. "*Get away?* Ansel was two cars behind you by the time you got on the Loop. He just didn't make it obvious because he knew you didn't want a chaperone. I took over at 1604."

Robbie headed to the sofa, and Festus followed me into my room. He crawled onto the bed and snuggled up beside me, resting his giant head on my chest, and I fell asleep stroking his muzzle, comforted by the warmth of his breath on my hand.

I slept through the night without a single dream for the first time since Kerabos showed up at my door. I got up with the sun and dressed, then scoured my email for any hint of a response from Dorinda's doctor. If I didn't hear something today, I would use the cell number for the psychiatrist I'd pulled off AccuData. I decided to give him until lunch. Munching on a bagel and sipping coffee, I watched with great joy as Festus romped in the backyard with a playfulness I hadn't seen since the poisoning.

I heard the front door lock grinding, and Robbie came into the kitchen and said, "You're up bright and early."

I sipped my coffee. "Don't you ever sleep?"

He put slices of wheat bread in the toaster. "I'll sleep when I'm dead. You hear from the shrink about Dorinda?"

"Not yet." I told him about my plan.

He offered me the toast. I shook my head. "Already ate."

He dug some strawberry jelly out of the refrigerator and spread it on the bread. "What's on the agenda for today?"

I refilled my cup and headed to the dining room table. "Finding Rose Morgan...come hell or high water."

Armed with her new name and those of her adoptive parents, I tracked the family to Lubbock. I found a 1972 newspaper article in the *Lubbock Morning Tribune*. "Local Girl Orphaned in Vacation Accident." The article described how the Hunter family was vacationing at Mount Rushmore when an eighteen-wheeler lost control and ran head-on into their Chevrolet Caprice on the outskirts of Rapid City. The obituaries for Roslynn Hunter's adoptive parents described them both as only children whose parents predeceased them. In a follow-up piece in the Rapid City paper under the headline "Orphaned Girl Begins New Life in Deadwood," I learned that, without family to take her in, the Division of Child Protection Services had placed the twice-orphaned girl with a Benedictine order of nuns in the town of Deadwood after the sisters there offered her a spot in their convent school.

I searched Google for the order and found a number. I dialed, and, after digging through a couple of layers of Benedictine bureaucracy, a woman who introduced herself as Sister Agnes came on the line. I told her what I needed.

"We all loved Sister Emily... Her religious name was Sister Jerome Emiliani after the patron saint of orphans. She was preparing to take her final vows in 1980 when she left the order. I have no idea how to reach her."

"I know that was decades ago, but do you have any idea where she went when she left?"

"I'm sorry. It was all very sudden. I was in her novitiate class, but the older sisters didn't tell us anything about it, and we didn't dare ask. However, I could pull the file if you'd like."

I drummed my fingers and tapped my heel while I waited on hold for what seemed like a couple of years, listening as Bach's Toccata and Fugue in D Minor was occasionally interrupted with messages about when the food pantry would be open. Fifteen minutes later, Sister Agnes came back on the line.

"Ms. Raines, I'm going to need to verify your credentials and call you back on a published number. Would that be all right?"

I forced myself to hide my impatience. Her request was completely reasonable—and it meant she had found something. "Certainly, Sister." I rattled off my PI license number and instructions for verifying it online with the Department of Public Safety. I invited her to refer to the cell number listed on my registration.

She said, "Thank you. I'll call you back in a few minutes."

I was sensing a crack in the brick wall I'd been slamming my head into since this search had started. Fourteen more torturous minutes passed before my cell rang.

"I'm sorry, Ms. Raines, but I needed to be certain who I was talking to. With your permission, I'd like to place you on speakerphone so Sister Frances can join our conversation. She is one of the most senior members of our community."

"Certainly." I waited...and waited.

Finally, Sister Agnes said, "Sister Emily was orphaned when her birth parents gave her up for adoption..."

I said, "Yes, ma'am. In Texas, in the absence of a will, children placed up for adoption still inherit from their biological parents. It is Sister

Emily's birth mother, Annabelle Morgan, who holds record title to the tract of land I'm working on."

Sister Frances said, "I see. Are you aware of Sister Emily's...personal situation?"

"I'm sorry. I'm not sure what you mean?"

Sister Frances paused as if choosing her words, then said, "Well, Sister Emily had some sort of cognitive challenge."

Inez had mentioned something... I flipped through my notes. "I spoke with a neighbor who lived next door to her birth parents. The neighbor said she had considerable difficulty recognizing faces."

Sister Agnes said, "Yes. It was very difficult for her in the convent... We all wore habits back then. So, while she was with us, we wore name tags. Her file contains no specific diagnosis of her disorder, but I believe the condition is now recognized as face blindness. Her case appeared to us to be absolute."

"Do you see any clues in the file about where she might have gone when she left your order?"

Sister Agnes said, "Since she had not taken her permanent vows yet, she could leave the order without dispensation from a bishop. So the paperwork detailing her situation was not required. Reading between the lines, I gather the elder sisters felt a man might have been involved."

Sister Frances cleared her throat and said, "Ms. Raines, shortly before Sister Emily left the order, a private investigator called here looking for her. He refused to say who had hired him, but he knew about her adoptive parents dying and mentioned information about her birth family. The Mother Superior at that time refused to even acknowledge Sister Emily was part of our order. But Sister Emily was an adult, and the Mother Superior felt it was her right to know someone was looking for her. I had been one of her teachers at the convent school, and we had developed a certain relationship. Sister Emily came to me. She was terrified the man might be working for someone in her biological family. She begged Reverend Mother not to disclose to him she was here. Of course, Reverend Mother complied." She cleared her throat again. "None of us ever knew the details, but we gathered something...awful...had happened to her before her birth parents gave her away."

I knew I was inches away from breaking through. "Is there any reference to this private investigator's name?"

Sister Frances said, "There is a pink message slip for the Mother Superior I found in the file. A Mr. Walter Kernan called for her at 2:35 p.m. on July 8, 1980. But we can't be certain he was the private investigator." She rattled off his callback number starting with an 817 area code. I had a death grip on the phone. After the hours I'd spent in the Wichita Falls city directories, I knew 817 had been the area code for Wichita Falls before the region split in 1997.

I thanked the sisters and hung up then logged on to the Department of Public Safety site for the Private Security Bureau and searched for Walter Kernan. Nothing. I pounded the keys and stifled my impatience as I called up my Ancestry account and searched his name. Walter Kernan had died in a car accident a week after he'd contacted the convent looking for Rose Morgan. The obit listed a surviving wife. AccuData spat out a phone number in San Marcos, and I dialed.

A woman with a strong North Texas accent answered. I introduced myself and told her why I was calling and asked her if by any chance she knew what had happened to her husband's files.

She laughed. "Well, honey, I know exactly what happened to them. Damn things are in my attic. I moved down here from Wichita a month after Walter died. With four little kids, I had to get a job—fast. My brother was a professor at the university here, and he got me a job as a secretary in his department. I was so upset about what had happened, I couldn't bring myself to throw any of Walter's stuff away, so I just brought it along with everything else. The whole kit and caboodle has been in the attic all these years. I kept swearing I'd clean it out...but I just never got around to it. Last year, I broke my hip. Now, I'm screwed. Can't get up the ladder."

While I couldn't imagine how, I knew in my investigative soul that Walter Kernan's file was going to lead me to Rose Morgan. The thrill I felt at the prospect of breaking the case—and being rid of Quinten Farragut—was making my hands sweat. "Ma'am, could those records possibly include a file for a case he worked on in July of 1980 right before he died?"

"Well, probably so. Walter was strict about keeping up his files. Whatever he had when he died, it's in my attic." She was quiet for a few seconds. "I've got a proposition for you, Ms. Raines. I'll let you look for that file if you'll help me get rid of all those records."

I would have painted her house if she'd asked me to. "Ms. Kernan, you've got yourself a deal."

Chapter 49

Friday, October 1, 11:00 a.m.

An hour later, Robbie and I pulled the GV80 into the grass and gravel driveway of a small white Craftsman in the historic district of San Marcos. The yard needed a good weeding, and the paint job was way past its stale date. A seventyish woman in lavender stretch slacks with a matching pullover top sat in a worn wicker chair on the porch, drinking iced tea out of a jelly glass.

We walked up the peeling wooden steps. "Mrs. Kernan?"

She leaned on an aluminum quad cane for balance as she hoisted herself off of the faded floral cushion. "Well, didn't you just get up here in a hurry?" I introduced Robbie, and she motioned for us to follow as she pulled the screen door open. "The window unit gave up the ghost last month. I spend most of my time out here. Damn fans in the house just don't cut it."

She showed us through a still, hot living room with worn, circa-1950s, clay-colored loop carpet and mismatched furniture stacked high with old magazines and newspapers and led us down a narrow hallway where she stopped and pointed a boney finger at the attic door. "It's all up there."

The attic was going to be an oven. Robbie pulled the rope that dangled from the hatch, and I climbed far enough up the rickety ladder to stick my head into the dusty space. Through a wave of suffocating heat, I shone my flashlight on three rows of torn and water-stained boxes bulging with files. They were piled three-deep, and the dust-covered stacks were all drooping and listing. But each box was labeled with dates in black marker.

Robbie followed me as I climbed the rest of the way up into the sweltering space. Crawling on all fours along roof trusses, we each took a row. Sweat poured down my face, and my blouse clung to my back as I lifted the warped cardboard lid and shone the flashlight on the contents of a box labeled May thru July 1980. Using my free hand, I inched through the tabs on the moldy manila folders. The stench of mildew and dust made me sneeze. But halfway through the box, I hit paydirt. In blue ballpoint, the tab read Case #80-325 Subject: Morgan, Rose. I dug through the other files in the box, but nothing looked promising. I called to Robbie. "I found it. You see anything interesting?"

"Nothing. Everything in this row is from the '70s."

I tucked the file into the waistband of my skirt and crawled back to the attic hatch. We climbed down the ladder and followed Mrs. Kernan back out onto the porch.

Once in the fresh air, I sat on a broken-down wicker loveseat and opened the file. It contained about twenty pages of notes, pictures, newspaper articles, and other research. I found Walter Kernan's intake sheet for the case. The client was a man named Jack Smith who claimed he was looking for his distant cousin, Rose Belle Morgan, in a last-ditch effort to locate a possible kidney donor for his ailing child. The file clearly identified Rose Belle Morgan and listed her biological parents as

Harrison and Annabelle Morgan. *Who the hell is the guy calling himself Jack Smith?*

I closed the file and looked up. "Mrs. Kernan, this is the file I need. Do you mind if I take it with me?"

She frowned. "What about our deal? I was planning on your taking a lot more than one damn folder."

I put the file in my briefcase. "I haven't forgotten." I brushed dust from my suit. "I didn't come dressed for attic cleaning today. And it's going to take a truck to haul all those boxes off. How about I send one of those document-shredding companies over here tomorrow to pull all of 'em down and destroy the whole lot?"

She smiled. "Now you're talkin'."

Chapter 50

Friday, October 1, 1:00 p.m.

As anxious as I was to identify "Jack Smith" and discover how he tied into the layers of secrets and dysfunction that plagued the Morgan family, I remembered my vow to call Dorinda's psychiatrist. While Robbie steered through the historic streets of old San Marcos, I spoofed a number from the hospital's area code and prayed the doctor would pick up. My celestial pleas were answered with a voice mail greeting asking me to leave a number. I hung up. Robbie turned to me with a raised brow. I shook my head. "I'll keep trying."

He merged onto 35 South and headed us back to San Antonio while I settled in with Kernan's file.

Back at the rental, I spent the rest of the day trying to figure out who Jack Smith was. Four hours later, I cashed in my chips and took Festus outside. It was the first day since the poisoning he had shown any interest in actually playing with his toys. In the weedy backyard, we pulled each other with his tuggy rope, and I tossed his ball a few times before he tired and moseyed back inside. I served up his prescription food, stuck a frozen lasagna in the oven, and took a shower.

After dinner, Festus and I plopped down on the rough plaid sofa and turned on a rerun of *No Way Out* while Robbie worked on his laptop at the fake oak dining table. Just as Kevin Costner was getting hot and heavy with Sean Young, my cell phone rang. My heart jittered when I saw the caller ID. Finneas Rhodes. Remembering Grover's admonition not to make waves, I squelched the inclination to decline the call, took a deep breath, and picked up the phone.

"Hey, stranger. I just wanted to see how you're doing." The deep, calming tone of his voice was just as attractive to me as it had been the first time I heard it. I hated the part of me that longed for the fun we'd had at the livestock show when he won me the stuffed kangaroo. I could still feel the strength of his arms around me as we two-stepped at the Silver Saddle. I thought of the sensation of my hand in his walking through the caverns on our date. But visions of Geare flashed through my mind, and the sledgehammer of reality smashed any more romantic fantasies I might have had about Finn. I forced myself to keep an even keel.

"I'm fine now. I've put a pretty good dent in the local Tylenol supply, but my nose is almost a normal size again, and you can hardly see my black eyes."

He laughed. "I've had Bella in town for a training session all day. We're down on the South Side. I thought you might like some Chris Madrid's."

I forced a casual tone. "That sounds great, and I appreciate the offer, but I've already eaten. I've got an early meeting in the morning, so Festus and I are packing it in early tonight."

His voice was tinged with rejection. "I understand."

Grover's warning to *Just maintain the status quo* echoed in my head and collided with a vision of a recording of this call being played in court. I said, "It's not that I don't want to have dinner with you. But I'm going to have to stick to my guns. I can't see you as long as you're legally married."

He cleared his throat. "Well, speaking of... The lawyers have worked out a truce. Her side has agreed to the divorce. We have a court date later this month to finalize everything."

"Congratulations."

He was quiet for a couple of moments. "I'd like to call you after that. Would that be okay?"

I hoped he couldn't hear that my mouth was as dry as the Bonneville Salt Flats. I licked my lips. "I'd like that—as long as you bring a note from the judge."

He sounded relieved. "It's a deal. I'll let you go, but before we hang up...how's Festus?"

I gave him a brief rundown, thanked him again for his help that night, and hung up.

I let out a deep, frustrated sigh and stroked Festus's silky head. He looked up at me with his jowly, freckled Saint Bernard face. I ran my fingers through his thick coat and said, "Why can't I find a human guy who's as good as you?"

I jabbed the remote to unmute the TV and returned to *No Way Out*—a movie about just one more hot guy who turns out to be a no-good, traitorous bastard.

Chapter 51

Tuesday, October 5, 7:00 p.m.

Sitting at the rickety dining table in the rental, I was paddling as hard as I could through the murky waters of the Annabelle Case mystery, having gotten exactly nowhere in four days, when Addison called. "Iris, you and Robbie should come over to the Cigar Club. We're celebrating."

Early that morning, Addison and Justis had led our eclectic duo of miscreants to the US attorney's office. Their pitch was a crazy quilt of evidence they hoped would free Darnell Washington Carter and Quinten Farragut of impending federal doom. I shut the lid on my laptop. "We're on our way."

The Cigar Club is nestled into the basement of Rick's. It's done up with coffered ceilings and mahogany paneling and oriental rugs dotted with oxblood wingback chairs and heavy brocade sofas. The walls are decorated with dark-toned hunting oils in ornate, gilded frames. Behind the bar, mahogany lockers hold the favored whiskey and cigars of each of the members who possess a coveted brass key to the heavy basement door of the club.

Robbie parked the Hellcat near the back door of Rick's, and we walked down the stairs. The speakeasy-style slider opened, and the doorman confirmed my identity and let us in.

My fathers were sitting at a corner table with Darnell and Quinten Farragut. Farragut's color had gone from ashen gray back to florid red, and the bags under his eyes were receding. I looked at Darnell. "The cleaners did a good job with your Hugo Boss."

He laughed and puffed on his cigar. "Glad you approve."

The sweet aroma of cigar smoke hung in the air as I walked over to my fathers' locker and poured three fingers of Macallan into two of the cut-crystal lowball glasses lined up on the bar. I carried our drinks back to the table, set one in front of Robbie, and sat down. "So tell us all about it."

Addison said, "Turns out the former army ranger, Bart Harkenson, fired the mouthpiece Allways sent to shut him up and took a federal defender who got him a deal. He's fingering Allways for all manner of crooked shit including hiring him to run the poisoning and blackmail schemes. In an effort to save those bazillion dollars in government contracts, Allways is flipping on Big Top like a pancake in a Teflon pan."

"Rats leaving the ship..." I said.

Addison sucked on a piece of ice from his drink. "Mysteriously, the assistant US attorney has received an anonymous tip directed specifically to him through the federal crime tip line pointing their cyberintelligence folks to certain files on Big Top's servers containing a series of coded messages that show Big Top in possession of instructions on how to culture *B. cereus* and use it as a poison."

I swallowed hard. When I opened my mouth, Justis held up his hand. "Don't want to know. Anyway, since the Big Top CEO was the one who hired Allways, I expect he will be charged with some variation of murder-for-hire tomorrow. Big Top is going to be folding their tent in no time."

"That's great."

Darnell sipped his drink. "Incidentally, I was fortunate enough recently to hear some reliable gossip regarding the location of your Mr. Ramirez who set the bomb at the grain elevator. And it seems some of my colleagues finally recognized the gentlemen in your surveillance photos down at the ranch and just happened to know their whereabouts, so we passed that information along to the good folks at the USA's office." He took a drag off the cigar and exhaled through his nose. "Unofficially, of course."

Addison adjusted his crystal glass on the cocktail napkin. "Robbie, you and Sean really helped us out with the Allways angle. We called Sean to ask him to join us here, but we didn't get an answer. I left a message. And we sure owe you one for keeping such a close watch on Iris during all of this. We know you're busy, and we appreciate you making Iris a priority."

Robbie said, "Speaking of...when do we think Iris will be safe to go back home?"

Justis looked at his watch and said, "Starting about an hour ago, using the names and IDs Darnell helped us with, Grover's multijurisdictional task force is out rounding up the drug dealers who got into it with Iris down on the ranch. They picked up Ramirez a few minutes ago."

"I can't believe the government is moving so fast," I said.

Addison smirked. "Yeah...you and me both. I think what we gave them today just pushed them over to go-mode on what must have already been an ongoing investigation."

I smacked the table. "The feds that were at the Wind Rose the night of the shootout..."

Addison nodded. "They already had a ball in play when it came to the drug dealers. We just choreographed the finale for them."

Darnell smiled a Cheshire cat grin. "Yeah...come to think of it...maybe that's how it went. How 'bout that?"

Justis glared at Darnell, who avoided his gaze by turning to me. "Those gentlemen downtown were so grateful for my help, they said they'd drop those spurious RICO charges they've been tormenting me with if I promised to be a good boy." The light glinted off of the gold cap on his front tooth as he smiled. "I told them I'm always good."

Justis refilled his glass and sat back down. "And Quinten is free of any charges relating to the drug sting."

Farragut took a drag off his Cohiba. "Addison called that witch at County Health and leaned on her to cut through all the red tape and get my stores open. Starting tomorrow morning, I'm back in business."

Darnell finished his cigar and took the last sip of his Scotch. "Gentlemen, it's been grand, but I have to go to work." He shook hands all around and left.

When I picked up my purse, Addison gave me a look and a minute head shake. I dropped my purse in Darnell's empty chair, and we all sat back down.

Addison cleared his throat. "While today was definitely a win, we aren't out of the woods yet."

Farragut shambled to the bar, refilled his glass, and settled back into his chair. "I'm still in bad shape, cash-flow-wise. The clock on that temporary restraining order holding those bloodsuckers from First National off my Fort Worth stores is ticking down like the timer on a bomb. The buyer on the Wind Rose sale is trying to get out of the deal because of the fire damage..."

Addison said, "We're holding that deal together for now. But we can't miss the contract closing date of October 14. Where are you on finding the Morgan heirs?"

I told them about Roslynn Hunter and the convent and Walter Kernan.

Farragut's jowly face was almost as sad and droopy as Festus's. "Iris, without the cash from that sale, I can't save the Fort Worth stores. That foreclosure happens, the rest of my financing will domino down, and I'll be screwed for good."

I took a deep breath. "I'm on it."

Farragut finished off the Scotch and looked into the empty glass. "I'm hanging by a thread here, Iris."

Little did I know—so was I.

Chapter 52

Wednesday, October 6, 8:00 a.m.

It was great to be back in my regular office, not to mention a big relief to not be looking over my shoulder every second to see if a bunch of narco-terrorists were coming to shorten my lifespan. I made my daily call to the prison shrink again. Still voice mail. I had been spoofing different numbers for the caller ID and hanging up when he didn't answer. I figured if he didn't reply to my email, he was unlikely to return my call. But this was my last-ditch effort with Dr. Robinson. I broke down and left a message. If I didn't hear back from him today, I'd drill through AccuData and find a cell number for the hospital administrator and use it to go over the yahoo's head. Meanwhile, I checked my email one more time, just to be sure he hadn't responded. Zippo from the shrink, but I did have a message from Carmine Pagano.

I had texted him after I left the Cigar Club the night before and told him I would be vacating the executive rental later that day. He had wasted no time sending over paperwork and the bill. I studied the invoice. Because Carmine was Carmine and had been known to cut a corner or two on financial matters, I pulled up my calendar to check the specific date I had moved into his dumpy rental. Scrolling through the entries, I could feel the wheels in my brain begin to turn. Then alarm bells were sounding in my subconscious. As I swiped through the days, my fingers were prickling like they do when I'm breaking a case.

The brake tampering and the poison gas and the snakes weren't about the drug cartel. They were about the Annabelle Morgan case.

I spun my chair back to the keyboard and tore into the databases.

I had to find Roslynn Hunter.

Chapter 53

Friday, October 8, 3:00 p.m.

After two more days of fruitless searching, I called Cheralyn to brainstorm every aspect of the Roslynn Hunter data we had amassed. I hoped fresh eyes could help me figure out where in the world the woman might have gone after she left the convent. When my cell rang with a blocked number, I told Cheralyn I'd call her back and picked up the phone. "Iris Raines."

"Ms. Raines, this is Dr. Edward Robinson."

My heart did a little staccato rumba. "Thank you for calling me back."

He cleared his throat. "I am making this call to warn you of a potential threat posed by an individual under the supervision of the Federal Bureau of Prisons." He sounded like he was reading from a script. "We convened the committee that reviews information such as yours regarding patients on conditional release. The committee conducted its own investigation and determined Dorinda Crandall should be returned to this facility for further evaluation and treatment. We scheduled a hearing with the supervising judge and advised the patient's attorney of the proceedings. The hearing was held first thing this morning, and the patient's attorney appeared and notified the court he could not reach his client."

"I'm sure she's here in San Antonio."

"We have already notified the marshals in the San Antonio office to pick her up based on a court order entered two hours ago."

"I appreciate your efforts."

He cleared his throat again. "During the hearing, the patient's attorney argued the photographs were contrived—Photoshopped—for the purpose of removing a woman against whom you have a personal grudge and whom you view as a rival."

"Dr.—"

He cut me off. "Ms. Raines, your name did not appear on any documents involved in the hearing nor did we use any of the photographs you submitted. We contacted security at the casino in question, and they provided us with multiple images of Ms. Crandall from their in-house security cameras. However, the defense attorney's arguments this morning imply that, contrary to his statements, he has been in communication with his client and that she is aware you made this complaint against her. In our judgment, Ms. Crandall poses a credible threat to your safety, and we have an obligation to notify you of such."

Despite the trembling fear that was coursing through me, I caught a ride on a freight train of rage that kept my voice clear and steady. "Thank you for your call. I will take immediate steps to improve my security. I trust you will keep me advised of any developments."

He cleared his throat one more time. "As the law requires." And the line went dead.

I took my Glock out of my desk drawer, slung the shoulder holster over my arm, and went to Addison's office to advise him of a potential threat to the firm as long as I was there. Just as I got back to my desk, my cell pounded out the "Eye of the Tiger" refrain. I snatched up the phone. Before I could say anything, Robbie said, "He knows."

I locked the door. "He knows what?"

"He knows we called the feds about Dorinda."

I slumped down in my chair. "I just talked to the prison psychiatrist." I told him about my conversation with Dr. Robinson.

Robbie said, "So word went from the hospital to the court to the attorney to Dorinda to Sean."

"So now, he's abetting a federal fugitive."

"And he's white-hot mad." Robbie's voice was tight, and he was talking fast. "About an hour ago, I stopped by the loft to pick up some things... He went postal. We had a huge blowup, and he stormed out. He's on his way to your office now."

Just then, Francine buzzed. "Iris, Mr. Galen is on his way back... I think something's wrong..."

My door shook on its hinges as Sean pounded on it and yelled, "Open up, Iris."

I said to Robbie, "He's here. I'll call you back."

I opened the door, and Sean barged right past me. "Who the fuck do you think you are?"

I stood gape-mouthed. I had no idea who this man was... It certainly wasn't the Sean Galen I'd known all my life. "Sean, please calm down."

He looked at me. His eyes were slits, and an artery was pulsing in his neck. His voice was eerily quiet. "I never ask you for a single thing. I bend over backward to help you with your cases, help you keep your shit together, help you with everything. And the one fucking time I ask you for something—that you trust me on this one issue—you can't do it. Instead, you involve a bunch of feds? Are you out of your mind?"

I could have sworn my heart was breaking. A terrible pain ripped through my gut and up to my throat. I swallowed hard and took two deep breaths. I was afraid of Sean Galen. I found my voice and managed to say, "Sean, the gambling is out of control. If you don't get help now, it's going to take everything you have and ruin you." I fought to calm the quiver in my voice. "Please don't let this happen. I need you. You're my family. I love you."

Suddenly, it was like all the wind went out of his sails. He stumbled back, collapsed into one of my client chairs, and buried his face in his hands. "Iris, I'm so sorry..." He rubbed his eyes and looked up at me. "I've been in a bad place. I can't believe I talked to you like that. I'm so sorry..." He pushed himself up out of the chair. "I'm asking you one more time—please leave this alone. I'll handle it." He kissed me on the forehead and walked out without looking back.

My knees felt like jelly, and I steadied myself against the desk. I made a quick call to Carmine. He agreed for me to return to El Dumpo Grande for a few more days. Then I dialed Robbie. Everyone around me was at risk.

Chapter 54

Saturday, October 9, 8:00 a.m.

I was eating a bagel and checking the morning news on my phone when a message from Sean dinged. *I'm sorry. I didn't mean any of it. I love you.* I stared at the screen. The recent events with Sean had shaken my reality, but I couldn't afford to get twisted off in that craziness.

I texted back, *I love you, too.* When no response was forthcoming, I was relieved. I was determined the passion play starring Sean and Dorinda wasn't going to tear up my morning.

Once satisfied I was safe, Robbie had left around midnight to take care of some business.

I topped off my mug and settled in at my dining table desk, firm in my commitment that today would be the day I would find the Morgan heirs. Before Sean's blowup the previous afternoon, I had come to a terrifying realization. All the bad shit that had been happening to me lately corresponded with times when I had discovered new information about Annabelle Morgan Case's family. The gas and fire at the cavern came right after Sol identified Luther Morgan as Lawton Meyer. The brakes on the Land Cruiser failed right after Robbie and I visited the

Meyer ranch in Gillespie County, and the snakes showed up in the lake house when we got home from seeing Inez Crain, the Morgans' neighbor from Wichita Falls. I had no idea who was behind it or what was driving it, but all taken together, it couldn't be a coincidence.

I took out Walter Kernan's file and read each page out loud, forcing myself to review every detail of its contents. About halfway through, I came to a pink message slip recording an incoming call from Jack Smith. The date was June 20, 1980. In neat handwriting, Smith's name was recorded above a phone number. As a Hail Mary, I called the number and got a grocery store in Fort Worth. I asked about Jack Smith, but the woman who answered the phone had never heard of him.

I logged into a database in Ancestry simply called US Public Records Index. The collection contained over three hundred million fragments of location information for individuals in the US from 1950 to 1993. I typed in the phone number and ran a reverse search, then scanned down the list of hits until my eyes fixed on a record with a name I recognized all too well.

My brain was buzzing as I switched to the Texas Marriage Index and entered the names. As the spinning circle resolved into a single search result, the facts of the Morgan case tumbled through my brain and fell into place like a series of jumbled puzzle pieces finally fitting together to show a picture no one would have ever imagined.

I looped my shoulder holster over my head, slid the Glock into the leather, and pulled on a jacket to conceal. I picked up my briefcase and headed to the garage. Once in the GV, I called Robbie.

When he picked up, I said, "I'm on my way to Gillespie County." I told him what I'd discovered in the databases.

When I finished, Robbie said, "Jesus Christ. Meet me somewhere in Fredericksburg. I'm going to go to the ranch with you. It's not safe for you to disclose you know about any of this without backup."

I thought for a minute. "Okay... I'll meet you at a place called Henrick's Peach Basket on Highway 87 coming into town. In the meantime, do you think Ansel could come to the rental this afternoon and check on Festus? I hate to leave him here alone if this takes all day."

Robbie said, "I'll call him from the road. He doesn't have a gig until next week. He'll be happy to handle that for us."

When I pulled up to the Peach Basket, I figured Robbie was fifteen minutes behind me. It was hot, so I walked into the store and bought a bottle of water.

Back in the Genesis, I cracked the top on the bottle and took a long drink. I pulled the Ancestry app up on my phone to review the documents I had found. As I studied the images, a shadow flickered across the front seat. I adjusted my position to keep the glare off the phone, and the reflection of a man crouching in the seat behind me appeared on the screen. Stifling a gasp, I was calculating my chances of reaching the Glock in my shoulder holster before he noticed I'd seen him when he pressed what felt like a pistol to the back of my neck. The metal was cold and hard, and the oblong shape of the muzzle cut into my skin. Terror shot through me when the pressure rocked against my neck as I heard the terrifying *click* of the pistol being cocked. In a high, feminine voice, the man said, "Drive to Lawton Meyer's house. Now."

My heart rate skyrocketed, and my mouth went dry. The way we were positioned, there was no chance I could reach my gun and get a shot off before he killed me. I scanned the parking lot. No sign of Robbie. I put the car in gear and pulled out onto 87. My mind raced as I drove to the ranch. *Who is this man and what does he want with me?* My eyes darted between the road and the rearview mirror. He was rail thin and thirtyish with sharp features and piercing green eyes that were tinged with insanity. His dark hair was long and unkempt. He hadn't shaved in several days and smelled of sweat and musk. His gun hand was trembling, and his breathing was a shallow pant. I could smell cigarettes and coffee on his breath. I knew him from someplace, but I couldn't recall where. All I could think was, *How can I keep him from killing me?*

Seven minutes later by my dash clock, I pulled through the main gate of Lawton Meyer's ranch. I stole another glance in the rearview mirror. Then it hit me...this was Andy, the guy who'd stopped to help us after the brakes on the Land Cruiser failed. *What the hell is going on?*

I could feel his breath on my neck as he said, "Take the left fork of the driveway and stop at the barn."

So he knows the ranch... I did as instructed and pulled the GV up to a large metal building.

"Get out. And keep your hands where I can see them."

I climbed out of the front seat, desperate for a chance to reach my Glock. But in seconds he was out of the SUV and in front of me, the gun in my face. "Turn around and go to the barn."

My hands in the air, I walked to the huge metal structure. He nudged me with the gun while I stood in front of a large roll-up garage door that was already open. "Inside."

A breath of cool air hit me. Giant industrial fans were running on either end of the building, and the overhead lights were on.

Once inside, he ordered me to turn around. His eyes darted around like a Komodo dragon's forked tongue. His gun hand was shaking, and sweat was dripping off his face. He said, "On your knees."

I knelt down, searching for anything in the barn I might use as a distraction to buy me a precious few seconds to reach my gun. Had I gone through hell with Kerabos and then with Geare only to die here at the hands of this psychopath? And for what? I didn't know who he was, but I was sure he had something to do with the connections I had just unearthed. I said, "I already told my colleagues everything. The documents proving it are on my desk. Killing me won't keep your secrets."

A terrible sadness washed over me that I might die right there, at odds with Sean, never having made peace with him. The man's high-pitched voice made my blood run cold. "Then I'll kill them, too."

His eyes were wild now. In a white-hot flash of clarity, I realized who he was...the only person he could be. I pressed my threat. "What about Maynard? When they can't find me, my family...my colleagues...they'll go to Maynard first. They won't let him rest until they find you. It'll destroy his career."

He fired the gun. I screamed as I threw myself flat on the ground. A cloud of dust flew up just feet from my face as the bullet hit the concrete floor and ricocheted into the barn's metal wall with a loud snap.

With my cheek plastered to the ground, I rolled my eyes to survey the barn. The roof was at least twenty-five feet high. A hay loft took up half of the overhead space, suspended over the rows of empty animal stalls that occupied the floor of the barn. I thought I saw movement in the shadow of a stack of feed bags.

Then a voice came from above. "I always worried they never found your body." Lawton Meyer stepped out of the shadows to the edge of the loft, a rifle aimed in our direction. He looked my captor up and down. "Can't say I've missed you, son."

Ambrose Meyer raised his pistol and fired wildly as he lunged behind a large wooden storage box. I rolled into one of the stalls as Lawton returned fire. A bullet nicked the box and ricocheted into the wooden railing right above where I was cowering. I crawled behind a hay bale near the edge of the stall to shield myself and drew my Glock.

As Lawton Meyer walked down the stairway from the hay loft, he spoke in a casual, terrifying voice. "Ms. Raines, I knew you were trouble the first day you showed up here. You had that awful tenacious way about you. No matter. I'll just make it look like you and Ambrose had it out and did each other in. Then, I guess I'll have to deal with those colleagues of yours..."

Panic surged through my jangled nerves as another shot rang out from behind the storage box. Lawton's head snapped to the side, but he stayed on his feet. When he turned back toward me, blood ran from a graze on his cheek. I forced myself to wait until he came closer. I didn't want to give my exact position away until he was in the same field of fire as his son. I was going to have only one opportunity to get them both.

My heart rate reached a staccato pace when a familiar man's voice boomed out from the area of the garage door. "Drop the weapons."

I raised my Glock and leaped out from the stall, my gun trained on Ambrose, and yelled to Finn, "Cover the rifle. I've got the pistol."

Lawton turned and fired on Finn with lightning speed. A bloodstain crept down Finn's left uniform sleeve and he staggered back and fell. A split second later, Ambrose fired his pistol. A gaping wound in Lawton Meyer's neck poured his blood volume onto the dirty floor of the barn in seconds.

As I trained the Glock on Ambrose, Mrs. Meyer ran into the barn. Ambrose called to her. "Mother, stay outside." Apparently recognizing the distinctive voice of her long-dead son, she raced toward him and blocked my shot. Taking advantage of the distraction, Ambrose turned his gun on me as Mrs. Meyer fell to her knees.

We stood locked in a Mexican standoff, guns aimed at each other at point-blank range. Neither of us moved a muscle, and the only sound was Mrs. Meyer, gasping out, "Glory be to the Father and to the Son..." I saw a flicker of movement in my peripheral vision. Finn rose up and fired on Ambrose, dropping him with a shot to the upper chest, before collapsing himself.

I ran to Ambrose Meyer and stuck his gun in my waistband before I dashed across the barn to Finn. He gasped out, "It's my arm. We've got to control the bleeding."

My fear evaporated as adrenaline hurled me into overdrive. I yanked off my jacket and used one of the sleeves as a tourniquet to staunch the blood pumping out of his wound. "Press the button on my collar mic," he said.

I fumbled for the lever. His voice was gravelly as he said, "Officer down. Shots fired. Multiple casualties. Meyer Ranch, barn on the west side of the main house." I released the lever, and a stream of orders and responses rattled through the speaker.

Finn's voice was getting weaker. "Take the cuffs off my duty belt and secure the one with the pistol."

As I fumbled for the handcuffs, the Hellcat swerved around the corner and fishtailed to a stop. Robbie leaped out of the driver's door with his gun drawn and ran to Lawton Meyer and checked in vain for a pulse. I tossed him the cuffs and sprinted back to Finn. Ignoring his wails, Robbie rolled Ambrose Meyer onto his belly and locked his hands behind him. Meyer was bleeding heavily from the chest wound, and his mother knelt next to him, weeping and stroking his head as she sputtered out a series of *Hail Marys* and *Our Fathers*.

Robbie knelt down next to us. Finn was barely conscious, and Robbie tightened the tourniquet on his arm. Then the barn devolved into chaos as sirens whooped and wailed and cops and sheriff's deputies poured into the metal building.

Medics elbowed their way past us to Finn. We stepped back to let them work, but an invisible force held me there, drawing me to him and not letting me loose. I followed when the paramedics raised the stretcher and jogged out of the barn, pushing the gurney into a waiting ambulance. An EMT pulled the doors shut from the inside, and the ambulance fired up its lights and sirens and sped down the ranch road in a cloud of dust.

I felt like a part of me was being torn away.

Chapter 55

Saturday, October 9, 3:00 p.m.

I raced to the Genesis and grabbed the handle of the driver's door. But before I could get it open, a shadow enveloped me, and a hand was on my shoulder. I whipped my head around to find Robbie. He edged past me and said, "I'll drive." I jumped into the passenger seat while he cranked the engine. As Robbie jerked the SUV into gear, the Gillespie County sheriff pounded on my window. I threw the door open. The sheriff's voice was deep and stern and dripped good ole boy redneck attitude. "Ms. Raines, I understand your concern for Ranger Rhodes. But I'm gonna need you folks to stay here and assist my detectives with their investigation. We need answers from you while the events are still fresh in your mind."

I resisted the urge to tell him the details of today's events would be fresh in my mind until I died. I shook my head. "We'll return later, but right now I need to see about Finn."

He assumed the posture all cops take on the street when civilians resist their commands—feet apart, hand on holster, death-ray stare—and shook his head. "I'm going to have to insist you stay here with Deputy

Rayburn." A beefy deputy with a buzz cut and a neck like a tree trunk stepped to his side, and he continued. "I'm going to the hospital myself, and I'll be sure you're kept informed."

I'd been shot at enough lately, and I was too tired to pick a fight I couldn't win. I was staving off a full-on PTSD episode with every weapon in my arsenal, but I was definitely going to pay the price when the adrenaline wore off, and this yahoo blocking my exit was only making it worse. I said, "Fine, but I need to make a call first." Robbie got out and lured the sheriff and Rayburn away while I worked my phone. Disappointment dropped through my chest like a free-fall carnival ride when I heard Madelyn's voice mail pick up. I cleared my throat and left a message briefly telling her what had happened and that I needed to see her. I took several deep breaths, climbed out of the SUV, and joined Robbie and the deputy.

Rayburn trailed us while we answered questions and walked crime scene techs through locations and timelines and event sequences for what seemed like an eternity. Periodically, staticky reports on Finn's condition would crackle through Rayburn's radio. "Still in surgery." "Moved to recovery." My heart surged when I heard, "Awake and responding."

Just as we finished up with the last of the crime scene crew and headed to the cars, Rayburn said, "The sheriff wanted me to let you know a medevac took off twenty minutes ago from the helipad at Peterson in Kerrville. The local docs got him stabilized, but they're airlifting Ranger Rhodes to main Santa Teresa in San Antonio where a team of surgeons is standing by to repair his arm. The sheriff says you're free to go."

I felt like a dump truck had buried me under a couple tons of suffocating emotion. My blood boiled that the damn sheriff, knowing he couldn't legally force me to stay at the crime scene, had obviously tasked the deputy not to tell me Finn was being moved to SA until the crime scene guys were done. At the same time, I was overwhelmed with relief that Finn was alive and stable and encouraged that he was on his way to a major hospital where great surgeons were waiting for him.

Underneath it all, I was swimming in a sea of all-consuming guilt that Finn had gotten shot protecting me. Visions of Geare shooting Grover flooded my mind along with thoughts of my neighbor, Ron, being attacked by a bad guy looking for me, then losing everything when the Victorian burned. Guilt seeped like a cloud of poisonous gas into every corner of my mind. I shook and shivered as the world tunneled down to a kaleidoscope of horrors. All of it my fault, all because of me...

Somewhere way off in the distance, I heard Robbie talking to me, but he sounded like he was underwater. I struggled to focus on him, but I couldn't seem to tune in to his frequency. Then I felt him helping me into the Genesis. The truck lurched into gear and bounced down the ranch road. I felt like I was drowning.

Around the time Robbie steered the SUV from 87 South onto 10 East, the smoke in my brain began to dissipate, and I started coming back into my right mind. I shook my head to clear it. "Please tell me I didn't make a scene back at the ranch."

Robbie turned the radio off. "I got you in the car before anyone noticed. You want me to call somebody?"

I looked down at my phone. Recalling the memory felt like I was pulling it out of a vat of taffy. "I left a message for my therapist before everything went wiggly. I'm fine for the moment." A shiver racked my body. "I'm just really cold."

When he reached down to jack the fan to High, I noticed the thermostat was already set on eighty-five degrees. "You must be suffocating."

He kept his eyes on the road. "You started shaking before we got off the ranch. I didn't have a blanket for you."

My mind was clearing, and by the time we hit the little town of Comfort, I had pretty much snapped back into shape. "We have to go to the hospital."

Robbie signaled to pass a slow-moving fifth-wheel camper. "Already on it. Ansel's at that rat trap of Carmine's with Festus. He'll hang out there until you and I see what's up with Finn."

Twenty-five minutes later, we were weaving through the parking garage at the Santa Teresa Hospital in the South Texas Medical Center. We parked and took the elevator to the first-floor information desk where a blue-haired lady in a striped smock dispensed a convoluted set of directions to a surgical waiting room. We traversed a maze of towers and sky bridges until we turned down a hall filled with cops and sheriff's deputies leaning on the walls and milling around. The actual waiting room was packed with rangers in jeans with white dress shirts and tan felt Stetsons. A chaplain from SAPD had set up shop at what was normally a volunteer's desk. I walked up and introduced myself. The man tipped his head and said, "Follow me, please."

He led us into a tiny carpeted room hardly bigger than a closet with three plastic chairs and a small shelf-like table built into the corner and equipped with a phone. I had an ominous feeling this room was reserved for delivering the kind of news I didn't want to hear. "I'm Father Rodriguez. Deputy Chief Delacourt told me to expect you. Ranger Rhodes is in the OR undergoing a shoulder reconstruction. He is out of danger and is expected to experience a complete recovery. Deputy Chief

Delacourt has asked me to inquire if you might need crisis intervention services. I can assist you myself or contact the on-call crisis counselor or the psychiatrist servicing the ER, if you prefer."

Since every cop in Texas had apparently heard about Finn being shot, it didn't surprise me that word had made it to Grover, and like the grousing saint that he was, his first thought was to make sure I was okay. "Grover is...a very kind man. But I'm all right, Father. Thank you, though."

The priest nodded. "The doctors have declared Ranger Rhodes off-limits for visitors until tomorrow night at the earliest. Meanwhile, I or someone from the officer's association will be with him every minute. You needn't worry."

I leaned in conspiratorially. "Father, being as he took that bullet for me, do you think there's any way you could use your...connections...to smuggle me in to see Finn tonight?"

He pursed his lips and slowly swiveled his head from side to side. "Ms. Raines, I doubt those doctors would let our good Lord and Savior himself in to see Special Ranger Rhodes tonight. Why don't you go home and rest?" He handed me a card. "Don't hesitate to call anytime."

He glanced down as the phone in his hand vibrated. He tapped the screen and studied the message, then looked up at me and said, "Special Ranger Rhodes is out of surgery and in recovery. He did well throughout. I hate to be rude, but I need to get back to the desk and update his colleagues."

We thanked him, and he left the little room and waded into the sea of rangers. Robbie shut the door behind him and sat back down.

"Iris, there is no reason for you to stay here. I want to take you home, get you something to eat, and let you get some sleep. You can call Father

Rodriguez every hour if you want. If there's any change at all, I can have you back here in fifteen minutes."

He had a point. If I couldn't see Finn, what good would me sitting around for twenty-four hours do anyone? We exited the carpeted closet, nudged our way through the crowd of cops, and slipped down the stairs. Once in the Genesis, Robbie headed east toward Carmine's shack.

He dodged down side streets, snaking through every shortcut he knew to avoid the brutal rush-hour traffic. When we rounded the corner to the rental at about 5:45, the street was clogged with a sea of police cars and ambulances and awash in red and blue strobing lights. Robbie braked the GV to a stop, and I leaped out the door and jogged toward the shabby tract home. My body choked out yet one more blast of adrenaline, and my heart thumped in my chest like a thrown tire tread slapping hot asphalt. Yellow crime scene tape stretched around the spindly trees in the weedy yard. An SAPD officer stepped into my path and assumed the I'm-in-charge position employed by bullies worldwide. "Police line, ma'am. You'll have to stay back."

I pointed at the rental. "I'm the tenant in that house. What's going on here?"

The cop shook his head and hardened his bully stance. "Step back, please."

Robbie stepped up beside me as I spotted Grover Delacourt coming out of the front door. I shouted. Grover waved and motioned to a tall man in a black suit with a gold badge around his neck standing next to him. Nick Ballard jogged over to us. "The deputy chief didn't want you to find out this way. The chaplain was supposed to call me when you left the hospital."

Thoughts of Ansel and Festus filled my brain. I wasn't going anywhere until I knew if they were okay. "A man named Ansel Highgrove was here with my dog. Are they all right?"

Nick ducked through to our side of the tape. "They're both fine. Mr. Highgrove was grazed by a bullet, but the wound is not serious." He pointed toward one of the ambulances. "The paramedics are patching him up right now." Robbie took off running toward the ambulance, and Nick went on. "Your dog is fine. He's in the rig with Mr. Highgrove. The intruder, a Dorinda Crandall, is deceased."

I felt like I had swallowed a bucket of sand. How could this day get any worse? "Dorinda Crandall was inside the house? And she shot Ansel?"

He nodded. "Made entry through a back bedroom window."

I was wildly curious about the details, but my concern for Ansel and Festus overrode everything. I ran after Robbie. Ansel was sitting on the edge of the rig with Festus perched beside him. The right sleeve of his T-shirt had been cut off, and a paramedic was putting the finishing touches on a bandage around his biceps. A thin line of blood was seeping through the gauze. Festus leaped off the floor of the rig and bounded for me. He stood on his hind legs and kissed my face, then bolted back to the ambulance, where he jumped up on the edge and resumed his protective position next to Ansel.

Robbie said in his strained, no-bullshit tone, "How bad?"

Ansel smiled. "Don't go gettin' your knickers in a bunch. It's just a scratch. Festus is the real hero. He's got nads of steel, that one."

I swallowed hard. "What happened?"

"Festus and I were in the livin' room watching the tube when out o' the blue, my boy here went berserk, jumped over the back of the sofa, and went hell-bent for leather toward the bedroom. I turned around to find that wee platinum devil, Dorinda, standin' in the door to the hallway with a .38 Special. She turned it on the hound, but he went airborne and knocked her to the ground. She fired as she was falling, and that's the shot that grazed me. I called Festus, drew down on her, and ordered her to drop the weapon. She raised the gun to fire at me, and I neutralized the bitch."

"Jesus in the morning." Dorinda was dead. I wasn't at all ashamed that my first thought was *Thank God*. "How bad is your arm?"

He looked down at the bandage. "I wouldn't care at all, but she cocked up my Legion tat. Sliced right through the top of the center flame. Bad enough, I'm going to have to live with that little fiend getting the drop on me, but having my Legion tat botched by .38 Special? A fuckin' snub nose, no less."

I pulled out my phone and called the twenty-four-hour hotline for the Raines & Raines criminal section. Grover and I went a long way back, but he was a cop, and Dorinda was dead. Killing someone was serious business, no matter what the extenuating circumstances were, and I wanted Ansel to have the best possible representation before he was interviewed. Satisfied a partner was en route, I wiggled my way between him and Festus and sat. "Ansel, I swear to you, I will find the best tattoo artist on the planet to fix that ink. We'll get a plastic surgeon if we have to."

Robbie said, "And I will personally fly you wherever it takes to get that done."

Ansel laughed. "Did I mention that I got the original work in Paris?" He winked at me. "May have to go back to the source."

Festus let out a chesty bark. We all turned and watched in silence as the medical examiner's techs pushed a gurney bearing a small black body bag down the cracked driveway, then shoved the stretcher into their hearse.

I felt nothing but relief as they slammed the back doors and drove away, removing Dorinda Crandall from our lives forever.

Chapter 56

Sunday, October 17, 7:30 a.m.

My fathers and I sat on the veranda of the main house of the Raines mansion munching on pastries and drinking coffee while Festus chewed on a rubber bone. The sun was just coming up, and the sky was a glorious pink. Addison checked his phone for a text and turned to Justis. "The birds were just released."

Justis nodded and started a stopwatch. "Loft to loft the distance is ninety-seven miles. ETA should be just after nine."

Their housekeeper, Ariscella, wheeled a cart filled with breakfast taco fixings onto the balcony. I poured another cup of coffee from the silver pot sitting on a wrought iron sideboard. We piled scrambled eggs and fried chorizo and grated cheese on fresh, hot tortillas and spooned salsa on top before we rolled them up and struggled to get our mouths around our giant creations. Addison swallowed, set his taco on the plate, and looked at the rising sun. "Well, this is one for the books."

Justis shook his head. "An almost unimaginable series of twists and turns in this case."

I used a paper napkin to wipe the red oil from the chorizo off my fingers. "But in the end, it was basically just greed and lust run amok drizzled with a hearty helping of good old-fashioned family dysfunction." I fed a tidbit of egg to Festus.

Addison pulled another tortilla from the warmer. "Yesterday, we corralled Quinten up at the office and finally got him to come clean. Turns out, when the Big Top CEO was still a midlevel manager at Circus Burgers, he caught Quinten screwing his wife. Fearing the fallout, Quinten broke it off with the woman and fired her husband on some trumped-up crap—all in a vain attempt to free himself of the whole mess. After the man lost his job, his marriage collapsed. Left with nothing, he swore revenge and finagled some funding to start Big Top."

I thought of Carmine Pagano stepping out on his nasty wife and ultimately being blackmailed the year before with pics of him and a stripper—and I remembered the torrent of hell that situation had unleashed on all of us. But marital infidelity was hardly limited to the modern cheaters rendezvousing in reserved parking spots at the San Antonio airport. PIs have made their livings off of it since the Pinkerton National Detective Agency opened its doors in 1850.

"It makes more sense now. I could never understand why someone would so flagrantly violate a noncompete agreement. He had to know Farragut would sue to enforce. I guess he was just too mad to care."

Justis said, "According to the AUSA, the Big Top guy took on too much debt to finance the start-up, so he had no capital to mount a meaningful defense against the suit to enforce the noncompete. Desperate to even the score with his archenemy, he got his fraternity brother, Emil Hatrock—CEO of Allways—to launch a dirty-tricks campaign of food poisonings and the drug sting to undermine Quinten's ability to prosecute the lawsuit and simultaneously destroy his business."

Addison made a finger gun and pulled the trigger. "Exactly. But it didn't matter to the drug dealers that Quinten had dropped the suit. They still wanted the money they'd been promised."

Justis spooned a few more scrambled eggs on one last tortilla. "After stalling the drug buyers for weeks, Quinten had finally promised them he'd be there that night to close. You walked right into a buzz saw when they thought you were part of a trap."

I shook my head. "Farragut actually believed he could somehow get us to resolve his problem with the cartel without us discovering his role in the deal. How could that even work?"

Addison shook his head. "Beats the hell out of me...but after all these years of clients lying to me, I've finally given up wondering."

Justis dribbled the last bit of the fresh-squeezed orange juice out of the crystal carafe into his glass. "Now the Allways CEO is facing criminal charges over the death of the Circus Burgers diner. So much for helping out an old college buddy."

Addison said, "How is Finneas?"

"He's going to be released this afternoon."

Justis said, "I still don't know how he happened to show up at the Meyer ranch that day?"

"Robbie called him from the car as he was coming to meet me," I said. "Finn was working close to Fredericksburg. That's how he beat Robbie there."

Justis said, "Thank God for that."

I nodded. "When he got to the appointed meeting spot and I wasn't there, Finn called Robbie back. God bless Ansel, he had stuck a GPS on the Genesis before I went on my date to the caverns with Finn, and Robbie used the tracking app on his phone to find me. Finn rushed there just in time to save me."

Addison said, "I'm not clear on how Ambrose Meyer heard about the ranch sale and knew to come after you?"

"News of the sale was in the media, as was word the deal was stalled over a title problem. One of the stories in the local press said the sale was being handled by Raines & Raines. Grover says Ambrose saw news footage of me coming out of the San Pedro Circus Burgers the day the health department closed down the stores. Once he knew what I looked like and the make and model of my car, he set up surveillance outside the firm and followed me home. The state crime lab found a cell phone tracking app set to my number on Ambrose's phone."

Addison leaned back in his chair. "I didn't know that was possible."

I shrugged. "Me, either, but Marvin explained it to me. Ambrose used a device called a Stingray to grab my cell and track it. He could also listen to my cell conversations using special software. Marvin found the equipment mounted on a tree limb overhanging the carport at the Victorian. Once the device connects with the phone the first time, the spy can track the phone's movement and intercept its signals wherever it is. The one mounted on my tree had Ambrose's fingerprints on it."

Justis said, "Undoubtedly, possession and use of such a device is a felony. That alone should keep him locked up for some time."

"I'm still confused about the events at the cavern," Addison said. "He needed time to plan that and set it up."

"Seems that with the proper skill set and malware, a cell phone can be turned into a listening device. My phone was on the kitchen island while

Ansel was setting up the protection plan for that night with Finn. Ambrose would have heard every word Ansel said during that conversation."

Addison sipped coffee. "Justis and I got in touch with Ansel through Robbie. We wanted to thank him personally for all he did for you. And Quinten has assured us he will make good on all the fees for Robbie's and Ansel's time on the case."

Justis said, "I just don't see why Ambrose Meyer would care if we approached his parents about buying their interest in a piece of real estate."

"Because, in the process of moving the record title from Annabelle Morgan Case into her children, there's no way we wouldn't have figured out Mr. and Mrs. Meyer were brother and sister. Apparently, Ambrose made it his life's mission to protect his mother and brother from the knowledge of what his father had done to all of them."

Justis said, "That poor woman. Sexually abused by that monster, given away when her parents couldn't protect her from him, orphaned again when her adoptive parents were killed, and then lured out of the safety of the convent by her abuser, who tricked her into an incestuous marriage. It's abominable."

The sun had crawled all the way over the horizon, and the sky was turning a cloudless blue. "Worse, the bastard took advantage of her prosopagnosia. Because of her disability, she never recognized his face, but there was nothing wrong with her memory. The Morgans didn't give her away until she was eight. She would have damn well remembered her abusive brother's name. That's why he changed it."

Addison scratched Festus's long, silky ears. "Does anybody know how he learned his parents were siblings?"

"Ambrose's psychiatrist had him undergo a DNA analysis to better tailor psychoactive medications to his particular condition. The results revealed he was the product of sibling incest. The shrink had a legal obligation to tell him."

Justis set his napkin by his plate. "I can't express how deeply I despise this man for trying to hurt you, but it's impossible not to feel some sympathy for him."

I nodded. "I agree. He confronted his father about the incest while they were out alone on the family sailboat. Did it there so there was no risk of anyone overhearing them. That's when his father tried to kill him—hit him over the head with a wrench and pushed him overboard. He would have died if a fishing boat hadn't picked him up. He told the cops staying dead was the best way he could think of to free himself of his abusive father."

Justis put his empty plate back on the cart. "Where has he been since he disappeared off the sailboat?"

I said, "He's been living off the grid in a travel trailer wandering around Bureau of Land Management land. To support himself, he built tiny, specialized photography drones for intelligence-gathering purposes and sold them over the dark web for blockchain currency. He picked up odd jobs in nearby small towns to generate enough cash to meet any needs he couldn't fulfill with his crypto earnings."

Festus pawed my leg, and I held my plate down for him to lick. "He apparently didn't need much money, even though he made tons of it with his drones. Amazingly, though, he managed to attend over a hundred of his brother's violin performances over the past decade and a half. The trailer was littered with ticket stubs and performance programs. The techs found a receipt where he made an anonymous donation of $100K to the Stradivari Society for them to loan his brother the Lady Tennant violin for a concert at Carnegie Hall."

Addison said, "The younger brother has come out strongly in support of Ambrose without regard to any impact it might have on his career. The *Texas Daily* had an interview with him. He talked about the terrible abuse his brother suffered at the hands of their evil father. Maynard was the old man's favorite and could do no wrong, while Ambrose showed the signs of his bipolar disorder very early with capricious and inappropriate behavior, trouble at school—all the issues faced by mentally ill children. Despite their father's favoritism, the brothers were inseparable."

I stroked Festus's chest. "It's even more amazing since Maynard has been a recluse for his entire adult life. Yet, he came out of the cave to publicly defend his brother."

Justis said, "My heart breaks for the boys' mother. I can't imagine where she'll go from here."

I smiled. "Well, that's a bright spot. Mrs. Meyer is once again Sister Jerome Emiliani. When she became a widow, she was eligible to rejoin the order and has returned to the Benedictine convent in Deadwood. She'll spend the rest of her life in the only place she ever really felt a sense of belonging. Last week, when I was talking to her about the Wind Rose title issue, I told her about Inez Crain trying to find her. I heard from Mrs. Crain yesterday that Sister Emily has contacted her, and they're striking up a friendship."

Addison smiled. "Working from that inventory Case's son sent you, Simpson has discovered Annabelle's estate owns an interest in several thousand acres acquired during her marriage to Case. As the sole surviving heir, all the interest goes to Sister Emily. Simpson's working on straightening it all out. Sister Emily wants all the money we can wring out of it to go to a program the order is sponsoring for survivors of childhood sexual abuse."

Justis sipped water from a sweating crystal glass. "So the problems with the brakes on Sean's Land Cruiser and that business with the snakes? And the gas at the cavern? That was all Ambrose?"

"Every time I got a step closer to figuring out who the Meyers really were, Ambrose tried to kill me. Turns out, he isn't any better at staging accidental deaths than his father was. Much as I wanted to blame it all on Dorinda, as far as we can tell her only crime against me was poisoning my dog."

Addison checked his watch and glanced at the sky then said, "I just can't figure why Ambrose stopped to play Andy the Good Samaritan after he had sabotaged the brakes on the Land Cruiser. Why stop to help if he was trying to kill you?"

"Grover found a diary in the trailer. In it, Ambrose wrote he was following us after he tampered with the brakes to be sure we were silenced by the sabotage. After the crash, he claimed to be a passerby just to see what condition we were in. He was planning on finishing me off with the knife he pulled ostensibly to cut my jammed seat belt, but the sheriffs showed up just as he was about to use it to slit my throat."

Justis massaged his temples and muttered, "Dear Lord," while Addison poured himself another cup of coffee.

He stirred in cream and sugar and said, "So how about you, Iris? Justis and I are worried about the effect all this violence may have had on your PTSD."

I fidgeted with my napkin while I collected my thoughts then looked up at my fathers, both of whom had their eyes locked on me. "Well, it wasn't without cost. But I'm holding my own. I'm back to seeing Madelyn twice a week, and that'll probably go on for a while. I was actually doing pretty well until that asshole of a sheriff from Gillespie County sequestered me at the Meyer ranch and made me relive the whole damn thing with those crime scene guys for three hours. I had an episode on the way back to SA afterward, but it was brief, and Madelyn thinks it was a one-off."

Justis said, "We are very concerned that we may have put you in a position where that hard-won progress you've made was jeopardized. There is no client or case that means more to us than your well-being. But since you became an adult, we have felt that it is not our place to limit your career advancement out of our paternal reservations about your safety."

Addison took a sip of coffee. "If it were up to us, we'd have you stuck in the office cranking out title work for Real Estate while we made it known we'd see anyone in hell who caused you so much as a paper cut."

As he often did, Justis seamlessly picked up Addison's thought. "But that's not the life you chose. You are a brilliant, inspired investigator, Iris. The best either of us has ever seen. And we feel like it's our own problem to deal with our anxiety about the risks you face doing your chosen work. But we are constantly torn about the possibility we may somehow put you in harm's way."

I reached over the table and squeezed both their arms. "I know you worry. And every day I'm thankful that you support my career just like you've supported every other thing I've done in my life. This was hard, but what I did was my own choice, and I'm okay."

Justis raised his binoculars and scanned the sky. "We have two approaching the loft." He passed the field glasses to Addison and checked his stopwatch. "Possible record time here."

Addison stood and stretched. "Come to the pigeon loft with us. You can see the birds come in."

I shook my head. "I've got some things I need to take care of." I looked down at Festus. "Besides, I do not like the way he eyes those birds like they're hors d'oeuvres."

Addison hugged me, then Justis leaned over and did the same. Addison said, "We love you, Iris. You're the best decision we ever made."

I smiled at them. "And I'm the luckiest girl in the world."

Chapter 57

Sunday, October 17, 10:30 a.m.

Festus and I were heading back to the Victorian when Grover rang my cell. "The mayor still hasn't gotten that damn short fixed in the Batsignal, so I had to use the Batphone."

"It's just as well. Robin and I are not in the Batcave at the moment. We've actually been over at Wayne Manor. What's up with you?"

He said, "I need to see you. Can we meet somewhere?"

My stomach swam. "Sure. Where are you now?"

"I'm on my way to Lions Field for a chess club tournament."

"Ron finally got back in town last night. He told me he's playing you first round."

Grover chuckled. "Yeah, and he's probably going to kick my ass just like he always does. We talked this morning. All things considered, it definitely worked out for the best that his adventure in Studebakerland took so much longer than he'd planned, but I hear rumblings he's looking at buying a 1962 Avanti."

"I heard the same noises. I'm preparing to get booted out of my covered parking spot."

Grover cleared his throat. "The match starts in about an hour. Why don't you swing by? We can talk before I go on the chopping block."

I found Grover with his oxygen concentrator sitting on a bench outside the main building. I sat down next to him, and Festus nosed him then lay down at our feet.

"I fucked up, Iris."

Grover Delacourt hadn't said those words to me since we got slammed in the finals of the Jefferson High School debate tournament when I was fourteen years old. "How?"

"Finneas Rhodes is not a crooked cop. He's a fucking hero. After the feds cleared him of any wrongdoing, he agreed to go undercover to help roll up the rest of the bad guys. Being married to one of them, he had the cred to do it. The intel I saw that said he was dirty was fed through the system as part of his cover. He couldn't tell you that part when he confessed to you about being investigated and cleared. But he came to you with the information he was authorized to share."

I cocked my head. "How do you know that?"

"Because once I got word about him being undercover, I called him. We met, and I told him about leaking the information about him to you."

My jaw dropped open. "Grover, you could go to jail for what you told me...or for what you're telling me now."

He turned to me. "Iris, Finneas Rhodes took a bullet for you. And I had leaked false information about him...making him out to be a corrupt cop."

I swallowed hard. "What did he say when you confessed to him?"

Grover shook his head. "He said I did what I should have done."

My eyes went wide. "He said *what*?"

Grover nodded. "I know—unbelievable. He made it clear he understands the broad strokes of what happened with you and Geare. He said he was glad you had a friend who would go all in to protect you."

I slumped back on the bench. "Holy shit."

He nodded. "Yep. There is at least one decent, moral cop left in the world."

I reached over, hugged him, and said, "No. There are at least two."

Festus and I climbed back into the Genesis and headed downtown. Robbie and I had spent the previous Sunday sitting vigil at the hospital waiting for news about Finn, going home only after we were allowed a five-minute visit. I hadn't talked to Sean since Dorinda's death, but Robbie had called several times to check on me, and I got the impression he still wasn't staying at the loft. I had no idea what was going on when Robbie had texted early that morning. *Loft at noon.*

When Robbie answered the door, his face was drawn and his voice was low. He hugged me and said, "Come on in."

The usual smells of blueberry pancakes and hickory-smoked bacon were absent. A tray of Starbucks cups and a box of Krispy Kremes sat on the table. I felt like a rock was stuck in my throat. "What's going on?"

Robbie turned and called, "Sean? Iris is here." Then he took Festus into the kitchen and gave him a biscuit.

After a few beats, Sean came down the stairs from the bedroom. His sponsor, X, trailed behind him. Sean's eyes were red and swollen. He walked up to me without a word and wrapped me in his arms. He held me so tight, I could hardly breathe. Then, he led me to the teak dining table. He pulled out a chair for me and sat down next to it. Robbie and X sat, as well.

I saw pain in Sean's eyes I'd never seen before. This was not the same guy who'd crashed the power grid for Kazakhstan and Photoshopped reindeer horns on Dick Cheney. I looked around the table at the somber faces and said, "What's wrong? You all are scaring the hell out of me."

Sean rested his elbows on his knees and covered his face with his hands. Robbie put his hand on Sean's back and said, "Go on, bud. Tell her."

Still covering his face, he said, "I am so ashamed I didn't realize she was a threat to you... I didn't see it." He lifted his head up and stared out the glass wall at the city skyline.

I reached over and took his hand. "It was a mistake."

He nodded. "As a condition of her release, she gave permission for the government to track her phone. From that tracking data, they can tell she was at your house the night Festus was poisoned."

I felt like I was in the Rotor ride where the barrel spins and forces you up against the walls before the bottom drops out. That works fine—provided the bottom comes back in place before the spinning stops. But looking at Sean, I was terrified the bottom was gone forever. Our only hope was to say the terrible truth out loud. I took a deep breath. "Go on, Sean. I'm listening."

When he looked up, he was a man I didn't know. "She went berserk when her lawyers told her about the pictures of her at the casino. She was convinced you were behind it. When I questioned that premise, she accused me of being against her. She demanded that I tell her where you were. She made it a point of loyalty." His voice broke, and he sobbed quietly, his hands back to covering his face. Robbie was silent but kept a reassuring hand on Sean's back.

After a time, Sean wiped his face and looked at me. He took a deep breath and said, "I told her where the rental was. I did it because I didn't think I could live without her, because I was so lost in the vortex of what we did together. With her, there was no constant pull to the addiction. No need to fight it every fucking hour of every fucking day. It was an orgasmic euphoria to just let go of the struggle and give in to the urges. She let go, too, and we just let it sweep us away. It took over my life..." Tears streamed down his face. "It became more important than anything." He took my hands in his. "Iris, I'm so sorry. She could have killed you or Festus... Christ, she almost got Ansel."

Robbie cleared his throat. "Sean has agreed to go back to Boston. I'm flying him up in the Citation this evening. He doesn't want to ask you, but we think it would be best if you came with us. I can fly you back here whenever you need me to. The hospital has arranged a furnished apartment. It'll do until we work out something better." He cracked a tiny smile. "And I promise it won't be that roach motel we stayed in a decade ago."

Sean was broken and ashamed and terrified. I nodded. "I'll go home and get some things together. I have to call my fathers and get Marvin lined up to take up the slack until we get a system going." I looked at my watch. "I can be back here by six."

I called to Festus, and we left the three of them sitting at the dining table with the cold coffee and sad, uneaten donuts.

I sped home and gathered up what I would need for a week. After we got Sean settled, Robbie and I would fly back and do a more thorough load-out. But now, we just needed to get Sean into treatment.

I called my fathers and told them what was happening. They were both sad and deeply concerned about Sean's health. Addison said, "We got through this eleven years ago. We'll get through it now. Marvin can handle any emergencies that come up until you get situated. Right now, you need to get Sean somewhere safe."

Then I dialed Finn Rhodes. There was genuine joy in his voice. "I am so glad to hear from you."

"Where are you now?"

He laughed. "I'm in town, staying with a friend. I'm still on a tight leash with the docs at Santa Teresa."

"I need to see you. Can you come by my apartment?"

I could hear him smiling. "I'm on my way."

Chapter 58

Sunday, October 17, 4:30 p.m.

I managed to throw on some decent clothes and a little makeup before Finn rang the doorbell. At the sound of the chimes, Festus went berserk, barking and whining and spinning in lopsided circles. He hadn't reacted to anything with that much enthusiasm since before the poisoning. When I opened the door and saw Finn standing there, a warm sensation of happiness spread through my chest. I stepped back and said, "Come on in."

Finn's left arm was still in a sling, but he squatted down and rubbed Festus's ears with his good hand. "It's great to see him all bright-eyed and bushy-tailed."

I said, "Shake, Festus," and the dog offered Finn his crippled front paw. They shook, then Festus wandered over to the sofa and climbed up.

I motioned Finn into the living room. "Please sit down. Can I get you something? A beer?"

He nodded. "Beer sounds great."

I returned from the kitchen with two Tecates and passed one to him. "I have some lime..."

He shook his head and took me by the hand. "I don't need a lime. I'm just happy to sit here and be with you."

My face felt hot, and I was pretty sure I was blushing. "How's your arm?"

He shrugged. "It'll be fine." He took a pull off the bottle then slowly placed it on a coaster. "Let's get the awkward stuff out of the way..."

I croaked out an "Okay."

"I've talked to Grover. I know what he told you a couple of weeks ago and what he told you today. I don't blame him for what he did. Grover loves you. He couldn't bear to see you hurt again. I hope I would have done the same thing. We fed that phony intel through the system because we were dealing with crooked cops. The story had to look good." He rubbed his thumb over the back of my hand. "I guess we hit that one out of the park."

"I'm just so ashamed to have believed the worst about you."

He shook his head. "I'm an almost perfect stranger to you. You've known Grover half your life. Considering Grover's role in the intelligence task force and your long-standing relationship with him, it was only natural you would take his word over mine."

I felt my eyes filling. "Thank you for that. And for saving me from Ambrose Meyer."

"I can't imagine how hard things must be for you after the experience with Geare..."

I turned away. "You don't know the half of it."

A long silence ensued. Finally he said, "I'll never ask you about it. You can tell me as much or as little about that whenever—if ever—you're ready."

"Thank you for that." I squeezed his hand. "I have to leave for a while. I'll be in Boston. It's family business. I don't know how long I'll be gone, but we can talk while I'm away...if you'd like that."

His eyes twinkled. "I would like that very much. And I have some news, too. My divorce will be final in a week."

I couldn't stop my smile. "That is great news."

He beamed. "But that's not all of it. I've gotten a promotion. I'll be moving to San Antonio in January. Starting next year, I'm moving into upper management."

There was a lightness, a joy in my heart I hadn't felt since before Daniel Kerabos had slithered into my life.

He held my gaze with his emerald eyes. Finally, he said, "I wouldn't ask until next week when I have my note from the judge, but since you're departing for the wild, blue Yankee yonder...would you mind terribly if I kissed you?"

"I would mind terribly if you didn't."

He pulled me toward him. I felt his arm around me, the same strength I remembered from dancing with him. Then his lips were on mine, and I took in the familiar scent of his cologne and arched my back at the feel of his body next to mine. The kiss was long and sweet. My attraction to him was so strong, I had to force myself to break the embrace, or I would have still been there when the sun rose. When I finally leaned back, he said, "I'll be waiting when you come home."

I checked my watch. "I wish I could stay here with you...now...all night, but I have to meet Sean and Robbie at the loft in twenty minutes."

He said, "Can I drive you?"

I smiled. "I guess I could just meet them at the airport."

He stroked my hair. "Call Robbie... Tell them I'll be taking you over."

Finn drove me and Festus to the private terminal. A porter carried my bags inside while Finn helped Festus out of the kennel in the back of his truck. Inside the small waiting room, a clerk said, "Mr. Galen and Mr. Hazelwood are already on the plane. The porter has taken your luggage out."

I turned to Finn, and he ran the backs of his fingers across my cheek. "Have a good flight. I'll miss you."

I took his hand in mine and kissed his palm. "Thank you...for everything."

I called to Festus, and we walked across the tarmac and climbed the stairs into the plane. Robbie pulled the door shut behind us. Out my window, I saw Finn standing on the tarmac, watching us taxi away.

In the cockpit, Robbie was in the captain's seat. Sean was riding shotgun. I'd never seen Sean in the second seat when they were both on a trip. Things were changing in our world. Robbie and I had always been friends, but now our relationship was different...deeper. I knew the truth about their breakup after Robbie was hit by the IED. I would never break his confidence, but for the first time in my life, I had a secret from Sean Galen.

And I'd made my own way in these early stages of my relationship with Finn. I'd found the new support group. I had called Evelyn, and, while we were gone, I, like the woman named Grace, would be joining the meetings by FaceTime. I had devised ways to take care of myself without always leaning on Sean.

Ultimately, it was that split second of weakness when he'd betrayed me that had brought him to the understanding of how sick he was and given him the impetus to go back to rehab.

But it was Robbie who'd stood with me through all of it. That would be with us from now on. And Ansel had taken the hit for all of us. He had been connected to Robbie and Sean before through war and business, but he was part of our clan now. And I was glad for that.

No matter how hard things have been, no matter how much they have changed, the clan has stayed together. We guard each other's secrets and watch each other's backs.

Because we're family.

Coming Soon

Enjoy this excerpt from Denise Diana Huddle's exciting new book in the Iris Raines Mystery series

DOUBLE TROUBLE

Don't look back—you'll turn into a pillar of shit. That's the advice I give to every adoptee who comes to me overwhelmed with an insatiable desire to dig down to their biological roots. Once I unearth the truth of their biological origins, the genetic genie is out of the bottle.

My search usually turns their vision of a biological parent—an astronaut or a movie star trapped in some convoluted, noble situation—into a hard look at a string of tragic characters mired in tawdry, awful circumstances. The reunions usually fall somewhere between a train wreck and a dumpster fire.

Me, I've never had the urge to search. I'd walked by the file cabinet holding the folder bearing my birth mother's name a thousand times, and I had never once even considered stopping and taking a peek—not until the cops kicked my door in to see if I was dead.

Chapter 1

Friday, August 20, 2:00 p.m.

I steered my gleaming black Genesis GV80 into the parking garage of the Bexar County Courthouse. My blouse was damp with sweat as I jogged through the crosswalk that connects the garage to the Bexar County Justice Center. The strap of the briefcase—stuffed with four hundred pages of certified copies of UCC filings I had just retrieved from the Texas Secretary of State—cut into my shoulder as I hustled down the sidewalk to the entrance.

I checked my watch as I ran. My father, Addison Raines—one of the brothers who adopted me when a client dumped me on their doorstep the day I was born—was in trial and had just discovered in testimony from the day's first witness that he was going to need the copies in court as soon as the lunch recess ended.

I had taken the mayday at 8:30 a.m. and left immediately for Austin. From the car, I called a hot-shot document retrieval service I used up there, paid the no-bullshit-gotta-have-it-right-damn-now surcharge and had them send a small platoon of specialists to start cranking the copiers and hitting up the clerks for certifications while I drove. I landed in the Secretary of State's office around 10:00 and pitched in.

By 11:30, the clerk finished the last certification. The muscles in my neck and shoulders felt like they'd shrunk in the dryer as I rushed to pay my bill. I took a deep breath and forced myself to slow down and match the stack of documents against my master list to be sure I wasn't missing anything. Satisfied, I stuffed my bounty into my briefcase and scurried down the stairs and out to the parking lot.

I hefted the heavy satchel into the back seat and raced the eighty-two miles back to the Bexar County Courthouse where Addison was waiting outside the courtroom, huddled with his client. The hallway smelled of old paper and dust and industrial cleaning solvent. His second chair, a litigation bone crusher named Bernie, was standing by the elevator waiting for me. I handed him the briefcase, and he hustled down the hall toward his boss. Addison turned to me. His jaw was tight, and he had on his hard-ass-litigator face. He gave me a thumbs up and mouthed "thank you" as he and the client hurriedly followed Bernie into the courtroom.

Since I had dropped everything to head to Austin, I had missed my usual stop at the donuts and coffee klatch in the break room of the Law Office of Raines & Raines, which was right down the hall from the smaller office of Raines Investigations.

Just the thought of the aroma of the coffee and the taste of the powdery sugar on the pastries made my stomach growl. I hadn't eaten since dinner the night before. With court back in session, the crowd at the cafeteria in the basement of the courthouse would've thinned, and I could get myself some lunch. I texted the firm's receptionist, Francine, and let her know the documents had been delivered in the nick of time and I was going to grab a bite downstairs.

The cafeteria smelled like grease and fried meat. I went through the hot line and chose enchiladas, pinto beans, and Spanish rice from the steam trays and sat down to dig in. For government chow, the Mexican food was pretty good, but the cheese had been sitting out too long. I was so hungry I didn't care.

I gobbled while scrolling through email on my phone. I was lost in a message about a document I'd been searching for since June when a sheriff's deputy rushed into the dining area and shouted out my name. *What the hell?* My chair legs screeched against the gray institutional vinyl floor as I scrambled to my feet. The few other diners were staring at me as I forced myself to swallow a gooey gob of enchilada and said, "I'm Iris Raines."

He loped over to the table. "Deputy Chief Delacourt has sent for you. It's an emergency."

A jolt of adrenaline shot through me as I grabbed my purse and briefcase. "What kind of emergency? Is my family all right?"

He looked perplexed. "I don't know anything about your family. There's a hostage situation at the Alamo."

Chapter 2

Friday, August 20, 3:00 p.m.

The deputy took me by the arm and guided me toward a door marked NO EXIT. He entered a code in a keypad and pulled me out into an alley where an SAPD police cruiser was waiting. A patrol officer stood by the open rear door. I jumped in, and he slammed it shut, slid into the front passenger seat, and hit the lights and sirens as his partner sped the mile to the Alamo. The back seat had the faint, lingering smell of vomit, disinfectant, and old vinyl. The expansion metal partition and the absence of interior door handles set my nerves on edge.

"I need you to tell me what the hell is going on."

The cop riding shotgun picked up the radio, "Dispatch—Notify Deputy Chief Delacourt we are inbound." He replaced the radio and turned to me. "The chief can explain."

The wailing siren amped up my fear of some unknown catastrophe. I grabbed the wire of the cage to keep from slamming into the door as the driver slewed the car to a stop on South Alamo, just north of Houston and half a block from where the massive RV that functions as SAPD's mobile command unit was parked.

A tall, handsome man in black jeans, a starched white dress shirt, and a perfectly knotted red tie hurried toward the patrol car. He wore a pistol on his hip and a gold shield on a chain around his neck. My heart dropped from Turbo to Overdrive when Grover's right-hand man, Detective Nick Ballard, opened the door and I got out of the stinky patrol car. He took my arm and said, "Grover's over here."

I longed for a deep breath of fresh air, but a giant generator was belching exhaust as it fed power to the RV. Nick opened the door and ushered me inside. The rig was packed with plain clothes SAPD specialists, all with gold shields hanging from their necks by beaded chains. Their overlapping conversations smacked of crisis managers struggling to get on top of a problem. Following Nick, I felt like I was inching my way to the concession stand during halftime at a Spurs game, edging past people sideways, as we made our way to Grover.

Grover was thirty-nine, around five foot ten, and balding. The ever-present toothpick in the corner of his mouth was bobbing between his lips like a harbor buoy as he barked orders into a walkie-talkie while watching a bank of monitors. He still sounded winded when he spoke—no surprise, given the near-fatal gunshot wound to his left lung two years earlier. The baggy khakis hanging off his frame were a testament to the forty pounds he'd lost during his recovery.

Grover waved us over to a table in the back. He sat the radio on the table and glanced at a bank of six camera views of the main entrance to the Alamo. In one view, snipers could be seen on nearby roof tops.

Nick let go of my arm, and I massaged my neck. "What the hell is going on?"

"Great to see you, too, Iris. Thanks for dropping by." He nodded toward the screens. "Seems we have a dipshit in the Alamo holding his brother hostage."

I stared at the screens. "What does this have to do with me?"

He fiddled with the toothpick. "Said dipshit would like to speak with you."

"Who's the dipshit?"

He used a mouse to rewind and zoom in on a video clip from one of the cameras focused on the entrance. I gaped at the grainy image on the monitor. A twenty-something man with shaggy hair and a scruffy beard in jeans and a T-shirt was holding a gun to the head of man about the same age dressed in the costume of the 1835 Texian William Barrett Travis. The look on the hostage's face said this was a no-bullshit deal. The armpits of the gunman's shirt were circled with sweat, and his gun hand was shaking.

It took me a second, but I recognized the guy with the gun. *Shit.* My stomach was rolling like a boulder caught in an avalanche as everything I knew I couldn't say slammed head-on into the life-or-death danger on the screen.

Grover leaned back in the cheap rolling desk chair. "You want to tell me how you are acquainted with these boys? And let me remind you that your PI license requires you to cooperate with law enforcement."

"Not if my investigation is attorney work product."

As if on cue, my father, Justis Raines, opened the door to the RV. He was dressed in his customary dark suit and Harvard tie. His shock of silver hair was neatly combed as he strode across the crowded room. Justis would have looked put-together on the beach at Normandy. Today was no different.

I looked back at Grover, stunned by Justis's fortuitous appearance. Grover just shrugged. "I planned ahead."

My father looked at me. "I have authorization from the client. Tell them what they want to know."

The whole interaction was moving so fast, I could barely keep up. Justis nodded for me to spill it.

"The kid in the costume is Felix Anderson. The guy with the gun is Gerard Maysenfelder. I was working a land title problem involving a dead guy who gave his child up for adoption—Maysenfelder."

Grover said, "Keep going."

"Bottom line. Maysenfelder's birth mother got knocked up by my dead guy who just happened to be her married graduate advisor. Mom gave the baby..." I tapped the gunman's image on the screen. "...up for adoption and vanished to finish her dissertation in Peru."

One of the radios crackled. Grover reached over and turned the volume down without breaking eye contact with me. "And..."

"Later, Dr. Mom married another archaeologist. Enter Baby #2, Felix Anderson, the hostage, who was raised while the little family globe-trotted in the name of science, all documented on Dr. Mom's personal website. Maysenfelder found the website, saw the happy family, and, voila, here we are."

Grover sat forward in the chair. "Fucking family drama."

Just then a large clunky cell phone on the table blasted out a ring. All eyes turned to us. Grover held up his hand for quiet, and the truck fell silent. He hit the speaker button and said, "This is Grover Delacourt. How are you doing, Gerard?"

The man's voice was shaky and breathless. "I'll fucking tell you how I am. If you don't get Iris Raines in here in the next ten minutes, I'm going to blow William Travis's head off. That's how the hell I'm doing."

Grover started to reply, but the line went dead.

I stood up. Grover just shook his head. "Iris, no way in hell are you going into the Alamo. Ain't gonna happen."

I looked at him without flinching. "Get me a vest, or I'll go in without one."

Grover was standing now. He eyed Nick, who stepped to block my path to the RV's door. The crowd in the rig fell silent as Grover used his best don't-fuck-with-me voice. "Iris, don't make me have these officers restrain you. Civilians don't go into hostage situations. You go in there, I've got two hostages to worry about him killing instead of one. I won't allow it."

I pulled my cell out of my pocket and dialed a number. Nick looked at Grover as if to ask if he should confiscate my phone. Before Grover could react, the breathless voice answered. The disembodied voice of Gerard Maysenfelder was tinged with equal parts insanity and desperation. Grover mouthed for me to put the call on speaker. I complied for fear he'd have Nick grab the phone.

"Iris, thank god. You have to come help me. I need you to come. Please. They're going to kill me. I've screwed up bad this time...there's no way out. Oh, God...what am I going to do...I..."

I braced my free hand on the edge of the table. Forcing my voice into a calm but commanding tone even as my pulse hammered in my ears, I shut him off.

"Listen to me! There is a way out—a clear way out. I want you to concentrate on what I'm saying. Can you do that?"

Long pause. "Okay."

"No one has been hurt. That's right, isn't it? Felix hasn't been hurt?"

"Not yet, but if my mother...excuse me, *our* mother... doesn't show up..."

I stopped him. "So, you screwed up the Alamo tour for a bunch of insurance adjusters from Toledo and interrupted that ridiculous living history exhibit they have going on in the back. There's no jury in this town that will give a shit about either one of those things. These are not real problems. Nothing has happened that can't be fixed. My father is here. He's an ass-kicking lawyer of the first order. He'll represent you for free starting immediately if you want...make sure you get a fair deal, that you're safe, if you'll just come out now."

Fear was transforming to desperation in his voice. "Fuck coming out and fuck safe. I saw snipers on the roof of the Weston. These assholes are setting up to pick me off like a Christmas turkey. No way I'm walking out of here. If Mommy Dearest doesn't show up and explain to me why she fucking dumped me like garbage while little Mr. Living History here got to tour the world with her, I'm going to do him. I swear I will, so you best get the bitch on the phone. And if you don't get in here yourself in the next five minutes, I'm calling it. Then we'll both be out of here, and God can sort it out." The line went dead.

Grover was shaking his head. "We do not volunteer additional hostages to mentally unstable hostage-takers. We do not and will not."

I wasn't getting anywhere with Grover, and I wasn't going to. But I had heard something in Maysenfelder's voice that told me he might just carry out his murder/suicide threat if I didn't join him. He was terrified and had somehow decided I was the only person he could trust. I let out an exasperated sigh. "Fine. I need some air to clear my head. You all figure it out."

I walked out of the truck and shielded my eyes against the bright afternoon light. I made a show of deep breathing and rubbing a crick out of my neck. Justis followed and stood next to me. The sound of the generator would ensure that nobody around could overhear our conversation. He looked out on the crowd as he spoke. "Don't do it, Iris. I know what you're thinking. Don't do it. This man is unstable, armed, and dangerous."

I looked at the plaza in front of the Alamo. Normally clogged with tourists milling around and taking pictures, the plaza was eerily empty. I said, "There is zero hope of reaching the mother. She's in the Andes. Even if she has a sat phone, it'll take all day for the cops to get the university to cough up the number. I already ran into that wall when I was working the title problem. I know what I'm doing." I turned to him. "I love you, Pappa J. Don't worry. I know him. He won't hurt me."

With that, I slipped around the truck and made my way through the crowd of cops and deputies milling around the plaza in front of the Alamo Cenotaph. I made a show of pretending that I was looking for someone in the crowd. At the Cenotaph, I broke through and raced across the empty plaza. I yelled, "Gerard Maysenfelder, I'm coming in."

Out of the corner of my eye, I saw Grover and Justis rushing to the plaza, but it was too late. I ran up to the big double wooden doors just as Maysenfelder cracked the left one open. My pulse sounded like Mexican cannon fire in my ears as I slipped inside the Alamo.

Free Bonus Materials

FREE *PANTS ON FIRE* BONUS MATERIALS

What you didn't see in *Pants on Fire...*

These bonus chapters take you behind the scenes of the case—revealing what was happening off the page while Iris was chasing killers, dodging lies, and trying to stay alive.

You'll discover how Iris got the lead that broke the case open—and what really happened after Finn Rhodes was shot and raced to the hospital in a lights-and-sirens fight to save his life.

Welcome back to the case.

Enjoyed Pants on Fire?

YOU CAN MAKE A DIFFERENCE!

Please leave your honest review of the book. As much as I'd love to, I don't have the financial capacity like New York publishers to run national campaigns for my books.

But I have something much, much more powerful—committed and loyal readers.

If you enjoyed the book, I'd be so grateful if you could spend five minutes leaving a review on the book's Amazon page.

Thank you very much.
Denise

Also by Denise

TRUE CRIME

ANTHRAX TO ZODIAC-
A SNARKY PI DELVES INTO THE MOST NOTORIOUS UNSOLVED MYSTERIES OF THE PAST 150 YEARS

ROMANTIC SUSPENSE

THE DEADLY SECRETS TEXAS TRILOGY:
A COLLECTION OF STANDALONE TEXAS ROMANTIC SUSPENSE NOVELS

STOLEN SECRETS

BURNING SECRETS

BURIED SECRETS

MYSTERY

HELL TO PAY—AN IRIS RAINES MYSTERY

Acknowledgements

I would like to thank Chris Parks, lawyer extraordinaire and author of the excellent adventure tale *Poco Bueno*, for his legal insights and all manner of other assistance.

Bestselling author Mariah Stoneand her husband Michael are always there to lend a helping hand and share their very valuable insights. Thank you both.

Laura Barth is always a great editor. She is positive and supportive while never letting me slide. I'm so fortunate to have her.

Beth Attwood is the eagle-eyed proofreader who can spot a typo at a hundred yards from a moving train. Any remaining errors are mine.

This book is dedicated to the memory of Harold Flemming Duncan, Jr., Esq. My life was forever changed in June of 1983 when he took me under his wing and offered to make me a landman. Whatever I understand about the law and real estate, I learned from him in the dusty courthouses of South and West Texas during the countless hours we spent chaining title and buying and selling oil and gas leases together. In a time when having a female protégée was not popular, he generously shared his vast professional capital to lift me up and never expected a thing in return. He was one of the great minds in Texas oil and gas law, and I am forever blessed to have known him.

About the Author

Denise Diana Huddle was born and raised in San Antonio, Texas. She graduated from the University of Texas at Austin with a degree in geology and a minor in accounting and went to work as a landman for her father's oil company.

After 13 years in the field, Denise got her private investigator's license and worked for the next twenty years as a PI and forensic genealogist servicing oil companies and law firms nationwide.

Now retired, she splits her time between San Antonio and Mobile with her significant other and their three rescue dogs while she writes mysteries inspired by cases from her colorful career. Two decades of discovering hidden secrets and unraveling complex family histories have left her with a lot of stories to write.

Visit her at denisedianahuddle.com for more information on her other books and news about upcoming releases.

www.ingramcontent.com/pod-product-compliance
Lightning Source LLC
LaVergne TN
LVHW090546110826
845146LV00001B/37

* 9 7 9 8 9 9 9 4 8 2 2 1 1 *